THE
GREEN
MAGE

The First Chronicle
of Tessia Dragonqueen

Michael Simms

MADVILLE
P U B L I S H I N G

Lake Dallas, Texas

FIRST EDITION

The Green Mage: The First Chronicle of Tessia Dragonqueen is a work of fiction. Names, characters, places, and incidents are entirely products of the author's imagination. Any resemblance to actual events, locales, businesses, companies, or persons, living or dead, is entirely coincidental.

Requests for permission to reprint material from this work should be sent to:

Permissions
Madville Publishing
P.O. Box 358
Lake Dallas, TX 75065

Author Photograph: Eva-Maria Simms
Cover Design: Andrew Dunn
Cover Art: Andrew Dunn
Maps: Jacqueline Davis

ISBN: 978-1-956440-18-8 paperback, ebook 978-1-956440-19-5
Library of Congress Control Number: 2022944363

For Eva-Maria

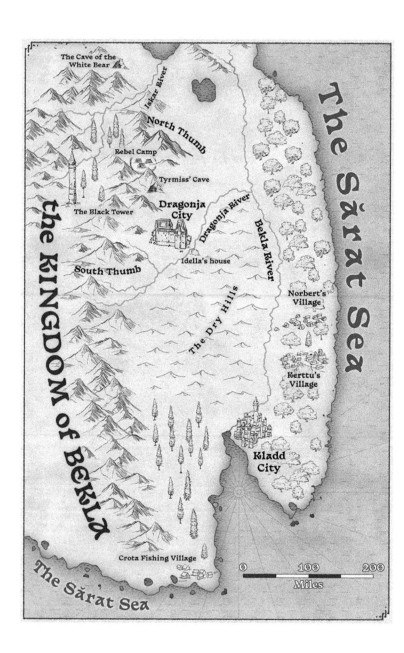

Prologue

*T*yrmiss crouched on the side of a high hill, listening. She could hear the Drekavacs on night patrol coming toward her, their thoughts jangling in their small skulls. Nonsense about their narrow lives in the barracks of Dragonja City. Poor little dears, their sergeants were mean to them. As their thoughts grew louder, Tyrmiss lifted a black wing to cover her body from view. She knew the purple scales on her throat and chest caught the moonlight, and she didn't want to give away her position.

When the Drekavac soldiers were close enough, Tyrmiss took a few steps, spread her wings and leaped into the air. She looked down and saw the soldiers marching, making enough noise so even the bandits they were chasing could hear them a league away.

Tyrmiss was trying something new tonight. She usually flew on moonless nights, coming down on her human or Drekavac prey without warning, silent as Death itself. But tonight, she would swoop down with the moon behind her, and in that moment when the soldiers could see her coming, she would hear their last thoughts. Tyrmiss wanted to take those precious thoughts from them, make them mourn their own lives. This was her revenge for a Drekavac having taken everything from her.

In her ten thousand years on earth, she had never killed for revenge until now—this summer of death she was creating, like an artist painting a mural. In fact, she had never known of any dragon who killed out of revenge, not that there were any dragons left, other than her, now that Rilla was gone. How many times had Tyrmiss told her wife not to sleep outside? *It's too dangerous,* Tyrmiss had said. *Someone will see you.* But Rilla often grew tired *of staying in the dank cave all day, and she would go outside to sleep in the pleasant meadow and listen to the birds and the singing stream.*

Men, Drekavacs, witches, mages, wizards—to Tyrmiss, they were all the same. They tried to control everything, and what they couldn't control, they destroyed. Why would a soldier murder sweet Rilla, a spear through her generous heart?

Tyrmiss turned in the air, and with the moon behind her swooped down upon the Drekavac soldiers. Their screams were like music to her.

Part One: The Quest

Chapter 1

When I first heard of Tessia, later known as Tessia Dragon-queen, she was a mere slip of a girl, running wild through the hills with the boys of her village. Her father, known as Kerttu Maker of Kettles, worked as a smith, a tradesman with thick arms and a deep kind voice. He was a man of tradition who despaired of his wild daughter who had no interest in learning the household skills that would make her a good wife. He did the best he could, but the girl's mother had died in childbirth, and he let Tessia have more freedom than families customarily allowed girls in those days. More than once I saw the village women cluck and shake their heads when Tessia's name was mentioned. Little did they, or any of us in those days, know what Tessia would become and how she would change the world. I'm an old man now, and I've seen many things, but none more remarkable than the way this girl became the champion of the Good and True and how we, the People Who Had Lost Hope, would rise to become what we are today.

As for me, I have been called many things—*The Healer, The Bard, The Green Mage,* but the name my blessed mother gave me was Norbert Oldfoot. My people are the riverfolk—farmers and craftsmen who've lived for many generations in the valley of the Bekla River. In the days in which this story begins, we were a simple and innocent people, and so the magic we practiced was of the practical kind. A farmer would ask that a field be blessed before it was planted. A fisherman would ask permission of the river to remove its bounty. Midwives and healers knew

1

that certain herbs would ease a fever, and certain spells would lessen the pain of a woman in childbirth. Jokes made a day's work shorter and a night's pleasure deeper while songs and stories helped people to remember and to forgive. We believed the Goddess Nilene would protect us if she were beseeched. Our broad feet kept us in touch with the earth, and our pointed ears helped us hear the voice of the wind. The sweet magic of ordinary life was all we knew. I was familiar with this Green Magic, but I learned at an early age that there were other kinds of sorcery, and some of it could be used for dark purposes.

In those days, I was a man of the shires, driving my cart from village to village, buying a few items in one place and selling them in another. I learned this trade from my father who'd learned it from his father. Villagers were glad to see me, for I brought news from other places and carried messages from distant kin. Also, in those days I had a fair singing voice, could pluck a tune on my lyre and knew a few of the old stories, so I made a good dinner guest. I'd picked up some local lore in my travels, so sometimes I was asked to gather a few herbs to treat a sick child, or to reset a broken bone, or to assist the local midwife with a birth. I tried to make myself useful, so I would be a welcome guest.

And yes, I could practice impressive magic if need be, but I preferred not to, having learned from my father that things are the way they are for a purpose, and rarely does it help to use extraordinary means to accomplish simple desires. Only once in recent years did I have a need for magic that defied the natural balance. It was a bright summer afternoon shortly after I took over the trade route from my father. I was leading my donkey Ottolo down the Bekla River Road when in the distance I saw smoke rising above the trees. I hurried to the farm where a farmer named Kis pointed at his barn which was on fire.

"My son is in the barn!" He shouted, recognizing me as my father's son. "Mage, can you help us?"

Without hesitating, I raised my arms in the air as a supplication to the Goddess, and chanted the invocation my father had taught me:

Zeita Nilene, te rog salvează băiatul!
Zeita Nilene, te rog salvează băiatul!
Zeita Nilene, te rog salvează băiatul!

No sooner had I said the incantation three times, then the roof of the barn flew off and the walls fell outward, revealing a boy lying on the dirt floor unconscious. The farmer ran into the smoking ruins of his barn, picked up the unconscious boy, carried him out and laid him in front of me. I put my lips over those of the boy and filled his lungs with my own breath. The boy started coughing violently and I gave him a sip of water from the flask I carried.

"The boy will be fine," I said to his father.

Kis invited me to dinner which I accepted, but after dinner when he tried to pay me for saving his son I refused, telling him that there were two rules that Green Mages must follow: first never accept payment for gifts that came from the Goddess, and second, never use magic to hurt a person. I might have added but didn't because it was no one's business but my own, that this was a singular event, not to be repeated. Years before, I had renounced magic in favor of a simpler life. In those days, I hadn't learned yet that whether you are a farmer or a mage, you cannot step away from your fate. And indeed, sometimes walking in the woods I could feel a willow branch vibrating near me, begging to be used as a wand.

Kis nodded silently, and we became friends. On the return trip down the Bekla River Road, I stopped at his farm and he bought my wares and never haggled over the price. This, as I learned from my father, is the way the Goddess rewards us, not with gold, but with friends and a sense of purpose.

My only traveling companion was Ottolo, named after our king, whom everyone thought was a fool. I didn't realize that if the king had known I'd named my donkey after him, his regent Ludek would have sent his minions to arrest me, but mocking the powerful was the only way we had in those days to show ourselves and each other that the king's regent had not completely intimidated us, whatever his heralds may have announced. But I was young and somewhat foolish and knew little of the cruelty of powerful men. Each evening I made a small shrine of stones and branches and paid tribute to the Goddess Nilene, mother of us all.

One day I was visiting Kerttu's shop on business. His copper kettles were much in demand through the region, and I wanted to buy a few. But Kerttu needed something other than silver as payment for his kettles. So, the day I visited, he was driving an especially hard bargain, wanting to trade his copper wares for the lumps of purple earth I'd brought from Dragonja City.

"Why do you need all this purple earth, Kerttu? It's not mined anywhere around here, and copper is better for making ornaments and weapons."

Kerttu ignored my question and continued driving a hard bargain for the purple earth. He and I were old friends—he'd known my father and had often traded with him—and we were enjoying the give and take of the haggle.

"You would cheat me, Norbert!" He bellowed, feigning anger. This was a dance many customers did with me, and I knew the steps well.

"Kerttu, you are the one cheating me!" I bellowed right back, and I dropped the lumps of purple earth in their leather pouch and acted as if I were about to leave.

"Wait, Norbert," Kerttu said, less harshly. "I'll give you the two small kettles, but for the larger one I'll need more purple earth."

"As I told you, Kerttu, I have no more purple earth. What else do you want for the large kettle?"

"What else do you have?" Kerttu asked, trying to hide a smile. He knew he had won a small victory in this skirmish of words.

"The next time I'm in Dragonja City, I'll buy more purple earth, and I'll bring you a lump the size of your thumb. That is," I said, almost challenging him. "If you trust me to fulfill my promise to do so."

Kerttu lifted his hands, palm up, as if to say *Of course I trust you. What kind of question is that?*

"And you will stay for dinner?" He said.

I hesitated. I had tasted Kerttu's cooking.

Kerttu saw my hesitation and knew what it meant, "Don't worry," he said, laughing. "I won't be cooking dinner. The widow who lives next door is bringing by a stew made with a rabbit my daughter shot with her bow. I did a little work on the widow's house, and so she's repaying the favor by cooking the rabbits. Please join my daughter and me. And you can meet the widow." He fumbled for words, "She and I are…" He looked sheepish. I held up my hand. He needed to say no more.

"After dinner," he continued. "We'll drink ale, and you can tell us the news from upriver."

Since we'd come to terms on the details of the trade, I was glad to accept his invitation, having grown tired of eating the weeds, nuts and berries traveling men like me survived on in those days.

The widow's name was Edelmira, and when I saw her, I almost laughed because she looked so much like Kerttu, both of them short and wide, and both of them highly skilled as

5

well. She was a plump attractive woman with high pointed ears and wide flat feet. The stew was delicious, and she kept filling my bowl and giving me more bread to mop up the gravy.

"It's wonderful to feed men who have healthy appetites," she said, nodding approvingly at Kerttu and me.

I noticed that she looked kindly at Tessia, who was not yet in full womanhood, but Tessia seemed to be ignoring Edelmira, and I wondered whether the girl resented the woman for taking over the household and occupying her father's attention. I hoped they could reach an understanding because a girl her age could certainly use the mentorship of an older woman. But I kept silent on this subject. I was merely a guest for the evening, not a family counselor.

As for Tessia, she was clearly not used to serving guests at their table—indeed by the look of her wild hair and dirty face, she wasn't much used to eating indoors at all. But she did the best she could with fetching things from the larder and was courteous and respectful to me, as she would have been to a visiting uncle. Out of respect for her father, I tried not to show too much interest in the girl. One thing I've learned in my travels is to leave the local women alone, especially the girls, if you want to be welcome in a village.

But there was something about the girl which kept my eye returning to her. She was tall for her age of twelve summers, and her arms were long and looked fit. Her fingers were nimble, and she put things away and cleaned up the table afterwards with a natural grace. She wore the singlet dress made from wool I'd supplied to the village some years before, and her brown legs were covered in scratches, no doubt from running through bramble bushes in the hills. She was pretending not to pay much attention to me, but I saw her casting quick glances in my direction every now and then. It wasn't unusual for people to be curious about me because travelers were uncommon in those days, the roads being full of bandits and wild animals. And there were rumors that dragons had been seen in the mountains near Dragonja City.

Although I returned to the village every year to trade my goods, I didn't see Tessia for about five years. Meanwhile, her father and I became close friends, haggling over the price of his kettles, drinking ale together, and eating at his fireside while Edelmira bustled between his house and hers next door. Often, the three of us ate a couple of rabbits or a haunch of elk that his daughter had brought home. Although he was clearly proud of Tessia's skill with a bow, he worried about her future.

"Those two friends she runs with... a boy and a girl. Hamlin and Anja are their names. They're from this village, and I've known them all their lives." He shook his head in disgust.

"Are they not of good character?"

"Oh, they're fine, I suppose. Hamlin is a big bear of a boy, strong but not very bright. His mother and father are old, and they survive on the meat he brings them. Anja is a small, dark, thin girl. A tomboy. Quick and silent as a fox. I've not heard her say more than two words her whole life. I've always felt sorry for the girl. Her father, who's far too fond of ale, beat the girl for years. There're rumors he did more to her, but what do I know? She ran away to live in the woods when she was young. What worries me is that neither of them, the boy nor the girl, have any prospects. They'll inherit nothing, and Hamlin has never learned a trade other than hunting. I suppose my daughter will marry him someday, and they'll have a brace of children as wild as they are. On the other hand, I've heard rumors that Hamlin and Anja are in love with each other, and if the rumors are true, then where does that leave Tessia?"

I offered no opinion. The only daughter of a man is a needle in his heart, and Kerttu did not need to be reminded of the pain of that love.

Later that evening, after Kerttu had had more than a few ales, he said to me in a hoarse whisper, "Can you keep a secret, Norbert?" I reassured him that I could. "Follow me," he said, and led me to his smithy behind his house.

He pushed aside some barrels and pulled out an object wrapped in cloth which he placed on the bench beside me. He carefully unwrapped a short sword as long as the distance from my elbow to the tip of my finger. I'd seen many short swords; in fact, at that moment I was carrying a copper one in a scabbard on my belt, but the weapon Kerttu had placed in front of me was not like anything I'd seen before. As I lifted the sword, the thin blade quivered, and light moved up and down its surface changing color from silver to purple and back to silver. The vibration caused it to hum. *A singing blade*, I thought. *How remarkable!*

"What is this metal?" I asked.

"It is Voprian," Kerttu answered proudly. "Much harder than copper, so the blade can be thinner, and it keeps an edge without being sharpened."

"And this is why you've needed the purple earth over the last few years?"

He nodded. "Voprian is nine parts copper and one part purple earth."

We went back in his house and sat beside the fire. Edelmira and Tessia had already gone to bed.

Kerttu explained that a stranger on his way to Dragonja City fell ill. Out of pity, Kerttu and Edelmira had taken him in and nursed him. The stranger, as it turned out, was dying and bequeathed the couple his sword as a reward for their kindness. He claimed that the copper axes and swords which had been in use since ancient times were now a thing of the past. The man said that the technique of casting the metal had been invented far away in an ancient city, and all the warriors in that part of the world were armed with Voprian swords, and their spears were tipped with Voprian. There was even talk of Voprian armor

8

although the alloy was expensive and had to be used sparingly. The man told him that the metal was made by melting copper and then slowly stirring in a small amount of purple earth. Over the last few years, Kerttu had been experimenting with the proportions, and just recently, he'd finally discovered the right formula.

"Who knows about this?" I asked. It had occurred to me that a king would be willing to pay a fortune for this formula, as well as being willing to kill people in order to keep the formula out of the hands of his enemies.

"I have not told anyone yet," Kerttu said. "But my brother is coming for a visit soon, and I may share the secret with him."

At that time, I didn't know Kerttu's brother, but later I came to know and admire him.

Chapter 2

The next time I saw Tessia was about five years later, and as it turned out, it was a meeting that changed both our lives. Ottolo and I were on the road that passes through the forest above Tessia's village when we were beset by robbers. There were three of them and they looked bedraggled and hungry. If they had approached me civilly, I would have shared what little food I had with them, but they no doubt wanted to steal Ottolo and whatever was in my cart. Although I carried a copper sword in my belt, in all my years on the road I'd never actually had to use it, relying instead on my ability to talk my way out of trouble. But this time, talking wasn't enough. They walked up to me on the road, eyeing me and my donkey, trying to sneak a look inside my cart which was covered from prying eyes by a tough hide tied down at all four corners. As I was exchanging cautious pleasantries with their leader, one of his friends came at me from behind, grabbing me by the arms, and a third one swung a cudgel, catching me on the side of the head. The next thing I knew I was on the ground being kicked in the ribs, and it was all I could do to curl into a ball while they roughed me up. I could hear Ottolo braying noisily, but the men were staying clear of his wild hooves.

Suddenly, the men stopped kicking me and I heard whooping, yelling, snarling and barking. Then the sound of running feet. Jeers and laughter. Then all was quiet. Gentle hands were laid on me, lifting me up until I was sitting in the middle of the road. I have never seen a lovelier sight than Tessia's smiling face, along with the faces of her two companions, a boy and a girl her own age, looking down at me. The two youths carried staffs; no doubt having used them on the men they'd chased away. Tessia, wearing leather boots and a man's leggings as well as the singlet I remembered from before, had a bowman's leather guard on her left forearm, and in her belt, she carried a short sword. At first, I assumed her sword was made of copper like mine, but as I looked closer, I recognized the thin blade and shimmering surface as that of a Voprian sword. I wondered how many of these swords her father had made.

"Why did you not draw your sword against the robbers?" I asked her.

She laughed. "It would have been too easy, and Anja and Hamlin needed the practice."

Tessia introduced me to her companions. Hamlin was a large blond muscular youth with an easy disposition and a joking manner. Anja was small, quick, dark and wiry, with a tendency to watch everything around her and keep her own counsel. The young woman had especially tall furry ears, which reminded me of a rabbit, a resemblance made more pronounced by the fact that her ears turned slightly in the direction of whoever was speaking. Tall ears were considered an attractive trait in Beklan women, but this girl's ears were almost comically tall.

Unlike Tessia who was dressed well because her father was prosperous, her two friends wore shirts and breeches that had been patched many times, scuffed leather boots worn down at the heels, and cloth peaked caps typical of farmers. Beside them was a dog named Bruin, a large mastiff bred in those parts for tracking and fighting boars. I could see why the ruffians ran from this small tribe.

That night, around the fire, the four of us shared the food we carried. I contributed berries and nuts I'd gathered earlier in the day. Hamlin roasted a brace of quail over the fire, and we drank water from the clear stream that ran next to the road. Bruin, having accepted me into the pack, allowed me to stroke behind his ears, showing his appreciation by vibrating his back leg in ecstasy and mooning his brown eyes at me. I hand-fed him a small piece of quail meat. Clearly, the mastiff and I were now boon companions. As I petted him, I relayed what news I had heard in other places, and Tessia told me what had happened to her father.

"A few months ago," Tessia began. "Drekavacs dressed as soldiers and carrying shields with the king's red dragon crest came to our village. They were led by a powerful wizard named Ludek."

"Yes," I said. "I know Ludek. He's the king's regent. He's known for his cruelty and his disdain for the folk of the valley."

Tessia nodded, taking this in. Raised in a village and spending most of her time in the woods, she was probably unaware of the politics of the kingdom.

"Several of our elders met Ludek and asked how they could be of service." Tessia went on. "He ordered the men, respected leaders of our community, to feed his Drekavac-soldiers and take care of his horse, speaking to the elders as if they were his servants."

"You were there in the village when this happened?" I asked.

"I was just then returning from a hunting trip in the hills. I walked into the village in time to hear the wizard insulting our elders. When the soldiers saw me, they grabbed my arms, catching me by surprise, and dragged me kicking and screaming to Ludek who said something like 'what an enchanting girl.' He stroked my hair and touched my breast. He was disgusting. I felt violated," Tessia shuddered at the memory. "I was able to pull one hand free and grabbing a knife from the belt of one of the soldiers, I slashed Ludek's face."

"Tessia can fight like a wildcat," Hamlin interjected, obviously proud of his friend's ferocity.

"What happened next?" I asked.

"Ludek's hood fell back, and I saw his white papery skin," she said.

"Hmmm, it sounds like he's changed a great deal since the last time I saw him," I mused, half to myself. "What happened then? You were able to escape?"

"The Drekavac-soldiers had started looting the village, but my attack on Ludek distracted them. Some of the villagers ran for the woods and the Drekavacs chased them, cutting them down in front of their families. I broke loose from the soldiers and ran as well." Tessia looked at the ground, ashamed. "I should have stayed and fought them, but I panicked and ran like a scared rabbit for the woods. A few soldiers chased me, but weighed down with their shields and swords, they were slow, and I outran them easily."

Tessia clenched her fist and said fiercely, looking at Hamlin and Anja, "I swear I will never abandon my friends again."

"I'm glad you didn't stay and fight the soldiers, Tessia," Anja said. "They would've killed you. Instead, you now have a chance to help your father." This was the first time I'd heard Anja speak in the hours since I'd met the group of friends.

"Have you returned to your village since the attack?" I asked. I was wondering what had happened to Kerttu, her father.

"That night I slept in the woods," Tessia continued. "In the morning I went back to the village…"

She grew silent, and I waited, afraid of what was coming next.

"When I came back, I found my friends and neighbors lying in pools of their own blood outside their homes. The house where I'd grown up and my father's smithy were both burned to the ground. I looked for my father's body but didn't find it."

"So, your father escaped as you did?" I asked.

Tessia shook her head.

Hamlin interjected, "We thought Kerttu must have been killed, but yesterday we talked to a farmer who said he saw him, his hands bound, escorted by soldiers down this road."

I wondered why Ludek would want to kidnap a copper smith. There were dozens of smiths in the valley. Why take this one? Perhaps Ludek had gotten wind of Kerttu's discovery of the Voprian alloy and wanted the smith to make weapons for his army?

"And what of Edelmira?" I asked, fearing the worst.

Tessia shook her head. "I saw her body," she said softly. "Poor Edelmira. She was nothing but kind to me, and I treated her with disdain." She hung her head.

"You were very young, Tessia. Sometimes children don't know how to accept change."

"I was afraid that she would take my father away from me, that he would love her more than me. I hated that good kind woman for the very reasons he loved her. And now I've lost both of them."

I looked at Anja and Hamlin. As Tessia was telling me of the murder of her neighbors, her two friends had been looking into the fire, their eyes welling with tears. Anja's ears were sagging.

"You were hunting in the woods when the village was attacked?" I asked them.

They nodded, and Hamlin made a small whimpering sound, and Anja patted him on the back. He was openly weeping at the loss of his family, but Tessia, who'd actually witnessed the murders, was dry-eyed. She was clearly a remarkably strong young woman.

After a long silence, I asked, "What are the three of you going to do now?"

"We're going north to the mountains, Norbert," Tessia announced with certainty. "Anja and Hamlin are going to help me capture a dragon, and I'm going to ride it to the king's castle to rescue my father."

To my knowledge, nothing like this had been done in recent memory. There were old songs and stories, of course, of heroes in the golden age who'd captured dragons, tamed them, and then ridden them into battle, but I never took those legends seriously. Tessia had heard me sing a few of the tales by her father's fireside, but I never believed they were true.

There was the story, for example, of Milon Redshield who chained the dragon Morf to a heavy cairn for forty days until the dragon consented to allow the warrior to fly on his back. In the great battle between men and dragons, Morf turned on Milon and the hero killed the dragon with a spear through his heart. And there was Edwige, the warrior-princess who kept a she-dragon next to her as she sat on the throne, establishing her dominance over all the fighters and elders of her kingdom. The dragon showed great disrespect for Edwige, so the warrior-princess had the dragon imprisoned for the rest of her days. I loved these stories, but, as far as I knew, they were told to entertain children, and whatever truth they held had been lost generations before.

Although I'd heard of dragons living in the mountains, no one I knew had actually seen one of the ancient flying beasts, much less ridden one. However, there were times when I was camped by the Bekla River, and I heard loud flapping noises and saw what appeared to be a very large bird skimming the surface of the water, catching a fish and flying away. But even if the old stories were true and there were indeed dragons in the mountains, the thought of capturing one seemed out of the question. Even as impressive as Tessia was, with her strong legs, long arms, and quick wit, even as determined as she was, even as passionate about saving her father as she was, the plan to capture a dragon seemed foolhardy and destined for failure. But I didn't have the heart to tell her this because with the burning of her village and the disappearance of her father, this wild adventure seemed to be the only thing left in her life.

She asked whether I knew the way to the mountains where the dragons were said to live.

"I do," I said.

"Will you be our guide?" she asked.

"I will lead you to Dragonja City at the northwest border of the Dry Hills," I said. "But no further."

She nodded and said, "Then we start tomorrow."

From where we were, my home village was an easy walk down the long slope of the hills to the Bekla River valley where we'd meet the river road and follow it for two days. Hamlin was walking next to me as I led Ottolo down the road. The young man was glumly looking at his feet as he walked. Just a few days before, he'd lost his family to the slaughter of the soldiers.

"Are you missing your family?" I asked.

He nodded. After a dozen steps in silence, he said, "I should have buried them."

"You were afraid the soldiers would return?"

Silence again, then, "Anja said there was no time. We had to save ourselves. So, we left them there. My mom, my dad, my two sisters. They were lying in front of our hut. My dad had a staff in his hand. He must have tried to fight the soldiers. My mom lay behind him, and my two sisters were in the hut. They'd been…"

"They'd been treated roughly by the soldiers," I said, so he wouldn't have to.

"Yah. They'd been… treated roughly." His eyes filled with tears.

"And now you're on a quest," I said changing the subject.

"A quest…" Hamlin returned to the present, looked around at the woods and into the distance where the road followed the river's curve. His large hands gripped his staff more firmly and his blue eyes steadied. He lengthened his stride until he was ahead of the rest of us, leading us down the red clay road of our destiny. I liked this young man.

In late afternoon, we stopped and made camp in an open meadow next to the river. Anja cut a dozen willow wands and quickly wove them into a net. She waded into a still place and stood with the water up to her thighs, put the net gently into the water and waited, her furry ears high and alert. She stood as still as a heron, thin legs and small torso, a white feather rising above her peaked cap. At that moment, she seemed remarkably beautiful. After a few long moments, she pulled the net out of the water and, behold! There was a silver salmon struggling in the woven willow.

While Anja was fishing, Hamlin had started a fire using a flint struck against a knife, the sparks caught in a wad of moss. He added twigs and bits of leaf until there was a small flame, and then a larger one. I went into the woods to gather garlic mustard for cooking the salmon. I also found rye grass that was in seed, dandelion flowers for tea, and a bird's nest with four small eggs. We would eat well this evening.

Nearby there was a large hill with a ditch around it. Once it had been a hillfort, but now it was just an odd feature of the landscape. At the top of the hill, Tessia stood looking off to the north. She was high enough so she could look beyond the forest and see the distant plains, and beyond the plains the two peaks known as the Thumbs of the Giant. And somewhere in those mountains were rumored to be dragons.

Tessia cut a fine figure on top of the hill. Tall and wiry. Leather breeches and high boots. A wool singlet covering her torso. A cape lifted behind her by the wind. Her long black hair was as wild as her ambition. Her ears were tall and pointed, her feet wide and strong. Then I thought about the quest and how ridiculous the whole thing was. If a mountain blizzard didn't kill these young people, and if ghost wolves didn't get them, and if outlaws didn't ambush them, and if Drekavacs didn't catch them, and they actually did find a dragon, then they would be killed for certain by the beast. Tessia, Anja, and Hamlin were brave, yes, but also foolhardy. Well, I thought, they are not my responsibility. I will take them as far as Dragonja City, and then they are on their own.

The next morning, I woke and saw that Tessia and her two companions were breaking camp. Hamlin had already unhobbled Ottolo and led him back to the cart. As he put the harness on the donkey, Hamlin said, "He wandered off downstream and was grazing on the river grass. Even wearing the hobbles, he can go pretty far, but I followed his tracks and brought him back. He's a fine animal, Meister Norbert, a fine animal. None too bright, but he's strong and trustworthy."

And I thought: *The same could be said of you, young Meister Hamlin.*

The six of us—Tessia, Hamlin, Anja, Bruin, Ottolo, and I—set off down the road, heading to my home village half a day's walk away. I've lived in the village all my life. My father was a shireman, as was his father, and his father, going as far back as I know. There's always been a need for men willing to travel, to bring news, tools and trinkets to the surrounding farms and villages. Maybe a song and a story as well. Every farm and village had too much of this and not enough of that, so it was up to the shiremen to trade a hammer for a saw, and a bolt of wool for a pair of scissors, as my old dad used to say. Since the soil in the river valley was rich and the people were adept at drying and pickling the summer harvests, there was always plenty of food, but made items were rarer and more in demand, and that's where the shiremen came in, providing the tools and materials people needed to have a better life.

"Might I become a shireman, Meister Norbert?" Hamlin asked, as we were walking.

"I don't see any reason why not," I said. "Perhaps when you finish your quest, you can join me for a summer of traveling, and I can teach you the trade."

"And what about being a wizard?" Anja asked, her ears turning in my direction. "Can girls become wizards?"

"Yes, girls can become wizards. Also, they can become witches."

"Can boys become witches?" Anja asked.

"I suppose so, but I've never heard of a male witch."

"What's the difference between a witch and a mage?" Hamlin asked.

"Witches and mages come from different traditions and use different spells, but they both use the power of nature to influence the world."

"Do you think I would make a good witch?" she asked. This was the most I'd heard her say since we met.

"Perhaps, Anja, but you, Hamlin and Tessia seem to be drawn to the role of warrior. So, you need to know it is usually not advisable for warriors to learn sorcery because they are often drawn to the dark arts. Warriors tend to see magic as a potential weapon, rather than as a force for good. It is best for a warrior, especially a warrior queen," I said, nodding to Tessia, "As I am sure you will someday be—"

At this, her two friends gave a hearty laugh.

"It would be best," I continued. "If you were *advised* by a wizard, rather than to be one."

"Meister Shireman," Tessia said hesitantly. "May I ask how it was that those three clods got the better of you? Are you not a mage? Why did you not use magic to fight them?"

"Well," I said. "I am not that kind of mage."

"There are different kinds of mages?"

"Yes, I am a Green Mage. Green Magic cannot be used to harm people, only to help them."

The truth, of course, was that I'd almost entirely given up magic in order to live a simpler life, but I didn't want to explain myself to these innocent young people who would never understand how I'd arrived at my decision.

"So, where does your magic come from?"

"All magic comes from nature. The way a tree grows every year, building ring after ring from nothing but water, soil and sunlight; or the way a child learns to speak simply by listening to her mother; or the way a salmon fights the rapids to return home. Earthquakes, lightning, blizzards, the rhythms of the day and the seasons. And even time itself. These mysteries make up the world as we know it. A mage or a witch is simply a person who understands these forces a little better than most people and sometimes can encourage the magic to work a certain way."

"And what is a Green Mage?" asked Hamlin, who now was walking beside us.

"Green Magic is closely connected to growing things. By blessing a field, a mage may help the farmer grow a better crop. By thanking a river for bringing fish, a mage is encouraging the river to do its chosen task. All living things need praise and encouragement. Green Magic can also be used to help a merchant accumulate silver, but only if the merchant is serving well his customers. Green Magic cannot help liars and cheats, and so they rarely prosper over the long term."

"So Green Magic can be used only to help living things?"

"That's right, Tessia. The healing arts are based on Green Magic. The healer cannot create health, only encourage it. The body has its own magic, and the healer listens to the body and helps it grow stronger."

"You listen to the body?" Anja asked, almost mocking me. "What does the body sound like?" She made a raspberry sound with her lips while lifting one leg, and she and Hamlin had a good laugh. Tessia rolled her eyes at their barnyard humor. I noted that Anja, despite her shyness and her cute furry ears, was certainly not girlish. She had the crude humor of an adolescent boy.

"It sounds like music," I answered, ignoring Anja's sarcastic tone and vulgar joke. "Music, song, spells, incantations, as well as painting, dancing, farming, cooking… they're all the same thing under their surfaces. They're all forms of prayer to the Goddess."

"Are there other kinds of magic?" Hamlin asked, clearly more receptive to the idea of magic than Anja.

"Yes, there are three kinds of lesser magic—Green, Red, and Purple. And two kinds of greater magic—White and Black."

"How does a mage make magic happen?" Tessia asked.

"Well, one of the ways that magic flows into the world is through gemstones. Each type of magic is sympathetic to a particular type of mineral. You see the green cat's eye ring I'm wearing? It was a gift from my father. Cat's eye, also known as Goddess Eye, encourages healing. Tourmaline brings passion. Chalcedony focuses power over other people. Rubies allow love to flow. And dark sapphires let loose violent disruption. The stones have no magical properties of their own. They act only as a bridge between the shadow-world and this one."

"Oh, this is all new to me, Meister Norbert. Tell us about the different kinds of magic," Tessia said, excited. Hamlin was listening intently, as well. Even Anja had dropped her cynical pretense and turned her ears toward me.

"Green Magic, as I just explained, encourages things to grow. Crops, herds, forests, children, songs, stories, and businesses all come from The Green. So, healers, singers, tradesmen, mothers, and farmers depend on Green Magic whether they realize it or not. All health and prosperity come from this life-force. Green Magic spells are gentle suggestions to nature that it rejuvenate itself.

"Red Magic spells are used to attract a lover, arouse desire, strengthen a marriage, enforce fidelity, mend quarrels, and encourage pregnancy. Red Magic spells can be gentle or strong, suggestive or coercive; what unites all Red Magic spells is that they encourage romance, love, lust, or fertility.

"Purple Magic has to do with politics and power. These spells are used to achieve personal success, attract allies, gain a favorable verdict, strengthen rulership, force others to obey, or to increase one's influence. Purple Magic can be gentle or strong, suggestive or coercive; what unites all Purple Magic spells is that they attempt to control other people, bending them to the will of the leader."

"What about what you called 'the greater magics'—White and Black?" Tessia asked, growing serious. "I've heard of these powers. White is good and Black is bad, right?"

"Not necessarily," I answered, carefully. "The greater magics, like the lesser magics, are gifts of the Goddess, and all gifts from the Goddess are good, but sometimes people employ Her gifts badly. The fault lies not in the Goddess's gifts, but in our own choices. Also, we tend to think that when we get what we want, the Goddess has blessed us, and when we don't get what we want, or things happen that we see as horrible or undesirable, then the Goddess has cursed us. But actually, everything that happens is part of the greater good."

"What about death?" Anja asked, growing angry. "Are you saying that what happened in our village a few days ago was good? Hamlin's entire family was murdered. His sisters were outraged by Drekavacs. How can anything like that be considered good?"

Hamlin blanched at the thought of his family. I stayed silent. His grief was very raw, and he would need time to heal before he could see that death is a necessary and even desirable part of life. Without death, there can be no life. Just as there can be no light without darkness.

"What other kind of magics are there, Meister Norbert?" Tessia said, trying to deflect Anja's anger.

"I've heard that there is Blue Magic which influences the weather, and there are people who claim this skill, but I think they are not actually mages, but just liars who are taking money from desperate farmers. The weather is far too large and important for a mage to have much influence in that realm. I have also heard of Orange Magic and Brown Magic, but again, I doubt they are real."

"Tell us about White and Black Magic, Meister Norbert," Tessia said.

"White and Black Magics are called *Greater* because they are a combination of the three lesser magics, and thus, they are much more powerful. To master White or Black Magic requires first to master the three lesser ones, and then to embark on a long and difficult path to master the Greater Magic and become a Wizard."

"So, a Wizard is a mage who has followed the path to master White or Black Magic. What is on the path?" Tessia asked.

"Each path is unique to a particular Mage. I know of one woman who began as a Red Mage and encouraged powerful men in her city to fall in love with her. Then she became a Purple Mage and became very powerful in her own right. Then she mastered Green Magic and helped her city grow prosperous. But then, she became disenchanted with these accomplishments, feeling they were meaningless, so she embarked on a journey, traveling around the world with the intention of becoming a White Wizard. Her task was to see only the good in people, even in people who had done evil things. She prayed ceaselessly to the Goddess to give her wisdom."

"Where is she now?" Hamlin asked.

"I believe she is now the queen of a southern city where the people are prosperous and at peace with their neighbors."

"What is White Magic used for?" Tessia wanted to know.

"White Magic spells are used to protect, bless, heal, and help those you care for. They can bless new ventures, help the mind and body, shield people and places from curses and hexes, reverse evil spells, transform bad conditions, and help good wishes come true. White Magic spells are powerful, but gentle; they are never coercive."

"And Black Magic?" Tessia was beginning to realize where this conversation was going.

I took a deep breath. I hated talking about Black Magic, but I knew that these three young people needed to know what they were up against.

"Black Magic spells are used to bring about sickness and unnatural illness, break up love affairs, punish enemies, destroy families, wreak vengeance, attract wrathful demons and disguise lies and harmful illusions. Black Magic hurts, harms, tricks, or brings misfortune. Black Magic spells are just as powerful as White, but whereas White Magic suggests, Black Magic coerces. Whereas White Magic reveals the truth, Black Magic disguises the truth. Whereas White Magic encourages happiness, Black Magic forces death.

"So Black Magic and White Magic are opposites?" Tessia surmised.

"No, actually Black Magic and White Magic come from the same place—the life-force that the Goddess has given us—but they are used for different purposes."

Hamlin looked confused, and Anja turned her ears away from me, not wanting to hear anything more about the paradoxes I'd hinted at. But Tessia was absorbing the ideas. I could see she was a practical person, so she was probably thinking about how to use magic to accomplish her ultimate goal to bring her father back to safety. I knew I should warn her, as well as Anja and Hamlin.

"My friends," I said, turning to look at each of them. "The Wizard Ludek is an accomplished master of Black Magic. You should stay as far away from him as possible."

"So, you know him?" Tessia asked.

"I knew Ludek many years ago before he became a wizard, but this creature he's become..." I looked into the fire and felt sadness come over me. "No, I do not know him."

Chapter 3

A s we walked past the farms and came to my village, people stared at us. They were used to seeing me and Ottolo, but strangers—now there was a sight. My neighbors, people I'd known all my life, waved at me and sometimes shouted a greeting. I knew they were curious about the strangers and what business and what trouble they brought, but the people of my village consider it impolite to ask questions, especially when the answers might be dangerous to know. Those were strange times when being curious could bring trouble to your family, not like the old days when the valley was a safer place to live. So, my neighbors simply stared at my new friends, bided their time and waited to learn the story.

When we arrived, I could see Tessia looking around at the houses and shops of the village and resting her eye on my small house, not critically mind you, but with a sharp intelligence typical of her. I opened the door and the four of us entered, leaving Ottolo and Bruin outside. I let the young people sit at my table and offered them ale which they accepted. Then I went outside to take care of Ottolo and Bruin—*always care for your animals before taking care of yourself,* as my father taught me. I scratched Bruin behind the ears and gave him a piece of dried venison. Then, I removed Ottolo's harness, led him to the manger behind the house, fed him a cup of oats and a few handfuls of hay and holding my face close to his so he could feel my breath mix with his, thanked him for his faithful service. I then brushed both animals with handfuls of dried grass while they sighed, showing their appreciation.

Back in the house, the young people had finished their ale. Hamlin, as was his habit, had started a fire for warmth. It was early summer, and an unseasonable chill had settled in the valley. Anja sat at the table, sharpening her short copper sword, a grim look on her face. Tessia was sitting opposite, watching her, but I could see her mind was elsewhere. She'd said very little during the two days in which we traveled here. I wondered whether she was planning strategy, thinking through the dangers that lay ahead, finding a way through the narrow path that led to finding and saving her father.

A kinswoman of mine brought bread, cheese, and apples for our dinner. I inquired about her children and her health and placed a silver coin in her hand to repay her kindness in taking care of the house while I was gone. I've always gotten along well with the people of my village, but I didn't like being there. The house, which I'd inherited from my father, made me feel trapped, as if the walls were closing in on me. There were too many memories of my mother and my brother. I never spent more than a few days in the house before going out on the road again.

After we'd eaten our fill, Tessia caught my eye and signaled that we should go outside to talk privately.

"I have to go check on Ottolo," I said, standing.

"I will come too," Tessia said and followed me out the door.

We actually did go to the manger, and Ottolo seemed glad for the company. Despite what people think, donkeys are social creatures and if there are no other of their kind around, will settle for human company. They're loyal and strong beasts, and in my opinion, better companions than most people. Ottolo had been my friend since he was a colt.

Tessia spoke gently while rubbing his ears, telling him how handsome he was and charming and smart. Ottolo, for his part, was falling in love with this young woman with her strong hands and confident manner.

"You think we're going to fail," she said. It wasn't a question.

I thought carefully before I responded. "You've chosen a difficult path."

"We need you with us," she said.

"I promised to take you to the far border of the Dry Hills," I said. "I will fulfill my promise."

"No, Norbert, we need you *with* us. We need you to come with us on the quest. We need your guidance. Hamlin is loyal and strong and has a sweet soul, and Anja is smart and skillful."

"And you are the perfect leader for them," I said.

She nodded. There was no false modesty about this young woman.

"I'm not much of a fighter." I laughed. "As you've seen."

Tessia looked puzzled. "You freeze up when faced with battle?"

"Yes," I felt a little ashamed. "Something happened when I was a child."

"What happened?"

"My mother was murdered in front of me. And ever since then, I've found myself frightened when I see people fighting."

"Your mother was murdered? Who did it? Was it your father?"

"Oh no, my father was a kind man." I looked away. "Although I think he was a little ashamed of me."

"Really? Why?" Her bluntness was a little off-putting, but I knew she meant well.

"My father thought that my older brother was a much more talented mage than I would ever be."

"Where is your brother now?"

"He is gone as well. He was taken by the man who killed my mother."

"Oh no, how terrible. I am so sorry," she said kindly.

Tessia thought for a while, and then gently said, "Hamlin, Anja and I are skilled at fighting, and we sharpen our skills with each battle, but you know more about the world."

"Well, I know a lot about the Bekla Valley, but the world is much larger than this valley. Or even this kingdom."

"Norbert, you know how to talk to people and how to listen to them. You're a healer who knows where to find the herbs that keep people in good health. And also, your songs and stories will open doors for us. People welcome you and trust you."

"Ah, there's the rub." I said. "I have responsibilities. People count on me to visit their villages and farms. My work is in this valley, following the Bekla River up into the hills, bringing people…"

"—Their pots and pans," she said with a hint of derision in her voice.

"What I do is important," I said defensively.

"Not as important as what you can do with us," she said, lifting her chin.

In the months to come, I was going to learn the meaning of her lifted chin, but at that time it seemed an oddly defiant gesture.

"And what is it that I can do with you and your companions?" I asked, trying to keep my tone from sounding mocking.

She narrowed her eyes at me, "We are going to bring down the king."

Surprised, I asked, "How many summers have you seen, my friend?"

"Seventeen."

"And Anja and Hamlin?"

"The same."

"And you, Anja and Hamlin, barely out of childhood, are going to overthrow King Ottolo?" I said, giving a little chuckle.

"Yes, but we're not alone. We're going to join Zygmunt's army."

"Zygmunt? You mean the bandit who lives in the mountains beyond Dragonja City?"

"So, you've heard of him?"

"Everyone's heard of Zygmunt the Rebel. I've even sung a few songs about him."

She laughed. "Don't believe everything that's in a song."

"There probably is a bandit named Zygmunt who lives somewhere in the mountains and fights the soldiers as best he can, but we singers have exaggerated his exploits, I'm sure. I don't believe all the songs and stories about him…" I glanced at her sideways and added "Just as I don't believe all the songs and stories about dragons."

"Dragons are real," she said with fierce insistence.

"How do you know?"

"Because I know people who've seen them."

"Like who?" I asked quietly. I was trying not to patronize her, but my attitude came through, nevertheless.

"Like Zygmunt," she said, imitating my tone.

"You know Zygmunt?"

"Yes, he's my uncle." She looked off into the darkness. The moon and stars were hiding behind clouds tonight, and there were only shadows of trees and houses to see.

"Zygmunt the Rebel is your uncle? Your father's brother?"

She nodded. "Zygmunt left home when he was just a boy and joined the bandits in the mountains. After a few years, he became their leader and made them swear to fight only the king's soldiers and never to rob from the people."

I remembered the conversation I'd had with her father years before. Kerttu had planned to show his brother the Voprian sword. I wondered whether the connection to his brother was what had gotten Kerttu in trouble with the king.

"I thought I knew all the kinships among the clans in these valleys and hills. Why have I not heard that Zygmunt is your uncle?"

"My uncle kept our kinship secret in order to protect us."

Now it was becoming clear to me what she planned to do. She was going to the mountains to find her uncle and join his band of warriors. But this business of capturing a dragon still didn't make sense to me. I was of the opinion that if there is such a thing as a dragon, and it was not just a children's tale, then it was best to make a point of not coming face to face with one.

O n the road, Tessia took the lead with Bruin at her side. The tall well-armed young woman and the large muscular mastiff made an impressive pair. I followed, leading Ottolo. We'd left the cart at my hut and loaded Ottolo like a packhorse with provisions for our journey over rough terrain. A donkey will not be hurried in his strong steady plod.

I'd packed dried fruit, barley and root vegetables for us to eat when we couldn't find enough meat or fish, as well as blankets and a few tools. Also, when Tessia and the others were asleep, I'd dug up the bag of silver coins I'd buried beside the oak tree behind my house. I didn't know what challenges would face us, but I thought it better to have money than not. The simple farmers and craftsmen of the valley rarely saw money, but I knew from experience that the people of the city valued coins more than trade goods.

The mountains, big and blue on the horizon, looked as close as the next field, but actually they were at least a month away by foot. We should reach them by midsummer, I thought, but it may be winter before the three young people found Zygmunt's rebel band. Wandering through the mountains in the fall and winter would be dangerous. Mountain bears, avalanches, renegade soldiers. Not to mention the dragon they were looking for. It was becoming clear that my young companions didn't understand the difficulty of the journey in front of them, and I grew more worried about them as we followed the Bekla River Road which grew narrower as we moved north across the plains.

In the evenings, we rested beside the fire, roasting roots we'd brought from my village, eating summer berries which were in season, and sometimes a rabbit or a trout that Anja or Hamlin had snared. Anja and Hamlin were almost always together, laughing at the same jokes and sharing bits of food. Beside the fire, they liked to sit together, their shoulders touching while Tessia sat a few feet away. They usually asked me for a song or story before they went to sleep, and I was glad to oblige. The stories usually began:

"There was once a giant who lived in a cave. A traveler came by..." Or: "Once a princess who lived in a Castle saw a man in the distance, crossing through her orchard..." Or: "A man wanted to cross a bridge guarded by a troll..."

These were old stories which I'd heard through the years, and I'd told them many times, polishing and improving them with each telling. Sometimes, I used my lyre to make the stories sound more beautiful. The giant's voice was in the low registers, the princess's voice in the high. The hooves of the horses were my fingers drumming on the frame of the lyre. The giant's footsteps were made by pounding on a log. This was actually my favorite part of being a shireman, entertaining my dinner companions with a song and a story.

One evening we'd just set up camp when a man approached us. He said his name was Caz, and he was a traveler from the south returning home after selling his cattle in the north. He asked if he could join us beside the fire. Not to be inhospitable, we agreed. Although King Ottolo ruled and there was much evil in the land, some customs were still observed, hospitality to strangers being one. He had several small bags of spices with him which he gladly shared with us. As we cooked dinner, we asked him what he'd seen in the north.

"I was chased by bandits yesterday," he replied somewhat

stiffly, as if he hadn't spoken the Beklan tongue in a while. "But I am fleet of foot and was able to evade them. I have heard ghost wolves howling at night, but I did not see any."

Tessia asked whether he'd heard of the dragons of the north. He looked at her with curiosity in his eyes, and answered slowly, "Yes, I have heard of such creatures."

"Who told you of them, and what did they say?" Tessia said, trying to make her voice sound casual, as if she were just making conversation.

At that moment, Hamlin announced that the beetroots were cooked, the trout had a nice crust on its skin, and he was ready to eat. He used a stick to pull the beetroots from the coals while Anja lifted the skewers of trout from the flames. We ate the spiced fish with our fingers off broad leaves. For dessert we had wild strawberries I'd gathered earlier. I've never had a better meal in my life.

After we had our fill, I said, "Well, Meister Caz, tell us of the dragons of the north," trying to sound like I was asking for a bedtime story.

Settling into a comfortable position beside the fire, Caz began, "I met a man in the foothills of the mountains. He said he had come from the northwest from the pass between the two high peaks known as the Thumbs of the Giant. He did not say what his business there was, but I thought he might be a trader of some kind, perhaps he was pursuing the gemstones which are said to be up there, or perhaps gold. He told me that in his travels in the mountains he came to a cave. Lighting a torch, he went in, wary of animals. The bears in that part of the world are very large and ferocious, and at winter's end, they would be waking from their slumber and looking for food.

"When he entered the cave, he did not smell bear, but he smelled something else, a mix of soot and rotten eggs. It was a strong odor, but not overbearing, so he descended down the path into the lower chambers. After a while, he saw a flicker of light up ahead, and he thought he might have found a human settlement of some kind. He had heard of such things, people taking shelter from the winter wind deep inside a mountain. But what he saw was something quite different.

"The dragon lay on its belly, eyes closed, head resting on its claws, wings folded against its sides. It was breathing deeply, and with each exhalation a small pair of flames came from its narrow nostrils. In the light of his torch and the on-again off-again light of the dragon flames, the man could make out the shape of the creature. The body, covered in red, purple and green scales, was the length of four horses with a long tail that curled around the body. Each talon was half the length of a man's arm. The beast was a frightening thing to behold.

"The man backed slowly away from the dragon, quietly followed the path to the mouth of the cave and ran as fast as he could down the mountain. He was following the road along the Dragonja River when I met him."

"Do you believe this tale?" I asked.

"I do," Caz replied. "The fellow did not seem to be trying to impress me. He was simply telling what he saw. And there was something else…"

After a pause, Caz, staring into the campfire, added, "The dragon was sleeping on a large pile of treasure."

After we broke camp the next morning, we said goodbye to Caz, and I watched him head south down the river road. He seemed a pleasant and reliable fellow, and I hoped we would meet him again.

"Do you believe his story about the dragon?" Tessia asked, standing beside me and watching Caz disappear around a curve in the river.

"I believe that he heard the story from the traveler. Whether the traveler was telling the truth, or just spreading a tale for his own amusement, I have no idea."

"But don't the old stories talk about dragons living in caves, breathing fire, and hoarding gold?" she asked.

"Oh yes, the stories do indeed say those things. They also say that dragons are wise, always tell the truth and live thousands of years. In the old days, they were advisors to kings, but then Milon Redshield betrayed them, leading many of the dragons to their death. He took their gold and made a name for himself as a hero and a great warrior, and eventually he became king of all the lands. But the dragons trusted men no longer and became the enemy of men and kill them when they can."

"Do you believe the stories, Norbert?" It was the same question I'd asked Caz, and I realized the answer is not as simple as it may sound.

"Oh," I said thoughtfully rubbing my beard. "Stories always contain the truth, but sometimes not in the way we expect. Things are not always as they seem. For example, what is my name?"

"Norbert the Shireman."

"Yes, that is what they call me now because I travel from shire to shire. But sometimes people call me Bard because I can sing the old songs. Or they call me Healer because I know the herbal cures, but I was born with a different name."

"And what is your different name?"

"It is Norbert Oldfoot. No matter now. No one remembers but me. My point is that what we call a thing is not the same as what that thing is. A story is a way of naming things, and that is the source of its power, but the name is not the thing itself, and in that way a story is always a lie and always the truth."

She shook her head in exasperation at me. "You're speaking riddles now, Norbert. What does all this have to do with our dragon quest?"

"We shall see."

And our stalwart band headed north, still following the Bekla River.

I had traveled this river road every year since I was a boy accompanying my father as he traded goods and sang songs at every farm and village along the way. It had always been a peaceful valley with big-hearted people who seemed content to farm and practice their crafts. In the summer, we could see children playing in the river and men and women working in the fields. Every house and hovel had smoke rising from the chimney, and a traveler was always welcome, especially if he had news from far away.

But now as Tessia, Anja, Hamlin and I walked along the road, people did not welcome us. No one invited us into their homes as welcome guests in the Old Way. No one shouted greetings to us as we passed, and when I stopped to trade with them, they acted suspicious, as if I intended to cheat them. Mothers herded their children indoors, and men held their rakes and hoes at the ready as if they were weapons. I thought about the men who had attacked me a few days before, how desperate and hungry they were and how easily my companions had beat them. I suspected the men had taken up highway robbery only recently because they were starving and did not have the hang of thievery yet.

At one farm which looked familiar to me, the old farmer spoke to me in grunts and indicated I should leave. I suddenly realized that this old farmer was Kis, the man whose son I'd saved from the burning barn the previous summer. I barely recognized him. He'd aged twenty years since I'd last seen him.

"I'm sorry, friend, why do you turn me away? Have I done something to offend you? Have I not always treated you fairly and with respect?"

He looked me coldly in the eye and said, "There has been much mischief in this valley lately, Shireman. I hear of girls being snatched when they go to the fields to call the cows, and boys are taken when they go out to hunt, and women are attacked in their homes and their husbands murdered."

"Has something happened to your son?" I asked him, suspecting that his anger had a deeper cause.

Kis jerked his head to the edge of the field where I saw a fresh grave, not more than a few weeks old. "They came in the night when I was in the hills pursuing an errant cow. He resisted," Kis said. "And so, they killed him."

"Who is doing this murderous mischief?" I asked.

The old farmer scratched his chin and said, "No one saw it happen. Neighbors say it was bandits, perhaps Zygmunt and his rebels, but I think it's clearly the king's soldiers, the Drekavacs who carry the red dragon shields, who are doing these things. We have no law in this land anymore."

"Why are the boys and girls taken?"

He snorted at me as if my question showed my stupidity. "Why do you think?" He grumbled. "They want the girls for the brothels in Dragonja City and the boys for the king's copper mines in the mountains."

He didn't invite us to stay, nor did I want to impose on his grief, so we continued on our journey.

After setting up camp that evening, I wandered downriver a short way to look for marsh reeds. This was a place where my father and I had camped many times. I waded out into the water and with my dagger I dug up a handful of reeds and found the tuber that had grown in the mud. I washed it in the river and stood for a moment in the shallow water and looked at the willow trees darkening in the dusk.

Willows always reminded me of my father because he carried a willow wand which he used for simple incantations. He was not a wizard, but just *a simple village mage*, as he called himself. I am grateful to him for teaching me about the gifts of the Goddess—which tubers we can eat and how to cook them, which flowers can be made into tea and what ailments they cure, what incantations to say to bless a field or to welcome a guest…. But after my mother's death, there was always a sadness clinging to my father. He wore his grief like a heavy cloak around his shoulders, and it weighed on him. Although he was never cruel to me as some fathers are to their children, I often caught him looking at me as if he didn't like what he saw. I sometimes suspected that he wished that I, instead of my brother, had been taken when we were young.

My father could have been a powerful wizard; instead, he chose, as I have, a simpler life. There were occasions, however, when I saw him cast life-saving spells. In fact, it was not far from this wide place in the river where I first saw my father's gift for magic. We were traveling this very road when a boy came running up to us.

"Please help!" He shouted. "A tree fell on my father!"

The boy led us into the woods where a man lay trapped beneath a huge oak tree that probably weighed as much as a house.

"He's still alive," my father said, having pushed branches aside to reach the man. "But he's trapped beneath the trunk."

My father pulled his willow wand out of the sheath on his belt and said, "I will lift the tree up a hand's breadth, and I want you boys to pull him free."

He waved his wand, pointed it at the tree and said an incantation that he later had me memorize:

Nilene Zeita
de viață
pe care le slujesc
restabili echilibrul
pentru a lumii
și să conducă viața

The tree lifted off the ground, and the boy and I pulled his father a few feet until he was safe, and my father set the tree gently down. Then he examined the man, saw that his arm was broken and his head was injured. He instructed me to go to the nearby meadow and gather yarrow root and other herbs. When I returned, my father was sitting beside a fire, whispering incantations over the man. My father crushed the herbs I'd brought, mixed them with the walnut oil he always carried and spread the paste on the man's wounds. He bound the man's broken arm to a wooden splint.

"Do you have kin nearby?" He asked the boy.

"Yes, my uncle and aunt have a farm upriver."

"Go to them and bring them back here. Tell them to bring a litter to carry him. We will wait for you."

The boy did as he was told. As we waited, my father taught me the incantations that stop bleeding and encourage the body to heal.

Since then, I have often used yarrow root and the healing incantations, but I've never been able to work the incantation that lifted the tree trunk. Many times, alone in the woods, I have tried to lift a log, but I have never been able to do much more than make the log tremble. Moving something that is stable is much harder than changing something that is full of energy. Causing the burning barn to explode was not a difficult spell because the barn was ready to explode; I merely guided the energy outward to save the boy rather than inward which would have killed him. I suddenly realized that I had never learned the boy's name, and now he was dead, and Kis, having lost his son, had become a bitter man. Not for the first time, I wondered whether it was wise to practice powerful spells. Encouraging a body to heal is one thing, but encouraging a barn to explode is something else entirely.

My father, although a gifted mage, never charged anything for his healing practice. He always said, "Magic is a gift from the Goddess. What She has given us freely, we should not profit from." I have always followed this practice in my own travels. Mind you, I am not above turning a profit; in fact, I charge dearly for the trade goods I carry, and I accept coins and gifts for singing my songs. But I've always offered healing to those who are ill or injured without regard for profit.

As my father used to say, "This is the way of the Green Mage."

Chapter 4

On the third day after we bid farewell to Caz, we left the Bekla River Road and turned west. I knew the Bekla River meandered to the East from here, and I told Tessia that we could take a shortcut across the hills and arrive in Dragonja City in a few weeks. She trusted me and, I'm ashamed to say, her trust in my navigation skills was a mistake. Nevertheless, we turned west toward the mountains, leaving the river to ascend into the Dry Hills, unfamiliar country for me. It was a hard slog up and down the steep slopes. We had to ration our water because streams were far apart. Also, the earth seemed to have recently suffered fire here, with gray ash mixed into the red clay and scorch marks on the trunks of the small thin trees. I told my companions to keep a careful eye on the surrounding terrain. The Dry Hills were known in those days for harboring bandits and wolves. Unfortunately, I didn't follow my own advice, and I was daydreaming when we were ambushed by a gang of men who sprang at us from hiding places beside the road.

One of the men walloped Hamlin on the head with a staff, which knocked him out cold. Bruin leapt at the man, biting him in the groin, which made him turn and run with Bruin close behind nipping at his heels. Another brigand charged me, but Ottolo took a bite out of his butt as he passed, and I took out my short sword and tried to look threatening, so the man backed away quickly. Anja drew her sword and did a credible job of parrying and feinting with two men who also had short blades. But it was Tessia who saved the day. As soon as the men jumped from the woods, her Voprian sword was drawn. She stabbed one man in the belly and slashed another across the forehead, blinding him with the flow of blood into his eyes. She seemed everywhere at once, dispatching the man who'd attacked Ottolo and me with a stab to the side of his neck—he ran into the woods, clutching his neck and limping from Ottolo's bite to his backside. Then Tessia was knocked down from a staff-blow to her shoulder. She rolled and leapt up to confront the two men who were fighting with Anja. Seeing that they no longer had an advantage, they retreated into the woods.

Tessia whistled for Bruin, and he emerged from the woods with a piece of cloth in his teeth and blood on his nose. The dog looked very pleased with himself. Meanwhile, Hamlin was sitting in the middle of the road, massaging a lump on the side of his head where the staff had landed. The whole fight had taken just a few moments, but it seemed to have taken hours. It would have gone differently, I was sure, if Tessia had not been with us. The young woman seemed to have a talent for skirmishing, and the Voprian blade was the perfect weapon for her.

But the real test of Tessia's abilities came a few evenings later when our camp was attacked by ghost wolves. These terrifying beasts are found only in the Dry Hills, and some say they are not wolves at all, but men who spent too much time in the wild and became wild themselves. Others say they are a cross between wolves and the great white bears of the snowy heights, the kind that live in caves and come out to hunt only at night. Some say they are merely white wolves like any other, just larger and fiercer. And still others say they are creatures of the underworld who live on the blood of men and the animals that men keep. Whatever they are, our little band fought them, and we lived to tell the tale.

We'd had a long day slogging up the side of a steep hill.

Ottolo, normally a docile animal, had balked halfway up the slope; perhaps he smelled something in the air. Bruin was acting strangely as well, sniffing every bush, every pile of stones, and suddenly stopping, his ears raised and his nose in the air, alert to something close and coming closer. In the evening, we built a small fire as we usually did. We missed the fish we easily caught at the river and were eating the roots and grains Ottolo had been carrying on his back. There weren't many edible plants or nuts in these hills either. But we were eating well enough and looking forward to reaching Dragonja City where we could rest and find new provisions. It was Anja's turn to stand guard, and the rest of us fell asleep around the fire. Although Ottolo and Bruin seemed restless, it seemed we'd have a safe and peaceful night.

If you've ever heard a donkey scream, it's not a sound you soon forget. It penetrates the heart of you. I was instantly awake, jumping to my feet, scrambling to find my short sword. Tessia was crouched, her Voprian blade pointed in the direction of Ottolo's scream. Hamlin was on all fours looking confused and dazed. I heard Bruin in the darkness snarling and fighting. Anja was nowhere to be seen. My first thought was that she'd fled, abandoning us to our enemies.

Tessia shouted, "Hamlin, get up! We're surrounded and under attack. Norbert, come over here! We need to get in defensive position!"

I ran to her, and she and Hamlin and I stood in a triangle facing outward, our swords ready.

Bruin came running toward us with two huge white wolves snapping at his heels. He stopped when he came to us and turned just as one of the wolves bore down on him. Tessia stabbed the wolf under the chin and lifted the canine clear in the air. It fell on the ground wriggling and gasping. The other wolf, a little behind her brother, stopped and backed up, staying clear of Tessia's blade. Half a dozen great white wolves closed in on us, cutting off any avenue of escape. I said a quick prayer to

41

the Goddess, asking for forgiveness for having neglected her in recent days, and I prepared for death.

Just then, Ottolo charged into the melee with Anja on his back swinging her staff, knocking the surprised wolves aside. And Ottolo was kicking and biting, braying like a donkey from hell.

Tessia seized the moment, lunging and slashing at the nearest wolves with Hamlin and me beside her. I missed the wolf I was attacking, but surprised by my lunge, he backed away. Hamlin swung his staff, hitting a wolf in the head. Bruin attacked another wolf, grabbing it by the throat and taking it down. The rest of the wolves, having lost their advantage, ran off into the darkness, whimpering in pain.

Tessia looked up at Anja, still astride Ottolo. "Thank you, sister, you saved us." Anja, perhaps for the first time ever, smiled, all ears. Tessia stroked Ottolo's muzzle, praising his courage. "You, my little sweet brave dear, will get an extra ration of oats tomorrow." Tessia leaned down and spoke softly to Bruin while stroking his ears. I couldn't hear what she said, but the big dog wagged his tail and looked up at her adoringly. Tessia nodded to Hamlin and me, "You fought well, both of you."

At that moment, I would have done anything for this young woman, our captain, our leader.

As we found out later, Anja had walked into the woods to relieve herself when she heard the ruckus at the campsite, and Ottolo had come running by, but for some reason, the donkey had stopped at the river and looked back at her. Anja had calmed him down and then rode him back to camp at a gallop. She'd hoped to surprise the wolves in order to give Tessia and the rest of us a chance to fight back. Her bold and brave strategy had worked, and she'd saved our lives.

The next day, Tessia asked, "Norbert, do you have a pair of scissors in the pack Ottolo carries?"

"I certainly do, my lady." This was the first time I addressed her formally, and she was a little surprised, but she didn't tell me to stop, so from then on, I always showed her the respect she'd earned as our leader.

"Would you cut my hair?" she asked.

It was my turn to be surprised. She'd always seemed a little vain about her thick black mane. She spent a good amount of time each evening brushing her hair until it shone in the firelight. She often swung her hair back with a gesture of her head which was obviously intended to call attention to its beauty.

"But my lady, your hair is so beautiful. Why would you want me to cut it?"

"Last night in the fight, one of the ghost wolves grabbed me by the hair and pulled me down. If I hadn't stabbed him in the eye, he would have killed me. If I'm going to be a fighter, I need short hair."

I admired her decision to give up part of her beauty in order to be a better warrior, so I agreed to cut her beautiful mane, but it would make me sad not to see it anymore. She sat on a log and I stood behind her, with a pair of sharp scissors in my hand. It was an excellent tool much in demand by women through the land, and I had sold many of them dearly. As I snipped her locks, letting the ebony hair fall on her shoulders, Tessia talked.

"When I was growing up, there was just my father. I never knew my mother. There were a couple of village women who helped look after me, but they didn't know what to do with this wild girl who had no interest in staying home. I didn't like playing with dolls or playing house. I just wanted to be in the woods, climbing trees, watching animals and scuffling with the boys. The other girls didn't like me and gossiped about me. As I grew older, some of the girls said mean things about me, that I was off in the woods pleasing the boys and that's why the boys liked me. But it wasn't true. Hamlin was the only boy I was close to, and he was my best friend, not my boyfriend. The other boys seemed a little afraid of me because I was better at running and fighting and hunting than they were. If it hadn't been for Hamlin and Anja, I don't know what I would've done. It would have been nice to have had a sister, I think, or maybe a girl I could be best friends with. At times I was very lonely."

"What about Anja? Isn't she like a sister to you?"

"Well, yes, she's like my sister, but…" Tessia hesitated, not wanting to say anything hurtful. "But Anja doesn't talk. She's there for me, you know, but really Hamlin is the only one she talks to… Hamlin told me that when Anja first ran away from her father to hide in the woods, she was mute. It took months of kindness from Hamlin before she said a word."

I was listening to Tessia and thinking about the mystery that was Anja, but mostly I was concentrating on shearing Tessia's locks. The first pass was easy, cutting big hunks of hair and letting them fall on the ground, but the second pass was harder, trying to shape the flow of her hair to fit her head. I knew that she'd made a decision to give up vanity in favor of practicality, but still I didn't want her to be embarrassed by the way she looked.

She was unaware of my desire to please her with the cutting of her hair, and she continued talking: "When I was little, my father thought it amusing that I wanted to work in his smithy rather than learn to cook, and he dismissed the concerns of the village women, but as I got older, he began to realize that my need to act like a boy was not just a passing stage, and that I was never going to be able to find a husband or have a home or do any of the things that the women of my village have done forever."

"I'm thinking of cutting the hair straight across. What do you think?"

"I don't care," she said dismissively. "Just make sure it doesn't

44

fall in my eyes in the middle of a fight. And the hair needs to be short, no more than the width of two fingers, all over my head. I don't want anyone grabbing me by the hair and slitting my throat."

She stayed silent for about twenty snips of the scissors, then said, musing: "I suppose I always kept long hair to please my father. He might think 'well, she can't cook, but at least she has beautiful hair. Perhaps some man will marry her anyway.'"

"There. All done. Would you like to see your new look?" I said, pointing at a pan of water beside the fire where she could see her reflection.

"No," she said waving her hand dismissively. "I am not interested in how I look anymore. Besides, I trust you to do a good job, Norbert. You always do."

As she got up and walked across the campsite, I admired the way her short hair showed off her high forehead, the strong line of her jaw and her high pointed ears. She was, I thought, even more beautiful than before.

A fter having rested a day recovering from our battle with the ghost wolves, we set off again across the hills. At the top of each hill, we could see the Thumbs of the Giant in the distance, but they didn't seem to be getting any closer. I was afraid we'd run out of food, and water was becoming harder to find. As the days passed, our journey seemed more hopeless and I thought we'd made a mistake in choosing this route. There were no people, no villages and no animals other than an occasional snake or mouse. There were vultures circling in the sky above us, and I wondered what they knew that we didn't.

About ten days after we left the Bekla River, we came to the remains of a strange massacre. As we approached, vultures lifted off from the bodies, flapping their large slow wings as they rose through the air. About two dozen charred bodies lay scattered on the hillside. Many of them were wearing helmets, and some had swords or axes in their clawed hands. Their tunics were turned to ashes, and their faces were blackened and burned to the bone, but it was clear from their long talons that these had been Drekavacs, not men.

Bruin sniffed each body, then looked up at Tessia confused.

"These are King Ottolo's soldiers?" Tessia asked me.

"Yes."

"Is this the work of bandits?" Hamlin asked, not able to take his eyes off the horror.

"I don't think so," Tessia said. "Bandits would have taken the weapons."

"A brush fire, perhaps," I said, picking up a handful of the ash and sand on the ground and letting it fall through my fingers. But I didn't actually believe a brush fire could have killed so many Drekavacs.

Anja picked up a chunk of glass from the sandy ground and held it out for us to see. "Whatever caused it," she said. "It was a very hot fire."

"Let's keep going," Tessia said, turning away from the burned bodies. "We need to find water soon." Bruin was close at her heels, his pink tongue hanging out.

Anja grabbed a dead soldier's copper sword from the ground, whipped it through the air a few times, testing the feel of it, and Hamlin picked up a spear, and they turned to follow Tessia. Ottolo and I brought up the rear.

No one suggested burying the Drekavac soldiers.

We made a fireless camp that evening. We didn't want to draw the attention of whomever or whatever had killed the soldiers. It had been a few days since we'd come across a stream, so we rationed our water, just a cup for each of us, including Ottolo and Bruin. As I held the bowl half filled with water to Ottolo's lips, he lapped it up quickly and then looked up at me gratefully. I rubbed his snout and told him what a good boy he'd been on this journey.

"Norbert," Tessia said. "Have you ever been in this dry place?"

"No, never," I answered.

"But this is the path to Dragonja City where you've been many times, no?"

"Yes, I go to Dragonja City every year to trade. I approach from a different direction, though. I follow the Bekla River upstream to a tributary called the Dragonja River and follow it west and south until coming to Dragonja City."

"So why did we come this way?" I was grateful that there was no accusation in her voice. The decision to cut across these dry hills had been mine, and it was becoming clear it had been a mistake that may get us killed.

"It would have taken several months to follow the Bekla River to the Dragonja River and then to Dragonja City. We saved a lot of time by cutting across the hills." I said. Both Anja and Hamlin were looking at the ground, not wanting to point out the obvious. It suddenly struck me, not for the first time, how kind these three young people were.

Without fire, we couldn't prepare food, so we ate dried fruit and had a sip of water. Ottolo chewed on dry grass without much enthusiasm. Bruin had found a bone to gnaw. It looked like a human femur, but I guessed it came from one of the Drekavac corpses. In any case, it was all the mastiff had to eat, and I certainly wasn't going to try to take it away from him.

When we woke the next morning, the sun was already fierce. Tessia gave each of us a mouthful of water, I strapped the pack onto Ottolo who gave me an accusing glare, and we started off again, walking up and down the steep hills. I had a small pebble in my mouth to encourage saliva and I suggested this trick to the others as well. At noon we stopped and Tessia told us to make camp.

47

"We'll travel only at night when it's cooler," she said.

I took the pack off Ottolo and hobbled him. Then I used a stick to make a tent of my cloak and lay down in the narrow shade, covering my eyes with the crook of my arm. I tried to sleep, but the guilt of having led our band into the desert perhaps to die weighed on me. I didn't burden them with my apologies. What good would it have done? Instead, I carried my shame silently.

After sunset, we broke camp and started walking again, Tessia in the lead with Bruin at her side, his head down and his tongue hanging out. The rest of us trudged along behind them, one foot after the other. The sky was lit with a full moon and a river of stars. We could see the outline of the Two Thumbs of the Giant far away to the west. We walked until sunrise. Tessia held up her hand, too tired to speak. We knew she was signaling us to rest here where a few scraggly trees gave meager shade. I relieved Ottolo of his pack but didn't bother to hobble him. He was as tired as the rest of us and was not going to wander off. We were out of water, so I felt as if I had a fever, my skin was burning and prickling. My mouth was as dry as the sand that surrounded us.

Suddenly, I remembered something my father had told me about this region. There's a small desert plant called the *wasserplanz* that has a tuber in which it stores water. He told me that after a rain it has a red blossom. I tried to think back over the last couple of days, but I didn't remember seeing any blossoms of any kind, just dry grass and scrubby bushes. He also said that it grew in gullies where the water flowed during a rain. I untied and opened the pack Ottolo carried and found a small wooden shovel. I walked down the hill to the gully. Tessia was lying on her back with her head turned in my direction, watching me. Anja and Hamlin were asleep.

In the bright light, it wasn't difficult to find a few small bushes in the gully. I picked one at random and dug it up, exposing a tangle of roots, none of which looked like it held any appreciable amount of water. I walked further down the gully, seeing similar bushes, and then I saw one that looked different than the others. It was just a bundle of thin twigs, but at the tip of one of the twigs was a dried flower bud, brown and barely distinguishable from the twig on which it sat. With my fingernail, I tore open the bud. And inside was a small bit of red fiber, perhaps the beginning of a blossom which never fully formed. I got on my knees and dug the hard clay aside and uncovered a gloriously round tuber, not much to look at, but looking beautiful to me. I used my short sword to slice it open to expose white flesh that oozed moisture. I licked the moisture which tasted starchy and slightly acrid. It was the best thing I'd ever tasted in my entire life.

"Are you going to share that, Norbert?" Tessia was a few feet behind me. She must have followed me from the camp.

"Of course, my lady," I said, handing her the split tuber. I used the shovel to dig up another one, and I could see more *wasserplanz* a little further down the gulley.

At first, we were greedy, collecting as many of the tubers as we could and loading our pouches and Ottolo's pack with them, but after a while we realized that the small inconspicuous plants were common in that area. Every gulley had a few, so we started leaving whole patches of them for the next traveler.

"You saved us, Norbert," Tessia said to me the next day.

"Thank you, my lady, but I have to remind you that I was the one who led us into the desert in the first place."

She gave me a sharp look. "No, Norbert, I am the leader here. You are the advisor. I value your opinion, but it is up to me whether I follow it. Taking this path was my decision."

I thought, how quickly she's taken up the mantle of leadership. She's very young, and yet she intuitively knows how to accept responsibility and to inspire loyalty. I was more than ten years older than she was, but I hadn't yet learned the skills

49

of leadership which she'd mastered so easily. I knew I wasn't a leader; instead, I had a gift for words and a shrewd knack for survival. She seemed to understand what each of us—Anja, Hamlin and I—contributed to our quest.

"Tell me, Norbert," she said after a while. "*Dragonja* is the name of the river we are coming to? The one that flows down from the mountains past Dragonja City?"

"Yes, my lady."

"*Dragonja* is an interesting name, is it not?"

"Yes, it is. I imagine it's a very old name. People have lived in this region a long time."

"Do you think the name has to do with dragons?'

"I do not know, my lady."

"Are not the names of things chosen for a reason?"

"I imagine they are, but over time the reason for the name may be lost."

She nodded, and I knew she was remembering the ashen soil and the charred bodies we'd encountered a few days before. Like her, I was beginning to believe these things were, as they say in the old stories, *dragon sign*.

Chapter 5

We came upon the Drekavac-soldiers unexpectedly as we topped a small rocky hill. There were only five of them, not a full company, about seventy paces down the slope. I guessed they were stragglers, perhaps the survivors from the company that had been incinerated. They saw us at the same time we saw them, and they quickly mustered a line with their spears pointed at us.

Tessia took charge of us immediately.

"Anja, cover the left flank. Hamlin, cover the right." She quickly unstrapped the pack from Ottolo and mounted him bareback. "Norbert, stay close on my right. Bruin, heel." She pointed at the ground on her left.

The dog and I did as we were ordered.

"My lady," I whispered. "There are five trained soldiers facing us, and only four of us. Should we make a run for it?"

She looked at me with disgust. "There are six of us," she announced loudly.

I realized she was counting the dog and the donkey as two of our soldiers, and I thought *This is not going to go well.* But she didn't need me undercutting her leadership right now, so I kept my fears to myself.

"Draw your weapons and hold position," Tessia said to Anja and Hamlin who were looking fit and strong. Hamlin had a firm grip on his spear, and Anja had set aside her staff and held her short sword ready, her ears so tall and stiff they resembled horns.

Tessia quickly strung her bow and let fly three arrows in succession. The soldiers caught the arrows on their shields. Seeing the Drekavacs unharmed, she unstrung her bow and slid it into the leather sheath on her back. Tessia drew her Voprian sword and held it above her head. Remembering that Anja and Hamlin had been honing their copper blades against whetstones every evening for days gave me some confidence, as did the memory of seeing them fight the ghost wolves. What are a few ragged soldiers compared to the ghost wolves of the Dry Hills? I drew my short sword.

When the soldiers realized that the squad they faced was made up of just two men, two girls, a dog and a donkey, all of us dusty and exhausted from our long trek, they started laughing, pointing at us and jeering. "Did you forget your other farm animals? Where's your cow and your chicken?"

The Drekavac-soldiers walked up the hill, their spears pointed randomly in the air, not even bothering to maintain close order. They obviously thought they could finish us off easily. My fear left me and was replaced by anger at their lack of respect. Do they not know who we are? We are Tessia's Guard, Heroes of the Bekla Valley! Now I was ready for a fight.

"Steady," Tessia said. "Hold your position."

When the Drekavac-soldiers were about ten strides away, Tessia yelled ferociously, "CHARGE!" and all six of us lunged at the soldiers who were so surprised by our attack that they froze and looked at us with big eyes. One soldier lowered the point of his spear at Anja who, striking it aside with a stroke of her sword, lunged and slashed the Drekavac across the face. Another went for Hamlin whose longer reach enabled him to jab the soldier in the chest with his spear before the soldier could get close enough to use his own spear. The three Drekavacs in the middle came for Tessia astride Ottolo, with me at her side trying to look dangerous. Ottolo and Tessia broke through their ragged ranks, knocking one soldier down. Another lifted his ax to slice open my head, but Hamlin, having dispatched his opponent, hit him with the shaft of his spear, knocking him down. I looked around and saw Bruin standing on a soldier's chest, growling, daring him to move. The man Tessia had knocked down was lying next to him, with the point of Hamlin's spear at his throat.

The battle had lasted only a few moments. Of the five Drekavac-soldiers who had attacked us, one was mortally wounded, Hamlin's spear having penetrated his chest. One was bleeding heavily from a slash to his face by Anja's sword. One had nasty-looking dog bites to his hands. Another had a lump on his head from Ottolo's charge, and he was also holding his gut, so Ottolo may have kicked him as well. And the soldier who'd lifted his ax to cleave my head was passed out cold from the blow from Hamlin's spear shaft. *We beat them easily,* I thought, and Tessia had held back, not even using the singing sword. I realized she was letting us get practice in fighting, preparing us for future battles. There were no casualties on our side, unless you wanted to count the mortal blow to my pride because I wet my pants when the man raised his ax to me.

"My lady," I asked. "Should I tend to the wounds of our enemies?"

"Yes," she said, pointedly ignoring the evidence of my embarrassing loss of control over my bladder. She added, "And when you're finished tending them, I want to find out what they know."

There was nothing that could be done for the Drekavac-soldier who'd taken Hamlin's spear through his chest. The tip of the blade was sticking out of his back, and his breathing had stopped. The Drekavac who'd been slashed in the forehead by Anja's sword was frightened because blood was running into his eyes. I had him lie down on the slope with his head higher than his feet and gave him a cloth to press on the wound. I would come back to him later after tending the other Drekavacs and sew up the gash with needle and thread. He'd carry a scar all his life, not an unusual mark on a man of his trade. The Drekavac with dog bites to his hands was not in bad shape. Bruin had torn the skin in both hands, but no bones had been broken. I stitched and bandaged his hands and told him he would be fine in a few days. Fortunately, dog bites rarely fester because canine saliva helps to heal wounds. The Drekavac with a lump on his head and the sore gut was not seriously injured although I doubted he'd tell the story of being bested in battle by a donkey. The Drekavac that Hamlin had bashed in the head with his spear shaft was awake, but feeling dizzy, and the welt on his head seemed to be increasing in size. I worried that his brain had been injured by the blow, but there was nothing I could do for him but give him water and tell him to lie still.

One of the biggest surprises of my life occurred to me that day when I realized that the differences between Drekavacs and men are merely superficial. Underneath, their bodies are exactly the same as ours. I wondered how this could be, and the only answer I could think of was that we're closely related. Drekavacs and men are, you might say, cousins.

I reported all this to Tessia who was looking at the weapons the soldiers carried. She distributed a sword to Hamlin and a spear and a helmet to Anja. Hamlin tried on helmets, but they were far too small for his large head. He looked ridiculous with a small helmet sitting on top of his large frame, and Anja was laughing at him, calling him "a mountain with a bucket on top." Tessia cleaned her Voprian blade with a cloth, even though she'd not used it in the battle, and slid it back into the scabbard on her belt. She looked dashing.

"Do you need a weapon for yourself, Norbert?"

I knew she was simply paying me a courtesy by asking. I shook my head, looking at the ground. She'd seen my incompetence on the battlefield a number of times now and knew an additional weapon would be wasted on me. She questioned each soldier separately, quietly, but in sight of the others. They would be less inclined to lie if they knew their comrades might tell a different story. She let me listen, knowing two memories are better than one. Later, she and I compiled an overview of what they'd revealed to us.

The five Drekavac-soldiers were, as we suspected, the only survivors from the massacre in the Dry Hills. Their company had been taking a shortcut from the Bekla River to Dragonja City just as we were doing. In the middle of the night, they woke to the sound of a loud flapping of wings, but much deeper than any sound made by a bird. Then came the rotten egg stench of sulfur. Suddenly their captain, who had stood up in surprise at the noise, burst into flames and ran off into the night screaming. The soldiers panicked and ran in all directions. Every now and then they would see one of their comrades burst into flame and fall down screaming and rolling in the sand trying to put the fire out.

The five survivors straggled west, hoping to get back to Dragonja City alive. Along the way, they stumbled across each other and decided it would be safer to travel together. Tessia asked each one what it was that attacked them, but none could say. All they'd seen was men bursting into flames. One Drekavac guessed they'd been attacked by wizards, and another said it was bandits with flaming arrows. Clearly, none of them had any idea who their enemy was. More important was the information about the regiment of soldiers stationed in Dragonja City's Black Castle. The Drekavac whose hand had been chewed up by Bruin was the most talkative. He said his name was Frezz.

"King Ottolo supposedly lives in the castle," Frezz said through parched lips. "But I've never seen him. The wizard Ludek is the one who acts like a king, if you ask me. He hears petitions, holds trials and dispenses what he thinks is justice, which usually means torturing and killing someone."

Frezz looked at the pack that Hamlin was strapping to Ottolo. "Do you have anything to eat?" he asked. "We haven't eaten in three days."

When Tessia shook her head, he asked, "How about water? Do you have anything to drink?"

Tessia glanced at me, and I fetched a couple of tubers from Hamlin and brought them back.

"What am I supposed to do with those?" Frezz asked. "They look hard as rocks."

I used my copper knife to slice a tuber into thin disks. I put one in my mouth and sucked the starchy juice. I handed the rest of the sliced tuber to the Drekavac who held it up to his nose and sniffed it suspiciously. Satisfied I wasn't trying to poison him, he put a slice in his mouth.

"Not half bad," he said. "These grow around here?"

"They grow in the gullies," I said.

"I wish we'd known about these things before," he said. "If you people hadn't attacked us, we would have surely died of thirst out here."

Tessia didn't bother correcting him on who'd attacked whom. Instead, she asked, "Is there a dungeon in the castle?"

When Frezz nodded, she asked, "Is there a prisoner named Kerttu there?"

"Don't think so," Frezz said, putting another slice of tuber in his mouth. "I've never heard that name."

"How many soldiers are there guarding the castle?"

"Two hundred total," Frezz said. "But usually there are about a hundred out in the field, divided into three platoons of twenty-eight each, plus officers."

"And what do the platoons do when they're out in the field?"

The skin of Frezz's white scaly cheeks twitched, and he looked nervously away.

"Oh, you know... Just keep an eye on things. Protect the citizenry... You know... protect the farmers and... service the

56

farmers' daughters…" He gave a wink, clearly trying to divert the conversation with an innuendo.

Tessia looked disgusted. "Protect the farmers and service their daughters?" As she drew her Voprian sword from its scabbard, the blade sang softly.

"What is that?" Frezz asked, his gray eyes widening. "A blue singing sword? Are you a witch? May the Goddess help me… Are you going to eat me?"

"I may," Tessia said, softly. Pointing the tip of her sword at the Drekavac's throat, she said, "Now tell me of the villages you burned, the citizens you massacred."

Frezz started talking quickly, telling a tale of terror, mayhem and mass murder. Ludek believed that the citizenry needed to be kept off balance, never knowing when the soldiers would show up or what they would do. Sometimes, to keep his hand in, the wizard led the expeditions himself.

Little else did the Drekavac-soldiers say that was of interest to us, just the usual complaints of soldiers—the food was bad and there was not enough of it, their officers were indifferent to the soldiers' fate or comfort, and the long marches to punish villagers sometimes went badly. But the soldier with the bandaged head said something which made Tessia's eyes light up.

"At the tavern," he said, sucking on a disk of *wasserplanz*. "I heard a drunk soldier repeat a rumor. A scout sent into the mountains to find Zygmunt's rebel camp had come across a she-dragon sleeping beside a waterfall that came out of a glacier. He'd run a spear through her side while she slept, and she'd killed him before she died. Another scout came across the two bodies later." As a reward for this bit of information, Tessia gave him a second slice of tuber which he carefully studied before putting in his mouth. "But I don't believe it," he said, shaking his head. "Everybody knows there's no such thing as dragons."

When Tessia was satisfied that the captives had shared all the useful information they had, Tessia said they were free to leave. She allowed them to keep their meager possessions except for the sword, spear and helmet she'd given to Anja and Hamlin. As the soldiers walked off, two of them carrying a litter on which their companion with the injured head lay, Anja narrowed her eyes and said, "Are we going to just let them walk off? They'll tell their commander they saw us, and he'll send an army against us. We should kill them before they get away."

By the Goddess, I thought, *this girl is quite ruthless.*

Tessia, watching the soldiers walk off, replied, "No, they're not going to tell anyone that they were beaten by four villagers, two of them girls, nor that they left their dying comrade behind. Instead, they'll tell their captain how valiantly they fought against a large army of bandits. They'll leave us out of their account altogether."

As we got closer to Dragonja City, the land became more fertile. We saw sheep and cattle in the pastures and the trees were taller and greener.

"What's wrong, Norbert?" asked Tessia who was walking beside me as I led Ottolo down the path. "You seem to be out of spirits today."

She let the silence stand between us until I felt I had to answer her.

"I feel I've let you down, my lady."

"In what way have you let me down? You have served our band well."

"Thank you, my lady, but I was completely useless in the battle. If it hadn't been for Hamlin, half my skull would still be on that hillside."

She laughed. "Hamlin is good with a spear, isn't he? I remember he did the same favor for me a few years ago. A large bear would have taken off my head if Hamlin hadn't run him through just in time." She looked at me full and square and said, "We each bring our gifts to the field, Norbert. Hamlin brings strength. Anja brings shrewdness. I bring leadership. You bring wisdom. And… Ottolo brings donkeyness!" She laughed, stroking his muzzle.

"My lady," I asked. "Where did you learn to fight?"

"Oh, my Uncle Zygmunt taught me," she answered off-handedly. "He thought I needed to know how to defend myself since I was spending so much time in the woods. He said I had a talent for it."

"Did your father approve of his brother teaching you these skills?"

She laughed ruefully. "My father has never approved of me. He always wanted me to learn how to cook and manage a household. How to sew and take care of children. He would have been happiest if I would have married a village boy apprenticing a trade and had a half dozen children and been content as a wife and mother. I love my father, so I tried to please him, but being a village matron was not something I could ever be. I needed to be out in the woods hunting deer and sleeping on the ground." She looked at me defiantly, "And why shouldn't I? Why does a girl have to stay home? I'm the best hunter in the woods, and my father never minded eating the meat I brought home."

"So, your uncle taught you how to use a sword?"

"And a bow and a spear. Also, how to use my hands and feet to fight. Most of all, he taught Hamlin, Anja and me how to work together, so we could fight bandits if we needed to." She looked off in the distance. "He told me three fighters could beat an army if they have a good strategy and know how to work together."

"And what makes a good strategy, my lady?" I thought about our battle with the soldiers a few days before. She somehow understood how to beat them as soon as she saw them.

She narrowed her eyes and answered confidently, "Deceit."

"Deceit? What do you mean?"

"You must make the enemy think you are less powerful than you are, so their guard goes down. Or you must make them think you are more powerful than you are, so they don't strike when they have the chance. They must think you are many, when you are few; and few when you are many. You must make them think you will attack from the front and then attack from the rear; attack them on the left when they thought you were attacking on the right."

Listening to her, I realized that in the battle with the soldiers what had defeated them was their over-confidence. They had no idea that they were up against a well-disciplined squadron of irregulars who had the high ground.

"And how is it that you can lead warriors so well, my lady?"

"Warriors must know that you believe in them. They must know they are not alone. And most of all, they must believe they are fighting for a cause worth dying for." She thought for a moment and added, quietly, "And they must believe that their captain will do everything she can to bring them home safely."

I looked at Hamlin walking beside Bruin in front of us. I turned my head and looked at Anja behind us. These two young people had known Tessia all their lives, and they were willing to fight, and if necessary, die for this young woman. And I wondered, what about me? What am I willing to do for this young woman?

L udek. *The dragon shaped the name in her mouth, letting her long-forked tongue ripple with the sound of the syllables.* Lu-dek. Luuuuuudek. *The first syllable stretched like a moan, a cry for help, a simmering below the surface of pain.* Dekekekek. *The short second syllable was like the click of a lid closing on a box. What was in the box? Nothing we want to know, she was sure. Nothing but darkness and suffering.* Luuuuuuudekekekek. *Was he still a man? Or had the years of pain, the abuse of the dark magic on his mind when he was a child turned him into a monster? That is, a real monster. Not a monster as men thought of dragons. Dragons are not monsters, but ancient noble beasts formed in the last age of ice, messengers of the Goddess, harbingers of history, witnesses to the ages. Ludek was something else. He had somehow come out of the depths of darkness, and now his soul threw a shadow wherever he walked.*

The Dragon had encountered Ludek only once. Once was enough. After her mate Rilla had died at the hands of one of Ludek's soldiers, the dragon had, she admitted, gone a little crazy. She and Rilla had always avoided humans, and the strategy had served them well for ten thousand years, but now all bets were off. She flew through the night searching for soldiers who looked like the one who speared Rilla through the heart. She was not going to take on a whole army, of course; instead, she picked off stragglers or attacked a platoon, swooping down on them and roasting them in their armor. Now who's the monster? *She thought as she listened to their screams.* No amount of pain and terror would be enough to quench her need for revenge.

But once, as she flew across the Dry Hills looking for prey, she had sensed a presence in her mind, a probing by a foreign mind. She had never experienced this before. In the past, she and Rilla had exchanged thoughts, meeting in the border area between their two minds, but this was different. Something was digging into her mind, like a surgeon slicing into flesh. She turned in flight away from the source of pain, flying as fast as she could back to her mountain cave. But in the few moments when she and the wizard were connected, she'd seen into his mind. It wasn't like listening to a dream of one of his soldiers, it was more like seeing into darkness suddenly illuminated by her presence. And what she saw horrified her. In his mind, pain was not a temporary condition as it was for other humans. Instead, for Ludek pain was everything, the entire universe. Pain was endless, permanent, infinite.

In the face of this kind of evil, there was nothing a dragon could do but flee.

But this summer, the dragon became aware of something else happening, something completely unexpected. She had recently become aware that Ludek has a brother, a silly little man who travels from farm to farm trading in household goods and practicing healing magic. His name, she now knew, was Norbert Oldfoot. She twisted her tongue around the name: Nordbutt, Nobutt, Oldfool. Oldfool Northbutt. *What a ridiculous little man, she thought. Unless, of course, he's a spy for Ludek.*

Part Two: The City

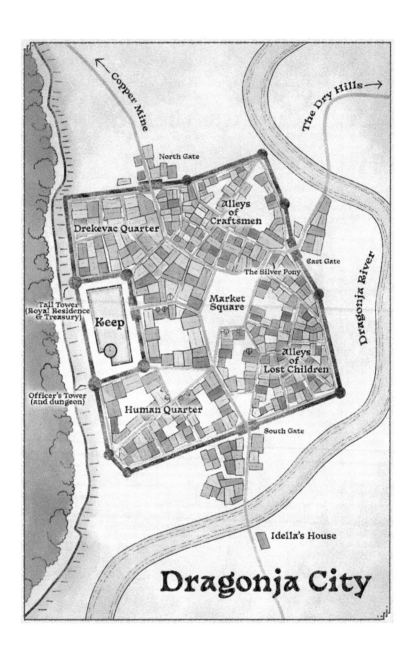

Copper Mine

The Dry Hills →

North Gate

Alleys
of
Craftsmen

Drekevac Quarter

East Gate

The Silver Pony

Dragonja River

Tall Tower
(Royal Residence
& Treasury)

Keep

Market
Square

Alleys
of
Lost Children

Officer's Tower
(and dungeon)

Human Quarter

South Gate

Idella's House

Dragonja City

Chapter 6

Dragonja City is in the lowlands beside the Dragonja River, a tributary of the Bekla. Here, gems and ore mined in the mountains are traded for grain and meat the farmers in the valleys produce. Smiths, weavers, potters, furriers, leather workers, miners and woodcarvers bring their goods here to trade in the markets. The streets are jammed with people jostling each other. Soldiers, rivermen, and fancy girls mix noisily in the taverns. Every year I came here to buy minerals and gems which I could trade for craft-goods in the valley. It was the largest city in the region, and the largest I'd ever visited although I'd heard of wealthy ancient cities far to the east.

On a clear beautiful day in midsummer, we approached Dragonja City from the Dry Hills. The outer city wall, the height of five men, stretched north and south curving out of sight. We could see the thatched roofs of buildings behind the wall and on a hill in the center a black Castle surrounded by its own inner wall, taller than the outer wall, with towers and turrets and banners flying on the spires. We walked past the beggars and cripples who were not allowed inside the city and approached the outer gate. It was market day, so the gate was wide open, two soldiers standing guard while a third examined each person wanting to enter, many of them carrying baskets of apples or leading carts loaded with hay. We tried to blend into the crowd and look like we belonged there. The soldiers stopped us at the gate.

"No weapons," one of them said curtly.

We'd already hidden our spears and swords, as well as Tessia's Voprian blade, in a hole we'd dug in the woods, so we handed our copper knives, our last remaining weapons, to the soldiers and walked through the gates. We planned to dig up the buried weapons later once we'd learned where Kerttu was being held.

I'd explained to my companions that there was only one main street which led from the East Gate where we entered to the inner gate of the Castle. There was one other street, much narrower, and it led across the city from the South Gate to the North Gate. The rest of the city was a bewildering maze of alleys, many of them dead ends and stairways leading to locked doors. Even the residents became disoriented and lost at times. I wanted Hamlin, Anja and Tessia to stay close to me, or we'd spend a lot of time looking for each other.

I led them to the Silver Pony, an inn on East Gate Street where I'd stayed a number of times before. The inn was easy to find because a large wooden sign displaying a rearing white pony hung directly over the oaken door. We left Bruin and Ottolo tied to a post outside the inn. May the gods have mercy on the man who tried to steal Ottolo or the pack on his back. Those two animals were seasoned warriors now.

The innkeeper recognized me because I'd paid him with silver at the end of my last visit.

"Norbert is it?" He said through the bushy black beard that completely covered the lower half of his face.

"That I am," I answered. "And your name is Heikum, as I remember."

"That it is," he answered heartily. His stock in trade was hospitality, and he knew his trade as well as I knew mine.

"Will ye be needing a room?" he asked, looking at the four of us. His eye caught on Tessia, as men's eyes always did, then he caught himself and looked back at me.

"She is our kinswoman, and we are honor-bound to protect her," I said to him meaningfully.

Tessia scowled at me because she needed no man's protection, but she understood that I was making the rules clear to the innkeeper, and her fighting skills were not the issue now.

"We'll be needing a room to stay until Spring," I said, and his eyes lit up with greed. I wasn't sure how long we'd be staying in the city, but I wanted us to have a safe warm place to sleep if needed.

"Oh, I don't know whether we have a whole room for you," he said, watching my reaction.

I treated him to a flash of anger before saying, "I think you could make arrangements."

I pulled a silver coin out of my tunic and showed it to him.

"Perhaps I could find room for you, but it would mean moving other patrons out of a room."

Calling the drunken Drekavacs and flea-bitten rivermen that occupied his beds "patrons" was flattering them, no doubt. I pulled another piece of silver out of my tunic and placed both on the plank that served as a bar in front of him. Both pieces disappeared into his apron pocket.

"It would actually be a piece of silver for each person," he said. I met his eye steadily and didn't move. "But those third and fourth pieces of silver would be payable at the end of the winter, of course," he said. When I gave a curt nod, he smiled and we shook hands, sealing the deal.

He also let us put our donkey in the barn in the back of the inn, but we had to supply the straw and feed for him. I'd instructed my companions not to let anyone know that he was named after the king; we didn't need to attract attention to our treasonous opinions at this stage. As it turned out, Bruin needed little care while we lived at the inn; he joined a pack of dogs behind the inn who lived off the scraps thrown on the midden.

For a few coppers, the landlord gave us tankards of ale which we took to a table in the corner where we could talk without being overheard.

"Stay here until next spring?" Tessia asked incredulously. "Why don't we leave now and go into the mountains?" She was so angry she was almost spitting.

"It is midsummer now," I explained calmly. "And winter comes early in these parts. If we were to leave now, we would be facing the first blizzards in the mountains soon. We need to wait until Spring before we go into the mountains. Besides," I added, dropping my voice and leaning forward, "This is a chance to find out as much as possible about the King, the wizard Ludek, his soldiers, and the Castle. If you do find your dragon, my lady, you want to know your enemy and the lay of the land."

Tessia considered what I'd said, glancing at Hamlin who nodded enthusiastically and Anja who didn't object. She could see she was outvoted, but I doubted she would spend more than a few weeks in the city before she headed into the mountains to find Zygmunt, his rebels and the legendary dragon. In the meantime, I knew she'd be testing the Castle's defenses and trying to get over the wall to save her father. As for me, I planned to stay in the city until spring at which time I could go back to being a tradesman visiting the farms and villages on the river. I'd had quite enough of fighting Drekavacs, robbers and wolves.

The room Heikum rented to us wasn't as bad as some I've seen. It was on the third floor and had a sloping ceiling with deeply recessed windows. The windows were open now, but in the winter the shutters would be closed keeping out the wind. The beds were wooden frames full of straw, and I made a mental note to ask Anja and Hamlin to fetch fresh straw from the farmers who sold it by the cartload in the market.

The first week we were in Dragonja City, we explored the streets and markets. The town was lively and prosperous. People seemed well-fed and there were children playing in the streets during the day. After nightfall, the inns filled with men and

Drekavacs, and the streets with soldiers and women who sold themselves to the soldiers. We discovered that not all soldiers were Drekavacs and not all Drekavacs were soldiers. We were warned repeatedly not to enter the maze of alleys off the main streets because gangs of youths were known to attack and rob strangers who entered their territory.

One morning, shortly after dawn, the black gates of the Castle opened, and a wizard, his face in the shadow of his hooded robe, emerged on horseback, followed by twenty Drekavac soldiers on foot, heavily armed. Each man carried a shield with the red dragon crest, the emblem of King Ottolo's family. They marched down East Gate Street and went out into the countryside.

"That's the Wizard Ludek, the king's emissary," Tessia said, under her breath. "He and his men are going out to the valley, *our valley*, to loot and burn."

I didn't tell her that I had a long history with Ludek and knew him well.

Looking back on those few months I spent in Dragonja City, I don't know why I was surprised every time love blossomed.

First, it was Anja and Hamlin. When we were traveling together, I noticed that they often would sit close together beside the fire in the evening, looking at each other intensely, but I thought nothing of it. After all, they'd grown up together, and they'd lived in the woods with each other for years. It never occurred to me that they were in love until I walked into our room at the inn, and they were sitting on the bed together kissing, and Hamlin was stroking Anja's tall furry ears, an especially sensitive area for Beklan women. After our long journey together, Anja and Hamlin had become my friends, and I was happy that these two admirable young people who had no one else to call family other than Tessia had found each other.

69

Next, it was me who was smitten. One day shortly after we arrived in the city, I was walking around the open-air market near the East Gate, looking at the fruits and vegetables, exhilarated by the cool morning air and the sights and sounds and smells of the open stalls. Ever since I was a boy, I loved going to the market in Dragonja City where my father took me every year. It was exciting to see the big piles of red and green apples, apricots the color of sunrise, pyramids of peaches and carts of turnips and rutabagas smelling of the rich earth still clinging to them. The Green Magic of the market was palpable, and I felt at home there. Wandering around, putting a little of this and a little of that in my basket made me happy.

The first time I saw Idella, she was standing behind a table stacked with barley loaves and sweetmeats which, I learned later, she'd stayed up all night baking in the clay oven behind her house. Every day, she showed up at the market, paid a penny tax to the alderman and set up her stall to sell her goods. I was immediately struck by her exotic beauty. Unlike the people of this region, who have pink freckled skin, Idella was dark, almost black. Her nose was aquiline, and her hair fell in a cascade of curls on her shoulders. A dark boy about ten, presumably her son, stood beside her, and when he made a joke, her laugh seemed to come from deep inside her.

I told her that the barley bread smelled delicious. I've long believed that the art of baking is one of the gentlest ways to practice Green Magic. Grinding the seeds of grasses into flour, mixing them with water, and growing the living yeast to nourish the body creates a pure form of love. I noticed that Idella was wearing an amulet on a chain around her neck. I recognized the stone as a Goddess Eye similar to the one in the ring my father gave me. Often people who are not mages wear an amulet with a magical stone as a way to encourage the Goddess to bless their work. I also noticed a copper bracelet of three snakes entwined in a circle. I told her I'd never seen anything like it.

"Oh, she said, shrugging. "It's nothing. Just a bracelet my mother gave to me."

I was later to find out that it was much more than a piece of jewelry. I was about to say that the bread smelled delicious, but she seemed to read my mind.

"You are right, sir. My bread *is* delicious," she said confidently, her voice almost singing, and she spread butter over a piece and held it up to my mouth. Our eyes locked and I took a bite. It was the most sensuous moment of my life. I was instantly in love.

I asked for four loaves of bread. She named a price and we bargained playfully. I ended up overpaying for the four loaves with four copper coins which she put in a leather bag she kept in her apron. I took the bread and fruit back to the inn and gave a loaf and an apple to each of my companions. As we sat in our room happily eating, Tessia looked at me out of the corner of her eye.

"Something is different about you, Norbert. What have you been doing?"

"Oh, I just went to the market. It makes me happy being there, that's all."

"Anja and I saw Norbert talking to a pretty Black woman," Hamlin said, as if he were a child telling on his big brother.

Anja nodded and gave a little laugh, a nice change from her usual dour countenance.

"Tell us about your pretty lady, Norbert," Tessia taunted.

"Oh, she's no one. How's the barley bread?" I asked, trying to change the subject.

Everyone nodded enthusiastically as they chewed.

"Norbert's new girlfriend made it," Hamlin said. "She has a stall down in the market."

"Oh, we shall have to meet her," Tessia said, waving her hand with a limp wrist, as if she were a duchess.

The next day I woke early and went to the market. Idella was setting up her stall. She and her son had driven a cart from her house not far from the city, and they were unloading the two barrels which held her loaves carefully wrapped in linen, as well as the small pot of butter which she spread on slices of bread to entice customers to buy the loaves. They laid a plank across the barrels to make a counter to display the loaves. Then, Idella unhitched the donkey that had pulled her cart and gently kissed the animal on the forehead. The donkey looked at her with undiluted love, then followed Idella without a lead rope to another stall where Idella thanked a farmer for the loan of the animal. I was fascinated with this beautiful baker who seemed to have a way of winning the trust of animals.

I didn't want to seem too eager, so I stood at the next stall, pretending to be very interested in the rutabagas and carrots the farmer offered for sale. Out of the corner of my eye, I saw Idella look at me, then look away when I looked at her. Then she brought her gaze back to mine, and I knew I had a chance with her. She turned to her son, said something to him and gave him a copper coin. His eyes lit up and he headed off to East Gate Street where a fire-breather who called himself The Dragon was performing. I walked over to her stall. I noticed she was still wearing the entwined snake bracelet, but she was wearing a different amulet today. She'd exchanged the Goddess Eye for an amulet with a red stone known as the Heart of the Flower, a love charm common in this region. So, Idella was trying to encourage someone to fall in love with her. Interesting.

"My friends loved the barley bread yesterday, so I've come back for more."

She buttered a slice and held it up to my mouth, as she'd done the day before. This time I lightly grasped her hand as I took a bite. Again, our eyes locked. "Is my barley bread the only thing that pleased you?" she asked provocatively.

"There is much here that pleases me," I said, brushing my lips against her hand.

She dropped her dark eyes, then slowly raised them in that age-old invitation a woman silently gives a man.

"You should come to see where I make the barley bread," she said casually. "My oven is very hot," she said, turning away and arranging her loaves on the table between us. "My son Alaric and I leave here usually by midday after we've sold all the loaves. Can you come back then?"

And thus, I began the great love affair of my life.

Anja and Hamlin hung around the market each morning, sometimes being hired to do odd jobs lifting barrels off carts, shoveling hay and manure, harnessing mules. They picked up an occasional copper coin, but usually they were paid in vegetables which they brought back to Femke, the innkeeper's wife, who ladled large bowls of soup for each of them. Anja and Hamlin became known as honest dependable workers, and they seemed content to stay in Dragonja City for the time being.

Heikum was the public face of the inn, tending the bar and taking care of business, but Femke was the real power, running the establishment with an iron hand from the kitchen. She was a large strong woman who oversaw the pantry, cooked a giant cauldron of soup every day and brooked no nonsense from anyone. I occupied my time by wandering down the shores of the Dragonja river, looking for edible herbs and medicines. I dried the herbs and gave them to Femke for her soup pot, and I showed her how to make teas out of medicinal plants and explained what illnesses they cured. She was grateful for the herbs, as well as the education, and every day she gave me a bowl of soup.

One morning I was at Idella's stall at the market while she ran an errand. A tall lanky Drekavac-soldier walked toward me.

He looked familiar but I couldn't place his face. Frankly, in those days, all Drekavacs looked pretty much alike to me.

"You don't remember me, do you, Healer?"

"Sorry, I do not."

"My name is Frezz." He held out both of his hands. There were red scars, still pink, on his gray skin.

"Ah, now I remember," I said. "You were one of the soldiers we met in the Dry Hills. Our dog Bruin gave you those scars. How are they healing?"

"I can use my hands, but sometimes they hurt."

"The apothecary over there on the square sells willow bark. Every evening you should make a tea out of the bark. That will help with the pain. And be careful using your hands. They are still healing."

"Thank you, Healer." He continued to stand in front of me, smiling. He looked a little scary. A fully armed Drekavac-soldier is not good for business. I noticed that the other customers were avoiding the table. I didn't want Idella to return to find I hadn't sold any bread.

"Is there anything else?" I asked pointedly.

"You know..." he said. "We were expecting you and your friends to kill us. Why didn't you?"

"Because it wasn't necessary. You were no longer a threat to us. Why waste a life?"

He looked at me, puzzled, and walked away shaking his head as if he had just talked to a mad man.

Every day I visited Ottolo in the stable behind the inn. I brought hay to him, groomed his flanks with a handful of straw, and spoke to him, praising his good nature and his great learning. You think, no doubt, that I'm joking, but actually donkeys are great philosophers, and we can learn much from them.

I also saw Bruin every day. He'd joined the pack that lived in the alley behind the stable. The dogs scavenged the refuse thrown out by housewives and innkeepers, and the canines killed an occasional rat or mouse for dessert, unless the feral cats caught them first. I often whistled for Bruin, and he left his half-wild friends and ran over to me. I gave him small treats of sausage and bacon saved from my meals at the inn, and I scratched behind his ears. I didn't want him to go completely feral because when Tessia left the Dry Hills to go into the mountains, she no doubt would want Bruin beside her.

Tessia was the only one of us who was clearly not happy in Dragonja City. The only work she could find was as a server at the Silver Pony Inn. Other than the leather pants and wool top she'd worn since we left the valley, she didn't own any clothes, having lost them when the king's soldiers burned down her father's house. She had to borrow a skirt and blouse from Femke, the innkeeper's wife, who'd taken a liking to Tessia. But Femke was a large woman, and the skirt was too big in the hips for Tessia, and the blouse was too big in the bosom. Tessia had never learned how to sew, so I used needle and thread to adjust the clothing to her tall lean frame.

Every evening the public house filled with men and Drekavacs who drank prodigious amounts of ale, bragged loudly about their exploits with women and competed with each other with dart-throwing and arm-wrestling contests. They thought it was great sport to say vulgar things to Tessia, making jokes about her breasts and her sexual tastes. They often slapped her on the rear as she walked by carrying tankards of ale, causing her to spill the liquid on her blouse or on a customer who was likely to curse her for being clumsy. She barely tolerated the harassment and would return to our room upstairs late at night, exhausted and angry. She never shed tears, but she often told me that we should depart into the mountains as soon as possible. The early winter be damned. But something happened that changed her attitude toward staying in Dragonja City, at least for a while.

Tessia met Taja.

Taja was the daughter of a wool merchant to whom I'd introduced Tessia, hoping he would have employment for her, so she could quit working at the inn. The merchant shook his head. He was sorry, but he didn't have work for her. I noticed Tessia was looking over his shoulder at a young woman sorting wool in the back room. She was paying attention to the task at hand and hadn't noticed Tessia. She was a tall attractive young woman with curly sandy hair. I noticed she had especially long fingers which, being a musician myself, made me think she'd be able to play the lyre.

In the mornings Tessia found excuses to drop by the wool merchant's shop. She claimed she'd lost a pendant and wondered whether anyone had found it. She brought her wool singlet and asked whether they knew someone who could mend it. She dropped by to see whether Taja could help her move her cart around to the back of the inn. And could Taja show her where she could buy the best apples in the market? Eventually, the two of them began spending time together without Tessia having to invent excuses. I would see Tessia and Taja holding hands in the market. They would feed each other bites of bread and cheese while looking deeply into each other's eyes. I'd see them sneaking off to the barn behind the inn which seemed to be their favorite trysting spot. When I went into the barn to bring hay to Ottolo, I would shout and wait a few moments before walking in so as not to embarrass them. I could hear the two young people whispering in the loft, pretending to hide while in each other's arms. Sometimes they emerged from the barn with their cheeks flushed, straightening their clothes, and trying to appear innocent. First love is a beautiful thing.

One afternoon, I went outside to visit Ottolo and saw Tessia sitting on the roof of the barn. It was a late summer day with the sweet smell of verbena in the air. She was looking over the rooftops at the black walls and towers of the Castle.

"What are you doing up there?" I asked, even though I knew the answer. This was the time when the soldiers came out of the Castle to go on night-patrol.

"Oh, nothing," She said. "Just enjoying the sunlight."

I climbed the ladder which was leaning against the barn and sat next to her.

Her dark hair had grown out since I'd cut it, and strands kept falling across her eyes. She never would have tolerated a distraction like this when we were traveling. At that time, she was always alert, ready for a fight. Since she'd met Taja, she'd become softer in her attitude, a little dreamier. I knew from my own recent experience that being in love changes a person quickly.

As we sat on the roof, we saw the black gates of the Castle open. Tessia stood up and waited intently. A mixed company of Drekavacs and men led by a Drekavac officer on horseback emerged from the Castle. The officer had his sword raised as he issued orders to the men behind him. They marched down East Gate Street and passed in front of the inn, a stone's throw from where we stood.

"Norbert, did you notice the captain's weapon?" She asked after the soldiers had passed.

I thought *Ah, here's the warrior woman I know.*

"What did you see, my lady?"

"His sword is a Voprian blade," she said and looked at me levelly.

As far as I knew, there was only one smith in the entire Bekla-Dragonja Valley who'd mastered the art of casting Voprian swords. "Kerttu is here in Dragonja City?" I asked. "But we would have seen him if he were here, or at least we would have heard of a smith who was casting a new metal. No one can keep a secret like that for long."

She turned and looked at the Castle again. "They're keeping him hidden in there." She lifted her chin toward the black walls.

After our conversation on the roof of the barn, Tessia became a different person. She lost her brightness and her sense of humor and became moody and angry. I'd see her walking through the market with Taja following behind or sitting on the bench in front of the inn with Taja sitting beside her, looking at her like a neglected puppy. I didn't see them sneaking into the barn anymore, and both of them lost the rosy glow in their cheeks.

Meanwhile the famous early snow of Dragonja had arrived. The wind swept through the pass between the Thumbs of the Giant and hit the town like a Voprian blade. Some of the farmers stopped setting up stalls in the market; and eventually only a few intrepid souls selling hay or firewood showed up. Femke started making two cauldrons of soup each day, sending Anja and Hamlin into the countryside to buy whatever roots and dried meats farmers had to sell. Heikum's public house became more crowded, especially in the evenings when Tessia served tables. I picked up a few coins with my lyre, singing songs and telling stories. People hunkered down beside the fire and drank ale and ate soup and spoke of dark tidings from the Castle. Sometimes, people said, there were screams coming from behind the black walls.

One evening when Anja and Hamlin were on one of their foraging expeditions, I was sitting in my accustomed seat next to the fireplace, warming myself, when I heard a commotion on the other side of the room. The room grew quiet and everyone turned to see Tessia, holding an empty clay tankard as if it were a club, standing over a large man who was sprawled on the floor.

I'd seen Tessia in battle before, and she always remained cool, but not now. She was furious.

"The next time you touch me, I will rip off your man-parts and stuff them down your throat," she said loud enough so everyone in the room could hear. The room was dead quiet for a long moment, then two of the man's companions stood up and headed for Tessia, obviously planning to teach this wench a lesson.

Big mistake.

Taja, who had the fighting skills of an angry kitten, leaped at one of the men who knocked her aside and Taja went tumbling over a table. Tessia lifted her skirt to free her legs and kicked the man in the knee and he fell. His friend tried to grab her, but she was too fast. She dodged his hands, jumped on the table next to him and came down hard with the heavy clay tankard on his head. He fell beside his two friends. More men stood up, whether they planned to defend Tessia or attack her wasn't clear. The melee was spreading across the room.

Heikum came from behind the bar with a large club and began to beat anyone in his path, and Femke emerged from the kitchen swinging a broom and cleared a path to Tessia who was standing over the men fighting beneath her, landing the tankard on the head of any man who ventured close. Eventually the two women were standing back to back on the table, battering every man they could reach. Men ran for their lives out the door, helping the injured escape into the cold night. Better to take your chances in a frosty wind than to face the fury of two women who'd tasted the blood of men.

When the melee first started, I'd grabbed my lyre and moved to a safe place against the wall next to the fireplace. Now that the fight was over, I helped Taja sit up. I took a look at the bruise on her forehead and the one beside her eye. She'd be swollen and in pain tomorrow, and she'd have a black eye for a week, but otherwise she was unhurt.

Heikum looked around his public house. Stools were broken,

tables were upended. An ale barrel had been upended and the black liquid spread across the floor. I could see his anger growing.

"You wench," he growled at Tessia. "You attacked a guest in my inn. How dare you?"

Femke moved to stand between her husband and Tessia. "It was not her fault," she said evenly, obviously not wanting to antagonize him further. "He laid his hands on her. She was defending herself."

"He laid his..." Heikum sputtered through his beard. "He laid his hands on her? SO WHAT? She's a serving wench. Of course, he laid his hands on her. It happens all the time. It's one of the reasons men come here... patting a pretty girl on the rump is part of the entertainment. Do you think men come here to listen to stories?" He gestured at me. "Do you really think they come to hear this fool?"

I stayed silent. There was more at stake here than my pride. We needed Heikum if we were to survive in this city.

"Who's going to pay for the barrel of ale that's on the floor? Look at it, dripping through the cracks in the floor into the root cellar. How much silver will we lose because of this silly girl's temper?"

"I can pay you for the damages, but I think..."

"SHUT UP!" Heikum bellowed at me. "You brought her here. She is, what, your niece?"

I nodded, seeing no point in explaining my devotion to Tessia right now.

"Heikum..." Femke said calmly. "The girl is truly sorry. Aren't you, dear?" She nudged Tessia with her elbow.

"Yes," Tessia said, clearing her throat. "I am truly sorry for attacking the patron. I felt I needed to defend my honor."

Heikum looked at her incredulously. "Your honor?" He said, shaking his head and turning away. "Her honor!" He lifted his palms in the air and rolled his eyes at the ceiling. "A serving wench's honor will ruin me, by the Goddess."

Heikum walked across the wet floor, the soles of his boots squishing, muttering to himself, and went upstairs to his bed.

"Will he evict us?" Tessia asked Femke anxiously. I was glad she asked because I was worried about the same thing. It was getting colder by the day outside, and if he evicted us, no one else would take us in.

Femke pursed her full lips and shook her head. "He will not evict you because if he does, then he will never be able to collect damages from you. Tomorrow he will be calmer, and we can talk about what payments you can make to him for the spilled ale. Right now, the two of you need to clean up this mess, so the damages he claims tomorrow will be reasonable."

Femke turned to go, then turned back to Tessia. "You beat three strong men senseless armed only with a tankard, girl. Where did you learn to fight like that?"

When Tessia didn't answer, Femke said, "Well, you made life better for serving girls in this house, haven't you? No man will be slapping a girl on the rear anytime soon around here."

Femke walked up the stairs, laughing quietly to herself.

Over the next few days, Heikum's anger passed. I negotiated a settlement of two silver coins for the barrel of ale and the ruined root vegetables in the cellar—a generous fee for him. And Tessia agreed never to assault a customer again, no matter how boorish he may be. It soothed her pride that Lugg, the big man who had insulted her, returned a few days later with his mother beside him. He sheepishly apologized to Tessia while his mother looked up at him fiercely. I guessed that she'd threatened to slap him silly unless he apologized.

Later that day, Anja and Hamlin returned to the inn with two large bags of turnips which they had come by in circumstances that they explained in only the vaguest way... something about finding the bags in the woods. I suspected they'd stolen the turnips from a farmer's barn, but I wasn't going to ask questions, not when the turnips were being delivered right after the ones in the root cellar had been ruined by ale dripping from above. Femke looked at Anja and Hamlin with narrow eyes, then decided, as I had, that too many questions would ruin the soup. She accepted the turnips and ladled as many bowls of soup as they wanted.

The fight at the inn did not hurt Heikum's business. In fact, it helped. A number of people, men and women, some of whom I'd never seen before, came to the inn to have a draught and get a look at the serving wench who'd fought three men and won.

Tessia must have realized that her indifference to Taja in recent days had been cruel. After the brawl at the inn, she thanked her in front of Anja, Hamlin and me for her chivalrous defense of her honor. She praised Taja for her bravery, and each day made a big show of checking her wounds. Meanwhile Taja began standing taller, walking with more confidence, and wearing her black eye as a badge of honor.

But sometimes, as the long days at the inn dragged on, I'd see Tessia looking at the black walls of the Castle with longing.

Finally, I said to her, "The time is not yet, my lady."

She turned to me with tears in her eyes, the first time I'd ever seen her cry, although not the last, and said, "Do you think they are torturing him, Norbert?"

And I answered, more confidently than I felt, "Oh no, my lady, they need him. I'm sure they are taking good care of him. He's the only one in this land who knows how to make a Voprian blade."

A few evenings later, I was playing my lyre and singing in the tavern when Hamlin showed up at the door and signaled that there was an emergency. I ended the song with a flourish and met him outside.

"Tessia's been hurt. She needs your help." He had a worried look on his face.

"What happened?"

"She fell from the Castle wall."

"What was she doing…" I stopped myself from wanting an explanation and instead concentrated on the emergency at hand.

"Does she have broken bones?"

"I don't think so, but she has a bad gash on her leg, and she hit her head."

"Is she conscious?"

"Yes, but she can't stand up."

I went to my room and got my healer's bag, and he led me to the far corner of the Castle wall where it meets the city wall. At the junction, there's a corner where an intrepid climber could conceivably scale to the top and gain entrance to the Castle. Tessia was lying on the ground hidden by shadows. Anja was nearby, also in shadows.

"How far up was she when she fell?"

"Almost to the top," Anja said.

I looked up and said, "You took quite a spill." Tessia nodded.

I examined the gash on her leg, cleaned the wound and put a yarrow compress on it to stop the bleeding. There was a large lump forming on the back of her head. I filled a cloth bag with snow and told Hamlin to hold it over the swelling on her head.

Just then, a Drekavac guard came upon us. "What is going on here, Bard?" Fortunately, he was a regular at the tavern, so I knew him.

"Oh, nothing, Snork. You know Tessia, the serving wench from the Silver Pony? She's had a little too much ale and slipped on the ice. She'll be fine. We're going to take her back to the tavern now."

Snork chuckled and walked off, shaking his head. A drunken serving wench. Nothing unusual here.

Hamlin carried Tessia back to the tavern and put her on the bed. I nodded to Hamlin and Anja, and they left.

"Tessia, you were trying to get into the castle?"

She stayed silent.

"And what were you going to do if you had gotten in? There are a hundred soldiers guarding the castle, and you don't even know whether your father is there. And even if he is, you don't know where he would be. Were you planning to search the castle looking for him? Once the alarm went out, you'd be fighting a hundred soldiers. You were lucky that you fell from the wall."

I waited for her to respond, but she said nothing.

"And you convinced Anja and Hamlin to go with you? You realize that they would have been killed as well? It's one thing to risk your own life, but to risk theirs in a foolhardy mission? You have behaved irresponsibly."

She turned her head to me, anger flashing in her eyes, "I didn't make Anja and Hamlin come. They wanted to do it."

"Tessia, those two young people would follow you any-where. If you are going to be their leader, then you have to take their safety into account."

"My father is in the castle," she said, changing the subject. "Before I fell, I was able to see over the top of the wall. There's a small stone building next to the keep. The building has two chimneys and one side is open. It looks just like my father's smithy back in our village."

Tessia lay back on the pillow, closed her eyes and yawned. "But you're right, Norbert. You can stop scolding me now. It's clear that three warriors cannot take the castle. We're going to need an army."

Chapter 7

Shortly after the equinox, the cold weather arrived in earnest. No sooner were the crops safely in granaries, then the winds blew down from the mountains, and people started spending more time indoors.

Soldiers, both men and Drekavacs, often came to the inn to drink and talk with their friends. Usually they kept to themselves. The townspeople were not fond of them because they were serving a king who was indifferent to the fate of his subjects. Sometimes, though, one of the soldiers would sit and drink and talk. He was always a lonely soul, far from his family and hungry for affection and conversation with regular people. He usually talked about his homesickness, how much he missed his wife or sweetheart, how his children were growing up without a father. These lonely soldiers seemed to be grieving for the lives they hadn't led. They wondered whether they should have stayed on the farm or continued working in their father's shop. They missed the tenderness of living with their mothers.

Late at night listening to drunken soldiers cry out of loneliness, I noticed something disturbing about myself. It became apparent that I felt far more sympathetic to the men than to the Drekavacs, and I wondered why. As a healer, I had cut open the bodies of both races and seen that under our skin we are identical. In treating the two races, I found that what healed men also healed Drekavacs. But there was something about the outward appearance of Drekavacs that made me feel queasy. Their sharp talons looked threatening. Their scaly skin disgusted me. It was difficult to listen to their raspy voices. But I knew these were superficial differences, and I wondered what it was that made people hate an entire race.

O ne evening a Drekavac-soldier sat by himself all evening drinking ale. He had a sour disposition and a missing ear. He drank quickly, deliberately, gesturing to Tessia to fill his tankard again and again. When he finally had had enough ale, he staggered up to the bar which Heikum was wiping off, and knowing truth can be found in ale, I moved closer to hear him. It was late, and the place was empty. I could hear Femke scrubbing pots in the kitchen. Tessia moved behind the bar and stood beside Heikum.

The soldier cursed the life he'd chosen. He cursed the mother of his captain. He cursed the king. He even cursed the Wizard Ludek whom most of the soldiers would never mention by name. Then he praised the men of his company, his brothers in arms, as soldiers have done since the first warrior picked up a spear. Then he put his head in his arms and sobbed.

"They were such fine brave lads," his muffled voice said, barely audible in the crook of his arm. "Now they are all dead. All of them." And he wept.

Heikum put a fresh tankard in front of the man, but it went untouched.

The man lifting his face from the bar, barely aware we were listening, said, "Once the snow starts falling, this is the dangerous time to be on patrol."

"Aye, Lad," Heikum said in the manner of barkeeps everywhere. He'd heard many soldiers' drunken tales before.

"Once the snow starts falling," the soldier repeated. "Zygmunt and his bandits are especially active. They come down from the mountains, dressed in white furs from head to toe. Even their eyes are covered with a strip of fur with slits to protect against snow blindness. Dressed in white fur, they're invisible as ghosts. They specialize in ambushing us on the river road."

Heikum was wiping out tankards, barely listening, but Tessia and I were paying close attention.

"Damn that Wizard!" the soldier said. He didn't seem to care that he could be executed for saying such a thing. He was past caring. "He assigned an inexperienced lieutenant to lead our patrol, and half a day's march from the city, we walk into a trap. The bandits suddenly surround us, coming out of the snow like ghost wolves, screaming and slashing and stabbing. And then suddenly, one of them whistles and the bandits disappear, leaving half our company dead or wounded."

The soldier stared at the wall behind Heikum. He was obviously still in shock from what he'd experienced. I thought he'd finished his story, and I was about to prescribe an herb infusion to help him sleep, when he shook himself out of the trance and continued.

"So, the lieutenant turns us around and we start back to the city, following the frozen road beside the river. Wouldn't you know, a blizzard blows in. With snow up to our knees, we slog along, barely able to see the man in front of us. Afternoon gives way to evening and evening to night. We have to believe that somewhere up ahead is the safety of the city walls, but we don't seem to be getting any closer."

The soldier notices the tankard of ale in front of him, but he doesn't seem to know at first what it is. Finally, he shook himself, lifted the tankard and takes a long draught.

"And what happened next?" Heikum asks, starting to show interest.

"So, we're way out there trudging through a blizzard, and I'm beginning to suspect that we'd somehow gotten turned around, and we're walking away from the city instead of toward it. I stop and let the company march past me. I've always had a good sense of direction, and I take a few steps to my right and realize I'm walking uphill, not down to the river like I should. I start to yell to my buddies who've continued marching that we need to turn around. I can barely see them through the blizzard, and the wind is loud, and they can't hear me."

Heikum and Tessia have stopped their chores and are listening. The Drekavac soldier is silent for what seems a long time, then says, not quite believing it himself, "And through the white air of blowing snow, I see an amazing thing, a ball of fire coming out of the sky. It hits a couple of men who burst into flame and they panic and run into other men setting them on fire. One of them runs toward me and I try to move out of the way, but my boots catch in the snow and the man on fire collides with me, knocking me over and my cape catches fire and I'm burned on the shoulder before I can rip off the cape. I look up the road and another ball of fire hits the men and another."

Now the soldier turns his back to Heikum and lifts his tunic. The skin of his back was red and blistered from his waist to the back of his head.

Femke, who'd come from the kitchen to hear the man's tale, said, "Oh, you poor dear. Take off those clothes and I'll get you some balm for those burns."

He did as she instructed, and she brought a jar of ointment made of lard and fennel she kept handy for accidents in the kitchen. As she spread the balm on the gray skin of the Drekavac's back, you could see the muscles on his face relaxing and he seemed to become smaller and softer as the pain subsided. I'm sure that the tenderness of a woman's touch did more to ease his pain than did the ointment.

He said that after the battle, he checked his comrades, but they were either charred from the fire, or they were gone, having run off in fear and flame. He headed back to the city, this time in the correct direction, and when he arrived at the East Gate, the guards told him they'd seen no one come from the direction he pointed. It's been two days and none of his comrades had returned to the city.

After the soldier thanked Femke for her kindness, he left to go back to the barracks in the Castle.

"What do you think happened to the soldiers? I asked Heikum.

"I have no idea," he said gruffly as we wiped down tables.

"It was a dragon that attacked those men," Femke said firmly.

"You don't know that," Heikum said.

"What else could it have been?" She retorted.

"It could have been anything," he said vaguely.

"'It could have been anything,'" she said, imitating him. "It was definitely a dragon. My people have lived in Dragonja Valley forever, and we know our dragons. What do you know of dragons, Heikum? Your people are from the coast. You know your whales, and we know our dragons." She nodded her head once affirmatively, as if she'd proved her point.

"It's just old wives' tales, if you ask me," Heikum muttered, stacking tables and chairs so Tessia could mop the floor.

"Well, you'd be wise to listen to your old wife, old man. This old wife goes out to the farms to buy turnips and bacon, and I listen to the other old wives. They've seen a she-dragon coming down from the mountains. She leaves the farmers alone, and the farmers leave her alone. But they say the dragon hates the king's soldiers."

Heikum laughed derisively, "The dragon has political opinions, does she?" He looked at me as if we were the only logical ones in the room, but I tried to look neutral, not wanting to anger either of them.

"The dragon hates the king, does she?" Heikum continued, "The dragon wants to overthrow the king and install a new regime, does she? My, what a sophisticated dragon we have in our valley! Perhaps the dragon should be our new queen?" He laughed uproariously at this new foolishness from his wife.

Femke was getting angry. She didn't like being mocked,

especially in front of Tessia and me. Tessia was mopping the floor, pretending not to listen to the married couple's bickering, but I was sure she was noting every word.

"And how do you explain the burns on the soldier's back?" Femke asked, raising her voice and pointing her finger.

"He probably just rolled over in his sleep into the fire and caught his cloak on fire. It happens all the time," Heikum said, shrugging.

Femke stormed upstairs, clearly exasperated by the stubbornness of her husband.

The next morning, Tessia and I walked to the market. There were only a few stalls open now. It was too cold to stand outside for long and all the farmers were sitting beside their small fires, repairing their tools, sorting seeds, and carving toys for their children. Tessia was meeting Taja at the market, and I was hoping to see Idella.

"What did you make of the soldier's story last night, my lady?" I called her "my lady" only when we were alone, of course. When we were around other people, I called her by her given name, or I called her "niece."

"I thought that Zygmunt's warriors ambushed the soldiers. They were probably just a small band, and so they attacked and left before the soldiers could fight back. Then the soldiers tried to head home and were attacked separately by a dragon."

"Do you think that Zygmunt's warriors and the dragon were working together?"

She squinted her eyes for a moment, thinking. "No, I don't think so. If they were working together, they would've coordinated the attack better. They would have used the dragon first, wiping out most of the company, then used the warriors to finish them off. By using the warriors first, they took the risk of casualties."

"So Zygmunt and the dragon have a common enemy, but they are not working together?"

She nodded. And I thought, not for the first time, that Tessia would make a brilliant general.

At the market, Tessia wandered off with Taja, the two of them holding hands and talking, and I stood in front of Idella's table, looking into the eyes of the most beautiful woman in the world.

I della and I began spending a lot of time together. Although I worked late most nights singing at the Silver Pony, and she woke early to start her bread, we managed to spend most afternoons together. I enjoyed being at her little house outside the city. Close by there was a willow tree beside a stream, and it amused Idella that the slender wands of the willow hummed and vibrated as I walked past. She understood that I had my reasons for having turned away from the practice of extreme magic, and she accepted my decision. Far from the bustle of the Silver Pony and the market square, I felt at peace and I was looking forward to helping her in the garden when spring came. Her son Alaric was a fine lad, and I tried to be friends with him. I'd noticed among the families I'd stayed with on my trading route that children often resented their mothers' lovers. They were afraid, I suppose, that their mothers would not love them anymore. And the men who came to live with these families often had a heavy hand, trying to make the children obey them. I vowed to treat Alaric with gentleness and kindness, rather than being stern and distant the way my father was to me.

One reason I fell in love with Idella was that she understood that magic, at least the simpler kind, is not something different than everyday life. She knew that when she baked bread, she was practicing Green Magic, as was the farmer who grew the apples she put in the bread. When she encouraged her son to learn to count or to bargain with customers or to talk gently to Ottolo, these too were the practice of Green Magic. When the body heals a cut or a cow births a calf or the moonlight makes the river

91

rapids look like snow-covered peaks, these too are the Goddess making gifts to us. Idella understood that what I did with my healing spells was not much different than what I did with the songs I sang at the Silver Pony. Both were words given to me by the Goddess, and I should honor them because they were signs of Her great love for us. Sometimes, I heard Idella mutter an incantation under her breath when she'd lost a button or the fire in the oven wouldn't start, and I could see she had a gift for magic, even though she never seemed to have developed it.

Idella had an air about her that inspired peace in both animals and people. Bruin and Ottolo adored her, and they seemed to know what she wanted from them without her having to lead or command them. Once in the marketplace, a mare spooked and ran through the square knocking over stalls and making people scurry for safety. Unlike everyone else, Idella didn't panic, but simply walked over and stood calmly in front of the rearing horse until the animal was as calm as she was. The owner who'd been chasing the mare, grabbed the reins and lifted the strap to hit the animal across the face, but Idella grabbed his wrist firmly, stopping him. The man turned angrily toward her, but when he met her eyes, he relaxed, thanked her and led the mare away.

Idella was also the most honest person I've ever known. Honesty was not a choice she'd made, as it was for me. I'd developed a reputation as an honest trader, and I guarded that reputation carefully. Since I often saw the same farmers and craftsmen on my river route every year, I needed them to trust that I wouldn't cheat them. So, my honesty was a business strategy that arose from the practical need to keep my customers happy. But Idella's honesty was of a different type altogether. Her world was coherent and seamless. Everything was connected to everything else, and to tell a lie would tear the fabric of her world in a way that would cause the whole cloth to fray. I believed that she could no more tell a lie than a bird could sing a false note, or a river could reverse its course. However, being honest is not the same thing as being forthcoming. There were things about her past that Idella refused to disclose.

I once asked Idella about the entwined snake bracelet which her mother had given her and she always wore.

"The three snakes symbolize Fate, Fear and Faith," she said. "Fate is your destiny, what you cannot control. Fear is what you want to run from but must look at calmly. And Faith is the belief in yourself and the Goddess, the acceptance of What-Is."

"Do you worship these snakes?" I asked.

She looked at me and laughed. "No, I'm not a snake-worshipper! The snakes are merely symbols of life."

"You were born in a land far to the south of here?" I asked, realizing that I knew little of her background.

She nodded and turned away. Clearly, she didn't want to discuss where she came from, nor anything else of her past. I wondered what hardships she'd endured that led her so far from where she was born. I wanted to honor her reticence about her past, but I thought it might be safe to ask about her beliefs.

"Do the people of your native land worship the Goddess Nilene, as my people do?" I asked.

"Yes," she said. "Although we call Her by a different name, I believe She is the same Goddess."

She then changed the subject to talk about the gossip of the market.

One day, Idella said she had something important to tell me. "Femke said I should tell you because people gossip, and it's better that you hear the truth from me instead of a version from someone who doesn't know what happened…."

Her voice trailed off. We sat in silence, and she traced the entwined snakes on her wrist, lost in thought. The silence went on so long, I wondered whether she was going to continue. Then she took a deep breath and began:

"As you know, I was born in a land far to the south of here, and when I was a little girl, my family hoping for a better life moved to the seacoast of this kingdom, two months travel from here. My mother passed away years ago. My brother still lives there, but I've not seen him since I left thirteen years ago when I accompanied my husband, Daras, to Dragonja City. He was a gem trader, and he thought he could make a better living here, close to the mountains where most of the gems come from, buying them here and then taking them to Kladd City to sell. When we first got here, we found this house which had been abandoned, but we thought we could turn it into a nice home for our family. Shortly after we got settled here, Daras came down with a fever. I took care of him, but I was pregnant at the time, and having a sick husband was difficult for me. After I spent the last of our savings, I didn't know what to do.

"One day, I went into labor. It was sooner than I expected, and I didn't have anyone to help me. I had the baby by myself with my feverish husband in the next room. After giving birth, I became very sad at our circumstance. We had no food and no money. I was so desperate, may the Goddess forgive me, I actually thought of drowning my baby. How was I to feed us? After two days of not eating and my milk running dry, I finally made a decision. I swore I would do anything in my power, no matter how vile or disgusting, to save my baby. So, I put on my best dress, left Alaric on the bed next to Daras and told this man whom I loved with all my heart that I'd found a job in the city, and he would need to watch our son for a few hours. This was the only lie I ever told my husband.

"It was evening. I went to the first tavern I saw, the Silver Pony, and sat at a table. There were Drekavac-soldiers there, loud and drunk. When they saw I was alone, I did the things a woman does to attract men. I wasn't subtle at all. It didn't take long before one of the Drekavacs came and sat at my table. He leered at me and invited me outside. We quickly negotiated a price. I made him give me the coins before I would go with him. We went into the alley and I satisfied him. Then I went back into the tavern and invited his friends to join me...

"With some of the coins I bought soup. I ate one bowl and took another bowl back to Daras. In a few hours, I was able to nurse Alaric. The next day, I went to the market and spent the rest of the coins on bread and vegetables. After a few days, we were again out of food, so again I put on my best dress and went to the Silver Pony. No sooner had I sat down, then Heikum walked over to me and told me I had to leave. I was so ashamed. I ran out the door and went around to the back of the building where I had serviced the soldiers a few nights before. There was no one there. I started retching. My stomach was empty, so nothing was coming up, but I was making a terrible noise.

"Suddenly, I felt a hand on my back. I turned my head and for the first time I saw the wide soft face of Femke. She said, 'Oh, my sweet girl. You certainly need a friend, don't you? Come along now. Let's get you inside where it's warm. I have some soup you'll love.'

"'But what about your husband?' I asked. 'He doesn't want a woman like me in the tavern.'

"Femke, may the Goddess always hold her in the palm of her hand, said, 'The kitchen is mine, dearie. Heikum has no say over what happens there.'

"I sat at her kitchen table, and she fed me soup and listened to my story. And every afternoon for months, I went to her back door and she gave me a pot of soup for Daras and me. I will always be grateful to Femke for her kindness."

Idella and I sat in the darkening bedroom, neither of us speaking.

Finally, she clasped her hands against her breast. Her eyes filled with tears, and she asked softly, "Do you hate me now?"

I turned to her and said, "Oh no, darling, I love you more now than ever. What a brave woman you are." And we fell into each other's arms.

Chapter 8

It was early autumn, and the snow was already up to our knees when I finally had a chance to meet Zygmunt. He'd heard from his sources in Dragonja City that there was an attractive young serving wench at the Silver Pony who'd fought three strong men with her bare hands and soundly beat them without so much as a scratch on her. He knew there was only one girl in the entire Bekla Valley who could best three men, and he was the one who'd trained her. He'd also heard she'd arrived in the city with three companions: a big blonde boy skilled with a spear, a small dark girl clever with a blade, and a shireman who could pluck a tune or two. Through his emissaries in the city, Zygmunt got a message to us at the Silver Pony.

It was too dangerous for the famous rebel leader to enter the city gates, so the four of us met him and a large well-armed man at a farmer's hovel down the Dragonja River. We sat at a rough-hewn table with Zygmunt while his bodyguard Wessel stood warily behind him. The farmer, who'd built a roaring fire in the hearth, brought out bread and apple cider for us with apologies that he couldn't provide better sustenance for such important guests. I silently vowed to leave the farmer with a silver coin when we left, so his family would not starve to pay for his hospitality.

I'd always assumed that Tessia had gotten her good looks from her mother whom I'd never met, but seeing Zygmunt, I was struck by the resemblance. He was tall, and even though he was still wearing some of the white furs that he and his warriors wore for warmth and camouflage in the snow, we could see he was a powerfully built man. He'd dropped his hood to reveal the same thick black hair that I'd snipped off Tessia a few months before. The uncle and the niece sat across from each other at the table and I noticed that her hair had grown out now, and the curls fell over the points of her ears, just as her uncle's did. He had taken off his gloves and his strong scarred hands rested on the table in front of him. He was wearing a ring with a chalcedony stone, the purple gem of leadership.

"I can't stay long. Someone may have seen us coming up the river. The king's spies are everywhere," he began. "I just wanted to see my niece," he smiled at Tessia who beamed back at him. "And find out why you've come to Dragonja City."

Tessia nodded at me, signaling that I should be the one who spoke first.

"Meister Zygmunt," I gestured toward Anja and Hamlin who stood with their backs against the wall where they could easily see the door behind Zygmunt. "My companions and I have accompanied your niece on her quest."

"And what is the nature of the quest?" Zygmunt asked, turning to look at Tessia.

Tessia related to Zygmunt the burning of their village, including their family home and his brother's smithy, and her belief that Kerttu was being held in the black Castle. When Zygmunt looked puzzled, she told him that Kerttu was seen being led away by the king's soldiers and some of the soldiers were later seen with Voprian weapons.

Zygmunt nodded, "My brother always was a genius at working with metal. He'd certainly be an asset to the king." The bandit chief narrowed his eyes at Tessia. "What is your plan?"

"We plan to capture a dragon and ride it into the Castle and save my father," Tessia said confidently.

There was a long pause in the conversation while Zygmunt looked incredulously at Tessia, then at me, then at Anja and

Hamlin. We all looked back at him without expression. Then he burst out laughing.

"Are you planning to muster an army of trolls to help you?" he asked straight-faced. "How about a regiment of warlocks and witches? Or perhaps a navy of whales?" He stood up. Clearly, he'd heard enough.

"Tessia, my niece, it's been a wonderful surprise to see you again. You know I love and admire my brother, but if the king is holding him prisoner in the Castle, there's nothing we can do to save him. Believe me, my spies and I have talked about storming the Castle many times, but there would be too many casualties." He shook his head in disgust. "As for enlisting the aid of the Dragon Tyrmiss…" He made a dismissive gesture, "It is impossible."

Tessia and I looked at each other. Zygmunt knew the dragon's name.

Zygmunt opened his arms to Tessia to give her an embrace before he left, but she did not move.

"Meister Zygmunt," I said.

"Yes, Meister Norbert?"

"Have you spoken with the dragon?"

"Yes, I have," he said, waving his hand, as if it were nothing to speak with such a beast.

Tessia, Anja, Hamlin and I stared at Zygmunt with wide eyes. "And if I may—what was the nature of your conversation?" I asked calmly.

Zygmunt sat at the table again. "Actually, I had the same idea that you have. I knew the dragon and I have a common enemy in the king, and I wanted to enlist her in our struggle. I thought we could coordinate our attacks, perhaps even storm the Castle."

"So, the dragon is female? And what was her response to your plea?"

"She laughed at me. Her laughter is a frightening thing. It

seems to come from deep inside the earth. And then she said I should go back to my tent." Zygmunt looked at Tessia. "You need to know that Tyrmiss hates men."

"What about women?" she asked, almost impertinently.

"I'm sure she hates women as well."

"Does Tyrmiss attack only soldiers?" I asked. "Surely you couldn't survive in the mountains if Tyrmiss didn't tolerate you."

"I will give her that," Zygmunt replied. "The dragon does tolerate us, and to tell you the truth we would never have survived if she were not keeping the soldiers away. I guess we owe her a great deal for her indifference toward us."

"So, the dragon can tell the difference between the soldiers and your band of rebels? How does she know the difference?" I asked.

"The same way you and I can tell the difference. The soldiers all carry a shield with the king's crest." He laughed. "I hadn't thought of it before, but the king's crest is a red dragon. Tyrmiss is simply attacking her own likeness."

"Please tell us about the dragon, Uncle," Tessia was clearly fascinated by the creature.

"Tyrmiss is an ancient being. Dragons live a very long time, and she says she's the last of her kind." Zygmunt became thoughtful, and then added, "And she is angry, very angry. Her rage is what is driving her to kill the king's men."

"What is the source of the dragon's rage?" Tessia asked.

Zygmunt replied sadly, "Last summer, one of my men came across the body of a female dragon beside the Poellat Gorge Waterfall. She had a spear in her side. Not far from the body was a dead Drekavac soldier who had been disemboweled by her talons. He must have snuck up on her as she was sleeping and run her through, and she killed him before dragging herself to the waterfall, perhaps to drink the water, or perhaps it was a magical place for her."

"And the attacks on the soldiers started after the female

dragon was killed? Was she Tyrmiss's friend? Is she getting revenge for the death of her friend?" I asked.

"I've thought the same thing myself." Zygmunt responded. "In any case, we have a useful, though undeclared, truce with the dragon. She leaves us alone and she kills our enemies. I do not want to invite Tyrmiss to reconsider the nature of our relationship. So please do not go looking for her. She is dangerous and temperamental, and she is not fond of men." Zygmunt looked meaningfully at Tessia. "Or women."

He looked at his niece and gave a long sigh. "But you were never one to listen to reason from your father, so why would you listen to me? I can see that you plan to search for this dragon despite what I say, so there's one more thing you need to know."

"And what is that, uncle?"

"Tyrmiss the Dragon will watch you for a long time before she speaks to you. If you travel in the mountains, you will feel her watching you. And when you sleep, she'll be listening to your dreams. And when you fight the soldiers, she'll let you die. She wants men to kill each other, so she doesn't have to."

There was a long silence as we all waited for what we knew was coming next from Tessia.

"Uncle, may we join your band?" Zygmunt didn't look surprised. He obviously had surmised that this request was the reason why his niece had traveled across the entire kingdom to meet him. He looked at his niece, and said gently, "It's not a soft life we lead, Tessia."

"I do not wish for a soft life."

"I heard how you took down three men in the tavern. We can always use a good fighter." He looked at Hamlin and Anja. "We can always use a spearman and a woman-warrior clever with a blade. You're both welcome to join us if you wish, but you must follow my orders. Is that clear?"

Anja and Hamlin each gave a single nod, agreeing to the terms. Zygmunt looked at Tessia who nodded as well. He walked over and gave Anja and Hamlin a robust hug, as did his man Wessel. Then Tessia stood and both men hugged her. And so, it was done. My three companions had joined the rebels.

The men started putting their winter gear on, preparing to leave. "Please wait one more moment, Uncle." Tessia pointed at me. "I need Norbert with us as well."

I was shocked. She hadn't discussed this with me, and I had no desire to join a band of rebels in the mountains. We'd been gone only half a day, and I was already missing Idella's warm bed. "My lady…" I started, but she gave me a sharp look that silenced me.

Zygmunt looked at me skeptically. Evidently, it had never occurred to him that I might be part of the package Tessia was offering.

"We've no need of a stringplucker or storyteller in the mountains," Zygmunt said bluntly. "Life is very hard there, and we have room only for fighters, hunters, scavengers, and cooks. This man would be dead weight we'd have to carry."

"I agree," I said, ignoring the insult and feeling relieved he thought so little of my art. "I would be of no use to you."

"I disagree," Tessia said. "Norbert has been invaluable in our quest. It's true he's no warrior, but he is a wise man who has guided us in our journey. He knows the herbs and medicines that can be found in the woods. He can set a bone and midwife a birth. And…" She looked guiltily at me and added. "Also, uncle, he has a bag of silver. He could buy supplies for us."

I felt betrayed. She knew my hoard of silver was a closely guarded secret, and now she had revealed its existence to the leader of a group of bandits! I stared at her in silent rage, and she looked at me and mouthed "I'm sorry" and looked down at her hands. But Zygmunt seemed more interested in my medical skills than in my supposed wisdom or my secret hoard of silver.

"Norbert, do you want to join us in the mountains? We could use a man who knows how to set bones and heal wounds."

"No, I do not, Meister Zygmunt. I wish to return to Dragonja City where I have people who are awaiting me."

"Then that is the end of it, niece. This man does not wish to join us, and I compel no man." Then speaking to his three new recruits, he politely instructed, "Please go back to the city, pack your kits and Wessel will come for you in a few days."

I looked at Wessel and realized that he hadn't made a sound the entire time he'd been with us. But he and Zygmunt seemed to be in complete harmony, understanding each other without saying a word. I wondered what had created such a strong bond.

Months later, when Zygmunt and I had become friends, he told me that he'd found Wessel living on the streets of Dragonja City years before. The boy, who was deaf and mute, was barely surviving as a petty thief and beggar. Zygmunt took the boy under his wing, named him *Wessel* which means *protector*, and brought him into the mountains to earn his keep as a camp tender, training him in weapons and combat and eventually making him his most trusted soldier. Being a deaf-mute was helpful because Wessel never became distracted by what people said, instead reading their intentions quickly by their eyes and their body language, a skill he'd picked up when he was surviving on the streets. Through the years, the two men had developed the ability to understand each other without talking. Zygmunt said that Wessel was fearless in battle and had saved his life more than once.

Through the doorway, I watched Zygmunt and Wessel walk away, following the river. Dressed in white furs and carrying spears tipped with Voprian, the two warriors quickly disappeared into the bright light of the snow.

Back at the Silver Pony, Tessia apologized to me repeatedly, swearing she'd not planned to offer my services to Zygmunt, but at the moment the words sprang to her lips unbidden.

I was skeptical of her explanation, but relieved that Zygmunt was not going to draft me into service.

Tessia, on the other hand, was trying to do just that.

"We need you to come with us into the mountains, Norbert."

I shook my head. "I'm sorry, Tessia." I saw her wince a little. I had not addressed her as "my lady." This was petty of me, I knew, but I was angry at her for the way she'd treated me in front of her uncle.

"For the first time in my life, I'm happy," I explained. "I love Idella and I'm fond of Alaric. I want to stay here and make a life with them."

"You'll be bored with them by spring," she said. We were in the kitchen and she started putting dried fruit and meat in her rucksack. I made a mental promise to pay Femke for what Tessia took.

"I think that Idella has put a charm on you to keep you close," she said.

"Tessia, you know that's not true. Idella does not use charms, well, not that kind of charm…. Staying here is my decision. Ever since I was a child, I've been living on the road. And now, I finally have a home. Idella is not keeping me here. She understands my work requires me to travel a good part of the year, but I'm wondering whether it's getting too dangerous to be a shireman anymore. You remember how frightened the farmers were on the river road."

She lowered her voice and said intensely, "And that is exactly why we need to bring down this king." She cast a quick disgusted look in the direction of the Castle. "You have resisted this quest at every turn, Norbert, and you're resisting me now as well. I should have foreseen this."

"I'm not resisting you, my lady," I said restoring her title. She rewarded me with a quick tight smile.

"Instead, I'm resisting the idea of fighting. You know I'm not a fighter. You, Anja and Hamlin are effective fighters. I'm a poet not a warrior. I sing songs about war; I don't go to war."

"My uncle needs you. I need you. Your friends need you. And you. Are. Letting. Us. Down." She said emphatically and stormed out of the house. I looked out the window and saw Tessia walking quickly across the market square in the direction of the North Gate. Beside her was Wessel with Anja and Hamlin following closely behind. I heard Tessia whistle for Bruin who ran to catch up, and then they were gone. I wondered whether I'd ever see them again.

The blizzard had passed, and the sky was clearing. A bright clear light shone down on the thatched roofs of the city. In the distance, I could see the mountains where the snow would be deepening by the day, the kind of weather that favored the rebels. Despite Zygmunt's quick dismissal of the feasibility of rescuing his brother, I had a feeling that his forces were preparing their attack on the city. There was menace in the air. Soon the war for the Bekla Valley would begin.

A nd then the weather surprised us. After the first blizzard passed, the wind changed direction, bringing warmth from the sea. People emerged from their houses, and the city came alive again. This was, as we used to say in those days, *Drekavac summer*, a time of warmth in the middle of autumn.

I was telling the truth to Tessia. I was very happy with Idella and Alaric. As the weather warmed, farmers started showing up in the town market again, laying out their baskets of carrots and rutabagas, their clay pots of honey, their burlap bags of grain. Idella would stay up all night baking her barley bread, carefully packing it. We would hang the bags of bread across Ottolo's back and lead him into town. The guards at the gate knew us, and Idella would reward their friendliness with a smile. At the market stall, people would approach, exchange pleasantries and gossip with us, then buy a barley loaf with a copper coin or trade a loaf for a bag of turnips or a small jar of honey. Alaric was growing tall and strong, and I enjoyed teaching him songs and how to add and subtract. And in the mornings, I would wake in the first light beside Idella, noticing for the thousandth time how beautiful she was, and I would thank the Goddess for my good fortune.

I've never been much of a farmer but decided, nevertheless, to try my hand at it. I dug a line of holes in the pasture beside the house, sawed logs in even lengths and put crisscrossed sticks across them to make a grape arbor. We talked about planting apricot and walnut seedlings in the other pasture behind the house. It would probably take at least three years for the apricot trees to be productive and five for the walnut trees and grape vines, but we were planning for the long term.

Working outside in the cool autumn, I often looked up at the Thumbs of the Giant in the distance, and thought of Tessia, Anja, and Hamlin. I wondered whether they were safe. Were they joining Zygmunt's raiding parties, or had they found life in the mountains too harsh? Did the discipline suit them? Had the other rebels accepted these brave young people from the valley?

Sometimes we heard about skirmishes between the soldiers and the rebels. Companies of soldiers returned to the city wounded and shaken from battle with incoherent tales of being attacked on all sides by wolves and bandits, and even the farmers, sick of being abused, were taking up arms against the king. One thing that struck me as odd, though, was that no one I knew had ever seen the king. All we saw was the cruelty and brutality of the Wizard Ludek, and I began to wonder about the king's role in all this oppression. Was he ruling the kingdom or was the Wizard?

I reluctantly decided that for the first time since I was a boy, I would not be following the river road with my wares come spring. Thinking about my being attacked the previous summer by robbers on the road, seeing Tessia's burned out village, and listening to the old farmer who told me about the boys and girls being kidnapped created a growing awareness that times had changed. It had become too dangerous to travel. I wondered whether the Bekla Valley which I loved would ever go back to normal.

When the maple leaves were in their autumn glory, Idella and I got married. We'd known each other only three months, but we were both confident that we wanted to spend the rest of our lives together. It was supposed to be a small ceremony with just family and friends, but once the word got out, many people said they were coming, and Idella, being a kind and generous person, couldn't say no. Although Idella had a brother who lived on the coast, the distance was too great for him to travel, and I had no family, so we decided to let the wedding be as large as our friends wanted it to be. Since our guests were expecting a feast, I paid Heikum to bring a barrel of ale and to slaughter a goat and roast it over an open fire in front of our house. Femke loaned Idella the dress she wore at her own wedding, and the two of them spent weeks adjusting and sewing the garment. I was not allowed to see it until the wedding day. I wore a black cape embroidered with a green willow, borrowed from Heikum. Alaric agreed to stand beside me as my best man, and Femke stood beside Idella.

We decided to have a traditional wedding. A shaman from a local village agreed to perform the ceremony, and he, Alaric and I stood beneath a spreading oak tree waiting for the women to approach us. When I first saw Idella, my bride, coming out of the house and slowly walking toward me, I was struck by her beauty. The white dress and white veil set off the black skin of her shoulders and arms in a way that was extraordinary in the light of the autumn morning. Her black curls had been braided into a crown and decorated with thin silver wire. The entwined snakes of her bracelet shone red in the bright sunlight. The shaman said the necessary words, and Idella and I exchanged gifts. As tradition dictates, she gave me a small piece of barley bread with a little salt, symbolizing a good harvest, and I gave her a small bag of grain, symbolizing wealth. Alaric handed me the gold band which had been my mother's, and I slipped it on Idella's finger. It fit perfectly.

Then Idella and I knelt in front of the shaman to show our respect for the Goddess, and again following tradition, I intentionally knelt on Idella's gown, as a funny way of indicating that I will wear the pants in the marriage. And then, when the shaman instructed us to stand up again, Idella took care to step on my foot, to let it be known that she, not I, will hold the upper hand. This, of course, is the ancient promise of marriage—that both people will feel empowered by the marriage, not diminished. Turning to Idella, I lifted her veil and kissed her.

As we turned to go, our path was blocked by ribbons. I was expected to ransom our way free by promising a feast to our guests—which I did. But before we could start the feast, we had to accomplish a task together. A log was sitting on sawhorses. The bride and groom are required to saw through the log together as a symbol of teamwork, a sign of how well they'll work together during their marriage. Fortunately, it was a thin log, so it didn't take long to cut through it. Then walking to the feast, we were showered with barley, symbolizing fertility. Legend says that every grain of barley that sticks in the bride's hair represents another future child. I announced to the laughing guests that I was worried that dozens of grains had caught in Idella's curly hair, so we were expecting thirty children. As we walked through the shower of grain, the guests beat on drums, blew horns and shouted, making as much noise as possible to drive off evil spirits and bring good luck. The last part of the ceremony involved setting fire to a line of pitch on the ground.

Idella lifted her wedding gown to show her shapely legs, and together we jumped over the fire, symbolizing that we would face any danger together.

Then everyone got very drunk. At one point, Heikum, swaying slightly, said to my new wife, "Well, as the man who supplied the feast, it is traditional that I get the first chance with the new bride." And he moved toward Idella with his hands outstretched toward her breasts. Femke slugged him with her tankard, knocking him down. The next day, Heikum woke up with a hangover and a black eye. He didn't remember what had happened, and no one told him.

Chapter 9

One afternoon a few weeks after the wedding, Idella, Alaric and I returned to our house from the marketplace and soldiers were waiting for us. Two soldiers were standing in the dooryard and one of them indicated we should go inside. I thought about running, but it would be foolish, they'd have caught us easily. Besides, even if we got away, where would we go?

Inside, a Wizard sat at the table, his hood pulled back to reveal his face. It had to be Ludek although he looked very different than the Ludek I remembered. The cruel mouth, the arrogant attitude, the sharp gray eyes—who else could it be? He also had a long scar, freshly healed, that went from the bridge of his nose to his left ear, a souvenir from the only time he had run into Tessia. The Wizard signaled the men behind us. I turned to see one man grab Idella's arm and lead her roughly toward the door. Another man did the same with Alaric. I moved toward them. My instinct was to attack the men and protect my family, but Idella said urgently, "No, Norbert, don't. Give them what they want, and maybe they will leave."

I realized she was right. At that moment, I was missing Tessia's skill with a sword, and I hated myself for not knowing how to fight. Feeling impotent, I watched the two men take Idella and Alaric outside.

I turned back to Ludek. "If they are hurt…"

The Wizard looked at me with a slight smile on his face. "Your woman is quite right, Little Norbert. Give us what we want, and we'll leave. We have no wish to hurt your pretty wife or her boy."

"What do you want?"

He stared at me silently. I knew that what he saw was a terrified young man of slight build, dressed as a farmer, who'd just returned from the market.

"You are not from this area, so what are you doing here? People tell me you're a shireman who travels up and down the river. What kind of trade goods do you carry?" He spoke slowly, almost gently, as if he were just making conversation.

I tried to keep my voice even although there was a sense of dread rising from the pit of my stomach. "Pots and pans, textiles, sometimes seeds… whatever is available that people may need."

"Ah, just like your old dad. You inherited the family business. How lucky for you."

He dropped his voice in a conspiratorial way. "Do you sell knives?"

"Sometimes. I sell knives, spoons, bowls… as I said, whatever people may need."

"And weapons? If your customers needed swords, axes, spears, bows, would you sell them?"

"Never."

"And why not?" He asked, as if we were having a philosophical discussion. "You are a shireman, interested in turning a profit. If your customers wanted, say, a dagger, why not sell it to them?"

"Because I don't want to be responsible if someone gets hurt."

"EXACTLY!" The Wizard slammed his palm on the table, making the plates jump in the air. "You are responsible, Norbert." He leaned over the table and looked at me with his cold grey eyes. "You are responsible for what others do. You brought this girl Tessia and her two companions to Dragonja City, did you not?"

"I traveled with them up the river. We were companions on the road, that is all." I hated how defensive I sounded, but I was starting to panic. I realized I didn't know how much he knew.

Ludek stared at me silently for what seemed a long time, letting my fear grow. I knew he could smell the panic I was feeling. The smell seemed to be coming out of my pores. I despised my cowardice.

"I am going to ask you a few questions, Norbert. And if you answer truthfully, then I will let you and your woman and her son go back to your sweet lives. But if you lie to me then I will know it, and I will go outside, and I will hurt your pretty lady in ways she will never forget. I will give her son a slow and painful death, and I will make your woman watch. And when she finds out that you could have prevented these terrible things simply by talking to me, she will hate you. Do you understand?"

I nodded.

"Now," he said gently. "Tell me about this girl Tessia."

And may the Goddess forgive me, I told him everything I knew.

I betrayed my friends."

"No, darling, you saved your family. Thank you."

"If anything I said helps Ludek find Tessia and Zygmunt, I will never forgive myself."

"What did you tell Ludek? That she is a fierce fighter skilled with a blade? Judging by the scar on his face, he's already aware of that fact. Or perhaps that she has two companions named Hamlin and Anja who are lovers? Or that the three of them went into the mountains to join the rebels led by her uncle? You told him very little that he didn't already know, darling. And you did so to save Alaric and me." She hugged me and I felt her tears on my neck. "Thank you so much, Norbert. We owe you everything."

Putting aside my shame, I took stock of our situation. One thing was clear. The three of us could not remain in this house outside the walls of the city. We were too vulnerable. We were at the mercy not only of Ludek, but also of outlaws and deserters. There was increasing anarchy in the countryside.

We talked about our options.

We might try to go to her brother and his family on the coast, but we decided that it was too dangerous at this time to travel so far. Also, there was no way to know what was happening with her brother. Were he and his family safe? Did they have a way to make a living there? Would there be room for us in his house? Would there be work for us? Is there enough food? Would his wife welcome us?

Another possibility was to stay here and fortify the house, but we decided that it wouldn't be possible to resist a siege from the Wizard Ludek and his men if they really wanted us. And moving to my house in the Bekla Valley was no safer than living here, considering what Ludek had done to Tessia's village. Finally, we decided that the best course of action was to move into the city and live in the Silver Pony; that is, if Heikum and Femke would have us. Our logic was that by living close to the Castle and living normal lives, Ludek would take less interest in us, perhaps see us as less of a threat. It was a feeble plan, admittedly, but given our options, it seemed the best we could do.

In the afternoon, I walked into the city and discussed the idea with Heikum and Femke. I explained that it had become too dangerous for us to live outside the city, with outlaws and soldiers on the loose, and I asked permission to move my family into the inn. I didn't tell them about the visit from Ludek and his soldiers, fearing that they wouldn't want us in their house if it appeared we were bringing trouble with us.

"Idella could work in the kitchen with Femke, baking bread which you could sell to customers. I could sing in the tavern, attracting a crowd in the evenings, and Alaric could make himself useful doing chores around the inn."

Heikum seemed hesitant, "We'll need silver from you for

our expenses." And he started counting on his fingers the ways he would be inconvenienced by our presence.

But Femke interrupted, contradicting her husband, "Of course, Norbert, the three of you can stay here. And you can pay us with your work; we'll not charge you anything." She shot her husband a stern look, and I took Heikum's silence as assent.

So it was that Idella, Alaric and I gave up our lovely house in the country, along with our plans for a grape arbor and a grove of apricot and walnut trees and came to live in the same room I'd occupied with Tessia, Hamlin and Anja in the summer. It was more crowded than our house in the country, and we missed the trees, birds and sunlight that made our lives so pleasurable, and the inn was noisy in the evenings; but at least, I thought, we were safe there.

Little did I know what was to come.

I was sitting in the public house, eating Femke's soup with a slice of Idella's bread, when I heard a tremendous commotion outside on the street. I tried to ignore it and concentrate on my afternoon repast, but the noise grew louder, and I thought I should find out what was going on. From the front door, I could see a crowd gathering next to East Gate where the Wizard Ludek sat on horseback at the front of a company of his Drekavac-soldiers, one of whom was leading a prisoner with a rope around his neck.

It was Hamlin. The left side of his head was covered in blood, and he was having trouble walking. When he stumbled, a soldier behind him gave him a shove. The crowd watching this small parade was boisterous. Some people were laughing, thrusting their fists in the air and jeering the prisoner. Others looked distraught. I saw one man who knew Hamlin from the marketplace where he'd worked for weeks, looking angrily at the Drekavac-soldier who'd shoved him. The soldiers marched down the street, their heads held high, obviously pleased to look like heroes with their rebel prisoner. They entered the Castle at the end of the street, and the great black gate closed behind them.

I realized that now two of my friends, Kerttu and Hamlin, were being held prisoner in the Castle.

That evening in the Silver Pony, Drekavac soldiers were in their cups, bragging about their victory over the rebels.

"And so, this big fella, the size of a bear, he was the size of a bear, I tell ya," The soldier looked at his companion, also half drunk, who nodded confirmation, before taking another draught.

"I tell you this rebel swung his great ax at my head," He burped. "And I ducked and ran him through with my spear. Ran him completely through. Then this other big fella hit me with a club from behind, and if it had not been for Gunza here..." he nodded at his companion who seemed slightly surprised to be singled out as a hero. "Then I would not be sitting here telling you about it." He took another long gulp of ale.

At another table, another drunken soldier was saying how they captured Hamlin. "There was this girl, a girl mind you, who was fighting beside them, and these two others, a small dark girl quick with her blade and this big blond fellow who handled a spear pretty well. And the three of them were covering the retreat of the rebels. And in the scrum, the big man got knocked down and a bunch of us jumped on him to keep him from getting up and the rebels had to retreat without him."

From what I could piece together from their drunken talk, which consisted largely of lies and exaggerations about their own heroics, Ludek had led an expedition up the mountain toward the copper mine and stumbled on a small group of rebels who were on patrol. A skirmish ensued and the rebels, badly outnumbered, retreated. Hamlin was captured and brought back to Dragonja City.

That evening, I played my set of songs while men drank in front of me. Neither my mind nor my heart was in the songs, but rather in the Castle with Hamlin. I thought of Tessia and Anja sitting in front of a fire on a mountain side and how they were undoubtedly thinking of Hamlin as well.

Meanwhile, life in the Silver Pony went on as if all was well in the world. Idella baked her bread. Alaric ran errands and fed the animals in the barn. Femke made her soup and scowled at Heikum who counted his money and worried about not having enough. I played my songs to drunken soldiers, laborers, farmers and shopkeepers. Sometimes they brought their wives and sweethearts who seemed to like my songs more than their men did. It was, all in all, a nice life for me and my family, but I knew it couldn't continue. There was something brewing in the air. No one spoke openly about the king, or the Castle, or the Wizard Ludek, or the rebels. Or at least, they didn't speak of these things when they were sober. Sometimes, a farmer who had too many ales would complain loudly about soldiers who came to his farm and demanded to be fed and paid him nothing for it. Or a shopkeeper complained about a soldier stealing a trinket for his sweetheart. When they'd said too much, the room grew quiet, and friends ushered the indiscreet man out of the inn.

It seemed to me that the citizenry of Dragonja City was divided into two factions. On the one hand there were burghers like Heikum—well established shopkeepers or tradesmen who'd found a way to thrive in the hustle and bustle of the city. And then there were people like Idella, Alaric and me, refugees from the countryside, farmers and villagers who'd fled from the valley where soldiers and marauders preyed on them. As lawlessness in the valley increased, refugees trickled in, most of them not as lucky to find work and a home as Femke and Heikum had provided for us. Many of the refugees turned to begging and petty theft to survive. Many of the girls, as well as some of the boys, stood on the edges of the marketplace, their sultry eyes lined with black and their hair dyed with henna, waiting for the soldiers to approach them. Femke sometimes gave a bowl of soup to a hungry person who came to the back door, but when Heikum found out, he demanded that she stop.

"We cannot feed the whole city, woman," he bellowed. She looked down at the floor, knowing he was right, but her heart was so large she could not stop herself from feeding someone who was starving.

One evening, as I was preparing to sing my first set of songs, I saw Wessel, whom I'd not seen since our meeting with Zygmunt in early autumn, sitting in the corner. He had an ale in front of him, but he was not touching it; instead he was watching the room intently, his muscular arms crossed, studying each man, especially the soldiers. The place was crowded and noisy, so no one seemed to notice him. Later, as I was singing to a relatively quiet room, I saw Anja come in, go to the bar and buy a draught from Heikum, who looked at her suspiciously, but said nothing. Anja settled into a seat in the opposite corner from Wessel. I tried not to look at either of them, but I wondered what they were up to.

Anja and Wessel sat quietly through all three of my sets, nursing their ales. Anja was obviously not interested in listening to my songs; instead, her tall ears were subtly moving from one group of Drekavac soldiers to another, eavesdropping on their conversations. Evidently, at least part of her mission here was to pick up whatever information she could about the movement of troops. At the end of the evening, when the public house was almost empty, Anja caught my eye and tipped her dark head in the direction of the kitchen. I covered my lyre with a piece of linen and placed it behind the bar where it would be safe and followed Anja into the kitchen. Idella, who was scrubbing pots, let out a squeal of delight when she saw Anja who put her finger to her lips to signal that her presence was a secret, and Idella silently hugged her. Anja and I went out to the barn where Ottolo nuzzled her hand and showed delight at the presence of our friend.

"What are you doing here, Anja? After that skirmish in the mountains, aren't you worried that one of the soldiers will recognize you?"

"Oh, that's unlikely, my friend," she said, feeding Ottolo an apple she'd taken from the kitchen. "In the middle of battle, no one looks at each other's faces. You're too busy looking at your enemy's sword."

What a battle-hardened veteran she's become, I thought. And indeed, she did look different than the lost girl I first encountered a few months before when she was living in the forest on squirrels and rabbits with her friends. How quickly she'd changed. The woman in front of me now was hard, lean, and confident. Her jaw was set, her eyes sharp and alert. I had the sense that she no longer thought of herself as prey, but as predator. The sparrow had become a hawk.

"Tessia sent me. We need you," she said tersely, turning to look me square in the eye. "I'm to take you back with me."

Well, I thought, nothing like coming to the point quickly.

"I really don't think that your rebel army has need of an alehouse singer," I said, laughing.

"Don't be coy with me, Shireman. You know I'm not talking about your skill with a lyre. We have injured men and women. We need you to set bones and heal wounds. Two of our women are pregnant, and we have no midwife. When Wessel and I leave here, you're coming with us."

"So, you plan to kidnap me?"

"No, you'll come willingly."

"And why would I do that?" I asked. Lacking true bravery, the best I could muster was insolence. I knew that if she and Wessel decided to tie me to Ottolo's back and take me up into the mountains, there was little I could do to resist them.

"You'll come with me," Anja said quietly, demurely, showing me for the first time her girl-sweetness. "Because Tessia needs you. And you love Tessia as much as I do."

Why are you going into the mountains with Anja?" Idella whispered angrily. "You're no warrior. You're a kind gentle man whose family needs him here."

We were in our room at the inn, Alaric was asleep on a pallet on the floor, and Idella and I were sitting on the straw bed having our first real argument. We'd bickered before, but nothing like this. I'd never seen this side of her. She was acting as if I'd suggested selling Alaric into slavery. She obviously felt that I was threatening everything we had, everything we had worked for in the months since we'd met. In her view, I was reneging on our plans for the future.

"I cannot believe you are running off to play soldier like Alaric and his friends." She put her face in her hands and sobbed. "We've been married only a few weeks."

I was distractedly throwing things in a sack—a change of clothes, my lyre, my surgical knives, my bags of herbs and medicines. My heart was breaking. Her heart was breaking. Why was I doing this?

"Tessia needs me," I suddenly remembered, stiffening my spine.

"*Tessia* needs you?" She asked. She looked up at me, her eyes narrowing. Obviously, I'd said the wrong thing.

"*Tessia* needs you?" Idella repeated. "What about me? What

about Alaric? *We* are your family. *We* need you here. *We* need you safe."

There was a pause, and then she asked suspiciously, "Are you in love with her?"

"No, absolutely not. I feel… loyal to her."

"And you have no loyalty to me?" Her voice was starting to rise, and I was afraid she was going to wake up her son. *Our son. My son.* I looked over at Alaric, the most perfect boy I had ever known, and tears welled up in my eyes.

"Idella, do you think I want to leave you and Alaric? There's nothing in the world I want more than to stay here with you. But you know what is happening to this country. If the citizens do not stand up for freedom, for some sense that we can live in peace, then things will continue getting worse. Already, soldiers are allowed to do whatever they want, and they want more and more. Tessia, Zygmunt, Anja and the others in the mountains are fighting for us. Hamlin is probably being tortured in the Castle as we speak. How can I sit by, enjoying my life, and let others fight for us? You are right, I am no warrior. The first time I fought bandits beside Tessia I wet my pants." *Oops, I had not meant to say that. I've never told anyone.*

She laughed. "You actually wet your pants because you were so afraid?" She laughed again, and despite my humiliation at confessing my cowardice to her, it was worth it to see her anger had disappeared.

"What happened?" She asked, wiping her tears away.

"A bandit came after me with a sword, and Hamlin hit him with the shaft of his spear."

"So, he saved your life?"

"Oh yes, if it hadn't been for Hamlin, my skull would have been cleaved wide open."

"Oh, my love," she said, taking me in her arms. "Thank you for telling me. Now I know you won't be doing anything brave and foolish up there with your friends in the mountains."

"Oh, you needn't worry that I'll be too brave," I said, laughing with her. "I'm famous for being a coward, as well as being completely inept with a sword."

I threw a few more things in my kit and went downstairs. Idella may have found my cowardice funny, but she would need time to get used to my decision to leave.

I went downstairs, told Femke and Heikum that I was leaving and asked them to watch over Idella and Alaric.

"You know we will, Laddie," Heikum said. "Don't tell anyone I said so, but I'm proud of you, joining Zygmunt and his band. People call them bandits, but I call them patriots. Someone has to make things right in this kingdom."

Femke, who believed in soup, not politics, brought me a large bowl and a slice of bread. "It's cold up in the mountains, dear. You need to fill your belly. Also, I packed some dried meat, hard tack and fruit for you," she said, laying down a cloth bag bulging with food.

As I was finishing my soup, Idella came downstairs and sat across the table from me. She stroked her snake bracelet for a moment, looking at me. She didn't seem to be angry anymore, just thoughtful.

"So, they need your skills as a healer, not as a warrior?" She sounded like she was extracting a promise from me to stay out of the fray.

"Oh, yes," I assured her. "I'll be the one who comes to the battlefield only to mend the wounded."

Reassured, or at least resigned to my decision, she put her face close to mine, and we kissed a long time. Then we went upstairs and made love quietly, knowing we may never see each other again.

If we'd known how things would turn out, I would never have left, nor would she have let me.

The next morning, I found Alaric in the barn, rubbing down Ottolo's flanks with a handful of hay. Ottolo seemed to sense that today we'd be leaving. Perhaps it was the presence of Anja the night before, or perhaps donkeys just know things without having to be told.

"I fed him oats and fresh grass this morning, and I've rubbed him down. He should be ready for your trip up the mountain," Alaric said, not looking at me. "May I come with you?" He asked matter-of-factly, as if he were asking the price of turnips.

His question surprised me. "No," I said firmly. "Your mother would never permit it, and besides I need you here." I'd seen Alaric and his friends practicing with their slings. Any of them could hit a bird in flight from twenty paces. I hoped the situation would not come to this, but if it did, the boy would not hesitate to protect his mother.

He looked out the barn door and into the distance. "You know, it's always been just my mother and me, and we managed fine. We always had enough to eat and a safe place to sleep. Then, when you came along, I was worried things would change, and she wouldn't love me as much as she loved you."

I remembered Tessia telling me she had felt the same jealousy for her father, and I realized that she'd never had a chance to say to Edelmira what Alaric was now saying to me, so I treated this conversation as somewhat sacred.

"It was never a competition, Alaric. Your mother's heart is very big. She can love both of us."

"Oh, I know that now. I'm just saying that it's been good having you in our family. I never knew my father. He died soon after I was born." He rubbed the tears from his eyes with the back of his hand. A few of his teardrops caught in the swirled pinna below the point of his ear, and I knew I'd remember that detail the rest of my life.

"Thank you, son." He looked up at me, startled. It was the first time I had ever blessed him in that way.

"I lost my mother when I was very young, so I know what it is to grow up with an empty space inside you," I added, touching his shoulder.

He nodded, then led Ottolo out of the stall and handed me the rope. We embraced, and I left the only family I'd known since my father died five summers before.

I stopped in the market to buy supplies. I had to guess at what the rebels might need. Probably everything, I thought. But I didn't want to burden Ottolo with more than he could carry up the steep trail, so I chose carefully. I decided to concentrate on enough food for myself for a week of travel and the common herbal medicines that I might need to practice rudimentary treatments. Thinking back, I realized I'd been a shireman selling pots and pans, an alehouse singer entertaining soldiers, and now I was embarking on a third career, that of an army surgeon. Life takes strange turns, no?

*S*ometimes the dreams of humans were so loud, the dragon could hear them. Nightmares, erotic dreams, flying dreams, dreams of clouds mixed with memories of being held in their mothers' arms, dreams of the anger of fathers, as well as the rare praise from fathers. Sometimes, the dragon wished she couldn't hear the dreams of men. It was all too much, how their short lives mattered to them. In dreams, their tedious days and tiny loves seemed so much more significant than they actually were.

Tonight, for example, as she made a wide sweep above the rebel camp half a league from her cave, the men and women seemed so full of themselves, their self-importance speaking loudly in their dreams. Their quaint idealism about forming a new society would be almost endearing if she hadn't heard it so many times before in her very long life. And their leader, this Zygmunt fellow, she'd met him, listened to his silly plans, his insulting attempt to recruit her for his revolution. She'd liked him at first. He had a noble bearing, his long black curls falling around his wide shoulders. He wore a peasant's garb as if it were royal robes. Now, there's a man, she thought, when she first saw him. She invited him into her cave, the first time a human had ever been allowed. She listened to him talk about his plans.

"With your help, we shall take the city of Dragonja!" he announced. "You will fly over the city with one of our archers on your back, providing support for our troops when they burst through the outer gates. You will rain down fire and terror on the Drekavacs fighting for the Wizard Ludek. Together, we will establish a new society where men and women will live with dignity, and all will share in the wealth of the land."

He was a very good orator, but he didn't realize the dragon had heard all this rhetoric before and for centuries had dismissed it as pig manure. A charming man gets the crowd stirred up with talk of equality and dignity. He appeals to their anger and their idealism and so they follow him, charging into the bristling spears and swinging swords of the corrupt ruler. People are killed. The leader is captured, tortured and hung. *And everything goes back to the way it's always been with the majority of the people under the heels of the rich and powerful.* Zygmunt was more charming and talented than most of the rabble-rousers she'd observed through the centuries, but the result would be the same, she was sure. Even if he were successful in this revolt, it wouldn't take long for him to be corrupted by power. In the end, he'd be every bit as cruel and oppressive as the rulers he replaced. After a short while, she grew impatient with Zygmunt's self-importance and ordered him to leave.

It always seemed to be the same with males, men or dragons. *Oh, the male can charm a girl easy enough with his confident manner, his courage under fire, his devotion to his mother, but once he'd gotten what he wanted, he dumped the girl like so much dirty laundry.* When she was young (was it really ten thousand years ago?) she'd followed her brothers and the other handsome young dragons into war against the men. *We saw what that led to, didn't we, my love?* she asked, forgetting for a moment that Rilla was gone. Yes, in that long-ago war only she remembered, the dragons had all been killed except her and the dragonling Rilla. But Rilla had grown up to be a beauty—pink scales scintillating in the moonlight—and they'd made a life together, hadn't they? A good life too, skimming the rivers for salmon at night, sleeping wrapped in each other's wings during the day. Rilla had always insisted they stay away from men and the world of men. *Let their memory of dragons fade,* she said. *Let them come to think of us as legends, not monsters.* Well, Tyrmiss thought, her eyes burning with tears as she passed over the ridge and looked down on the Bekla Valley, the world of men, *They want a monster to hate? I'll give them a monster they'll never forget.*

Part Three: The Dragon

Chapter 10

The guards at the North Gate had been at our wedding, so when I led Ottolo out of the city they asked in a friendly way whether I was starting my trading route in the fall instead of the spring.

"Oh yes," I lied. "I'll be going down the Dragonja River to where it meets the Bekla River and visit the villages along the way. I should be able to trade with enough farmers and tradesmen to make it worth my while. The closer you get to the sea, the warmer it is, you know."

"Be careful on your journey, Shireman," one of them responded. "There are outlaws on the road who'd be glad to have your trade goods and your donkey."

"Thank you, kind sir, but my donkey and I know the roads and how to avoid outlaws," I responded, stroking Ottolo's mane.

I led Ottolo down the road, following the river downstream. Then, looking back to make sure we were out of sight of the soldiers on the city walls, we left the main road and turned toward the mountains. Anja had said to meet her on the switchback trail that leads up to the copper mines. I knew the trail, having taken it with my father years before. He often traded with the soldiers' camp that guarded the miners, but after he died, I stopped going to the mines. I found it difficult to watch how the miners, most of whom were slaves, were mistreated.

Ottolo and I made our way up the steep switchback trail, stopping frequently to catch our breath. In late afternoon, the sun went down behind the mountain and a shadow moved across the valley below. From here, I could see most of the Drag-onja River, farms scattered along its banks, and further away the Dry Hills that Tessia, Anja, Hamlin and I had crossed in mid-summer, fighting the Drekavac-soldiers and the ghost wolves. Closer and to the right, I could see the city in shadow, lights coming on as lamps were lit and cooking fires were started. I could make out the thatched roofs although it was too far away to tell which one was the Silver Pony. I looked at the Black Castle and thought of Kerttu and Hamlin held captive there. I wondered if I'd made the biggest mistake of my life, leaving Idella and Alaric in order to embark on this fool's mission to help the rebels. I knew I could turn back now, and my family would welcome me home, but I felt very strongly that some-thing larger was at stake than my own happiness, so I turned with Ottolo to continue up the mountain.

When it was too dark to see the trail, we stopped and made camp. On this mountainside, a fire would have been visible from twenty miles away, so I unloaded Ottolo's pack, brushed him down with dry grass, gave him a cup of oats, and hobbled him in a grassy spot. I ate some dried apples and raisins, drank some water, spread my blankets and looked up at the stars.

Every evening, the star known as Vakr's Eye looked down. The story is Vakr hid the eye in the mead fountain of Mimir, the God of Knowledge, in order to watch him drink each morn-ing. In this way, Vakr became the wisest of the gods. I've heard of people praying to the star, thinking it will give them wisdom. Before going to sleep, I offered a short prayer to Vakr, as well as my habitual one to the Goddess Nilene. I was going to need all the help I could get.

In the middle of the night, I woke. Ottolo was braying quietly. I had never heard him make such a sound. He sound-ed terrified. I could hear something breathing in the darkness close by.

And I could see two red slits staring at me.

In the bright light of morning, the happenings in the night seemed nothing more than a bad dream. Ottolo seemed unusually skittish, but I convinced myself that he must have seen a snake. So, I brushed off my night-fears, and we continued up the narrow trail. I couldn't shake the feeling, though, that we were being watched. I remembered Zygmunt's warning that the dragon Tyrmiss could read our dreams, but I put that thought aside for now.

I expected to meet Anja on the second day, but we were coming close to the mining camp, and Anja had not shown herself. I stopped at a ridge above the camp and looked down. A scrawny boy not much older than Alaric emerged from the mouth of the mine carrying two buckets of ore on a yoke across his shoulders. A couple of soldiers, armed with swords on their belts and whips in their hands, lounged in front of a campfire in front of their wooden barracks. There were ragged tents scattered around the site. Two girls were sitting in front of one of the tents. I knew most of the boys were down in the earth, digging the ore under the whip of soldiers, and the girls, who were also slaves taken from their families, were held in the camp to service the whims of the soldiers. I hated this place and hadn't been here in years. It hadn't changed at all since I was a child, except that the boys and girls here were undoubtedly not the ones I saw back then. People don't survive long as slaves in this camp. No one comes to this mining camp for a visit, so I had no choice but to pretend I was here to trade goods. Otherwise, the soldiers would wonder why I was on the mountain.

"Hello, Meister Norbert!" One of the soldiers lounging in front of the fire shouted as I approached. He knew me from the times I visited his village, and I recognized him. His people were farmers in the Bekla Valley. "Why have you come way up here?" He asked in a friendly way. I joined him and his friend at their fire.

"I brought goods to trade," I said. "May I stay the night?"

"Of course, have a seat by the fire."

I had a seat on the log beside them.

"When was the last time you came to this camp, Meister Norbert?"

"It's been many years. I used to come here with my father when I was a boy." I looked around at the camp. It was almost deserted. I guessed that the boys were working in the mine, and the soldiers were down there as well, guarding them.

"How many boys do you have working in the mine, now?" I asked, trying to sound as if I were just making conversation. I knew this could be important information for the rebels to know.

"About fifty, I think," the young soldier said, scratching his chin. "But it's hard to keep up with them. We had a couple die last week."

"A lot of them die, I suppose."

"Ya, we get new ones coming in all the time, so it matters not how many we lose. They're replaceable," he said indifferently.

I looked at the whip coiled on his belt. There were blood stains on the tip of the lash. It was not long ago that this boy was playing in the fields and woods, helping his father on the farm and mooning over the local girls. And now, he'd become an overseer of slaves, an indifferent torturer, a soldier in the employ of oppressors. In a few short years, an innocent farm boy had become a tool of evil. How could this happen?

"I suppose that a lot of soldiers are needed to oversee fifty slaves," I said, casually. Here was the crux of it. I knew that this was information the rebels needed.

"Not really," the former farm boy said. "We have about twenty soldiers. We send ten at a time down the mine to keep the slaves working, and the other ten stay up here to guard the camp." He laughed, "But there is really nothing to guard. The slaves are so frightened, they do whatever we want. And the rebels never come here."

And I thought, *but we will, my young friend, we will come here, and you will never know what hit you until it is too late.*

The next day, I sold a few pieces of kitchenware to the camp cook and a few blankets to the soldiers, and then headed back down the trail, wending along slowly in order to give Anja a chance to find us. In midmorning, we came across her sitting on a rock beside the trail, waiting for us. She explained she'd been delayed the day before.

"This time of year, the snowfield is treacherous to cross, so I had to go the long way around."

Anja looked nervous and fatigued, almost fragile, her furry ears drooping past her jawline. The thought of Hamlin being held captive must be wearing on her, I thought.

Anja led us off the trail, across a hardscrabble slope where it was difficult for Ottolo to keep his footing, but we went slowly, and I was patient with him, and by noon we were on easier ground. We went up a slight slope to the top of a ridge, and I realized that this was a natural pass between the two Thumbs of the Giant. From here, we could see a huge valley on the other side of the pass, forested with streams and waterfalls, and at the bottom a broad river wended its way into the misty distance. There were a few farms and villages, but the valley seemed to be largely uninhabited. Although I knew from seafarers I'd talked to on the coast that there were other lands than ours, I'd spent my entire life in the Bekla Valley and never known that on the other side of the mountains lay a beautiful land. Strangely, once we were on the other side of the pass, the air was warmer. I realized that the cold wind from the mountain peaks must come down the east side of the slope toward the city, leaving this west side of the slope with a more temperate climate.

"What is the name of that sheltered valley?" I asked Anja.

"The river you see below is called the Iskar. It joins other rivers to the north and they flow together to the sea."

"What does 'Iskar' mean?"

"I've heard it's a very old name for *water*. But how would I know?" And I remembered that Anja, like most people, didn't share my interest in learning the true names for things. For her, words served simple purposes and had no power in themselves.

Ottolo and I followed Anja, carefully climbing down ledges piled on top of each other like a stairway for giants. We descended to a gulley cut by melting snow, and it led us below the timberline into the shelter of the forest. Here were white birches, and as the wind blew through the tops of the trees, the leaves flashed gray and green in the bright light. Descending the slope through the trees, we came to a stream which had cut a deep gorge through the rock. We stayed on high ground above the series of waterfalls and deep pools. Ferns and willows grew on the steep banks, watered by the mist of the moving water. It was the most beautiful place I'd ever seen. It was hard to believe that a day's walk behind us, the bare jumbles of rock were covered with snow.

"It's called the Poellat Gorge Waterfall," Anja said, in deference to my love for learning the names for things. "It's where the she-dragon was killed by a Drekavac-soldier last summer. A couple of our warriors found her beside the water with a spear in her side and the ripped-up body of a soldier nearby."

"What was a Drekavac-soldier in the king's service doing on this side of the ridge?"

"Probably a scout looking for our camp."

By evening we'd come to Zygmunt's camp, located in a clearing with a good view of the Iskar River below. Nearby was a small butte, ideal as a lookout post to warn of soldiers coming over the ridge from the Bekla Valley.

Zygmunt greeted us heartily. He pulled me into his powerful arms and hugged me. "You are most welcome, my friend," he said. "Thank you for joining us. We need you."

Tessia came running across the camp and leapt into my arms. "Norbert! I knew you would join us eventually."

"Believe me, my lady, if I'd seen any way not to come, I would have stayed with Idella." I held both of her hands and stepped back, looking at her. Her black hair had grown out and she wore it tied back like Zygmunt's. In Dragonja City, her face had turned pale from staying indoors, but now it was brown again. She looked the way I remembered from our time on the road. She wore leather leggings, the wool singlet I'd sold to her father years before, and a sturdy pair of high boots. She looked every inch a warrior.

"You must catch me up on everything," she said, taking me by the hand and starting to lead me away.

"How is Bruin?" I asked, suddenly realizing how much I'd missed the mastiff.

"Bruin I'm afraid has disappeared," Tessia said. "I've heard he's taken up with a pack of wolves. One of our warriors saw him in the Dry Hills a few days ago. And you've heard about Hamlin being captured, right? We—"

Zygmunt interrupted her, scowling, "Wait, niece, before the two of you start gossiping about your friends, I need to hear what news Norbert has brought from Dragonja City and what he's seen on his journey up the mountain. Come, let us break bread and talk." Tessia looked at the ground and moved away from me. Zygmunt's tone to her was dismissive, and I wondered what was causing the tension between Tessia and her uncle.

The camp was well established, with a stone cookhouse and beside it the mess tent, a covered area with tables and benches where people ate. The barracks were large low tents, and other smaller tents were used for storage. I could hear a stream nearby, and I saw a skinned deer hanging on a rack, ready for butchering.

Zygmunt, Tessia, Anja and I sat in the covered area next to the cookhouse. Wessel brought bread, cheese, and ale, and then stood off to the side watching us. There were half a dozen warriors whom I assumed were Zygmunt's lieutenants standing near us, listening. As Anja and I ate, Zygmunt asked me questions.

"Did you visit the mining camp?"

I told him what I'd seen and what the young soldier had told me.

"So, there are only twenty soldiers there, and each day half of them are down the mine?"

I nodded.

"Did the soldiers look ready for battle? Were they alert? Were they expecting an attack from us?"

"No, there were no guards posted. I saw only two soldiers, and they were lounging at the fire. The rest were either down the mine or in the barracks."

"Did they suspect that you were a spy?'

"No, it's well known I'm a trader who travels to sell my wares. One of the soldiers I've known since he was a boy, and I'm friends with his father. The young man trusts me."

"Did you see any patrols on the trail as you came up the mountain?"

I shook my head.

"When you were in the city, did you hear anything about patrols or about the mining camp?"

I told him everything I could remember about the conversations between the drunken soldiers in the Silver Pony, how they described the battle and their capture of Hamlin. I also told him about seeing Hamlin taken into the black Castle as a prisoner.

As I talked, Zygmunt, Tessia and Anja listened intently, and Zygmunt nodded every now and then as if he were putting the pieces together. After it was clear that I'd told him everything I could think of, Zygmunt slapped the table violently.

"We've been waiting for an opportunity like this! We strike the mining camp tomorrow."

Later in the women's tent, as Tessia was preparing for the expedition against the mining camp, she and I talked. I caught her up with the news of our friends. I told her how happy I was in my new role as husband and father, how Idella felt hurt and betrayed by my leaving, how proud I was of Alaric, and I shared the gossip of the Silver Pony. Tessia looked happy to hear about that other life she'd lived in the city, especially about Taja, but it was clear that this life she'd chosen, that of a warrior and a leader of warriors, was what she was meant to do.

She told me that she had been leading the reconnaissance patrol when it was attacked by soldiers. "There were only three of us—Hamlin, Anja and me. We were caught by surprise and badly outnumbered."

She shook her head, still in shock over the battle which had happened only a week before. "It was a terrible blunder on my part. Imagine being caught by surprise! Hamlin fought bravely but the soldiers swarmed him. Anja and I had to retreat, or we would've been killed. Now, I see I should have stayed and fought the soldiers and tried to save Hamlin. Poor sweet Hamlin who has saved my life and fought beside me! I abandoned him. I'm such a coward!"

I comforted her as best I could, but there was little I could say. She was learning the dark side of commanding warriors. If you make a mistake, others may pay with their lives or their freedom.

When she'd finished packing her kit, we sat in silence for a while in the dark tent. In order to take her mind off Hamlin, I told her about the night I spent on the trail, sleeping under the stars and having the sense there was some kind of large creature nearby, watching me.

She nodded, "I've had that experience as well, Norbert. The men say that it's the dragon watching us, listening to our dreams."

"Do you believe it is the dragon?"

She shrugged. "I do not disbelieve it," she said, enigmatically.

Early the next morning, Zygmunt and two dozen of his warriors left to attack the mining camp. Surprisingly, he ordered Tessia to stay behind and guard the camp. I knew she felt she was being punished for her blunder the week before when she allowed her patrol to be ambushed and a valuable warrior to be captured.

The only people left in the camp other than Tessia and me were women, children and wounded soldiers. I spent most of the morning grooming Ottolo, as well as unpacking and organizing the trade goods I'd brought. There were a few horses, as well as goats and chickens, that were kept in a field near the camp where they were cared for by a group of girls. I brought Ottolo to them, and they made a big fuss over him, praising him and brushing him with straw and giving him handfuls of grass to eat. I could see he would be well-cared for. I wondered what had happened to Tessia's mastiff Bruin. I missed his easy devotion, and I worried that wolves may have killed him in the mountains.

I was assigned a tent that would serve as a surgery. Almost immediately after I unpacked my herbs and knives, a woman brought her small child who had fever and a cough. I gave the mother a small packet of herbs, mostly ivy leaves and thyme, and told her to make a tea of it, add honey and dried apple, let it cool and have the child drink it three times a day. I taught her a short spell to say each time the child drank the tea. The woman went off happy. As every healer knows, children almost always get better by themselves. The treatment might help, but it is mostly for the purpose of giving the mother something to do that's harmless.

I also had one eye on Tessia. All morning she was restless. She sharpened her blades for a while, then she helped the women gather wood. She played with some of the small children, but her heart was not in it. She kept looking off in the direction that Zygmunt and the warriors had gone. Finally, she walked over to me and said, "Norbert, it is now time to complete our quest. Will you accompany me?" She spoke formally, in the manner of a warrior addressing a companion.

"I'm sorry, my lady. What are you saying?"

"A year ago, Norbert, we began a quest to find a dragon, capture it, and ride it into battle against the king."

I was stunned. "But I thought you'd given up that plan and now you're fighting as one of your uncle's warriors."

"My uncle clearly does not want me as a warrior, and I will not be put aside and treated as a…" she looked for the right word. "I will not be treated as a *woman*."

I almost said to her, "But you *are* a woman." However, I stopped myself when I saw that her hand was on her sword. She may very well have sliced me in half for stating the obvious.

She looked me in the eye and said, "Norbert, you and I both know what it is to be disgraced in battle. I need to prove that I am a warrior and not a coward. What about you?"

I realized she was right about me. One of the reasons I'd left my family and joined the rebels was that I had to prove to myself I was not a coward.

"Let us go, my lady." And we did.

Chapter 11

The location of the dragon's lair was well-known among the rebels. Close to the waterfall that Anja and I had passed the previous day was the cave Zygmunt had entered to speak to the beast. Zygmunt had failed to convince the dragon to ally with the rebels, but with her usual self-confidence, Tessia thought she would succeed where her uncle had not. I was still as skeptical of the whole enterprise as I'd been from the start of the quest. The only reason that I was coming with her was in order to prove that there was something more to me than just a trader and a tavern singer. Having wet myself in my first battle was still a humiliating memory. Besides, if Tessia was injured in this foolish attempt and I was not there to help her, as a healer if not as a warrior, then I would never forgive myself.

Tessia had brought a torch, and as she was striking flint to copper to light it, I checked the ground. There was a wide, well-worn path that led into the mouth of the cave, and there were marks that may have been the tracks of a bear. A very large bear. The largest bear I'd ever heard of. I peered into the mouth of the cave, but it was too dark to see anything. I felt fear rising in me, and I worried I was going to vomit. I steadied my breathing and followed Tessia into the darkness.

"Mistress Dragon!" Tessia called. She moved slowly forward with me close behind.

"May we enter?" Her voice echoed through the cave. I felt my knees shaking.

We followed the wide tunnel as it curved and descended.

And then we heard an extremely deep voice that seemed to come not from the mouth of any living thing, but from deep inside the earth. The stalactites seemed to tremble with the power of the voice.

"Ah, so a brave little girl and a frightened tavern singer have come to pay a visit. How sweet."

I fell to my knees, "Mistress Dragon," I quailed. "We mean you no harm. Please do not kill us with your fiery breath."

Tessia looked at me with disgust. "Mistress Dragon, please ignore my companion. He is a healer, not a warrior, and has no stomach for battle."

"Nor, from what I have heard, does he have a bladder for battle," the dragon commented wryly.

"By the gods," I muttered. "Does everyone know of my humiliation?"

The dragon laughed, and a stalactite was knocked loose from the ceiling and crashed to the floor bedside her. In the torchlight, her red eyes shone. I could make out the large bulk of her, the wide wings tucked at her side. The green and purple scales on her long neck caught the light. Then I saw that the dragon was lying on a huge pile of shimmering gold. I did not know that there was so much gold in the entire world.

"Gods, you say? What do you know of gods?" The Dragon rumbled. "There are no gods, only What-Is. There is everything and there is nothing, and together they are What-Is. So, speak no more of your gods, those silly creatures you tell stories about, those petty jealous ignorant fools who meddle in your lives and cause such misfortune and whom you revere more than life itself. There are no gods. There is everything and there is nothing, and where the two meet, there is death."

"Mistress Dragon—" Tessia started.

"You may call me *Tyrmiss*, my dear. Tyrmiss the Dragon they call me or used to call me when there were other dragons to speak with. In the old language, the first language I knew,

Tyrmiss means *Lady of Fire.*" Her voice grew softer, almost whimsical, "Actually, it was an old family joke, a nickname my mother gave me because I was always scorching my brothers' tails. My true name is *Onyntyss* which means *The Adorable One,* but I always hated that name." Her voice grew more threatening. "If you ever call me *Onyntyss* I will incinerate you where you stand." She laughed, and her laughter was frightening.

I silently swore to myself I would never call her *Onyntyss.*

"The names of things are an interesting artifact, are they not, Bard?" She turned her red eyes to look at me.

"Mistress Tyrmiss, I am not a bard, but only," I babbled. "As you said earlier, a trader and a tavern singer. That is, I know only a few old songs and –"

"SILENCE!" The dragon shouted. Her voice was so loud it shook the floor of the cave beneath our feet.

"I know who you are, both of you. The bard and the warrior-woman. I have watched you and listened to your dreams as you followed your pitiful little quest. You think you can convince me to join you in your fight against the king? Your Zygmunt, your vain arrogant uncle, thought he could convince me. He was lucky I didn't set his lovely locks on fire.

"Humans are so pathetic. Do you know where the name *human* comes from? Humus. Earth, soil, mud, dirt. You, my pretty little warrior, are nothing more than rotten stuff. Your body is like decomposed leaves that maggots crawl through. You are little mud-monkeys who love to stab each other with sharp sticks and talk about the gods as if you knew something, anything but your small short lives.

"On the other hand," Tyrmiss said, raising her magnificent head in pride. "In the language of your ancestors, the word *dragon* comes from *drit* which means 'light' and *adcondarc* which means 'I have seen.'

"So, there we have it, my dears. You are made of mud and offal, and I am made of light and vision. And that is the fundamental difference between us. How about that, my little mud monkeys?" She let out a tremendous roar of laughter which I felt down to my toes.

"Well, since I have so much time on my hands, and I have not had visitors in ages, I shall tell you a story. Please sit down. This could take some time."

And Tyrmiss began at the beginning:

"In the beginning there was ice. Great sheets of ice had pushed down from the north. Ice covered everything. By night, the moon shone on the ice. By day, the sun shone. And there was nothing else.

"What-Is grew tired of seeing only ice, so with fiery breath, she melted the ice and created the sea, and she created the land. And she divided one from the other.

"What-Is melted more ice, and so a river was made. And the river cut a valley. And green things grew in the valley. And fish swarmed in the sea and in the river. And What-Is enjoyed what she saw and called it Good.

"Then, What-Is discovered loneliness, so she created a dragon out of the boiling sulfurous water that bubbles out of the ground. She gave the dragon wings to fly over the ice, talons to catch the salmon, and a fiery breath like her own to melt the ice and stay warm.

"There were dragons in every valley. Dragons ruled the earth. And dragons lived in peace, happy in each other's company.

"But then, after thousands of years of dragons living in bliss, the mud-monkeys arrived. It is not known why What-Is created these creatures. They were disgusting little brutes covered in fleas who fought among themselves constantly. Always chattering and touching themselves. As soon as the mud-monkeys learned to speak, they started telling lies. But worse than the lies were the ways they invented stories about themselves. Their nobility. Their wisdom. Their god-like visage.

"The mud-monkeys divided themselves into races and

tribes. They inflicted the tyranny of small differences to justify their hatred of other races and tribes. The ones who had pointed ears and large feet lived next to rivers and along the coasts. The ones with gray scaly skin and taloned claws lived in the hills and called themselves Drekavacs. The ones who were large and stupid became trolls, and the ones who were small and quick began to live underground as gnomes. And finally, there were the ones who considered themselves the most beautiful of all the races, and they secluded themselves in the forests and called themselves elves. But I have found little difference between the races. They all bleed red blood when they are cut. They all cry in pain when they are burned.

"The mud-monkeys invented gods who looked like them and who acted like them. Petty, selfish, inglorious gods who told the mud-monkeys that the earth had been made for them. All the valleys. All the rivers. All the animals and trees and flowers were theirs for the taking, these gods proclaimed. And the mud-monkeys forgot What-Is and listened only to their new gods, the gods of their invention who told them what the mud-monkeys wanted to hear.

"And the mud-monkeys learned to hunt dragons, to follow them to their lairs and murder them in their sleep, to spear them like salmon as they swam in the rivers, and to shoot them with arrows as they flew overhead. Some men even ate dragons. It was said they tasted best if they were roasted alive.

"And the dragons learned how to use their fiery breath and their sharp talons to fight back, but it was too late, too many were dead, and the heart had been taken out of them with the destruction of the forests and the poisoning of the sea. Many dragons came to believe that What-Is had forsaken them. Perhaps What-Is was dead, some dragons whispered, having given up hope.

"Some of the dragons were captured and kept in cages. They were whipped into submission and their jaws were wired shut to stop them from using fire against the humans. I believe that you have sung about this, Bard?" Tyrmiss said, turning her great head toward me.

"Yes, I have," I said, again feeling my knees shake.

"You know the song of Milon Redshield who chained my brother Morf to a cairn for forty days until he consented to allow the warrior to fly on his back?"

"Yes, my Lady of Fire," I said, my voice trembling, waiting for dragon-flames to engulf me.

"And you have sung of Edwige, the warrior-princess who kept a dragon next to her as she sat on the throne. Did you know that the dragon's name was Tenwen and she was my sister?" Her voice was rising in volume.

"No, my Lady of Fire, I did not know that."

"MORF AND TENWEN WERE MY LITTERMATES, YOU IGNORANT MUD-MONKEY!"

The dragon's voice shook the cavern and stalactites tore loose from the ceiling, almost hitting Tessia and me. I worried that we would be crushed if the ceiling collapsed.

"You apes do not understand what it is to have littermates. There were six of us born at the same time. We were nursed by our mother who brought fish back from the river for us in her belly. She gently regurgitated the nourishment and offered it to us in love. We dragonlings slept in a pile, keeping each other warm at night. We ventured out of the nest together, learned to fly together, and felt the exhilaration of skimming the river's surface and sharing our first catch. You mud-monkeys are born alone, live alone and die alone. Not so with dragons. We are devoted to our mates and our offspring, our littermates and our tribe. When you humans tortured one of us, you tortured all of us."

"I'm sorry, my Lady of Fire. When I sang of the heroes –"

"HEROES?" Tyrmiss's voice boomed.

Her talon struck so quickly, I had no chance to avoid it. Her

143

bony claw lifted me to the ceiling of the cave, holding me over her open mouth the way a woman might hold a cluster of grapes she was eating. I looked down into a double row of sabre-like fangs, any one of which could easily pierce my soft body. I realized in horror she intended to eat me.

"PUT THE MAGE DOWN, MISTRESS DRAGON!" I heard the welcome voice of Tessia shout. Then in a soft growl, "Unless you want to lose your eye."

I glanced over and saw the shining purple blade of the Voprian sword, the tip just a hand's breadth from the dragon's red eye. The beast slowly shifted her gaze to the blade, then to Tessia's resolute face, and gently lowered me to the rock floor.

"My, you are a feisty little girl, aren't you?" Tyrmiss said evenly. "You realize I could have killed you both just now, don't you?"

"And you'd be flying lopsided for the next ten millennia, if you did," Tessia replied, just as evenly.

The dragon quietly chuckled. "I like you, girl. You've got guts. I'd heard stories of you, but I didn't quite believe them. Tessia, the little girl who would be a warrior. I've seen many warriors come and go through the ages, my dear, but they were all men—muscle-bound, arrogant, cruel. You are the first of your kind, I have to say. Well, I'm the last of my kind, so perhaps we should be friends?"

Tessia sheathed her blade and gave a small smile and a curt nod. The dragon and the warrior seemed to have reached a place of mutual respect.

"Heroes?" Tyrmiss asked quietly, picking up our conversation where she'd left off. "You call a man like Milon Redshield a hero? He kept a sentient being in chains and tortured him until his spirit was broken. And then Milon flew around on Morf showing off in front of everyone as if my brother were a pony doing tricks for a crowd. I watched this from a distance and could do nothing.

"As for Tenwen... my sister was put in a dungeon and starved to death because the spoiled brat of a princess had grown bored with her.

"YOU MUD-MONKEYS ENSLAVED MY KIND!"

The dragon put her large head on her taloned forearms and sobbed. Tessia reached over and patted the beast, stroking the very face that had nearly consumed me a few moments before. Remembering my past humiliation, I checked the front of my pants. Dry. I felt absurdly proud of myself—like a backwards boy who's finally mastered toilet training. Then I noticed that the fear I'd carried my entire life had left me, evaporating like sweat from my skin. And now things between the three of us were changing; it was happening so quickly I felt a little off-balance. I replayed the sequence of the last few moments. The dragon had almost eaten me. Tessia had stopped her. And now the dragon was sobbing in grief, and Tessia was comforting her. As for me, I was developing a degree of courage. It seemed that being together was changing all three of us. Could our odd trio become something never seen before? I wouldn't mind the three of us becoming friends, or at least friendly enough so I didn't have to worry about becoming a mid-morning snack.

After a long pause, Tyrmiss lifted her head, composed herself, and in a voice smaller than before, brought to a conclusion her recitation of the history of the dragons of Bekla Valley.

"And it came to pass, there was a great battle in which men came from far away to our valley and marched against the remaining dragons. The dragons fought bravely, but the men swarmed over them, stabbing and slashing until the dragons were defeated.

"And finally, there were only two dragons left."

The torch had gone out. We sat for a long time in the dark, then Tessia said:

"Mistress Tyrmiss, Lady of Fire, it frightens us to sit here in the dark. May I go outside to light my torch?"

The dragon grunted assent, and Tessia and I found our way out of the cave by following the wall.

Tessia and I sat beside the stream. The waterfall was a little way downhill. Tessia used a stick to scrape off some of the pitch left on the torch. She gathered moss and bark and spread the soft pitch over them, then with her hands pressed the mass into a punk which she stuck in a fork she had carved on the end of the torch. As she worked, her jaw was clenched, as if she were trying to work out a puzzle.

"Norbert, why do you think that Tyrmiss is telling us this story about creation and history?" she asked.

I had taken off my boots and had my bare feet in the water. The cool water felt wonderful. "I'm not sure," I said. "Perhaps she has no one to talk to and feels it's important for humans to know about dragons? She's the last of her kind and perhaps she wants someone to know that her kind were once great? Or perhaps she's just lonely. Anyway, it is a good sign that she wants to talk to us instead of just lighting us up."

Tessia smiled and lifted her torch which was now blazing nicely. "I think we should go back into the cave and hear the rest of her story, don't you?"

"I fought in the great battle between men and dragons," the dragon began again. "There were waves of humans—riverfolk, seafolk, Drekavacs, trolls, and elves—who descended on us. I did not know there were so many men in the world, much less that they would all come to our valley to kill us.

"My litter mates fought beside me. My brothers Gremrid, known as *Protector of the Forest*; and Eldradas, known as *The Gentle One*; and my sister Punnet whom we called *Puny*—we flew wing to wing against the invading horde. We floated high and dived into their ranks, roasting them in their armor where they stood. We swooped low over them, raking their ranks with our talons. Men's blood splattered high in the air. They shot arrows at us, tearing our wings and making us plummet to the ground where they speared our hearts and cut off our heads. It was a mighty battle with many men dead, and we fought bravely. But finally, flying above the valley I looked down and there were only men left alive. The dragons lay dead or dying, and I was the lone survivor.

"I was in pain. Arrows were stuck in my side, and I had a small tear in one wing that kept me from flying evenly. I knew I could fly down and attack one more time, or I could fly away to the mountains and hide. To my shame, I chose to quit the battle and flee.

"With only one good wing, I flew crookedly and fell exhausted at the top of the pass between The Two Thumbs of the Giant. I lay there in the snow, expecting to die of my wounds—alone, heartbroken and ashamed.

"I do not know how long I lay there, but when I woke my wounds were being tended by a pretty little dragon whose name, I discovered later, was Rilla Little Stream. She was too young to join the other dragons when they flew into battle, and her litter mates had all been captured or killed by men, so her mother had told her to hide in this cave. Rilla had watched the battle from the top of the pass and saw me fall to the rocks.

"Rilla helped me to walk here. In the first days, I was very ill with a high fever. Rilla carried water in her mouth and bade me to drink, and she brought bits of deer meat and chewed it for me, and slowly I healed. I stayed in the cave for months and when the first snow came, I ventured out into the chill air. The tear in my wing was healing and I was starting to fly again, but only at night. Men seemed to be everywhere, and we knew they would kill a dragon on sight.

"Dragons can live for tens of thousands of years, and we mature slowly. Rilla was too young for mating, so for hundreds of years, I lived with her as a littermate. This long period of living together as sisters was wonderful for both of us. I taught her how to hunt deer and how to avoid humans. She taught me the joy and wonder of being alive. We never dared to go out during daylight. I don't think either of us ever got over the shock of seeing our kind slaughtered on the battlefield. But we had each other. I loved her sense of humor, the way she would imitate the silly way that humans walk or the way they talk about the gods. And she was gentle. She had never harmed a human, and when I killed a deer, she would bow her head and thank the deer for giving its life to sustain us. She talked about What-Is as if it were her private advisor, which having seen what I'd seen on the battlefield seemed naive, but I never told her so. No dragon has ever been more kind, more reverent, or more companionable than sweet Rilla Little Stream.

"Through the centuries, we saw great changes in the Bekla Valley below us. Farms spread along the green parts of the valley. Almost as destructive as humans were the animals enslaved by humans. Herds of sheep and goats spread through the Dry Hills turning a high dry plain covered in cedar trees into a desert. Pigs, chickens, dogs, cats, and cattle spread through the valley consuming everything they could find. Rilla and I never hunted the animals of men for fear of being seen. We came out only at night. Every now and then, we would kill a deer or an elk, but mostly we ate fish, especially salmon and pike. Sometimes we would fly down to the sea and search for swordfish, or we would dive deep under the water to catch tuna. Rilla refused to eat birds because like us they are sentient beings with wings, she said. And she didn't want us to eat snakes because they are our cousins. I respected her wishes then, and still do today.

"When Rilla passed her two thousandth year, she was of age, and I took her as my mate. No dragon has ever had a better wife, lover, or friend than Rilla. I loved her with all my heart."

Tyrmiss lay her head down and grew silent.

"And men killed her." I was surprised by the rage in Tessia's voice.

Tyrmiss raised her head and looked at Tessia. Her eyes, red with rage before, turned a soft blue. I thought, *this is what the eyes of dragons must have looked like before humans arrived in this land.*

And Tyrmiss and Tessia wept together, wailing in grief and agony over the loss of a world that would never return. The sound of their grief filled the cave, and I thought of it rippling out into the Iskar Valley below. I thought such grief could turn the river in its course.

"I'm feeling a bit peckish," the dragon said, licking her lips with a forked tongue. "Why don't we go out and get a bite to eat?"

She looked at Tessia, "I never thought I would say this to a human, but, sweetie, why don't you get on my back and we'll fly down to the river and pick up some salmon?"

I was amazed. Tyrmiss seemed like a different dragon.

Once the three of us were outside, Tessia did not hesitate. Handing me the torch, she tied back her hair and climbed on Tyrmiss's back. There was a line of sharp spines that ran from the dragon's head to her wings with space on her shoulders for Tessia to settle in between the wings. Holding onto the spine in front of her, she seemed quite comfortable. Her eyes shone with excitement.

Tyrmiss turned to me and said, "Bard, you are to remain here. Frankly, I do not like the way you have sung about dragons in the past. All that nonsense about Milon Redshield being a hero and the beauty of the warrior-princess." She sounded disgusted. "For a long time, I've thought you were a spy for Ludek, but now I can see you are just a fool with a lyre.

"Stay here and compose a new song about dragons," she said, her eyes reddening as she looked me up and down.

"M-my lady," I stammered. "It takes me an entire summer

walking the road for me to compose a new song. I cannot compose a song in the time it takes for you to catch a fish!"

"Meister Bard," the dragon said, her red eyes traveling down my body and coming to rest in the area where my scabbard hung down. "Are you fond of your man-parts?"

"Oh, yes," I said, starting to tremble. "I am very… attached to my man-parts."

"Are you familiar with the term *barbecue?*" she asked as if she were my tutor.

"No, my lady, but I can imagine what it means."

"Good, then it is settled. When I come back, you will have a new song for me."

"My lady, I did not bring my lyre. I would not be able to find the right key."

"Very well, then, you may chant the words, but in the future, you will bring your lyre. A bard should carry his lyre everywhere. There is no telling when he will be called on for a song. Is that understood?"

Tyrmiss spread her great black wings, took a few steps and lifted off, picking up speed. She rose in the moonlight, made a wide turn and dropped steeply into the Iskar Valley below.

I sat on a boulder beside the stream. The moonlight on the aspen trees was beautiful. I tried to listen to what the water and the light and wind were saying about dragons. It was not the first time I had been coerced into singing a praise-song for my host, but it was the first time my man-parts were at risk.

I heard the great wing-flaps before I saw the dragon with Tessia on her back. They made a smooth landing in the glade. I was surprised by the graceful movements of this large creature. It was not like the nursery tales of a cow flying to the moon. It was more like a hawk returning to its nest. Tyrmiss had a large salmon in her beak.

Tessia dismounted. Her cheeks were flushed, and her eyes were wild. I have never seen her so excited, not even after battle.

"It was so…" She struggled for the right word but gave up. She turned to Tyrmiss. "Thank you."

Dropping the salmon on a flat rock beside the stream, Tyrmiss replied, "You are welcome, my dear. I have never carried a human before. You are so small and light, it was no trouble at all."

The dragon breathed fire on the fish, roasting it quickly. It smelled delicious.

"Bard," she said. "I know your kind like to have greens with your fish. There is watercress a little way downstream from here. Go fetch it, so Tessia can enjoy her meal."

When I returned to the cave, Tessia was using her dagger to divide the fish into three parts, offering the largest to Tyrmiss who swallowed it in one piece. She offered me a smaller piece of fish arranged on a wide leaf with watercress lying beside it. She and I ate heartily, the fat of the fish melting in my mouth.

"Tyrmiss," Tessia said with her mouth full of fish. "May I ask you a question?"

"Go right ahead, my dear."

"Where did you get all the gold that's lying in your chamber?"

"Oh, that. It means nothing to me. Rilla thought it was pretty, so we collected it through the years. We lived here for thousands of years, you know, and if you collect a goblet here and necklace there, it adds up over time."

The mention of Rilla's name seemed to make her sad, but she suddenly pulled herself out of her melancholy and looked at me.

"Now, Meister Bard, let us hear your song," Tyrmiss commanded, waving her taloned limb like a queen in her court.

In the short time they'd been gone, I'd made up a song I thought was passably good, especially since I'd composed it quickly while under duress. Without a lyre, I couldn't sing, so I spoke the song, trying to make it sound oracular.

"Mistress," I began. "This song is called *I am Dragon.*"

Long before you climbed
From the trees
I was formed by the gods
From clay and stone

When you were still a frog
Unaware and wriggling
I was flying over the river
Skimming the surface

Before you took the breath
That burned your lungs
I lifted my wings
And called the stars

When you were still a spark
I was breathing flame
I was moonlight on the water
And sunlight on the leaf

I am dragon

"Hmmm…" Tyrmiss said, musing. "I am not sure whether I like it. I am supposed to be the speaker of these words, right? You make me sound so vain. What do you think, sweetie? Does the song make me sound too full of myself?"

Tessia said, "Oh no, I think it's a wonderful song. Norbert is a great poet."

Bless Tessia's kindness, I thought. The truth is she does not care a whit for songs. In the Silver Pony, she never once stopped serving tables to listen to me sing.

"I am not sure…" Tyrmiss repeated, holding a talon up to her long lips as she looked at me. Her eyes were blue now, thank the gods. At least I had not angered her.

"Perhaps, you could change that last part and make it sound as if I don't take myself so seriously?"

Zounds, I thought, *everyone is a critic.* I'd had to deal with hecklers in the Silver Pony often, but this was the first time a poetry-lover was prepared to light me on fire for a weak line.

"How about this?" I said and recited the song in a quieter voice without changing any words. I let my voice die out at the end, as if I were overcome by sadness.

"Perfect!" The dragon said, clapping her forelimbs together, making her talons click. "I think you have captured me!"

After my audition as her bard-in-residence was completed, the three of us sat in the glade beside the stream and talked until dawn. I told Tyrmiss of my love for Idella and Alaric and my desire to return to them and live in peace the rest of my days. Tessia spoke about the love she held for her father, her misgivings that she had disappointed him by not marrying a village boy and having children. And Tyrmiss spoke of the huge emptiness inside her when she remembered she was the last dragon on earth.

"If Rilla had survived, it would have been bearable, this sense that we are at the end of all things. The greatness of dragons—our songs, our humor, our wisdom—reside in me in such a small way. I am not a poet or a philosopher. I am not even a clown. I am merely a being who has lived far too long and seen far too much and carries a burden too great to bear."

"Bard," Tyrmiss said, changing the mood. "We have time for one more song. Sing us something."

"Instead of singing of love or heroes, let me improvise a song based on what you told us earlier. I think I'll call this song *I am Water.*"

Water is essence
Clay is form
Fire is passion
Wind moves the wings

But water was the first
Of the elements
The gods gave us water
To be like them

We become what contains us
We take the shape of clay
We merge with air
And rise with fire

We are water
We are life
We are thought
We are the past

You are the future

I am water
I am dragon
The last of my kind

"Thank you, Bard. I think I am starting to like you," Tyrmiss said. "Ah look, the sun is coming up. If we stay here someone will see me."

The three of us returned to the cave and slept.

I n the afternoon, Tessia and I said goodbye and left the dragon cave and walked down the trail that led to the rebel camp.

"What was it like to fly on a dragon's back, Tessia?"

"It was unlike anything I've ever experienced. Flying down

into the valley was like falling through heaven. We flew over the treetops, staying low so people would not see us, except perhaps a glimpse, and we came to the Iskar River where we skimmed the water. Tyrmiss said she can hear the fish dreaming under the water, so she knew exactly where they were. When we came to a large salmon, she grabbed it with her talons. Then we rose through the air and came halfway up the slope to a meadow she knew of. We sat there for a while and talked. I think she wanted to get to know me, and also she wanted to give you time to compose your song."

As we scrambled down the shelves of basalt known as The Giant's Stairway, Tessia stopped, looked off into the distant Iskar valley, and said, "Norbert, I feel sorry for her. She's very lonely. Ever since her mate Rilla died last year, Tyrmiss has lived here by herself. And now, she and I are becoming friends. Until yesterday, the only human she'd talked to in ages was my Uncle Zygmunt. He came to the cave a few years ago and tried to convince her to ally herself with his fight against the king, but Rilla was still alive back then, and Tyrmiss was not interested in antagonizing humans. She still remembers the time when men hunted dragons. Besides, she did not like Zygmunt."

"Why not?"

"She thought he was arrogant. All he wanted was for her to fight the king. He was not interested in her. She tried to recount the history of dragons to him, as she did for us, but he didn't show much interest. Besides," Tessia looked at me sideways and said hesitantly, "She doesn't like men, especially since it was a man who killed Rilla."

"I thought it was a Drekavac-soldier who killed her mate."

"She does not see any difference between the human races." Tessia thought about it, then said, "I see her point. Drekavacs and riverfolk speak the same language, and except for the skin and nails, we are almost identical."

For some reason, I found that idea offensive. *I am not a*

Drekavac, I thought angrily, but I stayed silent, not wanting to argue with Tessia.

Changing the subject, I asked, "Is she hunting the king's soldiers?" I remembered the charred bodies we saw in the Dry Hills.

"Yes. She flies out at night, and if she sees soldiers away from the city, then she kills them. She understands that the rebels are doing the same thing, so she leaves them alone. Also, she leaves civilians alone. Since she can hear people's dreams, then she knows their plans, their fears, their politics. Everything about them."

Tessia looked off into the darkness of the woods.

"What else, Tessia?" I asked.

"She is very afraid of Ludek, but she wouldn't tell me why."

"Well, she certainly doesn't seem to be afraid of me. Should I fear her?"

Tessia laughed, "All that business of scorching your man-parts? That's her idea of a joke. Actually, she's been listening to you compose in your dreams for years, and she loves your songs. I'm sure she liked the songs you made for her."

"Well, at least my songs were good enough to save the family jewels." We both laughed, and I realized I had not heard Tessia laugh in a very long time. It seemed that becoming friends with the dragon had made Tessia happy.

Chapter 12

We entered the camp shortly before the evening meal was served. As we walked through the camp and past the men standing outside the mess hall holding their bowls, no one greeted us. A few glared, but most of the men just looked away. I gave a nod to Anja as we walked by, but she looked at the ground and said nothing. Someone must have told Zygmunt we'd arrived because he stuck his head outside his tent and looked at us. His stare gave away nothing, not anger, not disgust, not disappointment, just a flat stare. I knew we were in trouble.

Normally, Tessia would have gone into the women's tent while I went into the men's, but instinctively we knew we should stick together, so she followed me into the place where I'd slept the night before. Silently, she took out the copper dagger she kept in her boot, checked it for sharpness and held it briefly in her hand to remember its balance. She did the same for the slim copper ax she kept in her belt. Then, she removed her true weapon from its scabbard. Her Voprian sword given to her by her father was certainly the best weapon in this camp, and perhaps the best one in all the valleys of Bekla, Dragonja and Iskar. She tested its weight in her hand. She took out her whetstone and touched up a few places on the blade. When she was satisfied that the weapon was exactly the way it should be, she slashed it a few times through the air. She and the weapon were one. She looked up at me.

"I'm ready, Norbert. Let's go talk to my uncle." She was obviously expecting a fight.

We walked across the camp and entered the mess area. Before we could sit down, Anja approached us. I noticed that her ears seemed more rigid than usual. "Zygmunt wants to see you in his tent."

Anja seemed to have become Zygmunt's attaché, accompanying him everywhere, running errands for him. There was some gossip around the camp that Anja had become Zygmunt's lover, but it mattered little to me. Men and women are sometimes lonely and seek out love and companionship where they can find it. Of much greater concern was what Zygmunt was going to say to Tessia and me.

Zygmunt sat in his tent eating by himself at a small table. Wessel stood directly behind him, watching everything, and Anja stood next to the entrance. With the two of them standing protecting Zygmunt, I thought, it would take an army to reach him. Zygmunt gestured at the place across the table from him, and Tessia sat down. I stood behind her.

"Please forgive me for eating in front of you," he said. "There are so many people who want to talk to me in the mess tent that I cannot get a bite there, so I have to eat here." He finished his food, pushed his plate aside, and then looked at Tessia.

"Niece," Zygmunt said, shaking his head sadly. "You have disappointed me."

"I'm sorry, Uncle, I was only trying..."

He held up one finger, silencing her.

"You have disappointed me," he repeated with more intensity. "I left you here to guard the camp, and you deserted your post. And what is worse, you took the healer with you. What if my men had been wounded in the raid? Who would have attended them?"

I was startled and thought back to the men I'd seen as we walked across the camp. None of them had appeared to be injured, but I realized that Zygmunt was right. I should have stayed in the camp and waited for the raiding party to return.

I'd been thinking only of what Tessia needed and had neglected my duties.

"My Lord Zygmunt," I said. "I am very sorry that I abandoned the camp. Were there injured in your party? Are there men I should be attending to?"

"We will discuss your duties later, Norbert. Right now, I need to speak to my niece."

I wondered whether I should leave, but since he hadn't ordered me to, I stayed to listen to what he said to Tessia.

"Niece," Zygmunt began. "Do you remember when we talked in the farmhouse by the Dragonja River? I told you and your brave friends," he said, nodding at Anja, who stood a little straighter with the gesture of praise. "That you could join us, but only if you agreed to obey me. Do you remember that promise?"

She nodded.

"By abandoning your post and encouraging the healer, who does not understand the way of the warrior, to abandon his post as well, you could have brought disaster on all of us. Do you understand?"

She nodded. I could see her bottom lip trembling slightly, but I knew she would not cry, not in front of these warriors.

"Perhaps you thought I was punishing you by assigning you to guard the camp, but actually I was honoring you. I assigned you the most important task, to guard our camp and to protect the women, the children, and the injured who could not join us in the raid on the copper mine."

He paused, and then added, "In war, there are no small tasks, only small warriors. Learn from your mistakes and become a better warrior from what you learn. Now go join the others in the mess tent. You are dismissed."

I could see she was devastated by his criticism of her. She would have preferred that he had drawn his sword against her, so she could have defended herself. Instead, he had showed love for her. I knew she would never make the mistake of abandoning her post again. And my admiration for Zygmunt soared on that day. I could see why his men were willing to die for this wise man. Tessia, keeping a straight back and a neutral face, turned on her heel to leave. I started to follow, but Zygmunt stopped me.

"Healer, please remain. There is much to discuss. First, tell me what happened in the dragon's cave. Tell me everything and leave nothing out."

I realized that he would ask Tessia to report on the encounter with the dragon as well, but it was shrewd of him to have us report separately before we had time to coordinate our stories. He wanted facts, not a persuasive argument about what he should do. So, I told him about going to the cave, listening to the dragon tell the history of her kind, as well as her personal story about the great battle with men thousands of years ago. I related to him how Tessia had saved me from being eaten by the dragon. I told him of Tyrmiss's love for her mate Rilla. I also related to him what Tessia had said about her flight to the Iskar River to catch a salmon and the growing friendship between Tessia and Tyrmiss.

Zygmunt listened carefully, sometimes asking me to clarify or elaborate. After I finished telling him everything I could remember about the previous night's events, Zygmunt sat for a few moments in silence, his fingertips pressed together.

"This is a great opportunity for us, Healer. Imagine having a dragon fighting beside us."

"General Zygmunt." He looked at me startled. It may have been the first time that anyone had addressed him by that rank.

"Yes, Healer? What is it?"

"There's something I neglected to mention. I apologize for saying this, but the dragon dislikes men, and… I am truly sorry to say this, but she hates you."

Zygmunt's face dropped. He looked away, thinking through this new piece of information.

"Yes, I made a mistake when I talked to the dragon a few years ago. We'd lost an important battle, and I was afraid we were going to lose the war. I went to the dragon as an act of desperation. I was impatient and demanding. Obviously, I offended her."

"General, we now have a chance to correct that error. Your niece has become very close to the dragon. Let Tessia be the one, the only one, who talks to the dragon. Coordinating your warriors' attacks with the attacks by the dragon should be sufficient to win the war."

"Yes, it could be." He thought about strategy for a moment, and said, "Indeed, it could be. I will talk with Tessia about the dragon. Thank you. Now let's talk about your duties as a healer."

Zygmunt told me that the raid on the copper mine had been perfect. The rebels took the soldiers by surprise, and after a few were wounded, the soldiers fled. Zygmunt sent a squad to chase the soldiers far enough down the mountain so that it was clear they would go all the way back to the city and not return to the mountain any time soon.

The rebels had brought food with them which they shared with the slaves. After being told they were free, most of the boys left to return to their families. A few of the boys said that they had no place to return to, their families having been murdered and their homes and farms having been burned to the ground. These boys elected to join the rebels. On the other hand, none of the girls chose to return to their villages. They said that the way they'd been used by the soldiers had shamed them, and they didn't think their families would want them back. So Zygmunt and his rebels brought five boys and four girls back to the camp. The girls were being taken care of by the women, and the boys were to be trained as warriors. Zygmunt wanted me to take a look at the former slaves and to help them heal from their ordeal.

"But first, Healer, go to the mess tent and have dinner. You must be famished." As I turned to leave, he added, "By the way, I am assigning you the rank of captain, so the men will have to listen to you. And also, please do not leave camp without my permission. You are too valuable for us to lose you."

As I walked across the camp, I thought about the way that Zygmunt had treated my desertion compared to the way he had treated Tessia's. He'd appealed to her sense of honor and professionalism as a warrior, a tactic which completely disarmed her; whereas, for me, he'd made an offhand compliment about my value to the community and had phrased his order as a request. Zygmunt knew how to bring out the best in each of his followers. He was, without a doubt, the most effective and inspiring leader I've ever known.

While I was eating in the mess tent, Zygmunt came in. He went around to each group of men and talked casually with them, making jokes, asking about an old wound, praising men's courage in the battle of the day before, slapping men on the back and guffawing at their jokes, and then quickly changing mood to ask a man whether he'd received news of his family, and then with another man reminiscing about an old friend who'd died in battle years before. The men admired him, yes, but they also loved him.

I knew that Tessia could, in time, mature into a leader like her uncle.

After dinner, I intended to visit the tent where the new boys were. I vowed never to use the word "slave" again in relation to these young people. They were my patients, the people who depended on my skills, meager as they were, to help them heal. On the way, I stopped by the women's tent and asked if anyone had experience as healers. One of them, a plump young woman with red hair and a warm smile, said she'd helped a midwife several times in her village. I asked her to accompany me. Her name was Mina, and over time she became the best healer the Bekla Valley has ever known.

The five boys were undernourished and some of them had festering welts on their backs from the soldiers' whips. They also had many cuts and bruises on their hands and arms from working in the mines. Mina and I treated the injuries with an ointment and clean bandages. With lots of good food and kind treatment, the boys would completely recover.

The four girls were a different story altogether. They had been abused so many times that they had stopped crying, and instead, they sat silently, staring at nothing. When they spoke, it was as if they were having to come from far away, a place where there was nothing but pain, fear, and humiliation. It was as if their souls had been torn away from them, leaving only damaged bodies. Mina held each girl's hand as I examined them. She had a calming presence, and the girls seemed instinctively to trust her. Mina reassured them that I was here in the tent to help them, and they should not be afraid of me.

As I expected, the four girls had suppurating sores in their women parts, and their foreheads felt feverish. I left Mina with the girls and went outside to look for herbs that would bring down their fever and help heal their sores. By the time I entered the forest, I felt rage rising in me. Not for the first time, I was nauseated by the ways that men treat women. A man's desire for women is understandable, even beautiful, but the need to hurt them, to humiliate them, to use them in ways that destroy their spirit—this I could not understand.

In a meadow, I finally found the herbs I needed and returned to the tent. Inside, the four girls were sitting on the bed talking with Mina. All of them were sobbing as they spoke. Mina caught my eye and gave a small shake of her head. I placed the basket of herbs on the floor of the tent and left. I would treat their fever and sores later. Right now, Mina was doing essential work by helping the girls heal their spirits.

163

There was much healing work to be done in the camp, so I came to count on Mina more and more. Fortunately, she was a quick learner. I taught her how to set a bone and where to find the herbs to treat certain illnesses. She, in turn, taught me that healing is not primarily about the body, but about the spirit. If a person feels she is loved and has a place in the world, then the body will probably heal. But without love, no one can be fully present in the body, and the body will never have the strength it needs to recover. She also reminded me that songs, chants, spells and stories have magical qualities. They're not just for distraction or entertainment, but used correctly, they can rouse the spirit and heal the body. This was something my father had often said, but somehow, I'd forgotten this principle until I saw how effective Mina was as a healer.

One day when Mina and I were washing in the stream after helping a woman with a difficult birth, she confided in me that she was originally from Crota, a land on the southern coast. Her people were fishermen. She was a helper to the midwife who served a large region, and so Mina assisted her on a number of births. It didn't take long for Mina to discover she had a gift for healing.

"One day," Mina related, "Pirates came to the village and kidnapped all the girls. On the ship, we were abused by the sailors, then sold as slaves in Kladd, the city at the mouth of the Bekla River. I was bought by a man from Dragonja City who owned many girls. Living in a brothel in Dragonja City far from my home, I made the best I could of the situation, trying to help the girls who caught diseases or who needed to end pregnancies. The master of the house came to trust me and often sent me to the market to buy food. On a shopping errand last summer, I seized the opportunity to escape, passing through the East Gate and running into the countryside. I'd heard that the rebels welcomed escaped slaves, so I followed the river and ran up the trail to the pass. Zygmunt's men came across me asleep beside the trail. I was taken back to the camp and given work as a healer, but all I really knew was how to take care of women who'd been abused. Now I know much more about helping people heal."

I could see there was something else she wanted to say, so I waited.

After a few moments, she continued. "I thought when I came here, I'd be treated the way I'd always been treated since the pirates first kidnapped me, being raped and sold and passed around among men. Instead, in this camp, I've been treated with respect, at least as much respect as any woman receives. So, I've decided to stay here and develop my skills as a healer. I want to thank you for teaching me. My skills improve with each patient I see."

"You're welcome, Mina. It's a pleasure to teach someone with such a gift for helping people," I said, knowing the time was coming soon when she wouldn't be needing any more instruction from me.

One day, I saw Mina take out a small clay figurine from her apron pocket. When I asked about it, she said I was not allowed to touch it, but she could show it to me. She held up a small likeness of a female, wide-hipped and large breasted. She said it was Zelja, the earth mother, the Goddess of fecundity. In Crota, midwives, mothers, farmers, and healers—all who encourage life to flourish—worship Zelja. Mina said that whatever power she had as a healer is not hers but is entrusted to her by Zelja. Healing, she said, is not a trade, such as fishing or metal-working, but rather a sacred trust, and as healers we need to be humble in the face of the Great Mystery that is Life.

When Mina spoke this way, as she often did, I stayed silent out of respect for her beliefs and her skills as a healer, but behind my silence I was hiding my skepticism and my sense of superiority over her superstitious attitudes. Like most of my people, I was devoted to the worship of the Goddess Nilene, and Mina's belief in the deity of her tribe seemed at best unsophisticated, at worst sacrilegious. However, in time, I began to understand that Mina was exactly right in her attitude of humility in the presence of nature's wisdom. She did not have the power to heal; nor did I. No man or woman has that power. At best, I could encourage my patient's healing by prescribing herbs, stitching wounds or manipulating bones, but it is actually Zelja, She-Who-Is-the-Life-Force, who heals people. I also came to believe that Zelja and Nilene are different names for the same Goddess.

During the first week after seeing the dragon, I sometimes saw Tessia at a distance, but rarely had a chance to exchange more than a few words. Zygmunt had demoted her to the rank of private and assigned her to a platoon led by a grizzled old Drekavac sergeant named Zrul whom I recognized from the Silver Pony. He'd always been the first to raise his tankard to toast King Ottolo and to fight any man who insulted the king. Seeing the sergeant here was disconcerting, to say the least. He was the last soldier I would have expected to defect. According to camp rumor, Zrul had been a career soldier in the king's guard, but when he saw what soldiers had done to the village where he'd grown up in the Dry Hills, he deserted and joined the rebels. There were a number of these former soldiers, both Drekavacs and riverfolk, in the ranks of the rebels, and I couldn't help but wonder if at least one of them was a spy. But this was none of my concern, and I had my hands full taking care of the sick and injured in the camp, so I stayed silent.

Sergeant Zrul had a deep scar on his forehead which seemed to go deep into bone, a trophy of a long-forgotten war. Against his scaly gray Drekavac skin, the deep red of the scar looked terrifying. My guess is that he nearly died from the wound. Zrul emanated menace, terrifying everyone in camp, especially his trainees who did everything he told them to do. He fiercely believed in training and discipline, often saying that the unit had to function as one man. Coming back from a long night with a woman in labor, I'd see him at dawn drilling his platoon, having them run up and down the trail for an hour, then training with weapons. Although Tessia had never had this kind of training, she took to it easily, and after the first week, the sergeant promoted her to corporal, giving her the assignment of training the recruits in weapons. I was sure that she didn't see her assignment to the platoon as punishment, but rather as an opportunity to learn about the craft of soldiering. Her talent as a fighter could carry her only so far; she had to learn how to serve as part of an army.

And the men in her unit learned to respect her. A few days after her promotion to corporal, a man was carried to the tent I'd set up as a field hospital. The man was unconscious, and he had a large contusion on the left side of his head. I asked what happened, and one of the men who'd delivered him to me said, "He fell."

I scowled at the soldier and, using my rank as his superior officer, said, "Private, I order you to tell me what happened."

The soldier glanced at his companion, then looked at the floor and muttered, "She did it, sir. During weapons training, he made a remark about her rear end, so she hit him with the flat side of her sword."

I suppressed a smile and asked, "What did the sergeant say?"

"He pretended he didn't see it, sir. He just grunted and told us to take him here and tell you that he fell."

I told the men to go back to their platoon and I looked at the contusion. I put a bag of cold stream water on it to reduce swelling, kept him on bedrest for a day, and then sent him back to his unit with a suggestion that in the future he should show more respect for his corporal.

One evening, I was working late in the field hospital by torchlight, mixing herbs. It had been quiet in the camp that day, no illness or injuries, and I was enjoying the rest. There was a rumor going around that we'd be making an assault on the city the following week, and I was thinking that there might be time for me to sneak away, go down to the city and visit Idella. I thought about asking permission to do so, but I knew that permission would be denied. Perhaps, I thought, I could make up an excuse to leave? I could say that I had to go into the Bekla Valley to gather herbs for medicine? I was not fond of deceit, but I was missing Idella a great deal, and I was beginning to understand that I'd made a terrible mistake in abandoning her. I cursed the false pride that made me abandon my family to prove my bravery. Would Idella even want me to return?

My eyes became strained in the torchlight, so I went outside to take a break. On the edge of camp, I saw a figure in the woods returning to camp. I wondered who it could be because everyone was under strict orders to stay in the camp unless given permission to leave. I stepped behind a tree and watched the figure move toward me. It was Sergeant Zrul. I stepped in front of him, and he jumped, then calmed himself.

"Healer," he growled, seeming relieved. "I didn't see you there. What are you doing out so late?"

"I was about to ask you the same thing, Sergeant. As you know, we're under orders not to leave the camp without permission."

"Well, to tell you the truth," he looked sheepish. "I have not been able to move my bowels. I thought a short walk would do me good."

"Of course, Sergeant," I said. "I hope you are feeling better."

He nodded and hurried over to the latrine.

As an officer, I knew I was supposed to report the incident to the watch commander, but I decided not to. As the resident healer, I needed to have the trust of the men, and the fastest way to destroy trust was to report soldiers for minor infractions.

Tessia came to the field hospital where I was alone mixing herbs. I hugged Tessia affectionately, and holding her at arm's length, I looked at her up and down. She seemed taller than I remembered from our time in the city where she was making her living serving ale to laborers and soldiers. She stood straighter, kept her chin higher. Obviously, the fresh air and military training agreed with her.

"I've missed you, Tessia. What brings you here? You're not ill, are you?"

She put her finger to her lips, signaling me to keep my voice low. She said, barely above a whisper, "Norbert, what I am going to tell you is a secret, so you cannot tell anyone."

I nodded agreement.

"General Zygmunt..." she began. I noticed that she did not call him *Uncle*.

"... has ordered me to visit the Dragon Tyrmiss, and I need you to come with me. We leave tomorrow at dawn. I will explain everything to you on the hike to the cave."

She turned to go, then looked back at me, "And Norbert, you will need to compose a song for her. One that will remind her of why she hates the king and his soldiers. Her heart has gone cold, my friend. You need to make her burn with the need for vengeance."

Early the next morning, I went to the women's tent, and pulling Mina aside, I told her that I had to leave, but couldn't tell her why. She nodded, understanding that I must have a very good reason for keeping my mission secret. She said she would take good care of the health of our community while I was gone. I knew she would, too.

As we walked up the trail, Tessia explained. "The General is planning an attack on the King's castle. He's asked me to recruit Tyrmiss to help us by carrying me into the castle to open the gate while Tyrmiss creates a diversion by setting the tower on fire. He knows that I am the only one who can convince the dragon to be part of the attack."

"Why am I coming, Tessia? You know Tyrmiss hates me."

"Actually, you're the only man she likes, Norbert."

I thought about Tyrmiss's attempt to swallow me whole as well as her threat to roast my man-parts, and I realized how much she must hate men if I was her favorite.

Tessia looked uncomfortable. She had never been good at keeping secrets.

"I have to tell you, Norbert, that I was planning to go alone, but the general told me it was not a good idea. He always sends at least two people on every mission. So, he asked me to choose a partner, and I chose you."

"Thanks, Tessia." I could not keep the sarcasm out of my voice.

She gave a chuckle and asked, "I see you brought your lyre. Did you compose a song for her?"

"Yes, I did. Two of them, and I think they're good."

"They better be," she muttered. "We have to win her over, or Hamlin and my father will die in that dung hole of a castle."

If they are not already dead, I thought.

Chapter 13

T'essia! What a nice surprise!" The dragon exclaimed, ignoring me altogether.

"Don't be coy, Tyrmiss," Tessia said. "I've felt you listening to my thoughts ever since we left here. You probably know all about the reason why we've come."

I looked around the cave. There were flowers hanging on the walls, and the cave smelled much better than last time. Tyrmiss had been cleaning, anticipating Tessia's arrival.

"The place looks nice," I said, trying to sound cheery.

"Hello, Norbert," Tyrmiss said in a flat voice, underwhelmed by my presence. Obviously, she'd hoped to have Tessia to herself.

"Yes," she said to Tessia with more enthusiasm than she had shown me. "I knew you were coming, and I know why. But let's eat first, then we can discuss your uncle's little plan to get me killed in one of his foolish adventures. Look, I flew down to the river before dawn this morning and caught a lovely pike."

A large fish was lying on the flat scorched rock where Tyrmiss had roasted the salmon last time we were here.

While Tessia and I unpacked our gear, Tyrmiss breathed fire on the fish, checked it for tenderness by poking a talon in the flesh, then breathed fire on it again until the skin was slightly blackened on the tail and gills. "There! I believe it's done."

"Tyrmiss, I am so impressed with your fire!" Tessia said, generously, "How do you do it?"

"Oh, it is really nothing, my dear. Dragon anatomy is not much different than human anatomy, if you think about it. You

171

humans pass a mix of methane and sulfur gasses out of your back end while we pass similar gasses out of our front end. So, the flame is basically just a burp."

"How do you ignite it?" I asked, my professional curiosity aroused.

"We have very hard teeth, Norbert. We strike our back teeth together to make sparks, much like the way you humans make sparks by hitting a flint on a piece of copper." She opened her mouth wide, showing four long rows of daggerlike teeth. She seemed to have forgotten that I'd seen them before from very close up. "As the gas passes through our mouths, we click the back teeth together, igniting the gasses, then we open our mouths and exhale. Like this."

She closed her mouth, making a clicking noise, then opened her mouth and exhaled a small ball of fire in the direction of the cave entrance. "I suppose we are lucky as a species. We could have been designed with flames coming out of the back end, rather than the front end."

We all laughed at the mental picture of a dragon shooting flames out of her butt.

"Although sometimes as a joke," Tyrmiss said, "My brothers and I would have duels. We would stand back-to-back, take ten paces, and FIRE! We—" Tyrmiss stopped, suddenly serious, realizing that she'd been speaking of dragons, her own species, her own family, in the plural when she was the only one left. At that moment, I saw for the first time how lonely it must be for her to be the last of her kind.

Trying to recapture the light mood, I said, laughing, "When I was a boy, my friends and I would back up to the fireplace, drop our trousers, bend over and let one loose!"

My joke fell flat. The mood had shifted. Tyrmiss and Tessia were looking deep into each other's eyes, which were filling with tears. We ate in silence. Tyrmiss had thoughtfully provided dandelions and other greens for Tessia and me to eat with our fish.

After we finished eating, Tessia said, "Norbert has composed a couple of songs for you. Would you like to hear them?"

Tyrmiss nodded. I picked up my lyre, quickly tuned each string, and then I introduced the song simply by saying, "The song is called 'I am Tyrmiss.'"

The dragon seemed to perk up a little at hearing her name. I sang:

I am Tyrmiss the Dragon
Of Bekla Valley
My kind has lived here
Forever

Long before
Men came wearing skins
Carrying axes
Hunting

The great hairy beasts
Of the ice
Rilla and I
Flew over the green valley

Rilla my love
Purple scales
Catching the light
Was killed

Beside a waterfall

I have watched men
Burning and killing

I have grown to hate men
I am Tyrmiss
I am dragon

After the song ended, there was silence. Tessia who'd been watching the dragon closely while I sang, asked her, "That was a lovely song, I think. Did you like it, Tyrmiss?"

Tyrmiss was quiet, then she gave a deep sigh and said, "I need to go lie down now." And she went into the deeper chamber of the cave, leaving Tessia and me alone.

We waited quite a while, then I pointed to the mouth of the cave and Tessia followed me out. We stopped beside the stream.

"Should we leave?" I asked.

"No, no," Tessia said, shaking her head. "That would be unforgivably rude. She just needs a little time."

"What happened? Is she angry at me for singing about Rilla?"

"No. It was just a very emotional experience for her, I think. Remember, she probably has never heard a human other than you say Rilla's name. We should go back inside and wait until she's ready to come out."

We drank some water and went back in the cave. Eventually, we were hungry again and ate some more of the pike. We left only the head. Its eyes seemed to be following me around the cave. In late afternoon, Tyrmiss came out of her chamber and joined us. She seemed calm and composed.

"Norbert," she said. "Do you have another song?" Of course, she knew that I did.

"Yes, I do."

"Is it about Rilla?" She asked.

"Yes, it is."

"Sing it, Bard. I need to hear the music of her name."

I picked up my lyre, strummed a few notes, and said, "This song is called *Rilla*."

Rilla my Rilla
She was the flick
Of the tongue
Tasting the air

She flew through

She was the snake
With wings
That carried my heart

My Rilla
Was the fire
In the air I breathed
And burned

In death she crawled
To the water's edge
To breathe mist
A last time

Rilla my Rilla
I am Tyrmiss
The killer of men

I kill them for you

After a long silence, the dragon turned to Tessia and said, "I will fly you into the castle, so you can open the gates for Zygmunt and his men to enter. I will help you save your father and your friend. But I ask only one thing."

"And what do you ask, my dear friend?" Tessia asked.

"I will be allowed to kill as many of the king's soldiers as I wish."

Tessia and I were standing in Zygmunt's tent reporting on what had happened with Tyrmiss when the general stood up and started pacing back and forth.

"She actually said she'd fly you into the castle if she's allowed to kill as many soldiers as she can? Those were her exact words?"

175

"Yes, General," Tessia said emphatically.

"I asked her to help us a few years ago and she refused. Why is she willing to help us now?"

"It was Norbert's songs that did it, General," Tessia said generously.

"Actually, General," I quickly interjected, "Tessia has built a friendship with the dragon. My songs may have helped, but if the two had not bonded, my songs would have made no difference."

"Well done, both of you." Zygmunt gave Tessia a bear hug and shook my hand vigorously.

"Will the dragon obey you?" He asked, abruptly.

"Well, I do not... I mean things are not..." Tessia stammered.

Zygmunt looked at his niece, puzzled.

"If I may, General," I said. "The dragon is joining us out of friendship with Tessia and a desire to revenge the murder of her mate. Tyrmiss is not going to obey any of us."

Zygmunt nodded his head, taking this in.

"Let me rephrase my question. How dependable is this dragon? Is she an ally or just a random force of nature? I cannot have her turning on my warriors once she's finished with the king's soldiers."

Tessia and I stood in front of the general with our mouths hanging open. We had been so excited about enlisting the aid of Tyrmiss, we'd forgotten how dangerous she is. Tessia finally said, "I will speak with her again and ask her to promise not to hurt any of our warriors."

Zygmunt thought about it for a moment and then nodded his head. "She has not attacked us so far, and if you can exact a promise from her to continue restraining herself, then we'll probably be safe. I'll need you to go back to her tomorrow and discuss strategy. At that time, you can ask her to make the promise. If she refuses, then we have to change our entire plan."

After we left Zygmunt's tent, I turned to Tessia and said,

"It was very generous for you to say that it was my songs that convinced Tyrmiss, but we both know that it was her love for you that brought her around."

Tessia smiled at me. Her smile has always reminded me of the peach color of the sky at sunrise. "It was both of us, Norbert. What are the two most powerful forces in the world?"

"Pancakes and fart jokes?" I asked facetiously.

"No," she said, hitting me gently on the shoulder. "Loyalty and passion. I inspired her loyalty. You inspired her passion. She didn't stand a chance against our teamwork."

The next morning, Tessia and I returned to the dragon cave. Tyrmiss was not surprised to see us, of course. She'd overheard in our dreams what Zygmunt had said about her, and she was not pleased.

"So, General Dogbutt does not trust me?" she asked, her red eyes flashing.

"Please, Tyrmiss, he's just trying to watch out for his men."

"I should fly over his camp and set a few of his soldiers on fire."

"No, no. Please, Tyrmiss, don't hurt them." It was the first time I'd ever heard Tessia beg. I imagined that she was now realizing that we had, well, a dragon by the tail, but it was more than that. Tessia was softer when she was with Tyrmiss, and Tyrmiss was softer with Tessia as well.

Tyrmiss looked at Tessia, and the dragon's eyes gradually faded from red to light blue. "Oh, my dear, you remind me so much of my Rilla. When she was young, she used to beg me not to kill humans. She had such compassion." She sighed, "Very well. For your sake, I won't light General Dogbutt's britches on fire. But his distrust of me is very insulting."

She turned her eyes on me.

"And what about you, Bard? Do you trust me?"

"Yes, my lady, with my life."

She held my gaze for a moment, weighing whether I was mocking her.

"Very well, then, I will tell you something that will make you wish I were lying. Your wife's name is Idella?"

I felt a terrible dread descend on me. "Yes, my lady."

"She is in mortal danger."

"What danger? What has happened?"

"I don't know exactly. But I heard a dream last night that mentioned her name."

"Whose dream?"

"I'm not sure. This ability I have for listening to dreams is not very reliable. Sometimes I'm not sure who the dreamer is."

"Was it someone in the city? A soldier perhaps? The king? The Wizard Ludek?"

"Oh, no. The dreamer was not in the castle. I can't hear dreams so far away. It was someone closer. Probably someone on this mountain."

"A passing soldier perhaps?" I asked hopefully.

"No, you fool. It's someone in your camp."

"You mean we have a traitor in our midst?"

"It would appear so."

On the hike back to the camp, Tessia and I were both absorbed in our own thoughts. I felt a growing dread about Idella and the danger she was in. I was also thinking about what Tyrmiss had said about the traitor in the rebel camp. I wondered who it was. Sergeant Zrul came to mind. After all, why would a career soldier suddenly switch sides? The more I thought about Zrul, the more likely it seemed that he was the traitor. A rage grew in me. I vowed to tell General Zygmunt about my suspicions.

Tessia was obviously thinking about the rebels' imminent assault on the city. She knew, I was sure, that her uncle was entrusting her with a key part of the strategy. The success of the entire campaign rested in large part on her relationship with the dragon. Tyrmiss's love for Tessia was obvious, but whether Tessia could restrain the dragon from attacking our own warriors was uncertain.

Tessia and I went immediately to Zygmunt's tent where Wessel and Anja stood guard outside the entrance. Wessel looked us over, using his extraordinary ability to interpret people's intentions from the way they acted. Anja gave Tessia a curt nod and looked away which seemed to puzzle Tessia since the two young women had known each other since childhood. Both Anja and Wessel stepped aside, and we entered the tent to find Zygmunt sitting at the table looking at a map of the streets of Dragonja City. The map was crudely drawn with charcoal on a large piece of bark, and I guessed it had been sketched from memory by one of his men who'd lived in the city.

The General looked up at us. His face was tense with worry. He put his hand up, signaling that we needed to wait a moment. He walked past us, put his head out of the tent flap and spoke to Anja briefly, sending her on an errand.

"Tessia! Norbert! I'm glad you've returned," he said as he sat down again. He didn't invite us to sit, so we remained standing, Tessia at attention and me doing my best impersonation of an army officer. Since I'd arrived in the camp, it had become clear to me that I hadn't joined the ragtag band of malcontents I'd expected, but rather a professional army. I understood that the metamorphosis into a disciplined fighting force had been necessary if the war was going to be won, but truthfully, I was not comfortable in my role as an army captain. Tessia, on the other hand, seemed to have adapted well.

She reported about our meeting with Tyrmiss, giving me more credit than I deserved for winning over the dragon. She concluded by saying that she had complete faith in the dependability of Tyrmiss.

"You do need to know, General," I added, "That the dragon overheard our dreams and knows you do not trust her." Tessia gave me a sharp look. Clearly, she did not want me to make Tyrmiss look unreliable, but I worried that she had withheld information that Zygmunt needed to know.

Zygmunt looked at me, then turned his penetrating gaze to Tessia. "Why did you not tell me this, Corporal?"

Tessia went to full attention and replied, "Because I did not think it was relevant, General. I believe that the captain and I convinced the dragon to trust us. She will not betray us, sir."

So, now even Tessia calls me "the captain?" I thought ruefully. I would be very glad to be free of all this rank and discipline.

"A time may come, Corporal," Zygmunt said, "When it is necessary to kill the dragon. If she turns on our own people, are you willing to do what is necessary?"

Zounds, I thought, *I hope Tyrmiss does not overhear this.*

Tessia swallowed hard and said, "Yes, sir. I am."

"There is something else, General," I said, changing the subject.

"Yes, Captain. Tell me."

"Tyrmiss says we have a traitor in the camp."

Zygmunt leaned back, put his fingertips together to form a globe in front of his face. "And does the dragon know who the traitor is?"

"No, sir. But I have a theory."

Zygmunt raised his eyebrows in a silent invitation for me to speak.

"I believe it is Sergeant Zrul."

Zygmunt and Tessia both looked at me surprised.

"General," Tessia blurted out. "It could not be the sergeant! He's one of the most dedicated warriors we have. He has trained me and the other recruits, and he would die to protect us."

"Why would a career soldier abandon his regiment in order to join a guerilla band?" I asked the general, ignoring Tessia.

"Indeed, why would he? I will take what both of you have said about the sergeant under consideration, but I need to know whether either of you have told anyone about the dragon."

Tessia and I asserted that we had not.

"Has anyone seen you go in the direction of the dragon cave?"

Tessia and I looked at each other, and then told him that we did not think so.

"Good. It is very important that no one, absolutely no one, knows about the dragon. Am I clear?"

"Yessir," Tessia and I said in unison.

"Dismissed," he said, waving his hand and looking down again at his map.

Tessia saluted and turned to leave, but I remained in front of Zygmunt.

"Is there something else, Captain?"

"Yes sir, I need permission to go to Dragonja City."

"What?" Zygmunt looked at me incredulously. "We are on the eve of an assault on the city, and you want to go there? Why?"

"My wife, sir." I felt my voice trembling, but I was not ashamed. "My wife Idella is in mortal danger."

"How do you know this?"

"The dragon told me, sir."

Zygmunt looked at me disgusted. "Permission denied. Your skills as a healer are too valuable to risk your life right before battle. Now, get out of my tent and go get some rest."

As Tessia and I left the General's tent, Anja showed up carrying a large tray of food. Zygmunt must have sent her to the mess tent while we were talking. Not for the first time, I questioned the assignment Zygmunt had given Anja. The young woman was one of the best blade fighters under Zygmunt's command, second only to Tessia, and yet she was being assigned errands any private could have done. I wondered whether Anja was being side-tracked because she was young and female. Other than Tessia, who was obviously more gifted than Anja, there were no other women warriors in the rebel army; instead, women were assigned duty as cooks and nurses—which seemed to me a waste of talent. Well, I thought, it's just one more reason to get out of this army as soon as possible.

Tessia was obviously irritated at me. "Why did you tell him about Tyrmiss knowing he distrusted her?"

"Because it was something he needed to know. Tessia," I said, choosing my words carefully. "Do you feel your loyalty is divided?"

"What do you mean?" she asked, looking at me out of the corner of her eye.

"You love your uncle, right?"

"Yes, I love my uncle, and I also admire him. No one else could have led us this far in our fight against the king."

"And you also have grown very close to Tyrmiss, right?"

"Yes, but my loyalty to Zygmunt has nothing to do with my friendship with Tyrmiss."

"There may come a time when you have to choose between them."

For the second time that evening, Tessia looked at me angrily. "You do not understand, Norbert. Men always think every choice is completely clear. You are loyal to this person or that person, but not both. Well, choices are not always clear. Sometimes you have to make choices based on more than one loyalty. I will perform my duty to the General, and I will also love my friend. I will not choose between them." And she stormed off in the direction of the women's tent.

I returned to the barracks. The other men were already snoring. I tried to sleep, but I tossed and turned, worrying about Idella. Tessia was not the only one with divided loyalties.

A few hours later, Sergeant Zrul showed up in the barracks, shouting in his hoarse voice, "Wake up, men, we are going to war this morning!"

All of us jumped out of bed and hurriedly got dressed. Men

were grumbling that the assault on the city was supposed to wait until the moon was full, so they could see what they were doing. The sergeant was telling them that the march to the city was starting this morning, and they better to get ready or there would be hell to pay.

Turning to me, the sergeant said, "Captain, the general has said that you should join him in his tent to receive your orders."

I quickly walked across the camp. Though the sun had not come up yet, the camp was busy. The cooks were preparing food and handing it out as quickly as they could, and the armorers were distributing spears and axes to the men who were packing their kits and strapping on weapons.

Zygmunt was still in his tent where I'd left him. His face was drawn, and I guessed he hadn't slept all night. A group of officers gathered around as he pointed at the map and gave instructions. As each officer received his orders, he quickly left the tent to join his men.

I was the last officer to receive orders. Zygmunt greeted me. "Norbert, my friend," he said gently. "I apologize for dismissing you so curtly a few hours ago. I was worried about the plans for the assault."

"Not at all, General. I was worried about my wife, and I was probably disrespectful to you. May I ask what is going on?"

"We're marching to the city this morning, Norbert. The march is almost entirely downhill, so the warriors can reach the city by this afternoon, and then the assault on the gates ensues."

"And what is my role, General?"

"I want you to wait here in camp until all the fighting units have left, Norbert, and then leave with the auxiliary unit. By the time you get to the city, we will have wounded warriors for you to tend."

"And what about my wife, sir?" I was sure he could hear the disbelief in my voice.

"I am truly sorry, Norbert, but right now we must put aside

our personal concerns for the greater cause. Think of how many wives will suffer if we are not successful in our campaign."

I left the general's tent and walked like a ghost across the camp, barely seeing or hearing the warriors assembling into their marching formations. I went into the barracks and lay down, feeling completely empty inside. I thought of Idella and what horrors she was facing if no one helped her.

Having made a decision, I walked across the camp, which was eerily quiet now, and I went to the hospital tent and packed my bag with knives and herbs. I pulled out my short sword and tested the edge. Mina came in.

"You've been assigned to the auxiliary unit? So, you will be setting up a hospital to treat the wounded?"

I nodded.

"Will you be going?" She asked, intuiting my plan to desert.

"Well, actually I've been reassigned. A secret mission, you know."

She looked at me sardonically. "I heard about Idella," she said. When I looked surprised, she added, "There are no secrets in this camp."

"Mina, I have to try to find Idella." Panic was rising in my voice.

"Do you want me to go with the auxiliary unit and set up a hospital outside the city?"

"Yes, but what about your assignment?"

"What assignment? No one has said anything to me." She looked disgusted. "Zygmunt and his men never even see me. Most men don't see women. Except you… Thank you, for treating me with respect."

I realized it was true. People spoke of me as a healer but ignored her. I'd been given the rank of captain, but she held no rank, no title. People thought she was just my helper, but both she and I were aware that she knew as much about medicinal herbs as I did, and she was probably a better surgeon. I had more experience, but she was the one with a natural gift for healing.

"Mina, please take my place in the battle. The men will need your skills. And when they ask for me, tell them... tell them that I deserted."

She shook her head. "No, I will tell them the truth. You are a brave man who went into the city to save his wife."

Carrying my medical bag, I walked by the midden, but Bruin was not there. Tessia said she'd not seen him since shortly after she arrived in camp. *Too bad*, I thought, *I would have liked to say goodbye to him.*

I went into the field where Ottolo was grazing.

"Goodbye, old friend," I said, stroking the donkey's snout. "Thank you for your faithful service." Ottolo looked at me with his large wise eyes, then turned his attention back to the green grass.

I knew that this was probably the last time I would see him. It was unlikely I would survive the night.

In the cave, Tessia and Tyrmiss were sharing a roasted fish. Neither seemed surprised to see me. Tessia nodded in my direction. I noticed her spear, bow, quiver, short sword, ax and dagger were stacked neatly in the corner. She had never liked carrying a shield because it slowed her down. She was wearing a heavy leather doublet laced down the front, covering her torso and neck but leaving her arms free to move. Her Voprian blade was in its scabbard at her waist as it always was.

Tyrmiss said, calmly, "Hello, Nordbutt. We've been waiting for you. You better eat some fish and greens. It's going to be a long night."

*T*yrmiss was glad she hadn't eaten Norbert. The little fellow was turning out to be more interesting than she'd realized. It was obvious that Tessia didn't know that her pathetic friend was the brother of Ludek. Why did Norbert not tell her? Was he so afraid of his own power? Well, he'd better find his courage quickly if he was going to survive this war.

The dragon was feeling a little ridiculous, joining a human army to overthrow their king. She'd always let humans kill each other without interference from her. The fewer humans, the better, she'd always thought. And what would Rilla say about this childish adventure? No doubt Rilla would worry that flying into battle against humans is dangerous. As a dragonling, she'd witnessed a thousand dragons shot out of the sky by the weapons of men. And she would probably think that no matter who won this war, humans would continue killing each other, so what's the point of helping one side or the other? She and Rilla had seen hundreds of bloody human crusades that had, sooner or later, ended badly. Humans seemed to be fond of torturing and beheading their enemies, unlike dragons who'd never known violence until humans came along. So why help the mud-monkeys with their bloody chores?

She'd been offended by the way Zygmunt had asked for her help. He seemed to be assuming he was doing her a favor by offering a place in his ragtag army. He explained how important the rebellion was, but she could see through his rhetoric. The more he talked, the clearer it was that he was talking about himself, only himself. In his mind, he was the rebellion, and the rebellion was him. He thought of Tyrmiss only in terms of what he needed, and in his mind, she picked up a hint of the way he pictured her: a sad old lady in a dragon suit. He was lucky she didn't eat him on the spot. She'd tasted the flesh of soldiers and found it unappetizing, slightly mustelid like the meat of an otter, but she was willing to eat this rebel leader to make a point. Fortunately for him, the general had left before she'd been ready for dinner.

If anyone but Tessia had asked her to join this crusade, Tyrmiss would never have agreed. *It wasn't just that Tessia was beautiful—although judging by the number of men and women who dreamed about her, she must be extraordinary by human standards. It was that Tessia had a pure heart, and in this way, she reminded Tyrmiss of Rilla. The two were of course quite different. Rilla was not by any means violent. In fact, she'd always felt sorry for the fish they ate, giving heartfelt prayers thanking the Goddess for the gift of the salmon's life; whereas, Tessia was pure warrior through and through. Tyrmiss imagined that Tessia could easily slice off a Drekavac's head and then sit down to a hearty meal of bloody meat. But with Tessia, there was never any malice in her attitude toward the enemy. She didn't hate her opponent, she respected him, especially if he showed courage. Instead, she was practicing her trade as a warrior, the same way that Norbert cast healing spells and his wife Idella baked bread. Idella didn't feel sorry for the grains of barley she crushed because she knew they were giving their lives to nourish those she loved.*

Idella, *the dragon thought,* now there's an interesting human. *Tyrmiss chuckled to herself. Norbert has no idea whom he's married. All he sees is a loving wife and mother. Idella stirs warm feelings inside him because he lost his mother at a young age. Why is it that so many males want to marry their mothers? A desire to return to the womb? A desire to be suckled? A need to be loved unconditionally? Well, the Goddess has made males in this way and who is she, a mere dragon, to question Her wisdom? Tyrmiss suddenly felt a little guilty for denying the existence of the Goddess in order to put Norbert in his place. Of course, there is a Goddess. And who would know better than Idella?*

Part Four: The Campaign

Chapter 14

M istress Dragon," I asked. "Can you carry two of us along with our equipment?"

"Of course, my dear," she answered sweetly. Her attitude toward me had changed, but I didn't have the inclination to worry about her moods right now. It was enough that she'd agreed to help me.

"Zygmunt's warriors will be arriving at the city gates soon," Tessia explained. "His main force will be in front of the East Gate, with smaller forces in front of the North and South Gates. They'll stay far enough away from the city, so the sentries on the walls won't see them in the dark. When a flare goes up, partisans inside the city will attack the guards and open the outer gates. It's our mission to fly over the city shortly before dawn and set the tower on fire as a diversion. This will give Zygmunt's warriors an opportunity to charge through the outer gates, cross the market square and reach the Castle Gate. After setting the tower on fire, we'll fly down to the Castle Gate, kill or disarm the guards and open the Castle Gate for our warriors to charge through. Then we need to locate my father and set him free. It's not part of our mission to free Hamlin, but I plan to do that as well."

She looked off into the darkness of the inner cave and said, in a smaller voice, "If we are still alive."

Tessia handed me a heavy leather doublet like hers and helped me put it on. Standing in front of me, she put both hands on my shoulders, looked in my eyes and said, "I'll do my best to protect you, Norbert, but if the soldiers get past me, you will have to use that short sword of yours. Can you do it?"

When I hesitated, remembering my cowardice on the quest, she said, "For Idella?"

"For Idella," I said firmly and stood a little taller.

"Where do you think Idella is?" Tyrmiss asked me.

"I was hoping you would know," I said to the dragon, feeling a growing sense of hopelessness.

The dragon shook her head. "Who in the city might know?"

"Our son, Alaric, perhaps. Or perhaps Heikum or Femke, the landlords at the Silver Pony."

"Can we drop off Norbert on our way to the castle?" Tessia asked Tyrmiss.

"Of course," the dragon answered. "As long as you can recognize it from the air. But if Norbert's on his own in the city, you can't protect him."

Turning to me, Tyrmiss said, "Let me see you draw that sword, Captain Norbert."

I drew my sword and held it in front of me the way I'd seen Tessia do and scowled, thinking it would make me look fierce. I thought about growling, but I was afraid of looking ridiculous in front of these two man-killers.

"Don't scowl," Tyrmiss said. "It will cause wrinkles on your pretty face. Tessia, show him how to hold a sword. I'm afraid someone will take it away from him and remove his spleen."

Tessia adjusted my hand on the sword-grip and demonstrated how to stand, with the body turned to the side to make a smaller target and the front leg ready to propel the body forward while the back foot remained rooted in place, keeping the body stable during the lunge. I practiced lunging and slashing a few times.

"Very fierce, my dear," Tyrmiss said, obviously unimpressed with my efforts.

"He has a copper sword?" the dragon asked, turning toward

192

Tessia. "Most of the soldiers have Voprian swords. He won't stand a chance against them. Can you give him one of your weapons?"

Tessia shook her head. "The only Voprian weapon I have is my sword, and I need it."

Tessia looked worried. "Norbert," she said. "If the battle becomes too rough, it is perfectly fine for you to run."

Now I was really worried.

After packing our kits, we went to the ridge where we could see down into the valley. A flare arced through the darkness below.

"That's the signal!" Tessia said. "Zygmunt's warriors are close to the city gates!"

She and I climbed onto the dragon's back. I sat behind Tessia, arms around her waist, my leather doublet pressed against the quiver on her back.

"Tessia," the dragon said, turning her great head to look at us. "Be careful with your spear. Keep the tip pointed down so Norbert doesn't get impaled. Also, both of you should keep in mind that you're carrying a lot of equipment, so keep it balanced. Otherwise the weight may throw off my flying. Norbert, my dear, how are you doing?"

"I'm fine, Mistress Dragon. I'm ready for battle."

"Don't worry," she said to me. "Today you are brave and beautiful."

"Why is she being so nice to me?" I whispered to Tessia who shrugged.

"Why are you being so nice to Norbert?" she asked Tyrmiss.

"Because today he's willing to die for love," the dragon answered simply. And we rose through the air.

Flying on a dragon's back is the most exhilarating thing I've ever done in my entire life. A hawk dropping from the sky to strike a sparrow must feel the way I felt dropping into the Dragonja Valley on that moonless night. The stars were spread out like a blanket of light above us, and far away I could see a few lights which must have been bakers and cooks starting the day's work. As we followed the river, I saw below us the dark mass of Zygmunt's army moving toward the gates. There seemed to be far more soldiers than the ones in our camp, and I wondered whether the word had gone out to the partisans in the countryside to join the attack.

We flew quickly over the fields in front of the city gates, and I thought of Idella's lovely little house where we'd been so happy. And suddenly we passed the city's outer walls, and Tyrmiss turned her head to ask, "Which roof is it?"

I looked down and all I saw was a line of identical thatched roofs next to the market square. I'd never counted how many buildings were between The Silver Pony and the city gate, so I made a guess and pointed, "That one!"

A dragon cannot of course, hover in midair, so the best Tyrmiss could do was to slow down and skim the thatches. Suddenly, Tessia shoved me and I fell headfirst onto a roof.

And through the roof.

And landed on a bed where a man and woman were embraced in coitus.

The lovers were even more surprised than I was. "I swear I didn't know she was married!" was the first thing out of the man's mouth.

The woman covered her breasts with the sheet and said, "Where in the heavens did you come from?" All three of us looked up at the hole in the ceiling. A lovely panoply of stars shone down.

The man looked at her. "You think he came from heaven?" And cast his eyes to the stars again.

"No, you donkey." The woman replied looking at him as if he was the stupidest person she had ever heard of. "And how did you know I was married?"

"I... I didn't know you were married. I just thought... you know..."

"Is this the Silver Pony Inn?" I asked.

"No, the Silver Pony is next door," the man said, seemingly relieved to change the topic.

I left them quarrelling. I was sorry to have interrupted their tryst, but war is hell.

I threw a few pieces of dried meat to the dogs in back of the inn to quiet them and pounded on the kitchen door. Right now, I would give anything to have Tessia's mastiff Bruin beside me.

"Who's there?" shouted a female voice from inside.

"Norbert."

"Who?

"Norbert the Singer."

"Norbert Singer? Go away. We don't know you."

A deep male voice shouted, "Begone with you, or you will know a bat to your head. We open the door to no stranger!"

"Heikum! Open the door or I'll tell your wife about the serving wench!"

The door opened slightly and Femke stuck her head out and said, "What serving wench?"

I laughed and said, "Femke the Serving Wench! Were you not a serving wench when he married you?"

She opened the door and the three of us embraced, Heikum roaring that I was going to get him in trouble with my jokes.

"Where is Idella?" I asked looking from one of their faces to the other. "Where is Alaric?"

"Alaric is fine," Femke answered quickly. "He's asleep upstairs."

"And Idella?" When they looked at their shoes, avoiding my eyes, I asked, "Is she dead?"

"Not as far as we know," Heikum said slowly.

"What happened?" *I was too late. I should never have left her.*

"Just a few hours ago," Femke said. "Soldiers came and took her away."

"Did they say anything?"

"They asked whether she was your wife. She said she was not, but they took her anyway."

"Which direction did they take her?"

"Toward the castle gate," Heikum said.

I unbolted the front door and stepped into the street. Zygmunt's men armed with spears were running across the market square shouting, and I heard the clash of weapons. A woman screamed. I looked around the square, but I didn't see anyone who was wounded and needing my help. The king's soldiers must have retreated as soon as they saw the warriors coming through the city's outer gates. *Or they knew we were coming and barricaded themselves inside the castle before we got here.*

I looked at the black Castle and saw the tower in flames, but the castle gate was still closed.

Idella is behind the gate, I thought.

Where was Tessia? Where was the damned dragon? Why are the gates not open?

I saw Sergeant Zrul on the other side of the square. He and a group of soldiers were pushing a large catapult on wheels toward the castle gate.

Traitor! I thought.

I drew my sword and ran toward Zrul, planning to kill him.

Zrul saw me running toward him. He smiled and waved, but then, old warrior that he was, he realized my intention. He drew his sword and waited. When I swung my copper blade at him, he easily sliced it in two with his Voprian sword. Then he tripped me, knocking me down.

Sitting on my chest, he held the point of his sword at my throat, and asked, "Now, Healer, why would you be trying to remove my head?" His tone was jaunty, but his eyes were cold. It was clear that he'd killed many men, but he'd rather not kill me, at least not without good reason.

"You're a traitor!" I said, angrily. If I was going to die, then at least I would speak the truth.

"A traitor?" He asked, puzzled. "A traitor to the king, that's a fact, but why would that bother you?"

"You're a traitor to Zygmunt! You're a traitor to all the men you trained. You've betrayed Tessia! My wife will die because of you!"

"I'm no traitor, Healer. I am as loyal to Zygmunt as you are."

"Then why are you with them?" I moved my eyes to the Drekavac soldiers standing around the catapult. They'd stopped pushing it toward the castle and were looking curiously at the sergeant.

"Where else would I be but with my old platoon?" The sergeant said getting up from my chest and sheathing his sword. "They opened the city gates for us to come in. Last summer we decided to change sides and join Zygmunt, but he told us that only I should join him in the mountains, and the rest of the platoon should report me as having died gloriously in battle."

"And a regular hero he was!" One of the men shouted and his compatriots laughed.

"The General thought that the rest of the platoon was more valuable inside the walls than out. We could not have taken Dragonja City without them. And fine lads they are! After this battle is finished, the first round is on me! Now come on men." Zrul got behind the catapult and placed his hands firmly against the base. "We need to push this monster a little closer to the castle walls, and then we can test how far it can throw a rock!"

Turning a winch, soldiers wound a heavy rope around a spindle in the bottom of the machine, pulling the great arm back until it was eye-level, and a soldier slid a wooden pin in the frame to hold the arm in place. When the pin was removed, the tension in the rope would release a terrific force.

As the men worked, Zrul turned to me and said in his hoarse voice, "Why are you here, Healer? Why are you not with the auxiliary unit outside the city where you were assigned?"

"I... I deserted," I said, not knowing what else to say to him.

"Well, I've known many deserters, but never one that ran into the front lines of battle." The sergeant said, rubbing his chin. "Why are you here?"

"A few hours ago, my wife was taken by soldiers into the castle."

"Ah," he said, wryly. "And you thought you'd charge into the castle and save her. And you so poorly armed? Healer, you need to go back to your post. There will be injured men needing your care."

"And what will happen to my wife?"

The old soldier looked at the black walls and said quietly, "Better not to think about that, lad." And he turned his attention back to the catapult.

Four men lifted a boulder and placed it in the spoon-like cradle. The aim was adjusted until the sergeant was satisfied. "Pull!" He shouted. The pin was removed, and the arm quickly swung up, letting the boulder crash into the gate. The noise was deafening, but so far, the gate was holding.

"Good work, men!" The sergeant shouted. "Now, load her up again!"

I suddenly had an idea. "Wait! Sergeant, can that machine throw a man over the wall?"

The sergeant laughed and said, "Certainly, it can throw a man, but when he hits the ground on the other side, he will be splattered like a bug under a man's heel."

My mind was racing. "But what if he were well-padded? Could he not survive the fall?"

Zrul looked at me like I'd lost my mind.

"Please, sergeant. I'm willing to risk everything to find my wife."

He shook his head. "Love does make a man crazy." He thought for a moment, then said, "Corporal, gather as much clothing as you can find. Private, find me four shields and some rope."

In a few moments, I was donning layers of dresses the men had found in the home of a wealthy lady who'd fled the city. The soldiers were having fun putting frilly things on me and saying how pretty I looked. Over the clothing, Zrul strapped a shield on my back and one on my chest. He wrapped more clothing on my legs and strapped a second pair of shields over the bottom half of my body, front and back. He covered my head with a lady's undergarment and squeezed a helmet on my head.

"You will be needing this, Lad." He handed me his Voprian sword which, like me, was wrapped in a bundle of clothing. "Go save your lady," he said gently. I hefted the sword in my hand, and for the first time I understood why men would risk death for a sword like this one.

"Men, load him in the cradle. Careful now, we don't want him hurt before he's splattered on the wall."

Laughing, two men lifted me into the cradle. The rope on the spindle was wound tight.

For the second time that day, I was ready to fly into battle.

The last thing I heard before becoming a shooting star was Zrul's voice ordering, "Pull!"

Then I was flying over the wall and then…

…something grabbed me in mid-air and carried me up to a rooftop.

"What in the name of the Goddess are you doing? You could've been killed!" Tessia was shouting at me.

"More importantly," said the dragon. "What are you wearing?"

"I was coming to save Idella," I protested, starting to remove the shields.

"Disguised as a laundry basket?" Tyrmiss asked, wryly.

"How did you catch me in mid-air? I must have been traveling as fast as..." I realized that no one had ever traveled as fast I had, except perhaps a person falling off a cliff. When I realized how foolish and impulsive I'd been, my knees began to shake.

Tessia explained, "We watched you from up here. Everyone was watching you. There was a crowd in the square that gathered around the catapult to see what would happen to you. The soldiers on the wall were probably placing bets on where you would get splattered. Didn't you hear the cheers and applause when Tyrmiss caught you? By the way, Tyrmiss, it was a great catch."

"Yes, thank you for catching me," I said, a little belatedly.

"Thank you, sweetie. And you too, Laundry Basket. It was nothing."

Tessia went on: "After this war is over, Norbert, you two should take a tour of the river valley. People would pay good money to watch you break your neck. So, I ask again, WHAT ARE YOU DOING HERE?"

"I told you. I came to save Idella."

"Idella is not here, Norbert."

"What? Heikum and Femke told me..."

"No, Norbert. We asked a captured soldier about Idella, Hamlin, and my father. He said that the wizard took the captives out of the city yesterday. Ludek must have known we were going to attack the city today, so he took his cowardly leave. He probably is holding our people as hostages."

After I got over the initial shock that I may have lost Idella forever, Tessia explained the unpleasant fact that we had no way off this rooftop. Tyrmiss and Tessia had flown into a trap. Somehow the king's soldiers had known they were coming, and they had lined up archers on the castle wall. Even though a dragon is difficult to see on a moonless night, she'd not been invisible, and hundreds of arrows had been shot at them. My wits returning, I noticed that Tyrmiss had arrows sticking out of her hide. One wing was in tatters and she had a gash across her throat. I wished I had my medical bag, but I knew that even if I'd brought it, I wouldn't have been able to hold onto it, shot through the air by the catapult.

I did a quick examination of Tyrmiss' wounds. First, I tried to repair her torn wings. In places they were in tatters, but without needle and thread, I was not able to accomplish much. Perhaps, once this battle was over, I'd be able to get the proper supplies to help her.

"How did you fly in the air to catch me, Tyrmiss?" I asked, looking at her damaged wings.

"I can lift off the air, but can't fly very far, and I can't navigate," she answered between clenched fangs. She was obviously in pain. "I could probably glide to the ground, but I wouldn't be able to fly over the wall."

Another serious problem was an arrow that had grazed her throat. The wound was not deep, but Tyrmiss told me that the arrowhead must have damaged her fire-breathing gland. I thought the scrape would heal by itself, but whether her fiery breath would ever return had yet to be seen. There were also a dozen arrows sticking out of her tough hide. None of the wounds were life-threatening, but they needed to be treated in order to prevent festering. *Do dragon wounds fester?* I wondered. I thought it best to assume they did.

I had Tessia start a fire and gather tar that was used to patch the roof. I sharpened Tessia's copper dagger and started the slow process of digging out the arrowheads, cleaning the wounds and applying bandages made from pitch and the torn cloth from the dresses I'd worn for my flight. Dressed as a laundry basket, indeed.

Treating the dragon's wounds must have caused her excruciating pain. I saw her wince many times, but Tyrmiss never criticized me for causing the pain. I felt she and I now had a mutual understanding. We both loved Tessia, and that fact made us allies. I realized that the real reason I was here was not to save Idella—that may come later, or perhaps never. I was here to save Tyrmiss.

Meanwhile, Tessa was keeping watch. "Here they come," she finally said, as I was patching the last arrow-wound.

*Z*rul and his men were still using the catapult to toss boulders at the gates. It was making a terrible racket.

Tessia shot an arrow, hitting one of the soldiers below. Her last arrow hit the shield a soldier was holding over his head. Sliding her bow into the empty quiver on her back, she asked Tyrmiss gently, "Can you walk?"

"Yes," the dragon replied. "But not very well."

"We need to move to the other side of the tower. I've blocked the door, so the soldiers will have to come up the outside stairs if they want to attack us."

Tyrmiss and I followed Tessia to the top of the outside stairs. I drew my sword, and Tyrmiss bared her fangs. I thought *We may not be effective as fighters, but at least we look frightening.*

The stairs were narrow, so only one soldier at a time could face us. As each one made the last blind turn of the stairs, he was suddenly faced with a dragon and two armed soldiers. Distracted by the terrible visage of the dragon, he usually hesitated which gave Tessia a chance to deliver a mortal blow with her Voprian blade. It looked to me like we could hold this position indefinitely, or at least until Tessia's arm became too tired to swing the blade anymore.

When the castle gate burst open, a cloud of dust rose, and all we could see from below was a melee. We could hear the clash of swords and a deep humming as if an army of bees had descended on the castle.

"What is that noise?" I asked Tessia.

"Voprian swords clashing with each other," she answered.

The soldiers had retreated from the stairway, and we were safe on the rooftop for now.

As the dust began to settle, I could see that the rebel warriors had come through the gate and fighting beside them were a dozen ghost wolves.

"Bruin!" Tessia shouted, pointing at her mastiff fighting beside the wolves. "Where did he come from?"

Tyrmiss smiled, showing her large sharp fangs—a scary sight. "Yes, my dear, I introduced Bruin to my wolf friends a few weeks ago. He joined their pack, and I invited them to join us in this little picnic. Bruin led the wolves into the city to fight for the rebels."

Zrul and his Drekavac partisans were making effective use of the wolves. While the wolves were distracting the soldiers, the rebels were able to use their Voprian blades to kill them. It must have been confusing for the soldiers to be attacked by Drekavacs carrying the king's red dragon shields while being accompanied by white wolves. It didn't take long before it was a rout, the king's soldiers running away, chased by the white wolves.

And there was Bruin, fighting as fiercely as any wolf. I was so proud of him.

Chapter 15

"Norbert, come with me. We need to see whether there are any survivors among the captives," Tessia said, moving down the stairs toward the courtyard where I saw my donkey. He was being used to pull a cart full of dead Drekavac soldiers. I went over to Ottolo and stroked his muzzle. Despite the gruesomeness of his assigned task, he seemed in good spirits, and I looked forward to taking him back to the pasture beside our little house.

In the dungeon beneath the tower, we checked each cell. Most were empty, but in the far corner, we came to one where the door was open. Inside was Anja sitting on the floor. A tall extremely thin man rested his dark head on Anja's lap. Tears were running down Anja's drooping ears and falling on the man's face which she was gently stroking.

"Anja," Tessia said.

When Anja didn't respond, I walked over to her and looked down at the man whose head she was cradling. *Oh no*, I thought, *it's Hamlin*. He'd lost so much weight and his hair and skin had become so filthy, I hadn't recognized him. His face and arms were covered in cuts and bruises. Four weeks in this place had brought him close to death.

We searched the keep and the towers. Idella and Kerttu were nowhere to be found, but we did find King Ottolo.

When the fighting was over, General Zygmunt assigned mopping-up duties to his commanding officers. He gave field promotions to some of the warriors who'd distinguished themselves, including Zrul and Tessia. Privately, he reprimand-ed me for deserting my post, and privately I apologized to him, but publicly, he commended me for my bravery, and publicly I thanked him. I understood that he'd be glad to get me out of his command, and he understood I'd be glad to give up soldiering, a profession I'd shown no talent for whatsoever.

The General performed these leadership tasks quickly and perfunctorily, and then he ordered Tessia and me to accompany him to the King's chambers.

"There may be guards in the tower protecting the king, so be on your guard," he instructed Tessia. And to me he said, "If there are injured in the fighting, then we may need your skills as well, Healer."

We climbed a long stone stairway to the top of the highest tower in the castle, only to discover that the King's chamber was nothing more than an attic room. There were no guards at the door, only an old woman dressed as a chambermaid who let us in. By the rags she wore and her subservient manner, I guessed she was a slave. We entered the room and saw an old man with matted hair and beard sitting in a chair covered in frayed fabric. He was holding a black stone in his hand which he stroked fondly, murmuring to it as if it were a pet.

"Is this the king?" Zygmunt asked the old woman.

She nodded.

"And you are the chambermaid?" He asked.

She shook her head, and said softly, looking at the floor, "No, my lord, I am the queen. My name is Varvara."

The General looked at Tessia and me, as if he needed to reorient his sense of reality. Tessia's jaw dropped in shock. I imagine that mine did as well. This was the royal couple? They were filthy and dressed in rags. If I'd seen them on the streets of Dragonja City I would have assumed they were beggars. Where were the royal retainers serving them? Where were the guards protecting them?

Coming to his senses, the general addressed the Queen again, "Your Majesty," he said with a slight bow, giving her the dignity of her title. "My name is Zygmunt, and I'm the general of the rebel army that's taken over the city of Dragonja, including this castle. Do you understand what has happened?"

She nodded her head, so he asked, "Does the king understand what has happened?"

Still looking at the floor, she shook her head, "My husband the king lost his wits a number of years ago. I have taken care of him ever since."

"Then who is ruling the kingdom?" I asked.

"The wizard known as Ludek has allowed us to live in this tower as long as we did not interfere with his rule."

"What is the black stone your husband holds?" Tessia asked. "Does it have magical powers?"

"It is simply a stone, my lady. Nothing more. He thinks it is a cat that he was once fond of."

"Do you require anything, your Majesty?" I asked.

"If you could send someone to help us each day, I would greatly appreciate it, kind sir. I walk down the stairs to the kitchen and then back here each day to bring water and food. My legs are not what they used to be."

"I'm a healer, your Majesty. May I examine your husband?"

She nodded and assisted me in taking off the king's clothes. Thin as a twig, he sat in front of me, still holding the black stone, stroking it and muttering to it. I placed my palm close to the stone and felt a strange vibration. I put my ear close to it and heard a voice that sounded much like the king's. *Oh, my Goddess*, I thought, *it's a black sapphire the size of my fist*. I hadn't recognized it before because it was greasy and covered in dirt from the king constantly rubbing it over a number of years.

"Your Majesty," I asked the Queen. "Where did your husband obtain this stone?"

"The Wizard Ludek gave it to him."

"I believe that the black stone holds the king's soul," I said. Zygmunt and Tessia gasped.

"What exactly do you mean, Healer?" Zygmunt asked.

"The Wizard has used a black sapphire, the most powerful of magic stones, to absorb the soul of the King. No doubt the intention was to make the King easier to control."

"Your Majesty," I said, turning to the Queen. "You said your husband believes the stone is a pet cat?"

"Oh, yes," she answered. "He was very fond of the animal, always carrying and stroking it. Then one day the animal died, and the King started carrying this stone with him all the time, stroking and talking to it the way he used to talk to the cat. Do you think the wizard put the soul of the cat in the stone?"

"The soul of the cat and the soul of the King had a close bond, so the wizard may have used the cat to lure the king into the trance of the stone. In any case," I said, lifting my face away from the stone for fear of being pulled into its spell, "The stone has completely taken the King."

The Queen reached for the stone, but I grabbed her hand to stop her. "I thought I should take the stone from him since it has possessed him," she said.

"No, no," I replied urgently. "Let the King keep the stone in his hand for now. Removing the stone would probably kill him at this point. We'll try to find the wizard and make him release the King from this bondage."

"I've never heard of a black sapphire," Zygmunt said. "How does it capture a soul?"

"It is old magic, dark, powerful, extremely rare," I replied, looking at the stone but keeping my distance. "I've seen only one other in my life. It was fixed to the staff held by the wizard who killed my mother and kidnapped my brother."

"And Ludek inherited the wizard's powers?" Zygmunt asked.

"Yes, Ludek was trained by the wizard in the blackest of Black Magic."

I looked around the room but didn't see any other objects that could carry a magic spell. Soon after Zygmunt and Tessia left, one of the servants of the castle showed up at the door with bread, cheese, apples, a knife and a pitcher of water. She said her name was Herta and the general had instructed her to stay in the room and take care of the King and Queen from now on. After further examining the king, I told his wife that he seemed in good health and would probably live for a number of years. Since the Queen declined to be examined by me, I promised to send Mina to examine her. I left the tower, and later Mina and I discussed the situation of the royal couple in the tower and developed a plan for diet, exercise and herbal teas that would keep them healthy, but I was afraid we'd never find a way to make the wizard release the king from his bondage to the stone.

The politics of the situation were complicated, of course, but this was the general's problem, not mine. I was a healer, not a politician.

Of much greater concern to me than the health of the royal couple was the whereabouts of Idella. Tessia said she'd sent men to search the countryside to no avail, but they would continue searching. Meanwhile, I'd convinced myself that the most logical place for Ludek and his Drekavacs to have taken her and Kerttu was into the wilds of the mountains. The population was sparse there, and Ludek was no doubt planning to return to try to recapture the city.

I was packing my travel kit, preparing to go into the mountains to find Idella when Tessia showed up in my room.

"What's happening, Norbert?" she asked casually.

"I cannot stay here and do nothing while my wife is in the hands of that monster." I could barely talk, I was so out of my mind with worry.

Tessia sat on the bed and watched me. My hands were

shaking as I picked up my healing tools and herbs and put them in my bag.

"Norbert," she said. "You do know that Idella is my friend, don't you?"

I nodded.

"And there's one huge lesson I learned from the scrape that Anja, Hamlin and I had in the mountains when Hamlin was captured. The lesson was..." She paused, so I could finish the thought.

"Never abandon your friends?" I said.

"So, do you think that I would abandon Idella?"

"I suppose not."

Tessia's eyes flashed anger for a moment at my unenthusiastic response, then softened.

Not reassured, I mumbled, "What are you doing to find her?"

"I can't tell you right now, Norbert. But you need to have faith. We should each do what we do best. And what you do best is to heal people. Stay at your post, my friend, and I will let you know when we find her."

She stood up and walked out. Gradually, I began to feel a great weight lifting off my shoulders, and by the time I'd unpacked my travel kit, I felt a glimmer of hope. If anyone could find Idella, it would be Tessia.

The next week was extremely busy for Mina and me. In the month since we'd started working together, she'd shown a remarkable talent for surgery, and now was the time to put those skills to use. Many of the soldiers had been wounded, and she drew no distinction between rebels and loyalists or between men and Drekavacs. There were also civilians who were in need. Pregnancies, illnesses and accidents continued at their usual pace, so in addition to setting up a field hospital for the wounded soldiers, we also set up a separate clinic for the needs of the townspeople. The two tents stood side by side in the town square, so Mina and I crossed paths often during the day, depending on which patients we were seeing.

The only patient Mina refused to see was Tyrmiss. It was clear that Mina was terrified of the dragon, and Tyrmiss in turn disliked Mina, perhaps because the dragon had overheard Mina calling her "that beast." So, I took care of Tyrmiss without Mina's help. With her damaged wing, the poor dragon was in no shape to fly, and she was far too large and heavy to be carried down the stairway, so I ordered her to stay on the rooftop and had a tent constructed to protect her from the cold weather. I checked her recovery every day. The stitches in her wing were holding up well, and I was confident she would be flying again soon. The arrow wounds were also healing; her hide was thick, so none of the arrows had penetrated deeply. She did have a tendency to scratch her wounds with her talons because they itched. Once when I came up the stairs, I caught her rubbing her rear-end against the stone corner of the battlement. After I gave her a stern lecture, she promised to stop doing it, but I think she had her talons crossed.

Oh, well, I thought, *her hide is so tough, it probably doesn't matter.*

The biggest challenge to Tyrmiss' recovery was the slash on her throat. The exterior wound quickly healed, leaving a barely noticeable scar, but she still couldn't ignite her breath. One part of me was relieved that the last dragon in the world could no longer breathe fire; I'd seen what dragon-fire could do to a Drekavac. But as a healer, I wanted to help restore her to full health which, for a dragon, meant being able to decimate a platoon of soldiers simply by breathing on them. Her handicap left her depressed and listless. I told her that full recovery would take time, and we had to be patient.

Ever since the battle ended, I'd thought not only about Idella, but also about Alaric. I hadn't seen or talked to him since I'd joined the rebels although he was still living at the Silver Pony, or so I assumed. My neglect of this boy I called my son was as painful as a stone in my shoe. I knew the discomfort was caused by my having two fears pulling me in opposite directions. On the one hand, I feared he hated me for abandoning him, and on the other hand I feared he'd been injured in the fighting during the invasion of the city. Was he safe? Could he forgive me?

About ten days after the battle, Mina, whose wisdom I'd come to admire, taught me courage. One evening when we were walking back to the hospital tents after buying herbs in the market, I shared with her my fears about Alaric. The Silver Pony was in plain sight on the other side of the square.

"I hope he's safe," I said.

"Why aren't you going there now?" She asked, baffled by my waffling.

"Because I'm a coward," I felt such a deep self-loathing that I couldn't even look at her.

"Why do you call yourself such a thing, Norbert?"

"Because every time that Tessia and I faced danger, she did the fighting, and I stood by watching as if I were a helpless child." I told her about the time we faced robbers on the Bekla River Road. "I wet myself when a villain tried to slice open my head. I was so frightened that I couldn't move. If Hamlin hadn't saved me, I would have died on that road."

"You actually wet yourself?" Mina's heavy breasts shook with laughter. "Well, that was embarrassing I'm sure, but not cowardly. I think anyone would have been frightened."

She thought for a moment, then asked, "When your friends were in danger, did you ever abandon them?"

I shook my head.

"And you always volunteered when people needed your skills as a healer?"

I nodded.

"And did you not, as I've heard, allow yourself to be catapulted over the castle walls attempting to save your wife and friends?"

I nodded, slowly seeing her point.

"It seems to me that there are different kinds of courage," she mused. "Your courage is not Tessia's, which is like a lightning bolt. Your courage is more like the gentle rain that encourages life to flourish. Who else would have taken the time to teach me, an escaped slave, a penniless ruined woman, how to be a healer? Your courage lies in your faith in people. You think your fear of battle is a sign of cowardice, but it seems to me that wanting to avoid violence shows good sense, not lack of bravery. Your skills don't lie in causing bloodshed, but in preventing it, and your courage is a gift to people who've been hurt and need help."

I thought about what she'd said, and then asked, "If what you say is true, then why am I afraid to walk across the square to look for Alaric?"

"Ah, there, my friend," she nodded ruefully. "There you are being cowardly."

I hung my head in shame.

"Now, I want you to imagine you are sitting in the spoon of a catapult right now," she said, barely hiding her mocking tone. "And I want you to think of the castle wall you flew over. Except, this time it is not a wall you must fly over but merely two hundred paces. And it's not a catapult forcing you to fly, but the tip of my boot." She laughed heartily, turned me around and shoved me in the direction of the Silver Pony while giving me a light kick on my behind.

"Begone, then. Healer, heal thyself."

"But," I said over my shoulder, "I've things to do back at the hospital tent. My patients…"

"I'll take care of the patients, Norbert. They'll be fine. Take as long as you need."

I walked into the back door of the Silver Pony where Femke was stirring a pot on the stove. The familiar aroma of her soup filled me with soothing memories of my time here. The smell also brought back my grief at the disappearance of my beautiful wife.

"Norbert!" Femke shouted and embraced me. "We saw you fly over the wall during the battle. Heikum has been entertaining the guests with the story of the Flying Bard! You must come this evening and tell our guests the whole story!"

She hugged me so hard, I could barely breathe.

"Yes, I've heard a couple of those stories as well. The distance of my flight increases with each telling."

Turning serious, she asked, "What news of Idella? The last time we saw you was the early morning of the battle, when you came here looking for her."

Femke's deep concern for her friend moved me tremendously. I felt grief swelling inside me. I sat at the table, put my head in my hands, and wept.

She patted me on the shoulder. "There, there, my poor darling. There, there."

After a time, I composed myself, and wiped the tears from my face with the back of my hand. "All we know is that the wizard took her and Tessia's father Kerttu from the castle a few hours before the battle started. Somehow, he knew the rebel force was about to attack, and somehow, he knew we'd overwhelm the castle's defenses. He left only a token force to defend the walls."

"So, there must've been a spy in General Zygmunt's army?"

"Yes, the traitor had to have been someone high up in the command to know when we were going to strike."

Not for the first time, I wondered who the traitor had been. It was clearly not Sergeant Zrul, as I'd thought. He actually had been working with the partisans. The Drekavac-soldiers of his former platoon had been the ones who opened the city gates to the rebel army. We couldn't have been victorious without them.

So, who was the traitor?

Shrugging off these concerns of intrigue in the General's command, I brought up the reason for my visit. "What of Alaric? How is he? I've not seen him since I left."

Femke sadly shook her head and looked down at the table. "Ah, Alaric is not the boy you remember, Norbert."

"What do you mean, Femke? What's happened to my son?" This, I thought, would be more than I could bear. To lose both Idella and Alaric.

"Alaric has always been such a good lad. He helped Idella and me in the kitchen. He helped Heikum in the tavern. He fed and took care of the animals in the stable. He ran errands. He was truly a godsend. But the last week and a half, ever since his mother was taken by the soldiers the night before the battle, Alaric has not been himself. For a few days, he went out into the city looking for her. Then, he gave up and went to his bed and just lay there for days, refusing to eat, not talking to anyone. I was so worried about him. Then, a few days ago he just walked out the door and hasn't returned."

"Has anyone seen him? Or has he left the city?"

"We hear of him every day. A woman came to my door, complaining that Alaric had stolen a basket of apples from her table at the market. She wanted us to pay for them. Heikum refused, saying the boy was an orphan and no kin of ours. Later, I found her in the market and gave her a copper for the apples. The old bat said the price was two coppers." Femke rolled her eyes. "Imagine charging two coppers for a basket of apples this time of year when everyone has apples! I told her to be happy with the copper I'd paid her, and from now on, she should keep a better eye on her trade-goods."

Femke and I laughed at the gall of some people. Her face grew grim. "Norbert, the truth is that there are a number of orphaned children—both boys and girls—in the city now. They hide in the alleys and sleep in ruined buildings, living off what they can steal in the market. The General's rebels now control the city, but they don't protect the common people, and lawlessness is growing. Sometimes vigilantes from the marketplace go into the alleys looking for the orphans, but they easily disappear into the twisting mazes between the buildings. I fear that Alaric has joined the gangs of orphans."

"By the gods," I muttered half to myself. "We believed our troubles would be over once the king was overthrown, but now we see that our troubles are just beginning."

"Truly," Femke said, her shoulders sagging sadly.

Chapter 16

The next morning, I buried myself in work. Mina asked what had happened at the Silver Pony, but I pretended not to hear her, even when she asked a second time, so she dropped the subject. Unreasonably, I felt angry at her for insisting that I go to the inn to find Alaric, but I soon realized that the fault lay not with her, but with my confusion of loyalties which led to my abandoning the boy. Many times, I went over the events of the last few months trying to determine where I'd gone wrong. It became clear to me that the initial mistake happened when I agreed to join the rebel forces. I felt at the time I had to choose between my loyalty to Idella and my loyalty to Tessia, and by choosing Tessia, I'd betrayed both Idella and Alaric. I began to despise myself for trying to prove my courage by abandoning my family. In fact, I now understood that the responsibility of being a husband and father frightened me more than the dangers of battle. By trying to prove myself a hero, I'd actually proved I lacked the courage to face normal life. All of this self-reflection was exhausting, of course, so I was grateful for my work as a healer.

There were surprisingly few injuries among the rebel soldiers and only two deaths. General Zygmunt's brilliant strategy, scrupulous planning, and perfect execution had paid off. Also, Sergeant Zrul's training of the troops and his coordination of the partisan Drekavac-soldiers had made a huge difference in the outcome. I heard a rumor that the General had offered Zrul a promotion to the rank of captain, but the old soldier had refused, saying, present company excluded, he'd always thought officers were no better than donkeys, and he'd prefer, *if ye don't mind*, to remain a sergeant. Tessia was offered a promotion to the rank of captain as well, and, unlike Zrul, she accepted the promotion. Everyone agreed that her recruitment of the dragon, as well as her own valor in battle, had been decisive.

Meanwhile, Tyrmiss had disappeared. One day I visited the rooftop where she'd been recuperating, and she was gone. At first, I was worried, but then I accepted the idea that she'd felt well enough to fly back to her cave in the mountains.

I worried about Hamlin. He was still extremely thin. His skin was sallow and his eyes rheumy. Most worrying of all was that he seemed distant, uninterested in anything. Anja sat beside Hamlin's bed for hours at a time, trying to encourage him to drink water, eat soup, talk about the old days when they hunted deer in the hills near their village, but Hamlin showed no interest in anything. The big hearty man with the blonde hair and florid complexion who loved to joke and to clown was gone, and Anja was left with this gaunt listless man who barely recognized her.

Despite the lack of rebel casualties, our little hospital was very busy. Besides routine care of the elderly, the pregnant, and the accident-prone, we were seeing an increasing number of cuts, bruises, and broken bones coming from streetfights. As Femke had mentioned, vigilantes in the market square were on the lookout for thieves, usually homeless children who were stealing food or things they could trade for food. When the vigilantes caught one, the child was beaten badly to set an example to other thieves. People carried these children into the hospital and left them. We did the best we could, bandaging their cuts and setting their broken bones, but there was little we could do for a cracked skull or a gouged eye. Several times, Mina went into the market square and angrily denounced the leaders of the vigilantes, but people ignored her. They even laughed at her commitment to the orphans—which enraged her. She also went into the alleys and talked to the leaders of the gangs. These were boys and girls barely out of childhood, but they took their responsibilities to their younger compatriots seriously. They explained to Mina that the children needed to eat. There was no way to make money because the merchants hired only their own relatives, and certainly not an orphan dressed in rags. The merchants refused to share the food they had, so what could the children do but steal?

After one of these excursions into the maze of alleys, Mina seemed especially disturbed, so I asked her what was wrong. Reluctantly, she answered, "I talked to your boy Alaric."

One morning, several of General Zygmunt's officers, including Wessel, came to the hospital to arrest Anja. I tried to intervene, thinking they'd made a mistake, but the officers ignored me. Anja was sitting beside Hamlin's bed as she had every day since the rebels had taken the city. She'd taken excellent care of her lover, bringing him water, spooning him soup, sponge bathing him and turning him so he wouldn't develop bedsores. Largely because of Anja's care of him, Hamlin's health had improved dramatically in the weeks following his release from the dungeon, but his eyes were still vacant, his speech slurred, and his spirit dissolute. I thought it would likely take years for Hamlin to recover from his ordeal at the hands of the wizard's torturers. Anja did not resist arrest, nor did she seem surprised. As she left, she looked at me with imploring eyes which I interpreted to be a silent request to take care of Hamlin. I met her dark sunken eyes and nodded, and she seemed to understand and to accept my reassurance.

A few hours later, the general sent for me. He was sitting in his tent. His posture, usually straight and powerful, was slumped over, and his chest seemed shrunken. Despite his recent victory in taking the city, he seemed strangely defeated. He gestured for me to sit down.

"General, were you wounded in the battle?" I asked, realizing that something was not right about him. Normally, he was vibrant and vital, giving off an energy that inspired the people around him. He seemed to have become an old man in just a week.

I waited in silence, and when he finally spoke, it was with a much weaker and less confident voice than the one I was used to hearing from him. "Only a small wound, Norbert."

"General, as your Healer, I need you to take off your shirt, so I can examine you." As he opened his shirt, he winced. There was a gash across his chest. Several ribs seemed to be broken as well.

I looked closely at the laceration and gently touched the broken ribs. He involuntarily gasped. "Is this a sword wound, General?"

He nodded.

"You should have come to the hospital immediately after it happened, General. The wound is festering, and you're running a fever."

"There were others who needed attention more than I," the General said.

I applied yarrow ointment on the gash, then wrapped his chest with clean linen, sealing the edges with candle wax to hold it in place. Then I brewed willow tea to help him with the pain.

As he drank the tea, Zygmunt asked, "You know that Anja was arrested?"

I nodded, "What's she been charged with?"

Again, a long silence before Zygmunt answered, "Anja is a traitor. She revealed to the king's soldiers some of our strategies. Fortunately, Wessel figured it out and told me." Not for the first time, I wondered how he and Wessel talked to each other. Then, suddenly, a number of things that had puzzled me made sense. I remembered that Anja had been a day late in meeting me on the trail when I first arrived, and later she'd disappeared from camp a few times on flimsy excuses, such as "taking a walk."

"When did you discover her betrayal?" I asked, recalling that Zygmunt had sent Anja on an errand when Tessia and I were in the general's tent discussing the dragon's role in the strategy to take the city. At the time, I thought that Zygmunt was relegating her to lesser chores because she was a girl, but now I realized that Zygmunt must have suspected that Anja was a spy.

"Wessel came to me a few days before the invasion and told me of his suspicion. At first, I didn't want to believe that Anja would betray me. I thought that perhaps Wessel was jealous because he and I were once lovers. I immediately dismissed his accusation, but the more I thought about it the more it made sense. There were times when Ludek's soldiers seemed to know our plans and were waiting in ambush for our warriors. It's my fault for trusting her… There were times when I told her things, trying to work out problems, asking her advice."

I remembered the rumors that Zygmunt had taken Anja into his bed.

Zygmunt continued speaking in an uncharacteristically small voice. "Thank the gods I never told her about Sergeant Zrul's platoon having gone over to our side. They would've been slaughtered by the wizard's soldiers, and we would have had no way to open the gates of the city."

"Has Anja confessed?"

"Yes, once she was arrested, she told us everything. How the Wizard Ludek reached out to her in a dream soon after Hamlin was captured, and how Ludek told her Hamlin would die unless she revealed our plans. She told him about our defenses, that we watch the trail up the mountain and they would stand little chance with a direct assault. The wizard knew we were coming, and he'd heard from Anja about Tessia's friendship with the dragon, so the wizard fled the city and left some of his men to die defending the castle."

Zygmunt hit his fist on his forehead, "How could I have been such a fool? I fell in love with a girl who was using me! She cared only about protecting Hamlin and cared nothing for me..."

"May I speak to Anja?" I asked.

Zygmunt looked up, startled. He seemed to have forgotten that I was in the tent with him.

"Yes, of course. You're her friend. Perhaps the last friend she has besides Hamlin."

I got up to go.

"By the way," the general said, mustering the dignity to straighten his shoulders and stand a little taller. "The trial and execution will happen tomorrow. Nothing is served by prolonging this embarrassing ordeal."

Anja was being held in the dungeon below the castle tower, a few cell-doors down from where she'd found Hamlin the week before. At first, she avoided looking me in the eye. Perhaps she feared I'd come to her cell to accuse her. But I saw no point in further humiliating an ill-fated young woman facing execution the next day.

"Is there anything you need, Anja? I have some influence in the castle, and I can have food or ale sent to you."

She shook her head. "I think I owe you and Tessia an explanation. Could you tell her that I never meant to hurt her? I was just trying to help Hamlin, and I got caught in a web of deceit."

"I'll tell Tessia, but I'm sure she already knows," I lied. Actually, I was certain that when Tessia learned of Anja's betrayal she'd be enraged that her friend had allowed the Wizard to escape with Kerttu and Idella.

"It was strange how it started," Anja said quietly. "When the three of us were ambushed on patrol near the copper mine, the fight happened so quickly, I hadn't realized that Hamlin was captured until Tessia and I were a good distance away. I wanted to go after the Drekavacs to save Hamlin, but Tessia ordered me to stay with her. We were badly outnumbered, and she thought it was poor tactics to go after them. That is the only time I ever saw Tessia make a mistake in battle."

"She knows now," I said. "She wishes she'd tried to save Hamlin."

"I know. She's apologized to me for letting Hamlin be captured." Anja and I sat for a while in silence, then she said wistfully, "The night after the skirmish, I had a strange dream. The Wizard spoke to me. He said that Hamlin had told him all about me and how our love was the most important thing in the world to him. He showed me Hamlin sitting in his cell, and the big guy looked so sad it broke my heart."

Anja was sobbing, "You have to understand that I felt torn. I had to choose between Hamlin and Tessia. I love them both, but the Wizard made me choose between them."

I thought of my own divided loyalties, how I'd abandoned my wife and son in order to join Tessia in the mountains. Is love ever simple? In order to love someone, do we always have to betray someone else? I felt sympathy for this young woman whose love was used against her. I suddenly felt a surge of hatred against the Wizard Ludek who forced this innocent young woman to betray her friends.

"Tell me what you know about the Wizard," I said, thinking of Idella, my beautiful wife, being held in his grasping hands.

Anja paused, and I could see her gathering her wits. I was pleased to see a glimpse of the old Anja, the woman-warrior who'd fought beside Tessia and Hamlin, her quick blade slashing and stabbing in defense of her friends.

"He's the evilest being I've ever known," she said with a cold rage.

"What does he look like?"

"He looks like a Drekavac, but he's actually something else."

"Anja, tell me all you know."

"The day Hamlin was captured was when things started to turn bad," Anja began. "Hamlin was the great love of my life. He was like my other half. When Tessia and I got away and we realized that Hamlin wasn't behind us, I wanted to go back, but Tessia stopped me. She said it was too dangerous. She said we would go back to camp, tell her uncle what happened, and he would send a rescue party. But when we got back, the general was busy making plans for the raid on the copper mine, and he said we couldn't spare the warriors for a rescue mission."

"So, what did you do?"

"I didn't know what to do, but that night, I had a powerful dream. The Wizard showed me Hamlin. He was hurt, bleeding from his head and lying on the floor of a cell. Ludek said that if Hamlin was going to get help, I would need to find out what the General was planning. So, that same night I went to the General's tent. Wessel stopped me from entering, but Zygmunt said to let me enter. He and I sat for a long time, talking, and we kissed a few times. It was gentle and sweet, but I had to go slow in finding out his plans, so he wouldn't suspect I was spying."

"When you were late in meeting me on the trail when I first came up the mountain, where did you go?"

"There's a place off the trail where I'd meet one of Ludek's lieutenants and give him whatever information I'd gathered. Ludek could place ideas in my mind during dreams, but it wasn't a way to convey accurate information."

"Why didn't you warn Ludek about the raid on the copper mine?"

"I did, but the plan changed when you visited the camp. We

were planning to hold the raid in a few weeks, but when you told Zygmunt that the camp was an easy target, he jumped at the chance."

"And those times you said you were going out for a walk, you were actually meeting with Ludek's lieutenant?"

"Yes, I met with him several times, but Wessel, I think, was onto me and told the General I was a spy. I see now that Zygmunt was feeding me wrong information to pass on to the Wizard. I told him about you and about Tessia's dragon, and that we were going to attack the city, but I thought it would be later. And I didn't know about Sergeant Zrul's platoon in the city."

"Tell me about the dreams the Wizard gave you."

"The dreams seemed so real I would wake in the morning remembering them as clearly as if they'd actually occurred a few minutes before. And Ludek seemed to know everything about me, even things I've never told anyone.

"And Norbert," Anja said. "The Wizard asked me a lot of questions about you. I'm sorry, but I told him everything I know. How we traveled together on a quest, fighting bandits and soldiers and white wolves. How you hate to fight, and you freeze up in battle. I even told him about Idella and how much you love her. I'm so sorry. But he seemed to already know a lot about us. In one dream, I was standing in a large hall that looked like a royal chamber with a stone floor and timbered ceiling. The Wizard was sitting on a throne. He gestured for me to approach and as I walked toward him, he spoke, telling me things about my past, how my father used to touch me and if I resisted, he beat me, how I ran away to live in the woods, how my best friend Hamlin came to visit me, bringing me food, and how through the years, Hamlin and I became lovers and exchanged vows."

Anja looked at me with confusion. "How could he have known about our vows? No one, not even Tessia, knew what

224

Hamlin and I had promised each other. I don't think that Hamlin would have told Ludek willingly, so Ludek must have read our dreams. Perhaps those vows were so important to us that they were in our dreams even years later?"

Her voice changed from confusion to fear. "Norbert, I'm worried about Hamlin. Will he recover? Does he even know who I am anymore?"

The truth was that I had no idea whether Hamlin would recover, but I didn't have the heart to tell Anja, so I lied. "Oh yes, Hamlin will be fine, but it's going to take a while."

"I'm so glad," Anja said, relieved. "I love him so much." At that moment, she seemed like any young girl in love, and certainly not one facing execution.

The next morning, a huge crowd gathered outside the walls of the city in front of the East Gate. It seemed that everyone who lived in the city and the nearby countryside had shown up to see Anja's beheading.

General Zygmunt emerged from the gate and stood in front of the crowd. I wondered how many people noticed how much he'd aged in the last couple of weeks. Wessel, his bodyguard and devoted friend, was behind him watching the crowd closely. Tessia standing at attention, her eyes focused on the distant horizon, stood beside Wessel. Both were armed with their Voprian blades. In front of them was a wooden block with a basket beside it. And then Anja, wearing chains on her wrists and ankles, was brought out of the gate by two warriors. The crowd became raucous, booing and jeering the traitor, a few people threw rotten apples and cabbages at her. The general stood in front of the prisoner and moved his hands in front of him in a dignified horizontal gesture, signaling the crowd to be silent—which they did. This crowd clearly recognized him as a great man and as their leader.

Then Zygmunt stepped aside and nodded to Anja.

Anja, seeming much taller than she actually was, her chin held high, her ears erect, announced loudly and without hesitation, "I betrayed my friends, my general, and the cause of freedom. I apologize to my fellow citizens, and I accept my punishment." She laid her head on the block.

Wessel stepped forward. As he lifted his Voprian sword, it caught the morning light. He brought the blade down quickly, and Anja's head rolled off the block and fell in the basket. The crowd was silent, and those of us close to the front could hear the sword still singing from the blow.

*W*hen Tyrmiss flew down from her cave, she found Tessia waiting for her at the bottom of the trail next to the river, her silhouette barely visible in the dark.

"Tell me again why we're doing this?" Tyrmiss asked.

"Well, first because there's a family that's starving and we need to help them. The husband was killed in the revolution, and the wife has been ill and wasn't able to plant their field, and now the children are hungry." Tessia explained, "But we're also doing this because the Queen, advised by Norbert, told me that I should make a show of doing charitable things. The husband was a soldier in the king's guard. He died defending the kingdom against rebels like us. In fact, you and I may have killed him."

Tessia paused for a moment, thinking of the enormity of what they'd done, killing so many people.

"This is an opportunity to show generosity to our conquered enemies and their families," Tessia added, shaking off the larger issues of the morality of war.

"So, this is public relations for the queen?"

"No, Tyrmiss. These people really need our help, and the Queen wants to unite the kingdom. And also..." Tessia looked sheepish as she admitted, "Also, the Queen wants me to look like I will take care of the people when I take on more responsibility in the kingdom."

"So, the Queen has plans for you?"

"I guess.... Let's just go, alright?"

Tessia got on Tyrmiss's back and they flew up the mountain. The sun was beginning to rise behind them. When they got to the top of the pass, Tyrmiss banked to the north and landed in a glade that looked out over the Iskar Valley. Tessia looked out at the beautiful view. In the early dawn light, the Iskar River was like a shining green ribbon twisting through the forests of the north. A few farms and villages nestled among the trees, but the region was more sparsely populated than the Dragonja and Bekla valleys. Settlers from the kingdom had started settling in the virgin forests, but the region had not yet been formally claimed by any kingdom. Tessia imagined that the kingdom could someday expand in this direction without violating any boundaries. Something to consider for the future.

"There's a natural saltlick a little ways downslope from here," Tyrmiss said, bringing Tessia's attention back to the business at hand. "Of course, it's not fair to the deer to hunt them at a saltlick, but it saves a lot of time not having to stalk them through the woods. I'll wait here. Give me a whistle when you have a kill."

Tessia set off in the direction of the lick. A breeze was coming from ahead, so her scent wouldn't spook the prey. She moved through the woods in complete silence, not disturbing even the birds that continued singing in the branches above her, one of many skills she'd learned while hunting with Anja and Hamlin in the hills near their village. That life seemed an eternity ago, and the memory of her two friends made her sad, so she put aside those feelings for now. There was a task to do.

She took up a position behind a log and made sure she was covered in dappled shadow where she would be virtually invisible to a deer. She quickly strung her bow and slid an arrow out of her quiver. From long habit, she gingerly flicked her thumb on the point, checking its sharpness, ran her fingers over the straight shaft and smoothed the fletching although she had already inspected all her arrows before she'd left the city.

It didn't take long before a doe showed up at the lick, moving cautiously, sniffing the air. Tessia let loose an arrow which hit the doe exactly in front of her shoulder, piercing her heart and killing her instantly. Tessia walked over to the doe and looked at her eyes, open and staring at the sky, and as always when Tessia killed something, man or beast, she felt a quick but deep grief at having removed a life from the world. As she'd been taught by the elders of her village in what seemed a lifetime ago, she knelt in front of the supine body and silently thanked the deer for giving its life so others could survive. No one, not even Tyrmiss or Norbert, knew how Tessia grieved for those she'd killed. She then tied the back feet together and hung the deer from a branch overhead with the head down and the belly exposed.

Drawing her knife, she slit the throat, let it bleed out, then quickly field-dressed the animal. She wrapped the carcass in an oilcloth, so the remaining blood wouldn't make a mess, and she was ready to go. She put two fingers in her mouth and let out a quick sharp whistle. Within moments, Tyrmiss landed in the clearing, and Tessia tied the carcass on the dragon's back. Tessia gave a last look at the small meadow, realizing that her having bled the animal here would scare other deer away from the salt lick for a while, not a bad thing at all, considering how vulnerable to human predation they were in this clearing.

As Tyrmiss flew over the pass and came face to face with the early morning sun, she realized it had been thousands of years since she'd flown so far in the light of day. It had always been too dangerous until now. After the rebels had successfully taken the city, Zygmunt had made sure that people knew that the dragon was one of the heroes of the revolution, and anyone harming or interfering with her would be considered an enemy of the new regime. Since then, Tyrmiss had been free to fly around the kingdom as she wished, and often she saw people waving at her in a friendly way. It was a strange feeling to be loved by people, and she wasn't positive she liked it, but it was certainly better than soldiers trying to kill her.

She felt sad that Rilla couldn't be here now; the young dragon had always loved the light. In fact, Rilla's love for sleeping in sunlight was what got her killed. But Tyrmiss had to put aside thoughts of Rilla now because the memories brought up feelings that were unbearable. Tyrmiss would have to wait until she was alone to weep for her mate.

Following Tessia's directions, Tyrmiss flew up the Dragonja River and landed in an unplowed field next to a rundown house where three dirty children stopped their play to see an amazing thing: a beautiful young woman, dressed as a warrior, climbing down from a dragon's back and walking toward them carrying over her shoulder a large bundle wrapped in oilcloth. One of the children ran inside and her mother came out of the house, wiping her hands on a rag.

The young woman handed the child's mother the bundle, talked with the farm woman briefly, and walked back to the dragon. She whispered something in the dragon's ear. The dragon's eyes turned red and a puff of smoke spewed from its nose.

The dragon roared, "NO! I AM NOT AN OX! NO! ABSOLUTELY NOT!"

But the young warrior persisted. She spoke quickly, pressing her case to the dragon, urgently pointing at the house, the children and the field. Finally, the dragon nodded, relenting, and the young woman climbed on the dragon's back. The dragon took a few steps, spread its wings and carried the warrior into the air. Then the dragon made a wide turn and came back, flying low in the direction of the field next to the house. Turning her talons so they faced forward and swooping low over the field, the dragon dragged the talons over the earth, turning the soil like a plow. The dragon banked and passed several times over the farm until the whole field had been turned and was ready for planting.

As the dragon and the warrior-woman flew off in the direction of the city, the little girl asked, "Why did they do that, Mommy?"

Tears running down her face, the woman answered, "Thank the Goddess! Tessia and her dragon have plowed our field! Tomorrow we can plant our seed."

Part Five: The Tower

Chapter 17

"With General Zygmunt ill and King Ottolo useless, no one's in charge of keeping order in the city," Heikum complained to Tessia and me. "Farmers and tradespeople have stopped coming to the market square because it's unsafe. Those young ruffians who live in the alleys steal anything they can get their dirty hands on, and if you resist, they hit you on the side of the head with a stick. Just the other night, there was a woman dragged into the alley and assaulted. I tell you, people are afraid to come out of their houses. Drekavac soldiers do as they please and laugh in your face if you complain."

I agreed with Heikum, but as bad as the city was, it was even more dangerous outside the city walls, so I was living once again in the Silver Pony, earning my keep by singing in the tavern. It had been only a couple of weeks since the end of the war, but it seemed like years. Alaric showed up at the inn sporadically but avoided me. I heard from Heikum, master of town gossip, that Alaric spent most of his time with his friends in the alleys. I still hadn't heard anything about the whereabouts of Idella, but Tessia had said that Tyrmiss was searching the countryside and I should trust the dragon, so I was waiting for news, feeling as if I were dangling on a thin thread over a very deep pit.

Tessia was staying at the inn as well, although during the day she was usually at the wool merchant's shop where Taja worked. When Heikum told her gruffly that if Tessia wanted to continue living in the inn and taking her meals there, she'd have to resume her duties as a serving wench, she gave him a long level stare until he lost his nerve.

"Tessia," he said, changing his tone. "Perhaps you could just sit in the tavern in the evenings, and if the men become too rowdy, then you could persuade them to behave better?"

"You mean you want me to be your bouncer?" She considered the offer carefully. "So, I get room and board, and all I have to do is to sit in the tavern in the evenings and throw out anyone who misbehaves?" She looked around the inn and saw the serving girl, a niece of Femke's, wiping a table. "You know I'm not going to allow the serving girls to be mistreated, right?"

The girl looked at Tessia with a smile of gratitude.

Heikum nodded. "And perhaps you could protect the inn? Once it's known that you're living here, then no thieves or ruffians would dare to rob us."

In this way, Tessia became the protector of the Silver Pony. And Heikum, shrewd as always, quickly realized that her reputation for ferocity had a strangely calming effect. It was as if a magic charm had descended on the inn, keeping away those who would damage his property or harm those who lived there. The inn became like an oasis of civilization. Men brought their families to spend an evening in the tavern drinking ale, gobbling down Femke's soups and listening to my songs and stories. I'd never had a more appreciative audience. Outside the inn, the city was chaos, but inside, everyone was calm and happy, and no one more so than Heikum counting his coins every evening.

As word got out that Tessia's presence brought peace, she was invited to visit other shops and households, and the city gradually became a decent place to live again. Of course, it wasn't just Tessia's presence that brought calm, but rather she acted as a catalyst for a population ready for a sense of order.

When Ludek left the city and his spells had been broken, King Ottolo seemed gradually to regain his wits. But then, realizing what had happened to him and his kingdom over the previous few years, he became despondent and stopped eating. Mina was giving him excellent care, but she thought there was little that could be done other than to make him comfortable in his last days. She asked me to check on the king and see whether I agreed with her prognosis. So, the next day, I climbed the long stairway to the top of the high tower where the king and queen had lived for years.

As I examined him, he had, as often happens shortly before death, a few moments of clarity.

"I grew up in this castle," he said suddenly, looking around the room as if he'd just awakened. "In those days, this was Father's study. From here, he could look out over the river valley and up into the blue hills. He allowed me to play quietly with my toy soldiers and building blocks on the floor there."

He took a deep breath, letting it out slowly in a painful sigh. "I was a lonely boy with no playmates. Afterall, what children would want to play with the king's son? My father was busy governing the kingdom, my mother preoccupied with managing the castle, so I was basically raised by servants. They were kind to me but had no interest in my childish pursuits. The only person who took a real interest in me was an old stableman named Imre who allowed me to help him feed and groom the horses. I never had much interest in riding, but I loved caring for them, their huge faces close to mine, our breaths mingling on a cold day. Being with the horses always gave me comfort."

The King patiently answered my questions about his diet and his daily habits. I used a wooden tube to listen to his chest. His heartbeat was weak and irregular. His breath was shallow and wheezing. His lungs rattled as he breathed. I tested his strength and saw that his arms and legs were weak, and he couldn't stand or walk unassisted.

"Oh, don't bother with all that, Healer," he said, waving me away with his hand. "I know I'm dying."

I backed away from him a few feet and sat in a chair next to the window, facing him. There was little I could do for him but listen.

He peered at me from his bright blue eyes, "This young woman you are often with... Tessia? Is she a kinswoman of yours?"

"Not exactly, your Majesty. She's the daughter of a friend."

"She's very interesting, isn't she? She reminds me of my wife Varvara when she was young. Beautiful, intelligent, athletic, quite a horsewoman. Father wanted me to marry a certain noblewoman, the daughter of a political ally, but I held out for love. It's the only time I ever stood up to Father, and it was the best thing I've ever done in my life."

The King took a long rattling breath and said, a tear rolling down his cheek. "There were only three things I was required to do in my life. Protect the kingdom, serve the Goddess, and love my woman. I failed terribly on the first two, letting Ludek take over everything, but at least I succeeded on the third. I loved Varvara with all my soul..."

He turned to me, grasped my hand with strength I didn't know he had, and said to me with surprising urgency, "Mage, you must swear to me you will serve Varvara with all your ability."

I slid from the chair, knelt before King Ottolo and said, "I swear, your Majesty."

He let go of my hand, closed his eyes and seemed to shrink into himself. I picked him up from the chair easily—he was light as a child—and laid him on the bed. As I passed Queen Varvara who'd been standing outside the doorway, I said, "Let him sleep, your Majesty. When he wakes, give him only water to drink."

She nodded and quietly went to sit beside her husband. I

didn't need to tell her that he was dying. As I left the castle, I remembered all the times I'd mocked King Ottolo for being a fool, naming my donkey after him, never realizing that even a king is powerless to break free of his own fate.

"I hear that the king died," Heikum said late one evening as we were cleaning the tavern after closing.

I nodded, but said nothing, concentrating on mopping the floor. Heikum and Femke had been kind to me and my family, so I tried to help out where I could.

"I also heard that the Queen doesn't want the crown which would by law pass to her," Heikum continued. "Since she and King Ottolo never had children, then there is no heir. I suppose that she could choose an heir to the throne, but who would she choose?

"These are evil times, indeed," Heikum went on, half to himself. "We need a strong leader. Someone who knows how to keep order." He nodded approvingly at Tessia. "If Tessia and her men catch a robber on the highway, they just execute him on the spot. Many a headless robber has been buried in the Dry Hills." Heikum gave a small chuckle, then added, "Tessia and I have talked about reopening the copper mines, but we're not going to use slaves because then you have to hire Drekavacs to whip them. It's a lot cheaper to hire men, pay them good wages, and then set up a village where they pay rent and buy food from you. We're going to have a regular village up there supporting the mine."

Seeing Heikum's eyes starting to blaze with greed, Tessia reminded him, "We agreed that we'll charge the miners reasonable amounts for their food and lodging."

Heikum seemed a little disappointed to have his fantasy of profiteering interrupted. "Yes, yes, of course. We're not bandits, after all."

"Tessia," Femke said, changing the subject. "Are we going into the countryside to buy food tomorrow?" Tessia nodded. "Well then, would you mind if the wool merchant's cook and her helper came along? They have their own mule to carry the goods, so they wouldn't be any trouble."

Tessia shrugged indifferently, indicating it made no difference to her if more people joined them. A few months before, she'd started going regularly with Femke to the farms outside the city to purchase food. I'd loaned them my donkey Ottolo to carry the baskets. Seeing a business opportunity, Heikum had started inviting other householders to come along, charging them a small fee payable in fruits and vegetables. As more women came along, Tessia had recruited former soldiers, mostly Drekavacs, to accompany them as guards. What had started as a foraging party was now a regular caravan with a long line of people leading horses and mules and ten guards who watched over them. With the market closed, Tessia's caravan had become the most reliable source of food for the city.

With General Zygmunt's illness distracting him from the needs of the city, Tessia, under the mentorship of Queen Varvara, had emerged as the *de facto* leader. Men brought issues of justice and security to her, and women asked for her help in bringing food and household supplies to the city. She'd reunited a number of families who'd been separated during Ludek's rule. In order to deal with the gangs who lived in the alleys and preyed on citizens, Tessia and Sergeant Zrul went into the alleys to parley. When they were ambushed, the two veterans easily disarmed the dozen youths who'd attacked them. Tessia and Zrul met with the leaders of the gangs and extracted a promise not to commit any more crimes in exchange for daily shipments of food. No longer starving, the children and their teenage leaders became more cooperative, and the gangs began to break up. Many of the boys and girls, including Alaric, left the alleys and returned to their families. A home was set up to house the orphans.

Alaric bunked with a number of other boys at the Silver Pony who earned their keep by doing odd jobs and apprenticing with tradesmen who frequented the tavern. I was glad to see that Alaric had been traveling in Tessia's caravan. Tessia told me that he'd taken an interest in the buying and selling of goods, and he would make a good shireman. "Just like his stepdad," she said, nonchalantly trying to make me feel better about the fact that Alaric rarely spoke to me except in grunts and eye rolls.

Give him time, I kept telling myself. *He will grow out of it, and someday you can be friends with him.* I thought about how Tessia regretted the way she treated Edelmira, her father's paramour, after her death. *We all have our regrets and resentments,* I thought. *Perhaps someday Alaric will realize that I care for him.*

Tessia told me that the General wanted to see both of us in his private chamber in the castle. As we walked across the square, I noticed that the hospital tent was less busy than it had been in recent weeks, and a few stalls with fruits and vegetables had been set up and customers were crowding around them. People seemed relaxed. I sensed that it was just a matter of time before things returned to normal.

The guards, a mix of Drekavac-soldiers and rebel warriors, were standing around, passing the time. Seeing the two races getting along with each other was a nice change from the days when the rebels first took over the city. I remember seeing a gang of laborers and a group of Drekavac soldiers facing each in the market square, the Drekavacs hissing and spitting as they pointed Voprian swords at the glaring laborers who were armed with heavy work tools, mostly hammers and axes. It looked like the two groups were going to get into a brawl, but Tessia and Zrul stepped between the Drekavacs and the humans and stared them down, Tessia facing the laborers and Zrul facing the Drekavacs. No one dared to take on either of these warriors by themselves, and together, as everyone knew, they could outfight an army. The Drekavac soldiers left for their barracks, and the laborers went back to their work. Bloodshed was avoided on that day, but it was clear to Tessia that she was going to have to do something about racial tensions in the city.

One of the strategies that Tessia employed to bring peace to the city was to partner Drekavac-soldiers with rebel warriors in guard duty. The patrols in the countryside, which kept the roads open and safe, also had mixed personnel. As the former enemies came to depend on each other, tensions were diminished and there were fewer fights. Some of the men and Drekavacs even became friends. Another strategy was to speak with teachers to allow Drekavac children to attend school and later to encourage parents to invite children of the two races to play together.

"It may take a generation or two," Tessia said, confidently looking around the square at people going about their business. "But eventually, Dragonja will have a mixed population that doesn't judge each other on the basis of race."

I admired her idealism, but I wondered whether such a thing could actually happen.

Tessia and I nodded to Wessel and entered the General's private chamber. It was plain and bare, the only furnishings a narrow bed, a few chairs and a table which he used as a desk. The table, which I recognized from his tent in the mountains, was spread with maps. Zygmunt was still the most powerful man in the kingdom, and yet he lived like a Bekla Valley tradesman. I was reminded once again that this was a wise and humble man.

Zygmunt gave a tired smile and embraced both of us affectionately. He seemed to have aged years in the weeks since Anja had been executed. As he moved his arms, I could see that the wound on his chest still caused him pain. He also seemed to be ill, his cheeks flushed with fever. I was sure he hadn't treated his wound with the ointment I'd given him, and it had become infected.

"General, let me treat your wound…" but he interrupted me with a shake of his head. I've always obeyed the Goddess in not treating anyone who refused treatment, so I stayed silent.

The General gestured toward the chairs, a graceful but informal invitation for us to sit with him, and I noticed that, for the first time since I'd met him, he was not wearing the ring with the purple stone which was a sign of devotion to the principle of humility required of leaders.

"What is it, General? Is there news of my wife?"

"Or my father?" Tessia asked.

Her uncle shook his head. "Sadly, no. We've heard nothing of them. I asked you to come today on a different matter. I want the two of you to be the first to know that I'm turning all power over to Queen Varvara. I will be telling my lieutenants this evening and asking them to pledge loyalty to Her Majesty. Tomorrow Wessel and I will be riding across the Dry Hills to the Bekla River and from there to the coast."

Tessia and I were quiet for what seemed a long time. Then she said, "Can Queen Varvara actually rule? I've talked with her a number of times, and I appreciate her taking me under her wing, but she never seemed like someone who's interested in politics or warfare. Most of the time, she just sits in her private chamber and looks out the window at the city below. When she talks, it's almost always about the past when she and her husband were happy in the days before Ludek came."

"Be that as it may," Zygmunt replied. "With the death of her husband, she is the rightful ruler."

"General Zygmunt," I said, speaking carefully. "The city has just begun to recover from years of oppressive rule under the Wizard Ludek. We're finally beginning to feel safe. Today walking across the square, I saw a few farmers who'd set up stalls to sell food. They are able to do so only because Tessia's soldiers have made the river road much more secure for tradespeople and travelers. People are repairing their roofs instead of making plans to flee the city. Farmers are planting seeds, knowing they'll be able to harvest a crop in a few months. Fishermen can throw their nets without looking over their shoulders in fear at every sound behind them. When I walk around the streets of the city, I hear carpenters sawing wood and smiths hammering metal into plows and hand tools. Women are singing as they cook, and the ale houses are full. You, my friend, are responsible for bringing the beginning of peace and prosperity to the land. We all owe you our lives and the lives of our loved ones. Thank you."

Zygmunt smiled gently and tiredly at my words, and Tessia wiped away tears running down her cheeks as she looked at her uncle whom she admired more than any other person in her life.

"But General," I added, after a moment. "This is just the beginning of our recovery. We still need your leadership. I urge you to reconsider your decision. Continue to rule for a year, and then we'll see whether the country is ready to stand on its own without your strength to prop it up."

Tessia nodded and added, "Uncle, the Mage's counsel is wise. The kingdom still needs your strong leadership. A few days ago, I led the caravan into the countryside, and we heard that there are bandits in the dry hills, many of them former soldiers. They know when our patrols come, and they plan their attacks accordingly. Yes, the people in the city feel safe, but the reason is that our soldiers are everywhere protecting them. Without strong leadership, the city will again descend into chaos. The Queen is a kind woman, but she doesn't have the strength to lead the soldiers. I fear that a man with evil designs will again take over the city. We still haven't found the Wizard Ludek. Once he hears that you've left, he will return, take over the city again, and exact his revenge on all of us."

Zygmunt put his head in his hands. His pain and grief

had finally overpowered him, and I saw for the first time how the decades of leading the rebellion had been a terrible burden on him. And I realized he'd given everything—his youth, his health, even his love for Anja—to the cause of freeing his people from evil. All that Zygmunt had left was his bond with Wessel, and he'd come close to destroying even that love.

"I cannot... do this... task... any longer," Zygmunt said quietly.

He regained control of himself, and as he sat up, I saw what he'd kept hidden from his followers for so many years. He carried a great deal of grief. Many people had died at his hand, and even more had died on his orders. The execution of Anja, the lover whom he'd trusted, was the final blow. He simply could not continue as our leader. His grief had exhausted him.

Tessia spread her arms to her uncle, her commander, her mentor, and the two embraced for a long time.

I went into the hallway and using hand signals asked Wessel to bring water. When it arrived, I sprinkled some willow bark powder in the water, stirred it and gave it to Zygmunt. He drank it greedily, as if he were returning from the desert.

"Thank you, Healer," he said, and I saw his strength slowly returning. "As you can see, I can no longer lead. I need to retire to someplace quiet. And also," he said glancing at the door, "I've treated Wessel very badly. He's been beside me since we were very young. He's given everything to me, and I've repaid his love by chasing after the first pretty girl who showed an interest in me. Falling in love with Anja was a terrible mistake. I joined the rebel army when I was just a boy, and I'd never known many women, never been with one. Anja raised feelings in me I'd never experienced before, and I became confused. My foolishness cost good people their lives. People who trusted me." He shook his head slowly, sadly. "I cannot carry the burden of leadership any longer. Too many people have lost their lives because of me."

As we were walking back to the Silver Pony, Tessia asked, "What are we going to do? The queen cannot lead. Without a strong leader, Ludek will return and slaughter us."

I replied, "After the coronation tomorrow, I'll request an audience with the Queen. As her Healer, I have gained her trust. She may listen to me."

By request of the Queen, we had a small simple coronation. In attendance were General Zygmunt, Tessia, and I, as well as the household staff—an assortment of about two dozen cooks, maids, footmen, and gardeners. The Queen and the General had discussed the arrangements and decided that the traditional ceremony in which every citizen was invited would be a mistake. The high point of the ritual occurs when the High Mage, which would be me, holds the crown above the monarch's head and asks for the approval of the crowd. By tradition, it is unanimous, and a great roar rises from the city. The Queen, the practical daughter of a farmer, thought she had no credibility with the populace at this point and asking for their unanimous approval would make her look like a fool when they refused her. Her reign would be thrown into chaos and disrepute before it even started.

However, the coronation was dignified. I held the slim diadem over her head and asked the approval of those in attendance. They kindly mustered enthusiasm for their employer who hadn't paid them in weeks. I placed the crown on Queen Varvara's gray head. And we had a new queen. May God help her.

Queen Varvara was sitting beside the window in her usual manner, looking down at the bustling city below. From here, she could see beyond the city walls to the farms beyond. The cherry and apple trees were now in bud, and the brown earth was being plowed and planted. It felt as if the land, like the kingdom itself, was at the beginning of a new season. Winter was behind us, but spring had barely begun.

"My husband and I first met on a river barge," she said, speaking to the landscape that lay before her. "I was a country girl. My father was a prosperous farmer who was known for having the sweetest apples in the kingdom. Ottolo was a prince, and his father wanted him to marry a princess from the north, so the two kingdoms could merge. But Ottolo balked when he met her. She was a vapid pretty girl who knew nothing except how to order servants around, whereas I could ride as well as any cavalryman in his army. He was quite handsome you know, and all the girls wanted to flirt with him, but I caught his eye. And the rest is history, as they say.

"Of course," the Queen continued, turning to look at me slyly. "My wearing a love charm may have helped, as well as a girdle so tight I could barely breathe." She laughed pleasantly, "A girl needs all the help she can get."

I like this woman, I thought. *But can she lead an army, half of whom followed Ludek just a few weeks ago?*

"I suppose you heard from the General that he's leaving?"

I nodded. "Yes, your Majesty. He left this morning."

"And what do you think of his leaving?"

"I think, your majesty, that the kingdom is yours to rule."

"And what do you think of my ruling the kingdom?"

"Your Majesty, the kingdom is in a perilous time."

"No shit," she said, and for the first time I saw the country girl she'd once been. "Please be blunt, Healer. Think of the kingdom as a patient who is gravely ill. What does the kingdom need?"

"No one knows the future, your Majesty. All we can do is treat the illness that is in front of us. So, the first thing I would ask this patient is what are her symptoms?"

"The kingdom is ill from being ruled for years by a madman

who wanted nothing but to destroy everything good. Now the madman has fled and left a queen who is inexperienced as a ruler, but who has listened and learned. She has the practical intelligence of a farmer and the shrewdness of a politician, but she has no real power of her own. The only power she has is what other people choose to give her. She has no army to defend the kingdom, no gold to support her household and no ministers to carry out her commands. All the Queen has is a title."

"You are very wise, your Majesty."

"Right now, my friend, I have the wisdom of a cornered rat." She looked me up and down, assessing what I could do to help her. "Do I have your loyalty, Norbert Oldfoot?"

She surprised me. I was not aware she knew my real name. "Yes, your majesty. I pledge my loyalty to you." I kneeled before her and bowed my head.

"Arise, Sir Norbert," she said, tapping both of my shoulders with her teaspoon. "I hereby name you 'The Green Mage, Advisor to the Crown, Healer and Bard to the Kingdom.'"

I was surprised by my own tears. My first thought was of my father and how at last he may be proud of me. My next thought was of my beloved Idella whom I feared had died a horrible death at Ludek's hands. As usual when I had these thoughts, I pushed them aside because otherwise I would fall into a sobbing fit of grief.

"Your Majesty," I said, rising to my feet and shaking off my fear and self-loathing. "You said you need gold, an army, and ministers. I think I can help you acquire all three of those wishes."

"You want me to do *what*?" Tessia was incredulous. I had found her at the wool shop, playing dice with Taja while her father tied wool into bundles and glowered at the three of us from the back room.

246

"The two of you should talk in private," Taja whispered, flicking her eyes at the back room. "Politics can be a dangerous subject these days."

She was right, of course. Tessia and I left the shop and found a quiet place in an alley where no one could hear us.

"I have suggested to Queen Varvara that she adopt you, so you would be heir to the throne. While she's alive, she'll continue to rule."

"And what would be my role while she still lives?" Tessia was obviously suspicious of this new turn of events.

"She'll appoint you Commander and Heir-Apparent. You would be in charge of the defense of the kingdom."

"So, are we going to war?"

"By the Goddess, I hope not. At present we have no military unless you count all the lazy men wearing uniforms who steal fruit in the marketplace. Right now, the only defense forces are Sergeant Zrul's vigilante squads and the hired Drekavacs who accompany your caravan."

"So, I would have to build an army?" Tessia asked skeptically. When I nodded, she rolled her eyes. "And how am I going to pay the soldiers? Does the Queen have gold or silver I can use?"

I shook my head. "I was hoping that Tyrmiss would give us some of her hoard. She has no use for it."

Tessia looked at me and she gave a slight tremble. I realized that she was feeling something rare for her. Fear. "Norbert, I have not seen Tyrmiss in a week. I don't know where she is. I'm so afraid that she's hurt and needs our help."

"I will go first, Norbert," Tessia said, taking the torch from me. She had seen me trembling at the thought of walking into the dark cave.

I'm such a coward, I thought. Then I followed Tessia into Tyrmiss' lair.

"I didn't see any dragon tracks outside, and nothing seems amiss," Tessia said. "And the smell of smoke and sulfur is not in the air. So, I don't think she's been here in a while."

I followed Tessia into the inner chamber and saw the huge pile of treasure. Crowns, chalices, necklaces, rings, coins.... I was transfixed by the thought of what all this wealth could buy. Lit by torchlight, the gold, silver and gems seemed to be radiating wealth, as if a small piece of the sun had landed here. For the first time in my life, I felt dizzy with greed.

"Should we take some of it?"

Tessia looked at me aghast, "NO! What are you thinking, Norbert? This treasure is not ours. It belongs to Tyrmiss."

"I'm just thinking of how much good this wealth could do if we give it to Queen Varvara. You would be able to build an army to defend the kingdom. The Queen could rebuild the city, help the poor, send delegations to foreign kingdom to improve trade..."

"Norbert, you of all people know the old stories of what happens to people who steal dragon treasure. The only way we can take this treasure back to the castle is if Tyrmiss gives it to us."

"What if she's dead? We've not seen her in weeks. As far as I know, no one has. If she's dead, she'd want for you to have her treasure."

"Norbert, what has come over you? You've never been greedy before."

"Sorry, Tessia. You're right," I said, coming to my senses. "We can't take the gold unless we're sure Tyrmiss is gone for good."

I realized that trying not to think about what had happened to Idella was making me slightly mad. I needed to accept the likelihood of her death and try to come to terms with it.

Tessia was looking at the hoard, trying to puzzle something out. "What if someone finds this cave? They'll take the treasure for themselves, and the Queen will have nothing. But if we try to move it, then we may be seen." Tessia turned to me and asked, "Norbert, how was it that you kept your silver coins in a bag on Ottolo's back and I never saw it until we got to Dragonja City?"

"Oh, I used a simple invisibility charm to protect the bag from thieves. You know how a mirror bounces the light back to you? Well, an invisibility charm is similar. It bends the light around an object, so you see only what is on either side of the object and not the object itself."

"Can you make the cave entrance invisible?"

On the long hike back to the city, Tessia and I had a chance to discuss a strategy. We'd wait seven years before claiming Tyrmiss' treasure, and in the meantime, we'd develop an alternative source of wealth in order to finance the kingdom.

One evening I was sitting at a table in the tavern with Caz, the merchant we'd met on the river road when we were on our quest. He'd done quite well for himself in the year since he'd told us about the traveler who discovered the dragon lair full of treasure. Caz had traveled to foreign lands, buying spices and trading them for gold, silver and gems. He now traveled with an armed Drekavac who right now was standing against the wall with his hands on the pommel of his Voprian sword, eyeing everyone in the establishment as if we were robbers.

"Caz," I said. "Don't you think your guard should sit down at a table and have an ale? He's scaring all the customers. People can't listen to my songs if they're afraid any minute they may be sliced in half."

The merchant signaled the Drekavac, and he slid into a chair, but it didn't help. He was still scaring the customers.

Caz shrugged. "Sorry. I have to keep him close by."

The merchant and I had become friends since he'd moved to Dragonja City a few weeks before. We had a lot in common. Both of us had lost our mothers early in life and had been raised by strict fathers. We both had supported ourselves as traveling men, living by our wits. We both loved songs and stories, and sometimes he joined me in entertaining the guests at the tavern. I admired his worldliness, and I think he was in awe of my healing magic. Mutual admiration and a shared love of song had brought us together. But there were differences between us as well. He was much more interested in gaining silver and gold than I was, and I had been very attached to Idella, whom I was beginning to think of as *my late wife*, whereas he preferred to stay single. Another difference was that he'd traveled to far lands, whereas I'd never left the kingdom of Bekla and Dragonja.

"Caz, I've been wanting to ask you a question," I said carefully. "I've been composing a song and I want the story to sound as if it really happened."

"Well," he said laughing. "I've never been asked to help compose a song. I'm all ears." He flicked the point of his right ear. "Tell me what you have so far."

"In the song, there's a king who knows where a hoard of gold is hidden."

Caz leaned forward. He was always interested in stories of gold.

"But the hoard of gold is under a magic spell, and it appears only every seven years."

"Does the gold disappear during those seven years," Caz asked. "Or is it simply invisible?"

"No matter. What's important is that the king can't get his hands on the gold for a long time. Now the king is at war with the neighboring kingdom, and he needs gold to pay his soldiers. I'm wondering whether in all your travels you've come across a problem like this."

Caz looked at me shrewdly. "By the Goddess, you've found the dragon hoard in the mountains," he whispered excitedly. "So, it is true! The traveler I told you about did indeed find the dragon lair." He narrowed his eyes at me, "Was it where I said it was? In a cave between the Thumbs of the Giant?"

Tessia, who had been eavesdropping from the next table, looked at me with pure anger. I realized she was right to be angry. I'd been too clever by half.

"Caz," I said, trying to salvage the situation. "There is no treasure. It's just a story." But I've never been a good liar, and he saw through me immediately.

"You have to take me there!" He was almost crazy with excitement. I glanced at his Drekavac-guard who looked as if he was about to attack me.

Suddenly, Tessia stood up, grabbed Caz by his left arm and started to escort him to the front door. Caz's Drekavac-guard jumped up and drew his sword to protect his employer. Tessia tripped him and hit him in the chin with the heel of her hand, knocking him to the floor. Without missing a beat, Tessia goose-walked Caz out the door with me following.

Outside, she turned Caz over to two of her Drekavac-soldiers with orders for him to be locked in the dungeon. Tessia pointed her finger at me and said, "I should arrest you as well, Norbert. You've revealed a secret you were sworn to protect."

She stormed off, leaving me standing in the street without my cloak while a winter wind was bearing down on the city.

The next morning, I visited Queen Varvara and told her what had happened. Tessia had already told her about the dragon hoard, and she agreed with Tessia that we had no right to take the treasure until seven years had passed without hearing from Tyrmiss.

"And who is this man you call Caz?" she asked.

I told her how I'd met Caz and that I considered him a friend.

"In your judgement, is he of good character?"

"Yes," I said. "I've never known him to lie, or to cheat

anyone. Even though it is common in his line of work to take advantage of the naïve, I have never seen him take unfair advantage of his customers."

"And is he a successful merchant?"

"Yes, your Majesty. I believe he's accumulated a fortune by traveling the world and trading spices and gems."

"So, what we have is a rarity," the Queen said. "An honest man who's traveled the world and in so doing has become wealthy. I would like to meet this man," she said and called to Tessia who had been standing outside the chamber, seething. "Please bring this man Caz to me, Commander. I should like to talk to him."

A short while later, Tessia returned with Caz. Although he'd spent only one night in the dungeon, he seemed to have aged five years. *How did Hamlin survive a month in that place?* I wondered.

"Meister Caz," the Queen inquired graciously. "I apologize for the rough treatment that the Commander has shown you." She gave a sharp look at Tessia. "Have you broken your fast yet?"

Caz shook his head, somewhat dismayed to have been transported from a tavern to a dungeon to a royal chamber in the space of a dozen hours.

"Well, then, won't you join me?" She walked into the next room and sat at a long table set with a feast. The custom was that the Queen ate first, and then after she retired to her private chamber, the royal retainers feasted. But the Queen broke precedent, and asked Caz to sit with her. Tessia, her fiancé Taja and I sat at the table as well, listening.

"I suggest you try the duckling, Meister Caz. It's one of the specialties of my chef."

After they both had finished eating, the Queen said, "I believe that the Bard asked you to help him compose a song that tells a story. I'm curious about the devices that storytellers use. The story must be believable, or it is nothing at all. Don't you agree?"

Caz nodded his head, completely bewildered by what was happening to him.

"I appreciate your help in this, Meister Caz. So, let us suppose that a royal personage has a great treasure that she cannot spend for seven years. But she needs money now to build an army, repair her castle, feed the poor, and hire ministers. Have you ever heard of a situation like this?"

Caz slowly nodded his head, keeping a careful eye on Tessia who was looking like she wanted to feed him to the dogs.

"And was this royal personage able to solve the problem?"

Again, Caz nodded his head.

"How was it solved, good Meister Caz?"

"Through a promise," Caz said. "The Queen makes a promise."

"A promise?"

"Yes, your Majesty. She has coins made out of pottery and declares that each piece of pottery will be redeemable for a ring of gold in seven years. And she spends the pottery coins at whatever rate people are willing to accept. At first, perhaps, a coin is worth only an apple, but after a few months, a coin may be worth a bag of apples, and as the seven years pass, the coin will eventually be worth a ring of gold."

"But pottery is fragile. How could it last for seven years?"

"Mix copper filings into the clay, your Majesty. And fire the clay with a hard glaze also containing copper."

"And people are willing to accept these pottery coins as payment?"

"Yes, your majesty, but only if they trust the Queen to honor her word."

"What is to prevent someone from making their own pottery coins?"

"Each coin has the royal seal on it. Counterfeiting the royal seal is a crime punishable by death."

"I see. And, Meister Caz, would you be willing to oversee

this process? I would make you Minister of Finance, and you would be paid well. In pottery coins, of course."

Caz, keeping one eye on Tessia, nodded his head. And in this way, the Queen found her Minister of Finance. And Caz faithfully served Queen Varvara for the rest of her days.

But now many years later, I realize that I should have seen the significance of Caz shifting his gaze from Tessia to Taja, whom he obviously desired. I thought little of it at the time. Taja was very beautiful in those days, and often I'd seen men transfixed by her shapely figure, her slender white neck and her blonde curls piled high like a treasure. How was I to know at the time what tragedies would come from Caz's desire?

Chapter 18

I was surprised by Tessia visiting me in my quarters. I had not seen her since the incident with Caz. In the meantime, she'd quit her job as a bouncer at the Silver Pony and started her duties as a queen-in-training, and I'd wondered whether the slow pace of building an army and mastering the politics and rituals of royalty bored her, or whether the new role suited her and was a welcome respite from the rigors of battle.

We hugged and exchanged pleasantries. "How's Taja?" I asked.

Tessia smiled sweetly, looked at the floor and demurred from speaking about her new bride. She'd always kept her love affair private, and I respected her discretion. A few weeks before, Tessia and Taja had gotten married in a small ceremony in a lovely mountain glade. I presided over the ceremony which had been witnessed by Heikum, Femke and Queen Varvara. The queen's two guards stood at a discreet distance.

"How's Hamlin?" Tessia asked, looking around at my spare room. She was polite enough not to ask why I was staying here instead of my house outside the city which Idella and I had shared. the truth was that everything in the house reminded me of my missing wife.

"There's little change in his condition," I answered. "His body is recovering, but he shows no sign of engagement with what's happening around him. One of the women who assists Mina has taken over his care, and I check on him daily. He seems not to notice that Anja no longer sits with him and takes care of him. The only sign of hope is that Bruin has started lying beside the bed, and Hamlin seems to be responding to the dog, but only listlessly. It's as if he has no soul anymore. I'm not sure what the wizard did to him, but Hamlin is no longer part of this world."

Tessia nodded, "I've visited him, but he doesn't seem to recognize me." Her eyes filled with tears. "He was my best friend for so many years and now he's gone."

"I do see some response from Hamlin when Bruin is with him. The two used to be very close, and sometimes developing a friendship with an animal can help a patient recover."

I wondered what it was that brought her here. She had never been one to socialize. "It's always wonderful to see you, Tessia." And I let the silence grow heavy between us, and I waited for her to say what she'd come to say.

She looked me in the eye and said, "Tyrmiss may have found Idella and my father."

The shock of hearing these words made my legs shaky. She pulled a chair closer and helped me to sit down. I had completely given up on ever finding Idella. In fact, I'd convinced myself that she was dead because the thought of her in the hands of the Wizard Ludek was more than I could bear.

Tessia explained, "Every night since Tyrmiss left your good care, Norbert, she's been flying low over the land listening to the dreams of riverfolk and Drekavacs. She started by following the Dragonja river, then the Bekla River, then the seacoast. She listened to animals as well, the deer and bear in the forest and the white wolves in the Dry Hills. Then she went back to the pass between the Thumbs of the Giant where her cave is, flew down into the Iskar valley and searched the dreams of those who dwell there. And finally, she heard a faint dream of Idella, barely audible. She was dreaming of you, Norbert, and her son Alaric."

"And where is she?" My voice was urgent and desperate. "Tell me where the Wizard has taken her!"

"Tyrmiss believes that she's in a tower on a cliff on the other side of the Iskar River. And my father may be there as well."

"Then we must go to them," I said, rising from the chair and starting to pack a few things for the journey.

"We'll be flying tonight, Norbert. I wanted to go alone, but Tyrmiss said I should bring you. She said we'd be needing the healing power of your magic, so bring your lyre and your kit."

I told her I needed to do a few things and to speak with a couple of people first, and then I was free to go. Tessia said she and Tyrmiss would meet me at the river crossing where the mountain path joins the river road. After she left, I sat on the edge of the bed and thought about how my brother would defend a tower from unwanted guests. He would certainly have hidden the doorway, so I thought back to what my father had taught me about locator spells. And I was also certain Ludek had recruited trolls, screechers or disguised Drekavacs to act as sentries at three key locations inside the building, three being the most powerful number. I thought about what strategies I would need to trick the monsters in case Tessia's sword was not enough. I prepared a grab bag of various objects and potions, and then I was ready. Before I left, I took a few deep breaths, gave a short prayer to the Goddess, found my calm center, and walked out the door.

I stopped by the hospital tent to tell Mina I would be gone for a few days, and she agreed to take care of my patients. Then I walked across the market square to the alley where the children's gang posted lookouts. Alaric had run away again, and I'd heard he was living in the alleys with his gang of friends.

"I need to talk to Alaric," I said to a scruffy boy who'd barely seen a dozen summers.

He looked at me with hard gray eyes, and I thought, *a child should not be so embittered.*

"Who are you?" he asked, looking me up and down as if inspecting a goat for sale.

"His fa—" but I stopped myself. Had I any right to call Alaric my son? I was married to his mother for only a few weeks before I abandoned her. Had I any right to even think of myself as a husband and father?

"I am Norbert Oldfoot, the healer."

The boy disappeared into the alley and came back almost immediately.

"Alaric doesn't want to see you," he said indifferently, as if he'd known the answer all along.

"Could you give him a message, then?"

"What is it?" he said looking over my shoulder at the market. He clearly didn't care what I said or what I needed.

"Tell him... please tell him..." I searched for the right words. "Tell him I'm sorry."

He gave a grim chuckle. "Yeah, yeah. All you adults are sorry. A sorry lot you are. Now get out of here before we teach you how sorry sorry can be."

Half a dozen children, as well as a few older boys, had gathered around and were staring belligerently at me. Some were armed with heavy sticks. I moved away, back into the open market.

What have we done to our children? I wondered.

After the sun went down, I followed the Dragonja River Road north from the city. I could see Tessia standing at the bottom of the mountain path, and behind her was a large dark mass which I assumed was Tyrmiss.

"Get on my back, Bard," Tyrmiss said abruptly. "We can't stay here without being seen."

"Why are you doing this, Tyrmiss? You don't even know Idella or Kerttu."

"In a weak moment when I was in extreme pain lying on the roof of the castle a while ago, I made a promise to Tessia that I would find her father," she answered impatiently. "And as for you, Nordbutt, when I saw you catapulted through the air to save your lady, I thought, this has to be the stupidest man on the planet. He certainly needs all the help he can get."

I climbed on her back and sat on her shoulders, wrapping my arms around Tessia who leaned forward and held onto a sharp spine.

"Besides," Tyrmiss added as she lifted and stretched her wings. "I despise that Wizard."

The flight up the mountain was much slower than the flight down had been. The flight down had felt like riding on the back of a hawk striking a sparrow far below. The flight up the mountain was like sitting in a bucket being pulled out of a well. Each wing beat seemed like work for Tyrmiss. I tried to take a look at the wing that had been injured, but it was moving invisibly through the dark.

Finally, we reached the dragon-cave. Settling in, Tyrmiss folded her great black wings to her sides, and said, "We'll first eat, then I need to tell you what I know about the tower and the Wizard. By the way, Nordbutt, quite a clever trick with making the cave entrance invisible. It took me quite a while to find it."

"Tyrmiss," Tessia began. "We need to tell you something about your treasure hoard..."

"Let me guess, my dear. Your precious Queen Varvara needs gold to administer her kingdom, but you told her that I might roast little Norbert here if you took even a single ring without my permission. Am I right?"

Tessia nodded hesitantly. "Something like that," she answered.

"Take it. Take all of it. I don't care about the gold. Rilla and I collected it because she thought it was pretty. I couldn't care less about it."

She blew a short breath of fire onto the large pike laid out on the flat cooking stone. When it was brown and crispy, Tessia drew her copper dagger across the fish dividing it into three pieces. She piled dandelions and a small piece of fish on a flat leaf and offered it to me, and she did the same for herself. The rest of the fish, a piece as long as my arm, Tyrmiss lifted in the air and swallowed in one gulp.

"I see your fire has been restored, my lady dragon," I said, looking at the jagged gray scar where the wound in her throat had been.

"Yes, thanks to your excellent care and the gift of time, I'm fully myself again," Tyrmiss replied. "Although I find I'm not as quick as I once was, a little stiff when I wake up in late afternoon, and sometimes a fish that once would have been an easy catch gets away."

Once we were finished eating, Tyrmiss told us about the Wizard's tower.

"The first thing you need to know is that there is no door into the tower," the dragon said, picking her long teeth with an oak branch.

"No door?" Tessia exclaimed. "Then how do we get in?"

"Exactly, my dear," Tyrmiss answered. "And that's not the only challenge. I'll fly you to the tower, but I can't go in." She smiled. "I've been on a slimming diet, lately—only one fish a day and lots of exercise flying around at night—but I'm afraid I'm still too thick in the waist to squeeze through the halls of a tower. Also…"

The dragon paused, adding reluctantly, "I hate to admit it, but my powers are no match for Ludek. A Wizard like him can be defeated only by another Wizard." She looked at me meaningfully.

"I'm not really… I mean I don't…" I stammered.

The dragon dismissed my insecurities with a wave of her talon.

"So, assuming you find a way into the tower, you're on your own. Tessia, your fighting skills will be essential in this mission. And Norbert, bring your lyre, your magic powders, your magic wand—"

"I don't have a wand," I said, feeling completely inadequate for the task in front of me. Then I thought about Idella and realized that any trepidation I had about using magic needed to be set aside. Idella needed me.

"… And whatever else you require to enter the tower and find your friends. And, of course, the chances of either of you surviving this task are slim."

Tessia looked at me. "How do we find the door, Norbert?"

"We can try a locator spell… but I'm sure the Wizard put a block on the usual ones."

"So, what do we do?" Tyrmiss asked.

"First, we need to cast a spell that will remove the invisibility spell protecting the door. Then, before the Wizard can restore the invisibility spell, we'll need to cast a locator spell to find the door. But there is a big problem with this strategy."

"By removing the invisibility spell, we've let the Wizard know we're coming," Tess pointed out.

"Exactly, so we need to go to the tower, work the spell and get in the door before the Wizard realizes we are coming for him."

"And what about finding Idella and Kerttu in the castle?" Tessia asked.

"Once inside, we'll have to cast the locator spell again."

"But by then, the Wizard will know we're in the tower." Tessia was squinting her eyes as she thought about the fight that was coming. "I suppose we won't have time to squeeze more warriors through the door before the Wizard attacks us?"

"Probably not."

"Very well, then. The one time I saw the Wizard I slashed his face with his own dagger. The next time I'll slash his throat."

I thought, *Tessia is the only warrior I need beside me.*

Tyrmiss flew us down the slope to the Iskar Valley and followed the river north. The moon shone down on huge trees, broad snowy fields, wide evergreen forests, and small villages with smoke rising from chimneys. The sparsely populated valley was much larger and more verdant than I realized. I vowed that if I survived this wild adventure, then I would like to come back to the valley and explore it. Before my first trip to the rebel camp, I hadn't realized there was a whole new world beyond the mountains to the north and west of the Bekla and Dragonja valleys.

Finally, I saw the black tower below. It sat on a cliff that overlooked the river. The dragon circled it twice, so we could get a good look at all sides. As she had said, there was no door or gate visible. She flew upriver some distance and landed on the gravelly bank.

"Is this close enough? Can you do your spell from here?" Tyrmiss asked.

"No, I'll have to be closer. It helps to be able to see the tower."

"Very well then, we should take a quick rest here," she said.

Tessia and I dismounted. She stretched her arms and legs, then turned her head from side to side, limbering up. For the thousandth time, I noticed with amazement how strong and athletic she was. Tyrmiss was looking at her fondly with wide blue eyes.

"Be careful, my dear. I want you to return to me with your pretty head on your shoulders where it belongs." Tyrmiss said to Tessia, and then the dragon turned to me, and I saw her eyes gradually narrowing to slits and changing from blue to purple to red. "And you, my friend, had better return her to me safely. I am holding you responsible."

"Tyrmiss," Tessia said, "Of course, Norbert and I are going to protect each other, but threatening him is not helpful." She and I quickly ate a chunk of bread and a handful of dried apple slices and gulped down a mouthful of water, then Tessia looked at me. "Are you ready?"

When I nodded, she swung herself onto Tyrmiss's back, and I climbed up and sat behind her. The dragon took a few quick steps, spread her wings, and we were quickly in the air, following the river. Tyrmiss landed us on the cliff next to the tower. It was still dark, the moon shining down on us, a perfect night for casting spells. I picked up a stick from the ground.

"Is that a wand?" Tessia asked.

"No, it's a stick. Just a stick." *Why do people always think magic requires a wand?*

With the stick, I drew a small square in the dirt to represent the tower. I drew two lines through the middle of the square, connecting the four corners. I took out four candles which had the sign of the Goddess carved into them, and I placed them on the corners of the square representing the four cardinal directions. I sat cross-legged facing the square and gestured for Tessia to do the same. We held hands so that our arms encompassed the square. In a quiet calm voice, I said, "Breathe deeply. Now close your eyes and think only of the castle. If your mind drifts, bring it gently back to the castle." After a few moments, I said, "Now I am going to let go of your hands, but you need to keep your eyes closed."

I took a pendulum out of my pocket and held it spinning above the center of the square where the two lines crossed.

pătrat frumos
a castelului negru
Unde ţi-e uşa?
lasă pendulul
arată-ne unde

No sooner did I say the words, then the pendulum slowly moved to the middle of one side of the square.

"The door is over there, right?" Tessia asked, opening her eyes and pointing to the side of the castle facing the river. I nodded.

We walked along the wall, Tessia tapping her dagger against the stones until she came to a place in the middle of the wall where the dagger penetrated stone as if it were merely air.

"Here's the door," Tessia said, her dagger tracing the shape of the aperture.

"We're going to need light in there," I said, tearing a piece of cloth off my shirt and wrapping it around the stick in my hand. I held it up and Tyrmiss gave a small burp of fire to light the torch.

"Ready when you are," I said.

"Stand back, sweetie," the dragon warned as she pushed her head into the dark hole. We heard the swoosh of her fiery breath, and then she pulled her head back. "Just want to discourage anyone from attacking you before you're ready."

Tessia leaped into the darkness, her sword drawn.

"Well, Nordbutt, what are you waiting for?" Tyrmiss said, using her claw to push me into the darkness behind Tessia. The torch in my hand gave a feeble flickering light, but it was enough to see that we'd entered a long narrow passage. The walls were still warm from Tyrmiss's breath. A light shone from ahead. Dropping my torch which had gone out, I followed Tessia slowly down the passage toward the light. I realized we'd already walked further down this passage than the width of the castle. The black tower was larger on the inside than on the outside. My brother knew his craft.

We entered a room that was huge, much larger than the entire castle, and the ceiling seemed to be as high as the top of a pine tree. Chained to the far wall was a mountain troll guarding a doorway. He beat his wooden club on the floor a few times, inviting us to approach him and fight. Tessia didn't hesitate. Holding her sword in one hand and her dagger in the other, she strode up to the troll and stood just beyond the length of the chain that held him by the ankle.

"Meister Troll," she addressed him. "May we pass?"

He beat his club on the floor a few more times, then held it ready. Clearly, he wasn't going to let us pass. Tessia backed up a dozen steps until she stood beside me.

"How do I defeat such a creature, Norbert?" she asked, not taking her eyes off him.

"Trolls are strong and brutal, but notoriously dim-witted," I said. "Try to trick him into exhausting himself."

Tessia carefully walked forward until she was within reach of his club. When he swung at her, she leaped back. She stepped forward again, and he swung the club again. She repeated this a number of times, and the troll began to show fatigue. She continued until sweat was streaming off his bald head and his hairy chest. Finally, she stepped forward, but the troll was too tired to lift his club. Tessia calmly walked up to him and cut off his arm. Blood spurting from the stump, the poor troll looked stupidly at his arm lying in front of him and then fell forward, hitting the floor like a felled tree.

The second room was somewhat smaller, and against the back wall was chained a three-headed yellow horned beast guarding the doorway. All three heads were snarling, showing their vicious teeth. When Tessia walked up to the demon, it lunged at her, and she cut off the nearest head. Immediately a new head grew in its place and let out an ear-piercing scream.

Tessia covered her ears with her hands and backed away until she was standing next to me. I noticed that she had blood on her left hand where the creature had scratched her. I took her hand in mine and inspected the wound. It wasn't deep, but blood was running onto the pommel of her dagger. I reached in my bag and pulled out a yarrow poultice which I'd prepared back at the Silver Pony, pressed it on the laceration and wrapped her hand in a bandage. "What is this creature, Norbert? How do I defeat it?" she shouted, trying to be heard above the noise of the beast.

"It is *vreel*," I yelled back. "Known as *The Screecher*."

"Where did the monster come from?" Tessia shouted, looking at it in disgust.

After a few moments, the demon grew quiet and I explained, "It's believed to be the ghost of triplets who died in the womb. There is some debate about whether it's actually alive or whether it's just a nightmare of guilt and torment. In any case, it's the demon that guards the doorway of the underworld. You cannot defeat it, Tessia."

"How do you know, Norbert? Have you ever seen it before?"

"No, I've never encountered one, but my father made a study of monsters, and he taught me what he knew. In some strange way, he seems to have been preparing me for this task."

"Then what shall we do? Does the quest end here?"

"No, no. The quest is merely part of the journey that began when we were born and continues until we die, Tessia."

She looked at me in exasperation. "This is not the time to discuss philosophy, Bard. How can we get past this demon?"

"You must make friends with it, Commander. Like the other creatures that the Wizard has brought forth, vreel thrives on your fear."

She looked at me, puzzled.

I reached into my bag and pulled out a piece of dried meat. "This is a piece of the uterus of a goat which has been dried over a fire of amaranth and calaria, Tessia." I handed her the piece of meat. "Go make friends with Drekavac."

"You just happen to travel around with the dried uterus of a goat, Norbert? What else have you got in that bag?"

"A mage must always be prepared, My Lady."

Tessia rolled her eyes, walked up to the three-headed demon

and sat down just out of reach of its triple set of snapping jaws. She tore the dried uterus meat into small tidbits and held out a piece to the creature. Smelling the meat, all three heads lunged, but banged their heads together. Then she placed three pieces of meat on the floor, an arm's length apart, just out of reach of the demon. The vreel lunged at the meat but couldn't reach it. It sat back and looked at Tessia with all three heads cocked. I had to laugh. I had seen Bruin give this look many times. It was the universal signal that a creature was puzzled about what the human wanted from it. Tessia spoke gently and encouragingly to the vreel, telling him what a good demon he was. She praised him for guarding the door to the underworld for so many thousands of years. She called him her brave and faithful monsterling. The vreel wagged his tail and sat back on his haunches. He used one of his tongues to lick his front paws, while a second head looked imploringly at Tessia and whined. His third head looked away at the far wall, pretending not to be interested in the dried meat at all.

Tessia slowly and gently pushed the pieces of uterus meat closer while continuing to praise the vreel. The vreel wagged his spiky tail while the three heads snatched the tidbits and swallowed them. Tessia moved a little closer and scratched each of the heads behind the ears.

"Follow me, Norbert," she said, standing up and heading for the doorway.

We entered a room where a single candle burned. And sitting at the table, staring into the candleflame were Idella and Kerttu.

"Wait," I said to Tessia. We stood for a moment looking at the beautiful faces of our loved ones. Something was not right here. I felt a terrible fear rise from my gut, pushing out any semblance of calm. Idella stepped toward me, her arms wide, and feeling a spell descend over me, I stepped toward her and pulled her closer. We kissed long and deep. She lifted her strong hands to my face, the hands I knew so well, and wrapped them around my neck, at first affectionately and then she pressed hard, viciously choking me. I grabbed her wrists, breaking her grip on my throat. I looked at Tessia with alarm. Kerttu was smiling at her as he pulled a copper ax from his belt. She kicked him hard in the knee, knocking him to the floor. "It's a trap!" She yelled, quickly turning toward the doorway behind us just in time to block a Voprian sword from descending on her head. Tessia turned to her father who rose and held out his arms to her. She seemed to be struggling, caught between her fear of a trap and her overbearing desire to embrace her father. She slowly walked toward him.

Idella stretched her arms to me, her eyes meeting mine. "Oh, my love, I have missed you so much," I said, feeling myself drawn to her perfect face. Then, I noticed the hand stretched toward me—the serpent bracelet she always wore was missing. Suddenly, Idella's face became enraged. She drew a dagger and lunged at me. I jumped back to avoid being stabbed. She lunged again, this time nicking my hand as I blocked the blade. She slashed at my belly, but before I could bring myself to hurt my beloved Idella, Tessia had cut off her head.

I turned to Tessia, horrified that she'd killed my wife, but Tessia nodded toward the bodies on the floor, and I saw, not my friend Kerttu and my beloved Idella, but rather two dead Drekavacs and a third one beside the door.

"Ingenious," Tessia said, wiping the blood off her sword. "Disguising the assassins as our loved ones."

"Yes, Ludek has made us destroy the images of those we love. He is truly evil."

When we went through the final door, we stepped into a beautiful green meadow that sloped down to the shore of a river. A large oak tree spread its limbs over the water. A rope hung from a heavy branch. I recognized this place. My brother Ludek and I played here as children.

"What do you see, Tessia?"

"I see the village where I grew up. Over there is my father's smithy where I spent many happy days helping him. This is the place where I first became strong by pounding metal into shape."

"It is not real," I said. "Ludek has created this illusion to trick us, just as he created the illusion of our loved ones in the last room. Be on your guard."

My brother, a boy about eight years old, appeared and started playing on the rope, swinging it far over the river and dropping into the water with great joy. He was exactly as I remembered him before he was taken away.

"What do you see?" I asked.

"I see Anja and Hamlin. They're holding hands. They look happy, the way they looked before our village burned and the quest began."

My mother was standing on the riverbank, calling to my brother, telling him to be careful.

Tessia said, "I see my mother, putting her head in the doorway of the smithy, calling my father and me to dinner."

"Tessia, the wizard is summoning our dreams of the dead to beguile us. Do not be fooled."

She didn't seem to have heard me. Transfixed by the illusion of seeing her mother, who had died while giving birth to her, Tessia walked toward her loved ones.

"Stop, Tessia! What you're seeing is not real."

Despite my entreaties, she continued walking and I had no choice but to follow her. As I moved in the direction of my mother and brother, I felt a growing sense of peace. My grief which had been gnawing at me so many years was evaporating, being replaced by joy. *Love*, I thought. *Love is the answer to everything.*

Beside me, Tessia drew her sword. "Valor," she said intently. "Valor is all."

"Tessia," I said, grabbing her arm. "What do you see?"

"My enemies," she said. "I see an army of Drekavacs!" She slashed her sword through the empty air. "I must protect my mother!"

My own mother, long dead, was in front of me, beckoning. I felt a surge of love for her, then when I realized this was nothing more than a dream and I'd lost her forever, sadness overcame me. Then self-pity. Then anger. My mother had been taken away from me when I was a child, and I'd been deprived of her love. And my father had become distant and angry and finally had died of heartbreak. And ever since, I've been afraid and full of self-loathing. I felt overwhelmed by the waves of emotion crashing over me. I was drowning in my own feelings.

Chapter 19

When I woke, my hands and feet were tied, and I was lying on the floor of what looked like a dungeon. A small square of light from a high window fell next to me. Tessia was leaning against the wall, struggling to untie herself. She winced in pain as the rope rubbed against her injured hand.

"By the spit of the Goddess, I hate being tied up," she cursed. Despite the pain, she kept working the bonds. When she was free, she untied my hands and feet as well.

"What happened back there?" she asked me.

"I'm not sure, but it appears the Wizard used our own memories against us. He created the illusion that the dead ones we love were in front of us, and the sight of them alive evoked our deepest feelings, including the fears we've never allowed ourselves to experience."

"Whatever," she said. Ever the pragmatic one, she'd never shown much interest in the inner workings of the soul. Right now, she was looking around our cell, searching for a way out.

"Is this dungeon real, Norbert? Or are we being fooled again?"

"Reach out and touch the walls," I said. "Can you feel the texture of the stone?"

When she nodded, I asked, "Can you smell the dankness in the air? Sight is easily fooled, but scent and texture are almost impossible to duplicate in an illusion. This prison is real. We are still in the black tower."

When no strategy for our escape presented itself, Tessia sat down beside me.

"Norbert," she said, "Who is Ludek? I need to know more about him if I am going to fight him."

"Ludek is..." I said hesitantly. "He's my brother."

"What?" She asked, incredulously. "Why haven't you told me this before?"

"Because it isn't important," I said. "Ludek is not who he was. The boy I knew died a long time ago. This Wizard, this evil creature, is not the brother I knew."

"Tell me what you know about him," Tessia said urgently.

"I'm not sure I know what happened. When I was a boy, my father was a shireman who traveled up and down the Bekla Valley selling his goods. He was also, like me, a Green Mage who provided his simple skills and charms to the farmers and villagers whom he met in his travels. He'd never had the chance to get any formal education in magic, but he hoped that his older son Ludek would have the chance to study and become a true Wizard. Of the two of us, my father always said that Ludek was the more gifted, having picked up the basics of magic at an early age. I'd always been a somewhat backwards child, so my father taught me enough to be a shireman, a trade which I eventually came to enjoy, but I was always jealous of the gifts that my brother had. Because of my father's work, Ludek and I stayed at home for months at a time with my mother. In those days, not much happened in the village, so she felt safe.

"One day a cloaked stranger came to our house. He wore a hood that kept his face in shadow, and he carried a staff with a black stone fixed to it. He said he had a message for us from my father. My mother opened her door to the stranger, and following the custom of our people regarding guests, she poured ale and sliced bread and put them in front of the stranger. He said he'd met my father upriver and had bought cloth and copperware from him. They decided to make camp together. Sitting at the fire that evening, my father told him of his family, and how proud he was of his beautiful wife and strong sons..."

My voice trailed off as grief overcame me.

"Go on, Norbert. What happened?"

"Sorry, Tessia," I said wiping the tears from my eyes. "This is difficult to say."

"I understand, but I need to know who this Wizard is."

"The stranger asked whether he could meet this remarkable boy who showed such a talent for Green Magic. My mother gestured to Ludek and presented him proudly to the stranger and confirmed that he was the most gifted boy in the valley. As usual, nothing was said about me, and I pretended not to care that I was once again being ignored.

"The hooded stranger said that my father had instructed him to bring Ludek to him at the fork of the Bekla and Dragonja rivers. My mother, of course, was hesitant to release her son to the care of a stranger, so she politely declined. The stranger insisted, and my mother grew more firm in her refusal. They argued, and finally, the stranger grabbed my brother by the arm and started dragging him to the door while Ludek resisted, kicking, scratching, biting and trying to use magic against the stranger, but he was far too powerful for the boy. I was very frightened and shrank back into the corner of the room. My mother screamed at the man to let go of her son, but the man continued dragging my brother to the door. My mother grabbed the knife she had used to cut the bread and threatened the stranger who laughed and pointed his staff at her. My mother lunged at him and there was a huge flash of light and a thunderous noise and my mother fell down. The stranger picked up my brother who was screaming for help and carried him out the door. The neighbors came to the house to find out what was happening, but by then, my mother was dead and the stranger and Ludek were gone."

"What happened to Ludek?" Tessia asked.

"I don't know." I said, tears streaming down my face. "It was the last time I ever saw my brother. The next I knew of him was a few years ago, when I heard that he led a company of

Drekavac-soldiers who burned and pillaged the villages of the Bekla Valley."

We sat in silence for a while, and Tessia said slowly, "So when Ludek was a boy, he was kidnapped by a Wizard and taken to a far land. The Wizard trained the boy in the black arts. And when he was grown, he returned to his native land and enchanted the king?"

"It would appear so," I said sadly.

"But you are so kind and gentle, Norbert. How could you have a brother who is so evil?"

Before I could answer, the door opened and a Drekavac-soldier stood in the doorway, squinting at us in the half-light of the cell.

"I heard that there was a Green Mage and a feisty girl handy with a blade here. I wondered whether it was the two of you." He looked at me. "Healer, you're wanted by the Wizard."

The Drekavac seemed to recognize us, but I'd treated dozens of Drekavacs after the war, and I didn't have much interest in this one right now.

The Drekavac accompanied me down the stone passage to a pair of heavy oak doors which he pushed open to reveal a large chamber. Ludek sat on a wide throne, holding a staff which held a smooth black stone identical to the one I'd seen in the hands of King Ottolo, except that Ludek's stone was polished and gleaming, obviously a black sapphire. A pair of Drekavac-soldiers stood at attention on either side of the Wizard.

Ludek looked at me with an evil smile on his face. "Hello, little brother," he rasped. "It has been such a long time. It is nice to see you again. Family reunions are always so pleasant."

He wore a black cloak. I wondered whether it was the same cloak worn by the stranger who had taken him away twenty years before. Ludek's skin was gray, and he had a deep pink scar that ran from the bridge of his nose to his left ear, the souvenir

Tessia had given him at their first meeting a year before. *It's only been a year since Tessia, Hamlin, Anja and I started the quest,* I thought, irrationally. *So much has happened since then. It seems like a lifetime.*

"I have grieved for you, Ludek," I said, pulling myself back to the present and looking for some kind of advantage over my brother.

"Grieved for me? Why would you grieve? As you see, I am doing well."

"No, you've lost your soul in the pursuit of the dark arts."

"There is no such thing as soul, brother. There is only power."

"What happened to you, Ludek? Why have you chosen this path?"

"I chose nothing. One thing happens, then another, then another until we die. That is all."

He looked at me as if he were considering buying a calf in the market. "As I said, I am fine, but what has happened to *you*, Norbert? Have you actually chosen to be such a little man? My spies have been watching you. A shireman who traipses from village to village with his pots and pans, his dresses and toys. Always looking to profit a copper coin here, a bag of apples there. Are you not ashamed of this pathetic life you lead?"

"No, I am not," I replied, straightening my back. "It was our father's trade and his father before him. The shire men are necessary. Without us—"

"Without you, a wife may have to cook in an old pot instead of a new one." Ludek laughed. "You showed talent for magic when you were young, Norbert. Why did you give it up?'

"Because I decided the best way to serve the Goddess was by—"

"By singing songs and making herbal teas." Again, Ludek laughed at me. "You could have been a great Wizard. And yet you chose a small life."

"I chose life, Ludek. You chose death. All things must die.

Death is part of life, but you who are not my brother, have chosen to serve death. The Goddess is not pleased with your choice."

"The Goddess? Where is this Goddess you speak of? Show her to me." He waited. When I stayed silent, he said with a smirk, "Yes, just as I suspected. You have no more influence over the Goddess than a goat has over a milkmaid."

"You should not blaspheme this way, Ludek. The Goddess—"

"Where was your Goddess when the Wizard carried me from my mother's arms?" Ludek's voice rose in anger. "Where was your Goddess when he left me in a dark cave, a place where there was not a single ray of light. Not even a star shone its light in that cave. He kept me there for years. Every day, he brought me food and water and told me about the world outside. All the kings, the warriors, the castles. All the farmers, fishermen and craftsmen. The rivers and forests. It could all be mine, he said, but first I must embrace the darkness, take it inside me and become the darkness. He taught me spells and enchantments. He gifted me this weapon." He held up the staff with the black sapphire. "He taught me how to use it to control nature. And what I could not control, he taught me to kill."

"You are mad," I blurted out. "You are not my brother. My brother died in that dark cave, and you took his place."

"Oh, but I am your brother, Norbert. Just as night is brother to day, and death is brother to life. We are different sides of the same force. You serve Nilene Zeita, Goddess of Life. I serve Ytgein Zeitu, God of Time. Come here, brother. Since you value life so much, let me show you something." He walked over to a window which had suddenly appeared in the wall. Outside it was night. There was no moon and only a few stars. He gestured at the black sky. "From here, you can see a glimpse, only a glimpse, of eternity. In all this distance, all this darkness, how much light is there? In eternity, there is far more darkness than light. Life is merely a spark in the vast night of death. Life is insignificant compared to death. Norbert, my brother," Ludek said, his voice softening. "I am asking you to join me. You have power over the girl and the dragon. Together, we can rule these valleys and extend our power beyond."

I finally realized what this conversation was about.

"I have no power over Tessia, nor over the dragon. Tessia and the dragon will never join you, Ludek!"

The Wizard who called himself my brother looked at me with cold gray eyes, ascertaining whether I was telling the truth. Then, he pointed his staff at my face, and I felt a strange chill come over me, as if all the warmth in my soul was being drained out of my life. The people I loved—Idella, Tessia, Alaric, Mina—were being pulled away from me the way a thread is pulled from a spool. I felt myself falling into blackness.

The Drekavac returned me to the cell and laid me gently beside Tessia. I slept. When I woke, he was again standing over me. I could see Tessia coiling her muscles, preparing to leap at him, but the Drekavac gestured toward the open door and said, "You two better get running if you want to get away. I imagine the Wizard's got nasty plans for you if you stay."

"Why are you releasing us?" Tessia asked.

The Drekavac looked from Tessia to me with a puzzled look on his gray scaly face. "You don't recognize me? I'm Frezz."

When we didn't show any sign that we knew him, he said, "Remember me? Frezz… I was one of the soldiers who attacked you in the Dry Lands last summer. Your dog chewed up my hand." He held up his right hand and indeed there were pink scars. I recognized the stitch marks as my own handiwork. Now I remembered him.

"Oh yes," I said. "You came to the market and bought bread from Idella's stall."

"That's right," he said, nodding enthusiastically and show-ing his pointed teeth in a wide smile. He acted like he wanted to hug me but stopped himself and checked the cell door behind him to make sure the other guards were not listening. "Turnabout is fair play," Frezz whispered. "In the Dry Hills, you had the chance to kill me and you let me and my mates go. So, I'm returning the favor."

"Won't you get in trouble when the Wizard sees that we escaped?" I asked.

"My mates and I are deserting today. We've not been paid in weeks, and the Wizard treats us like slaves. So, I thought I'd do a good turn before I left. Out the door you go. Go left and at the first door, you can exit the tower. Here you go, girlie, you can have my sword—I've had enough of soldiering to last a lifetime. Oh, I suppose you need a wand, sir. So, I brought you this."

He pulled out a willow stick about the length of my arm, the same stick I'd used to draw the quadrangle in the dirt.

"I found it in the hall," he said. "I've heard that you Wizards like willow sticks."

He seemed very pleased with himself. Not having the heart, or the time, to explain to him that a wand was not just any stick, but one that a Wizard had imbued with special powers, I accepted the stick and put it in my belt.

As I walked past him, I nodded and said, "Thank you, Frezz. Now can you tell us whether the Wizard is still in his chamber?"

With Frezz's Voprian sword shimmering in her hand, Tessia pushed open the heavy oak double-doors and walked into a large chamber with me following a few steps behind, staying alert. The floor of the chamber was made of wide stones, and the ceiling of heavy beams. I quickly reached out to the wall beside me and felt the rough texture of wood and leaned down and felt the cold stone. I took a deep breath and smelled... something fetid.

"Is this room real, Norbert?" Tessia whispered. "Or is it an illusion?"

"It's real. We must have surprised Ludek. He's not had time to prepare an illusion."

And indeed, Ludek was sitting on his large throne at the opposite end of the chamber with a startled look on his face, two Drekavac-soldiers standing beside him, equally surprised. Ludek was holding his staff.

Tessia, hoping to seize the initiative, charged toward the Wizard who lifted his staff and let loose a fireball from the black sapphire. Tessia ducked and the fireball hissed as it flew through the open doorway and exploded in the passage behind us. I kept my eyes on Ludek. He grunted at the two guards, and they charged Tessia with Voprian swords drawn. She feinted toward one with a lunge and as he lifted his sword to ward off the expected blow, she pivoted toward the other Drekavac and cut off his hand. The first one was so taken off guard by this deft maneuver, he was slow to start his lunge, and in the moment he hesitated, she leaped toward him and sliced off his head and sent it rolling toward the throne. Then she turned to Ludek.

She was too close for him to shoot a fireball—the conflagration would have consumed both of them—so he pointed his staff at the detached Drekavac head in front of him and it flew toward Tessia, hitting her hard in the face and knocking her down. She lay there, not moving, blood pouring from her nose and ears and trickling across the gray stone floor.

I felt the old terror rising in me. I flashed back to the time twenty years before when the cloaked stranger had killed my mother and taken my brother while I hid in the corner, doing nothing. And I remembered the times on the road when Tessia, Hamlin and Anja had fought the robbers and wolves, and I'd done nothing. And the attack on the city when brave men and women died to take back their city, and where was I? Then I remembered being catapulted through the air, and my courage began to stir. And now Tessia, who'd saved me so many times before, needed me. *The Wand! The Wand!* I heard a voice say, and I remembered the willow stick Frezz had given me. I pulled the stick from my belt and it became my father's wand, the one he used to speak to the river and the trees.

Ludek and I pointed our wands at each other at the same time, and his fireball was met in midair with a giant snowball of mine that put out the fire. He sent a bolt of lightning at me and I caught it in the space between my wand and the palm of my left hand, juggled it back and forth until the bolt sputtered, threw off sparks and died. He tapped his head with his wand, turning himself invisible, and I threw a large bucket of aquamarine dye at him, turning him into a blue Drekavac. He snarled, his long canines showing in his blue dyed face and crouched like a leopard to leap at me. I lifted the willow wand, now shining like a Voprian blade, pointed it at the ceiling, and invoked the Goddess Nilene, the One I have served my entire life:

Nilene Zeita
de viață
pe care le slujesc
restabili echilibrul
pentru a lumii
și să conducă viața

And the great wooden beam above Ludek began vibrating. Pieces of the ceiling fell around him, and as he looked up, the beam cracked and fell, crushing him and his throne.

I bowed my head and thanked the Goddess for her gifts:

Vă mulțumim pentru cadouri

I looked up and, seeing that the other wooden beams and the rest of the ceiling remained intact, I rushed over to Tessia. She was still breathing. Again, I thanked the Goddess.

Suddenly I heard the swooshing of wings, and Tyrmiss flew through the gaping hole in the ceiling and landed beside Tessia.

I quickly constructed a litter from two spears and a cape, and then I lifted her onto the dragon's back and secured her with rope so she wouldn't fall off in the flight back to Dragonja City. Tyrmiss's eyes were filling with tears and a few drops fell on the beautiful face of the young warrior we both loved. Dragon tears are said to be magical, a cure for fever and madness, but I didn't try to catch any of the liquid because there were more important tasks to be done at present.

"Fly her to the hospital tent in the city. Tell Mina that Tessia has suffered a severe blow to the forehead. Mina will know what to do." I kissed Tessia on the forehead and laughed at myself for my sentimentality, a feeling that Tessia rarely allowed herself. "Heal well, my lady," I said and watched Tyrmiss spread her wings and fly carefully through the broken ceiling and into the sky.

I thought back over what had happened in the last few minutes and I realized that the fight with Ludek had been quick. Too quick. I searched through the fallen timber, but Ludek was no longer under the beam, and the throne room and indeed the entire tower was dissolving around me. I looked around, but Ludek was nowhere in sight. He'd somehow survived and escaped. I felt a lump of fear rising in my throat because I was sure we'd see him again.

However, when he left, the spells he'd created lost their power. The chamber where I stood had now reverted to its true appearance—a ruined keep with crumbling walls. I scrambled over a pile of rocks and through a hole in the wall and found myself in a beautiful meadow where Idella and Kerttu were sitting, looking around, puzzled at the transformation of their prison cell into a place of grasses and flowers. Seeing me, Idella waved excitedly, and I knew she was real because she was wearing her bracelet of entwined snakes. She and I ran to each other, and I lifted her high in the air. We hugged and cried for a long time.

It was nice to see Kerttu as well.

Chapter 20

When Tyrmiss delivered Idella and me to our house, Alaric was waiting in the front yard. When he saw us, his face went through a series of expressions from stunned to ashamed to angry, then it settled into the insolence which had become his habitual expression of late.

"I didn't think you had it in you," he snarled at me and turned his back to go into the house.

I saw Idella, who had seemed in shock from her ordeal, shake loose from my embrace and march over to her son. She grabbed him by the back of his shirt and yanked him so hard he fell into the dirt.

"I raised you better than that!" she yelled. "How dare you treat your father with such disrespect!"

"He's not my father," the boy said, his eyes wide in shock at his mother's anger.

"By the Goddess," she growled. "He is the only father you have, and you will treat him the way he deserves. He has never been anything but kind to you, and you have made me feel ashamed to be your mother!"

Alaric started crying, "I'm sorry. I'm sorry..." he murmured softly, getting up and running into the house.

Idella turned toward me, her anger starting to dissipate. "I should not have blown up that way," she said.

"Do you want me to scorch his pants for you, My Lady?" Tyrmiss asked, drolly.

Idella laughed ruefully, "It's tempting, Tyrmiss, but let's save corporal punishment as a last resort, especially if it involves fire."

Idella and I thanked Tyrmiss and bade her farewell. She'd been flying almost nonstop every night for weeks looking for Idella and Kerttu, and now the dragon needed to return to her cave and rest. As we watched her fly off, Idella looked at me and said, "I need to talk to Alaric."

"Let me do it," I said. "Although I appreciate your standing up for me, the issue is between him and me. There's nothing you can do."

She nodded and I went into the house, stopping at the doorway of Alaric's room and asked, "May I come in?" When there was no answer, I presumed to enter. Alaric was on his bed. I pulled the chair a little closer to him and said, "You know, Alaric, you and I have one big thing in common."

After a pointed silence, he asked, begrudgingly, "What's that?"

"We both love your mother." Alaric looked out the window at the Dry Hills stretching into the distance.

"Do you remember when you and I said goodbye in the stable last winter before I joined the rebels?" Still nothing from him. "Do you remember what you said to me?"

"All I remember was that you left us, and the soldiers came and took my mother. Why would you leave us when you knew the war was starting? Didn't you care about us?"

Ah, I thought, *here's the crux of it. I abandoned my family when they most needed me. This poor boy has been through torment, and it's largely my fault. I should have protected them.*

"I'm so sorry, son."

He looked at me with tears in his eyes. "I'm not your son," he said, almost inaudibly.

"Yes, you are, Alaric. You will always be my son." I stood up, and he almost leapt into my arms.

It's a beginning, I thought, kissing the top of his head. *I have much to make up for.*

Everyone in Dragonja City tried to pick up their lives again. Idella located her helpers and went back to baking. Kerttu set up a smithy downriver from the city and got busy hammering out copper pots and pans for the local trade. Tessia went back to being a commander in the King's Guard and the unofficial protector of the merchants of the city. Tyrmiss returned to her cave in the mountain pass, and I… I didn't want to go back to traveling the river road as a shireman, so after a great deal of soul-searching and conversations with Idella, I started a school for mages in the city. At first, I had only a few students, but I was expecting the school to grow and perhaps someday my students would make a difference in the kingdom by serving the Goddess.

After school one day, I was walking home, and as I came out of the woods, I saw Idella being dragged by the arm through the dooryard by a man in a hooded black cloak. Behind Idella was a figure lying motionless on the ground. I sized up the situation quickly because it was exactly what I'd been dreading ever since our return from the terrifying events in the Iskar Valley. Ludek had returned to try to take Idella away again.

I looked at the willow tree next to me and willed a stick to break off and fly into my hand. The stick instantly became a wand, my father's wand, and sparks of rage flew from its tip. My reluctance to commit violence evaporated in my growing determination to protect my family. With the willow wand in my hand, I ran toward the figures scuffling in front of the house. Ludek must have sensed my presence because he turned his head in my direction. Idella, my beautiful Idella who has the muscular arms of a kneader of bread, swung her right fist in a round-house punch that caught Ludek in the side of his head, knocking him down. Then Idella yelled "BRUIN! OTTOLO!" And the mastiff and the donkey came charging from behind the house. Bruin leaped at Ludek while Ottolo reared back and swung his hooves at him.

Meanwhile, I scooped up a large rock with my wand and threw it at Ludek who ducked. As he reached for his wand, I threw a bigger rock at him, delaying him long enough so Idella could drag Alaric into the house and slam the door. Ludek, trying to fend off Bruin and evade Ottolo's hooves, managed to point his wand at me and shot a fireball which I deflected. Ludek turned and ran through the fields and was quickly out of range of my wand. I watched him disappear over a hill chased by the two animals.

Idella stood in the doorway and called Bruin and Ottolo back to the house, so Ludek wouldn't hurt them.

"Is Alaric alright?" I asked urgently, walking past her.

Idella had placed Alaric on the kitchen table. He was unconscious and had a laceration across his forehead which was bleeding. She said, "Alaric tried to protect me, and Ludek used a spell to knock him down."

I closely examined the wound, then checked the rest of his body. When I was satisfied that the wound to his head was his only injury, I said, "He has a nasty bump but fortunately our son has a hard head."

Idella was in no mood for jokes. "It's bleeding a lot. Is he going to be alright?"

"Yes, he will be. Just keep his feet lower than his head." I stitched the wound, spread a balm of distilled wine and yarrow root on it and covered it with a bandage.

"Let him rest now," I said. "He should be fine tomorrow, but he's going to have a scar." I looked at Idella who was shaking with anger and shock.

"That was quite a punch you gave Ludek," I said, still trying to lighten the mood although I was feeling anything but jovial.

"I'm going to kill him," Idella said, looking at me. Her eyes had narrowed to slits. She was enraged to a degree I'd never seen in her before. Or in anyone.

"What are you going to do, Idella?" I felt a terrible dread.

"I'm going to ask Tessia and Tyrmiss to help me find Ludek and I'm going to kill him."

"You realize that Tessia already tried to kill him, and Ludek easily dispatched her, and Tyrmiss is no match for Ludek either."

"Then I will go alone to kill him." My wife looked at me steadily. "Do you know what the greatest force in the world is, Norbert?"

"Tell me."

"Mother Love. When Ludek attacked my child, he unleashed something inside me that I've never known before. Do you know anyone else who's been able to take him on without a weapon and slug him in the face, knocking him down?"

"No, I don't, my love." I took her by the hand and said, "We need to stay with Alaric now, but when it's clear that he's recovering, then you and I will find my brother and kill him."

"So, it's a family thing?"

"That's right. It's a family thing."

When Alaric was awake and alert, I talked with him for a few minutes to make sure he was coherent, then I moved him to his bed where he fell asleep. During the night, Idella and I took turns checking on him. The next morning, she was slicing bread and fruit for our breakfast when we heard the heavy flapping of wings in the yard. I looked out the window to see Tessia dismounting from Tyrmiss. When I went outside, I saw Tyrmiss's blood-red eyes inflamed with anger. Tessia had a steely look on her face which I recognized.

"You know what happened yesterday?" I asked her.

"Yes, Tyrmiss told me."

I looked at the dragon. "I heard Idella's dreams last night," she said. "And I know where Ludek is."

"Can you take me to him?" I heard Idella ask from the doorway behind me.

"Wait," I said. "I'm confused. Tessia and Idella are going after Ludek?"

"No, Nordbutt," Tyrmiss said. "You and your wife are going after the wizard."

I looked at Tessia who shrugged. "I had my chance to kill Ludek and failed. I don't think a sword is going to be effective against him. If he's going to be stopped, it will have to be with magic."

"Well, then, shouldn't I go alone?" I asked.

"Nordbutt, you are the slowest man I've ever known—which is saying a lot," Tyrmiss said, looking at the ground and shaking her head.

"Tyrmiss," Idella said. "Please show more respect to my husband."

Tyrmiss looked at Idella, obviously startled by her mild rebuke, then the dragon bowed her head to my wife and said, as if speaking to a superior, "Yes, My Lady." It was the only time I'd ever seen Tyrmiss defer to a human other than Tessia.

Then Tyrmiss turned to me and said, "Didn't you hear your wife yesterday when she told you that the strongest power in the universe is Mother Love? What do you think the Goddess is? Who do you think you've been worshipping all these years? What do you think holds together the universe? Don't you realize you never became a true mage until you met the Lady Idella? Do you really need for all of this to be explained to you, Norbert? With this lady at your side, you are ten times stronger as a mage than when you're alone."

"It's going to require very deep magic to defeat Ludek," Idella said in a voice I'd never heard from her before. She was looking off in the distance where we'd last seen Ludek running over the hill, and she was twirling her snake bracelet around her wrist again and again. Tessia and Tyrmiss didn't seem to notice the change that had come over my wife.

"We need to go now, Nordbutt, er... I mean Norbert."

Tyrmiss said. "I'm not sure how long Ludek will stay where he is."

Realizing the dragon was right, but worried about my family, I turned to look at the house where Alaric was asleep in his bed.

"Don't worry about your son," Tessia said. "I'll stay here with him, and I'll guard him with my life."

Idella handed me my bag of potions, and I checked my new willow wand at my belt. I noticed that Idella also carried a bag, but hers was bulging with bread and fruit—our uneaten breakfast—and strangely she had a rolling pin in her belt. She was wearing a smock over an old pair of leggings and on her feet was a pair of beat-up boots. She looked as if she were going on a picnic in the wilds. This was certainly the oddest quest I'd ever been on, but I was willing to trust the judgment of my friends, so I climbed on Tyrmiss's back, and Idella seated herself behind me. Tyrmiss ran a few steps, spread her wings, and we rose through the air, our small house growing smaller and smaller below us.

We circled over the house twice, gaining altitude, then headed west toward the mountain pass. Once over the mountains, we followed the Iskar River and rose up the slopes until we were above the tree line. Tyrmiss landed on a rocky ledge and let us dismount. We'd been flying for hours and my legs were stiff. Idella and I stretched and then stood in front of Tyrmiss, waiting for her to speak.

"Ludek is about half a league from here. Just follow the path along the rock ledge and you'll come to him. I can't go with you. As you know, Norbert, a dragon is no match for a wizard. And you need to be aware he knows you're coming, so be on your guard."

Idella and I started walking down the narrow path, the

Iskar Valley a long way below, and a steep cliff rising above us. I saw why Ludek had chosen this spot, anyone approaching him would be trapped between the cliff and the precipice. Suddenly, Idella grabbed my arm and pulled me roughly against the side of the mountain. No sooner did we have our backs pressed tightly against the rock, than a rumble came from above and a large boulder hit the path in front of us, missing my shoulder by a hand's breadth. Somehow, Idella had known the boulder was about to fall on us. I looked at her face. Her eyes were narrowed, and she was nodding slightly as if listening to instructions.

The path in front of us had been demolished by the falling boulder, leaving a gap. We could see where the path continued past the gap, but there was no way to get across to the other side. Idella was again undeterred. She simply closed her eyes and gave a small nod as if someone were giving her instructions and continued putting one step in front of the other until she was walking on empty air. When she stood safely on the other side, she gestured for me to follow. It may have been the scariest thing I've ever done, stepping onto the invisible path. I looked down, and below my feet I saw an eternity of nothingness between me and the valley below.

"Don't look down," Idella said. "Have faith. Just walk to me."

It was the greatest feeling of my life to be on solid visible ground again, hugging my wife.

We walked further down the path, and as we came around a turn, we encountered a large white she-bear standing on her back legs in front of us, growling. I reached for my wand, but Idella put her hand on my arm, stopping me. She slowly stepped toward the bear with both hands open, palms facing upwards. The closer to the bear she got, the calmer the bear became. As the bear lowered herself to place all four feet solidly on the path, she raised her ears and stretched her huge head toward Idella who gently scratched the bear behind the ears.

"Tayra, Tayra," Idella said soothingly.

The bear, whose name was evidently Tayra, moved past Idella, and I pressed myself against the rock wall, letting her pass. Her massive presence pushed me against the rock wall, and I smelled her rich ursine odor. With a gentle smile on her face, Idella calmly watched the bear walk away. I wondered how she knew the bear's name. Idella seemed completely unsurprised by everything that was happening.

"There, my love," she said, lightly touching her bracelet entwined with three snakes. "We have passed three tests: we have accepted fate, we have made friends with fear, and we have discovered faith."

"Ludek made these challenges for us?"

"No, no, my dear," Idella said to me, sounding surprised, "The Goddess gave us these tests to prepare us to confront Ludek."

No sooner had Idella said this, then I heard a fireball whistling toward us. We ducked and it passed over our heads and exploded harmlessly on the rocks behind us. I looked ahead and saw Ludek ducking into a cave. I kept my wand ready as we rushed in his direction.

"You must go into the cave alone," my wife said to me, squeezing my hand. "Ludek is not only your brother, but in the shadow world beneath this one, he is also you, or a version of you. Only you can battle your shadow self."

"How do you know all of this?" I asked, completely baffled at what had come over my wife.

"I'll explain later, my love," she said and kissed me deep and long on my lips. She took her rolling pin out of her belt and handed it to me. "Use this rolling pin as your wand. It's been empowered with Mother Love. Now go and do what you must."

I entered the darkness with the rolling pin, my new wand,

in front of me, walking slowly straight ahead. I felt baffled and afraid. I started to speak a spell to dispel darkness, but then I heard a whispered warning to stay in darkness. Yes, I thought, I will depend only on fate, fear and faith to guide me. However, I hoped that folly was not guiding this strategy as well.

As I moved through the darkness, I could feel a thousand small breaths above me, and I realized that the ceiling was covered in bats hanging upside down. This cave was a nursery, a cauldron where the flutter-mice raised their young. Bats, of course, are magical creatures, and like whales and dragons are favorites of the Goddess, but these particular bats didn't seem benign. I wondered whether Ludek had somehow infected them with dark magic. No sooner had the thought occurred to me, than the whole ceiling seemed to descend on me with black wings hitting my head, and small teeth biting me, tearing at my skin. I knew I had to keep my wits, to panic would only feed their frenzy. So, I stood still and let them bite me until they grew tired and flew toward the deeper darkness of the cave. I realized that it had been only a few bats who had bitten me, not the entire cauldron. Ludek's spell over the bats was not powerful enough to kill me—the point of the attack was to cause me to panic and run.

I followed the sound of the bats deeper into the cave, leaving the last particles of light behind me. The darkness inside me expanded until it filled my emptiness completely. The apparition of my father came, chiding me for being a coward and a failure. I ignored him. The apparition of women who'd died in childbirth while under my care, the soldiers I'd seen die in the siege of the castle, my mother who died while protecting my brother—as each ghost appeared, I allowed the grief to inhabit me. I embraced the pain, feeling the heaviness of guilt and the paralysis of self-doubt, and just when I was about to break, I felt the heaviness of the rolling pin in my hand and the apparition of Idella came to me, speaking of our love and her pride in me, and I felt strength returning and my heart filling with purpose. I remembered I was here in this cave because Ludek had harmed my family, and if I didn't stop him, he would harm them again.

I raised the rolling pin like a torch, feeling the power of Mother Love. Suddenly, I sensed Ludek in front of me. A fireball whistled in my direction, but the rolling pin caught it, absorbing its power until it glowed. I remembered Idella telling me that Ludek was me and I was Ludek and only *I* could fight him. I reached out to him with my mind, and I felt what he was feeling. A tidal wave of rage and jealousy went through me, and a thousand images of the people he'd hurt filled my mind. The spearing of Rilla was his doing. The torture of Hamlin. The burning of Tessia's village. The war with the rebels. On and on, all the evil he'd caused washed through me, and it was as if I had done those things, and I felt ashamed. I held the glowing rolling pin in the air, lighting the cave with Idella's love, and I saw Ludek's face in front of me. And then a voice came to me, a voice which sounded like Idella's:

You must become him. He is you. You are him. You must embrace him, so you can know.

Know what? I asked.

To become a wizard, you must know good and evil. Only then, can you choose.

I breathed the darkness in, accepting it, making it part of me. I felt the poison of Ludek's hatred, his jealousy, his resentment, his envy and most of all his loathing for every living thing. He was offended by joy, by light, by love. Rilla lying in the sunlight by the stream was intolerable. My love for Idella and Alaric, Tessia's love for Taja, the fishermen pulling in their heavy nets, the farmers harvesting barley, the deer in the glade, the blacksmith at his anvil—whispered to Ludek in the darkness of what he would never have, never be. My brother was beyond redemption. The years spent in the darkness of the cave, this very cave, had turned him into a cesspool of evil. This cave was the very place where he'd lost his humanity, and now I was losing mine.

And the voice said,

Now you know what evil is. And now you know what good is. You must choose.

I choose.... I choose, I said, unable to finish the thought. I felt myself sinking into the darkness, and I knew I would never return if I couldn't find something to hold onto. Then Alaric's voice came to me.

Father, he said, *Come home. Come home. Come home.*

Behind me I smelled a musky ursine odor and felt a massive presence. It's Tayra, I thought, as the beast knocked me aside and went for Ludek.

When I woke, I was lying outside the cave. Idella's face was leaning over mine. Ludek was beside me, dead. His chest had been ripped open, and his putrid yellow heart lay beside him.

"What happened?" I asked, holding my head which seemed to be the size of a small ox.

"Tayra returned and entered the cave. She came out dragging the body of Ludek, her snout and claws covered in blood," Idella replied. "I went into the cave with a torch and found you. You could barely walk. Then you passed out here."

"Idella," I said weakly, reaching out for her hand. "I heard your voice in the cave."

"Yes," she said, matter-of-factly. "The Goddess has been speaking to both of us." She looked at the ground, tracing the copper snakes on her bracelet. "There's a great deal I haven't told you about me."

"Yes, I know," I said. "Are you a witch?"

"Not exactly," she said. "My mother was a brown witch—she could speak to animals. My mother's powers were considerable, but unfortunately, she was ruthless and ambitious. I never knew my father, but my stepfather, a powerful warlock in a southern kingdom, was a cruel man. My mother, my brother and I escaped and fled to Bekla when I was a girl. I saw what my mother's ambitions had done to her and I swore never to be like her. So, I never took training as a witch and never developed my talent. Instead, I tried to live a simple life as a baker, a mother and a tradesman's wife, practicing only simple magic."

"When you saw Ludek hurt Alaric, something woke in you?"

"Yes, I felt a power come into me which I can only explain as being the source of mother-love."

"I felt the same way when Ludek kidnapped you."

"Norbert, I wanted to marry you because I felt that in some basic way, we're the same. We both have turned away from magic in order to have a simpler life, but..."

She paused, looking off into the distant valley.

"But now, we find we cannot escape who we are," I said, finishing her thought.

We sat for a while on the side of the mountain. It was cold up there, but the sun felt good on our faces.

"Idella, did you send the bear into the cave to save me?"

"Well, let's say I suggested it to Tayra, but it was her decision. I've always had a way with animals."

I thought of how devoted Ottolo and Bruin had always been to her and how they leaped at Ludek to protect her.

"Why didn't you just send the bear into the cave to kill Ludek. Why did I have to go?"

"Tayra needed you to capture Ludek first. She could never have gotten close to him by herself."

"Is that what I did? Capture Ludek?"

"My dear, your soul battled with his and you won. You are now a Wizard."

I thought about all that had happened in the course of one day, and I realized that both Idella and I were more powerful than I'd ever realized.

"Thank you, my love," I said. "We make a good team, don't we?"

"Well, that depends," Idella said, looking sternly at me. "Did you lose my best rolling pin?"

We both laughed. "Ow," I said, feeling the cuts on my face. "It hurts when I laugh."

While Idella applied ointment to the bat-bites on my neck and shoulders, I looked out over the valley. It was filled with sunlight, and I could hear wild geese passing overhead.

Chapter 21

Hamlin was healing more quickly than Mina and I had expected, considering the terrible tortures he'd been subjected to in the dungeon of the castle. Bruin sleeping beside his cot at night may have helped; as everyone knows, an animal's love can be therapeutic. As Hamlin began to take an interest in things around him, he and I had long conversations. He spoke often of Anja—the fun they'd had, the hunting and fishing expeditions, the long quest to Dragonja City. He never spoke of Anja's betrayal, but I was fairly sure Hamlin was aware of what Anja had done since people often referred to it. I tried to keep our conversations hopeful while filling him in on what he'd missed. I told him of the weeks that Tessia and I spent in the rebel camp, our becoming friends with Tyrmiss, and our part in the assault on the castle. As he gained strength, the rosy bloom in Hamlin's cheeks returned, and he occasionally smiled. And one day in late summer, when I saw his eyes following a pretty young woman walking by, I knew Hamlin was ready to move out of the hospital bed and into the Silver Pony.

Kerttu showed little distress at having been Ludek's prisoner. As long as he produced Voprian swords, he was given plenty to eat and a comfortable place to sleep. He said that when he first was taken prisoner, he had balked at the idea of working for Ludek, so the Wizard had taken the metal smith into the dungeon and made him watch men, including Hamlin, being tortured. Kerttu was told that the torture would stop as soon as he agreed to start producing swords—which he did. Kerttu, of course, had tremendous value as the only smith who could make Voprian swords. He must have forged a great many blades because once the war started almost all the Drekavac-soldiers were armed with them. After the war, many of them found their way into the hands of pirates and highwaymen which made Tessia's job of enforcing the peace much more difficult.

Idella's value to Ludek was of a different kind than Kerttu's. Unlike Hamlin, she hadn't been tortured, but nevertheless, I could tell from her dark moods and vacant looks, she'd suffered in confinement. Shortly after she got back to the Silver Pony, she said there was something she had to tell me. She said Femke had said that she should because people like to gossip –

"Wait, my love," I said, interrupting her. "We have had this conversation before."

"No, no," she said. "That other time I was starving, and I had to, you know, do what I did to get food. This time was different."

"How was it different?"

She grew silent and she traced the bracelet of triple snakes, exactly as she'd done the last time we'd had a conversation like this.

"Ludek…" she began in a small voice. "He said he would hurt Alaric if I didn't do as he said."

"Darling, thank you for telling me, but I'm sure you did what you had to do to protect yourself and your family. You really need to talk to Mina about all this. She has gone through it herself and has helped many women recover as well. Only a woman who has been through it is going to understand. Now, will you go to Mina tomorrow and tell her what happened?"

She nodded. "There's something else you need to know."

"What is it?"

"I'm pregnant."

I thought about the implications of what she'd said, then asked, already knowing the answer, "Who is the father?"

"Ludek." She looked in my eyes imploringly. "I need to know. Will you accept the child as your own, just as you've accepted Alaric?"

"Of course, I will," I said hollowly. I tried to smile at her as if it was an easy decision, but she saw through the deception.

"Norbert, how could you blame me? Ludek forced me to sleep with him!" She looked at me with her brown eyes filling with tears.

"I don't blame you."

"Yes, you do. I can see you do. Oh, by the Goddess, I thought you would understand."

"I do understand. You had no choice. You were trying to protect Alaric."

"Oh, no. No, no, no. You are going to hate the baby. You will always see Ludek when you look at the child."

"I promise I won't see Ludek."

"Please leave," she said, pointing at the door, her hand shaking.

I walked out the door and went to the hospital to work. Mina could see that something was wrong, but intuitively, she knew I wasn't ready to talk about it yet. And indeed, I felt so much anger that Idella had slept with my brother that I wasn't able to talk about anything, especially not the irrational feeling that Idella had betrayed me.

In the following months, I did everything I could to make peace with Idella, but I could feel her anger at me growing by the day while my anger compacted into what felt like a stone in my throat. We never again spoke of Ludek, nor of what she'd gone through at his hands.

One day seven months later, I returned home from the castle where I'd been meeting with the Queen. Femke stopped me at the door.

"It's best you stay in the kitchen until the baby is born," she said. "Sit at the table, I'll bring you a bowl of soup."

After what seemed an eternity, Mina came into the kitchen and gestured for me to follow her. I rushed to my wife's bedside, and lying there in her arms was Ena, the most beautiful baby girl I'd ever seen.

She looked exactly like my mother.

Epilogue: The Coronation

"How long has it been since you and Tessia first showed up at the inn?" Heikum asked, wiping the surface of the bar.

"Four years, almost to the day," I said, after a quick calculation.

"We've seen a lot of changes since then, haven't we, Laddie? Under Queen Varvara the Wise, the city is thriving," he said, with a gleam in his eye and I knew he was thinking of how many copper coins he was making every day at the inn. "Caz knows a thing or two about how to encourage honest shopkeepers while putting dishonest ones out of business, doesn't he?"

I nodded. As Finance Minister, Caz had enforced laws that made sure that merchants acted in good faith. He had also increased wealth in the kingdom by establishing trade relations with neighboring kingdoms. Heikum took my tankard and filled it again with ale, and I put a copper coin on the bar in front of him, but he ignored it. Heikum drew an ale for himself, breaking his own rule against drinking with customers.

"Yes, and Tessia has served the kingdom brilliantly as well," I added, burping. As Commander, she'd used dragon gold to build an army to guard the borders, increase security on the roads, and establish a militia that protected citizens from thieves and ruffians. She also sent emissaries across the pass into the Iskar Valley to establish friendly relations with the residents, and already families were making the difficult trek from Dragonja over the mountains to establish homesteads in the new lands.

Heikum and I nodded. This was a weekly ritual for us, taking an inventory of what we both knew, but the facts seemed so unbelievable we needed to refer to them out loud to reassure each other that they were still true. The kingdom was safe and prosperous—more so than at any time in history, or at least that's what everyone was saying.

"We miss you at the inn, not like the bad old days when you had to stay here for protection," Heikum said. "When are you going to have us out to your place for a meal? Your missus makes the best turnip soup—even better than Femke's, but I'll deny it if you ever tell her I said that."

I laughed. "Sorry we haven't had you and Femke over for a while, but we're very busy. We planted apricot and walnut trees, and Idella has expanded her bakery." Heikum nodded.

"I know that Idella's now supplying most of the taverns. My customers love her bread and pastries." Heikum took a sip of ale, and asked, "Kerttu, Tessia's dad… his foundry is flourishing too, isn't it?"

"Kerttu is getting rich," I replied. Following Caz's advice, the Queen gave some of the dragon gold to Kerttu to expand his new smithy downriver from the city. Now he had over forty people working for him, some of them orphans who used to loiter in the alleys. They hammered out copper tools and household goods, from knives to doorlatches to kettles. He also had a lucrative agreement to produce Voprian swords, but only for the Queen's soldiers. Each sword was catalogued and licensed.

"Owning or selling a Voprian blade without the Queen's permission is a serious offense, I'm told," Heikum said. "The Council of Elders loves the reforms the Wise Queen has made, bringing peace and prosperity to the kingdom. Femke and I…" He stopped, realizing that he was about to boast of his importance on the Council, something his wife had warned him against.

Heikum pulled his large shoulders back and stood a little

301

straighter. He was obviously proud of his prominent role now in the city. The Council of Elders, whose role was to advise the Queen, was made up of an equal number of men and women. Both Heikum and Femke had been appointed, and their angry debates in council were a source of great amusement, as well as educational merit, for the whole town. Following the advice of the Council of Elders, Queen Varvara had the dungeons converted to ale cellars. People who committed a serious crime such as murder, rape or grand theft were banished from the kingdom, and since there was nowhere else as wonderful as the Wise Queen's realm, no one wanted to leave. Immigrants were welcomed, and if they showed themselves to be productive and law-abiding residents, they were given citizenship in a large festivity held every year in the marketplace. At this same festivity, old soldiers were celebrated by their comrades who told tales of their bravery. The bravest were given the task of guarding the Queen's residence, a desirable appointment since they ate from the Queen's table.

One of the innovations that the Wise Queen instituted was a way of dealing with delinquent youths. It was based on something Caz had witnessed in a faraway land to the south. When a young person committed a crime, he or she was taken into the market and forced to sit in a chair and listen to his parents, grandparents, uncles, aunts, neighbors and teachers praise him until all the good in the child had been brought into the light. The child was then returned to the family and given the opportunity to live up to the high opinion they had of him. This enlightened strategy almost always worked.

When Alaric was caught stealing shortly after his sister was born, he was brought home to us by a militiaman, a tall fierce-looking Drekavac, who held the boy firmly by the arm.

Before the Drekavac had even let go of the boy, Idella

pointed her finger in Alaric's face and announced, "I intend to follow the law set down by the Wise Queen."

The next day, the same Drekavac showed up at our door and escorted the boy to the market square followed by Idella, me and several neighbors. By the time we got to the market, a crowd had gathered to watch the ordeal. Alaric was forced by the militiaman to sit in a chair in the middle of a chalk circle.

His mother briefly told the story of his birth, the loss of his father, and her own disappearance at the hands of the evil Wizard Ludek. "My son," she said, "Has lost his way, but he's a fine person, and I love him more than anyone else in the world." She looked around the market square. "Most of you remember how he used to help me sell my bread in this very square, carrying boxes for me and watching the stall when I had to make deliveries. He showed a talent for talking to customers and could always be trusted to treat them fairly. But when I was kidnapped by Ludek, Alaric took up with the children of the alleys and fell under the influence of thieves. I no longer know what to do with him."

Idella sat down, weeping out of love for her son.

Next, I spoke of how Alaric had helped take care of the animals at the inn. How loving and kind he'd been to my donkey Ottolo. "He's a brave lad. He volunteered to go with me when I joined Zygmunt's rebels, but he was too young. I'm so sorry I abandoned him, and I wasn't here when he grieved for his mother when she was kidnapped. I love him as my own son, and I blame myself for the mistakes he's made."

Then, Tessia spoke to the crowd. "Alaric has helped us in the food caravan, using his skills at trading. I've seen him helping the old women who have trouble walking."

At this, an old woman in the back shouted, "YES! He often helped me."

And many people in the crowd nodded and muttered about what a helpful boy he'd always been. Many other people—Heikum, Femke, Hamlin, neighbors, even the shop-keeper who had caught him stealing—spoke of what a good, kind, generous, talented, hardworking boy we had in front of us.

We spent all afternoon praising Alaric, and by the time the shadows were lengthening in the market square and all the farm-ers and tradesmen had closed their stalls, loaded their donkeys and left the city, poor Alaric, overwhelmed at being shown so much love, was weeping. His mother and I went to him, wiped his tears away, and took him home to eat his favorite foods.

Alaric was one of the lucky ones. Noticeably absent from this conspiracy of benevolence were Alaric's friends from the alley, no doubt fearing that they also may have to go through this ordeal someday, and no one would step forward to speak for them. Many children and adolescents still lived in the alleys, and it was clear that we would spend many years trying to bring them back into the fold of the community. We'd had success in finding apprenticeships for some, and others had been taken in by family members, but there were still many who had not found a place, and their presence in the alleys and the ways they often disrupted life for the citizens was an ongoing problem. The years of oppression under Ludek had created a dark shadow in the city that we had to learn to live with.

Such was the Reign of Love that the Wise Queen created. Her kingdom was truly the best place to live in the world.

When the Wise Queen died, people came from all over the kingdom to stand beside the road and weep as the cortege passed. She was buried in her family's apple orchard beside her husband, King Ottolo the Befuddled, whom she loved. Years later, Kerttu forged a statue of her and erected it in the middle of the market square. It portrayed her as the Goddess Nilene with children at her feet looking up at her adoringly.

Against my advice, the Queen had held onto the black

sapphire with which Ludek had imprisoned her husband's mind. Perhaps she needed it to remind her of the unanticipated dangers of monarchy. After she died, I gave the stone to Tyrmiss who carried it far away from the kingdom and dropped it into the deepest part of the sea.

For the coronation of Queen Tessia, I dressed the part of the Green Wizard, with my long dark green robe and my light green conical hat. Tying my sheathed willow wand on the green rope that served as a belt, I looked in the mirror and laughed.

"You look wise and powerful," Idella said kindly.

"I feel like a fool dressed like this," I said.

"Have I thanked you today for being so wonderful?" She kissed my cheek.

"Only twice," I answered.

"Well, when you get back from Tessia's coronation, I will thank you again," she said with a small suggestive smile and a glint in her eye. What a wonderful woman I was married to! Now, fifty years later, after all that happened in our lives and Idella buried beside our grape arbor, I look back at those years with her as the greatest blessing of my life.

As I left our house, Alaric waved at me from the field where he was planting more walnut seedlings. They would not bear for at least five years, but we planned to stay for a long time in this snug house outside the city walls. Idella now had seven brick ovens behind the house, and her stall in the market did a brisk business under the watchful eye of Alaric. He'd become a shrewd haggler, and for several years I'd taken him and Hamlin down the river roads to teach them the shireman trade, and they were ready to take over the business. *But they'll need to buy a new donkey*, I thought, glancing at Ottolo grazing in the field;

he was getting old and would, no doubt, be glad not to have to carry trade-goods through the countryside anymore. Bruin was getting old as well, but he still enjoyed occasionally running through the Dry Hills with the white wolves.

Idella had been encouraging me to dress more like a wizard, or at least more like the way that people thought wizards dress, but wearing a tall conical hat and a long robe made me feel ridiculous. So, except for official state functions when the Queen wore her crown and mantle and wanted her Green Wizard to dress his part in the theatrics of political ritual, I wore what I'd always worn—a linen blouse and leather breeches. I did start carrying my wand in a leather scabbard though because using a wand to cast spells was not just theatrics, although it certainly did create an effect in an audience, but, as I had learned in Ludek's tower, waving the wand focused one's energy, directing the will toward a certain end. Magic comes from nature, not from the Wizard; magic is the life force flowing from the elements through the Wizard and into the world.

The battle with Ludek had changed me. Certainly, I had more confidence in my abilities now, but it was more than that. I had come to a reassessment of my relationship to magic. I'd begun to understand that serving the Goddess meant nourishing life, certainly, but it also meant being willing to defend life. As Idella says, "When a wolf defends her cubs, is she not serving the Goddess? If a man such as Ludek is destroying life, should you not fight that man? And would the Goddess wish for you to fight bare-handed? The wand is nothing in itself, just as a sword, even a Voprian sword, is nothing in itself."

The fact that it was the hapless Frezz who had given me the willow stick proved that it was not the wand that carried the power. Frezz had seemed to understand that any old willow stick would work as a wand, and now I saw that true power lies not in the wand, nor in the mage, but in the Goddess. The wand, the wind, the weather, even the dirt under my feet, are merely conduits for the will of Nilene Zeita, the Goddess I serve.

Walking across the market square dressed as a Wizard is not a way to be inconspicuous. The crowd parted. People stared. Children pointed. Looking around, I noticed once again how the space had changed. The farmers had moved their trading space to the field outside the South Gate because they needed more room. Replacing them in the market square were merchants from faraway lands selling silks, gemstones and other amulets. Queen Varvara had instructed Mina to move the hospital to the castle and had used dragon gold to lure the most gifted healers from around the world. Mina ruled over the health of the city with a strong hand that, I recently noticed, now displayed a ring with a purple stone, instead of the red stone she'd worn for years. There were rumors she'd taken an oath as a witch.

And in the middle of the square there was a new altar, made of green stone. Today it was piled high with fragrant birchwood, said to be the favorite scent of the Goddess Nilene. In the place where the hospital tent used to be, there was a raised dais that was draped with purple fabric. I walked past it on my way to the Castle gate which now always stood open, guarded by a single pensioner who had been a hero in the war against Ludek. I remembered him as the first rebel through this very gate when Tessia, Tyrmiss and I were trapped on the roof of the tower. The guard bowed his head to me as I passed, and I acknowledged him with a slight nod.

I found Tessia engaged in a fierce argument with Caz. Taja sat on a chair nearby, quietly observing. As the wife of the Heir Apparent, Taja was already an important advisor in setting policy. Once Tessia was crowned Queen, Taja's role would become even more important. The two young women balanced each other nicely, I thought. Tessia's impulsive and aggressive ways of dealing with people were tempered by Taja's kinder gentler nature.

"I will not do it!" Tessia shouted at Caz.

Caz, who through the years had learned to stand up to her, was quietly insisting, "You must, my Lady. The queen must make a speech to her people. She must inspire them in the common enterprise of building and defending the kingdom."

"I will not." She crossed her arms and tried to stare him down. "I do not make speeches. I inspire my troops by example, not words."

"Words are the tools of governance, my Lady." Caz flashed his purple ring, signifying that he took his administrative duties seriously.

"I am the queen, and I order you to –"

"No, Tessia. You are not the queen until you are crowned," Taja pointed out.

"And you will not be crowned until you agree to make a speech," Caz said.

Tessia looked at Taja who gave a small shrug.

Tessia lifted her chin, narrowed her eyes at the Minister of Finance and said, "Very well. I agree to make a statement. A very bold statement."

"And you agree to light the altar as a sign of your respect for the Goddess?"

"I do."

They both turned to me, and Caz said in his formal voice, "Healer and Bard of the Kingdom, are you ready to proceed?"

I nodded, and the four of us walked out of the castle through the Castle Gate and mounted the dais. It was midsummer, and the weather was perfect, not a cloud in the sky. The purple fabric on the dais rippled in the wind. My two apprentices had roped off an area in front of the dais, as well as an area around the altar. Tessia had told me what she planned to do, so I'd asked my upper-level students to keep the crowd away from these two areas, so no one would be hurt. The crowd had gathered in the square, crowded shoulder to shoulder, waiting to watch the coronation.

Caz, dressed in a white robe with purple fringe, made a speech welcoming the crowd, praising Tessia for her courage. He listed some of her accomplishments, such as leading the assault on the castle to free the city from the clutches of the evil Wizard Ludek, building an army, organizing the militia, securing the roads and rivers from thieves, and faithfully serving our blessed Queen Varvara the Wise to bring peace and prosperity to the Kingdom. He reminded them that the Wise Queen, not having any children, had adopted Tessia as her daughter, and in this way, Tessia, having inherited the crown, is the rightful ruler of the Kingdom of Dragonja and Bekla. He went on to speak at some length about the wealth of the kingdom from trade and manufacture, the fecundity of the farms and pasturelands, as well as the increasing trade with foreign kingdoms. He kept mentioning his position as Minister of Finance, taking credit for the growing wealth of the kingdom. This unsubtle bragging was wearing thin, and as the day grew warmer, I could see that his listeners, some of whom had been standing in the square all morning, were growing restless, shifting from foot to foot and whispering to each other. Finally, Caz concluded his speech and stepped back.

Tessia and I stepped forward. Taja took her place beside Tessia. The crowd grew quiet. In my official duty as Royal Advisor, Healer, and Bard, I lifted the small, elegant diadem, crafted of gold wire and a single stone of chalcedony, and held it high for the people to see. It was the same crown worn by the Wise Queen and generations of royalty before her. In a ritual as old as the kingdom, I shouted loud enough that all the people in the square could hear:

"DO THE PEOPLE OF THE KINGDOM ACCEPT QUEEN TESSIA AS THEIR RULER?"

As a loud roar of affirmation rose through the air, I lowered the crown on Tessia's head.

Tessia lifted her arms wide above her head:

"I SWEAR TO SERVE AND PROTECT THE PEOPLE OF THE KINGDOM WITH ALL MY STRENGTH AS THE WISE QUEEN HAS TAUGHT ME!"

The roar was deafening.

Then there was abrupt silence. People, their eyes wide and their mouths agape, pointed toward the sky behind Tessia. And I heard the familiar wingbeats thudding toward us. Tyrmiss flew low circling over the square, descending until people fell on the ground to avoid being hit by her talons, and as she passed over the altar in the middle of the square, the dragon breathed out a short burst of fire, lighting the birch. As the flames rose, the fragrant aroma was released into the air, pleasing the Goddess Nilene. Then, Tyrmiss gracefully landed in the roped-off area in front of the dais. The dragon folded her wings and bowed her head to the new monarch. Tessia slowly stepped down from the dais and, lifting her skirt, climbed onto the back of the beast. Tyrmiss lifted her head and smiled, showing her frighteningly long fangs, and gave me a sly look. People in the crowd gasped in terror. I thought *Tyrmiss is enjoying this.*

Tyrmiss again spread her great wings, took a few steps, and lifted into the air. Tessia, her back straight, her eyes straight ahead, lifted her shining Voprian blade and shouted:

"FOR DRAGONJA! FOR BEKLA! FOR ISKAR!"

The crowd roared as Tyrmiss carried Tessia, her golden crown catching the sunlight, three times around the city to land on the highest tower of the castle. Tessia, the Dragonqueen of Dragonja, was radiant. People fell to their knees in awe.

"No speech?" Caz whispered to me. "She said she'd make a speech."

"No, Caz. She said she'd make a statement. A bold statement."

He and I—and the whole city—watched as the dragon extended her wings and lifted our Queen ever higher into the perfect sky.

FINIS

The author would like to thank Kim Davis, Jacqui Davis, Liz Evans, and Cat Smith for their tireless and brilliant attention to the publication of this novel.

About the Author

Born and raised in Texas, Michael Simms has worked as a squire and armorer to a Hungarian fencing master, stable hand, gardener, forager, estate agent, college teacher, editor, publisher, technical writer, lexicographer, political organizer, and literary impresario. He is the author of seven collections of poetry and a textbook about poetry. In 2011 Simms was recognized by the Pennsylvania State Legislature for his contribution to the arts. Simms and his wife Eva live in the Pittsburgh neighborhood of Mount Washington overlooking the confluence of the Allegheny and Monongahela rivers. *The Green Mage* is Simms's second novel.

CPSIA information can be obtained
at www.ICGtesting.com
Printed in the USA
JSHW081911051122
32623JS00002B/78